THE
HOOK
UP

First Published 2014
First Australian Paperback Edition 2025
ISBN 978 1 038 93441 3

THE HOOK UP
© 2014 by Kristen Callihan
Australian Copyright 2014
New Zealand Copyright 2014

MIX
Paper | Supporting
responsible forestry
FSC® C001695
www.fsc.org

Published by
Emblaze™
An imprint of Harlequin Enterprises (Australia) Pty Limited
(ABN 47 001 180 918), a subsidiary of HarperCollins
Publishers Australia Pty Limited (ABN 36 009 913 517)
Level 19, 201 Elizabeth Street
SYDNEY NSW 2000
AUSTRALIA

Printed and bound in Australia by McPherson's Printing Group

KRISTEN CALLIHAN

THE HOOK UP

emblaze

For additional books by Kristen Callihan,
visit her website, kristencallihan.com.

The Hook Up

Kristen Callihan

emblaze

To all those who've found love amid crisp fall days
and the ribald cheers of college football games.

PROLOGUE

ANNA

I'M LATE, and it's the first day of class. I'd like to lay blame on something—car problems, couldn't find my way to the room, got attacked by a swarm of bees while crossing the quad, anything. But I ride a scooter. I'm a senior, so I know where I'm going by now. And the bees kept to the flowers.

The truth is, I stopped to down a strawberry smoothie and a bag of cashews before heading to class. Because I was hungry, and some things can't wait. Even so, I hate being late. It sets a bad precedent.

Painfully aware of my professor's stare, I berate myself as I scurry down one of the aisles between the rows of desks. I slide into a seat in the back just as a guy barrels down the aisle in the same hurried fashion and sits in the desk next to mine. Keeping my head down, I pull out my notepad and try to look organized and ready for the lecture. I don't think I fool my professor, but she doesn't say anything to me as she starts the introductory roll call.

Soon it's my turn. I'm saying my name and year when I hear a sharp intake of breath to my right. The shocked sound has me turning.

That's when I see him. The second our gazes connect, hot tingles zap through me, making my breath catch and my insides dip. The sensation is so unnerving that I can only sit there, my hand fluttering to my chest where my heart struggles to break free.

Oddly, the guy gapes back at me, as if he too feels the strange kick. Which must be wrong; no guy has ever gaped at me. So maybe it's just that I'm staring at him. Only, he's staring at me too, and he doesn't look away.

Stranger still, it feels as if I know him, have known him for years. Which is ridiculous. Even though he looks oddly familiar, I'd remember if I'd met him before. A guy this gorgeous isn't easily forgotten.

I don't know why I feel the connection, but I don't like it. Nor do I like the way something inside me gives a little happy squee, as if I've been mentally shopping for men and have just found the perfect one.

Still looking at me, he suddenly speaks. I'm so addled; it takes me a second to realize that he's responding to Professor Lambert. "Drew Baylor. Senior." His voice is dark chocolate on a hot summer night.

And it causes a stir. People snap out of their morning fog, turn, stare, and start whispering among themselves. He ignores them, watching only me. It flusters me.

Drew Baylor. His name is a ripple through the room. Recognition sets in. The quarterback. I haven't paid much attention to the members of our legendary football team, so I only know of him in that vague way one knows there's a Student Union or that the library closes at 7:00 p.m. on Sundays.

Disappointment is swift and sharp. I have zero interest in getting to know the star quarterback. Chest tight, I turn away and try to ignore him. Easier said than done.

As soon as class ends, I attempt to flee. And nearly run into a solid wall of muscled chest instead. I don't have to look up to know who it is. We stand facing each other in silence, me staring at his chest, and his gaze burning a hole through the top of my head. Annoyed, I straighten my shoulders and force myself to look aloof. Shit, what does "aloof" look like? It doesn't matter because our eyes meet again.

Mistake.

I think my knees go weak. I'm not sure because my brain has screeched to a halt.

Holy hell, he's potent. Heat and vitality come off him in waves. I think I sway a bit. He is close enough that I notice the faint stubble along his strong chin and the glints of gold in his brown hair. He wears it cut short, and thick clusters of it spike along the top and front. It's flattened a bit on one side as if he'd rolled out of bed and forgotten to brush it. But I doubt that was the case, because he smells fantastic—like warm pears and crisp air. I almost lean in for a better whiff, but manage to control myself.

The silence between us grows awkward until I can't stop myself from glancing up, just in time to catch him jerking back, as if he too had taken a covert sniff. Doubtful. He's casually stuffing his hands into his jeans pockets and smiling with ease, the gesture pulling a little dimple in on his left cheek.

I almost smile, start to rethink my earlier stance of avoidance. Then he opens his mouth and ruins everything.

The warm cadence of his voice rolls over me before the words fully make sense. "Hey there, Big Red."

My world grinds to a loud, screeching halt. Big Red? What the ever-loving knuckle fuck?

I gape up at him, too shocked to even form a proper glare. And he squints back, that inane smile still in place, as if he's waiting for me to answer. My mind is stuck on one thing.

He'd called me Big Red. *Big* Fucking Red.

His comment is a punch to the gut. Yet not entirely out of left field. I'm a redhead. Being called "red" goes with the territory. It's not the "red" part that bothers me. It's the "big" part. Having been chubby for most of my adolescence has left me sensitive. It doesn't matter that I'm now more curves than chub; that I like my body. One freaking word from this guy and I feel the pain all over again, damn it. Somehow, I find my voice.

"What did you just call me?"

The corners of his eyes crease in what might be a wince. "Ahh... If I say 'nothing,' can we move on and pretend it didn't happen?"

I almost smile at that one, which irritates me further. "No."

He shifts his weight to his other foot. "Relax, I was only trying—"

"Do not—" I point a finger at him "—tell me to 'relax' when you've insulted me, bud."

"Bud?" He makes a strangled sort of half laugh.

"I'm not 'big.'" There's more hurt in my voice than I'd like to admit. I hate that too.

His head jerks back like I've surprised him. It's a small movement, one that he tries to hide by putting his hands low on his narrow hips.

"I wasn't trying to insult you. Believe me, I was referring to the best of places." His butterscotch gaze drifts down and roves over my chest. Instantly, my breasts feel exposed, heavy yet tight. And to my utter humiliation, my nipples go stiff. As he is staring, he sees and sucks in a sharp breath.

Fuck this. "Eyes up, asshole."

He flinches again, his attention snapping up to my face. "Sorry," he says, not even a little sheepish. "I'd like to say it won't happen again, but I honestly can't promise that, Red."

"Jesus, you're unbelievable."

He scratches the back of his neck, squinting at me as if I've become a painful sight. "Look, can we start over?" He thrusts out a massive hand attached to a forearm corded with muscle. "Hi, I'm Drew."

I don't take his hand, and he's forced to let it fall.

"I know who you are."

His smile returns. This one far too pleased.

"You said your name less than an hour ago," I remind him.

His confident attitude falters, but he tries again, I'll give him that. "Well, at least you remembered. I remember too, Anna Jones."

I ignore the surprise washing over me and cross my arms in front of me. "And I don't need to start over. I'm not interested in talking to some egotistical meathead who ogles my breasts and calls me obnoxious names."

I ought to walk away, but I've worked myself into a lather now. "I mean 'Red'? Seriously?"

He just gapes at me. This time dumbfounded, as if he can't believe some unhinged chick is berating him.

"Why not be original?" I go on as if I'm not unhinged. "Why not call me Blondie?"

White teeth flash in a quick smile. "An esoteric approach, eh? Could work. Though it veers a bit too much toward sarcasm for my taste."

I blink. His response sends a tingle through me. A pretty face is one thing. A quick mind is nearly irresistible to me. Especially when paired with that grin he wears. No anger there or even triumph, he simply waits for the next volley, enjoying it.

Stranger still, *I* enjoy it. I fight to maintain my bland look as I respond. "I'm not sure if anyone's told you, Baylor, but there's this thing called a person's name." I find myself leaning in closer, and as if on cue, he does too. His scent and his heat surround me, making my knees weak as I finish. "You might try using it."

Little white lines fan out at the corners of his eyes from where he's spent months squinting in the sun. Those lines deepen now as his voice drops to a murmur. "So no to *Red Hot*, then?" It's clear he's fighting a laugh.

I grit my teeth. "You're just fucking with me now."

Wrong. Thing. To. Say.

His nostrils flare on an indrawn breath, and his gaze goes liquid hot. "Not yet, *Jones*."

Point two to Baylor, because he's managed to unnerve me and give me a nickname in one stroke. And somehow I walked right into his trap. Heat rises to my cheeks as I stand there, staring back at him, speechless. But then I'm saved from further comment when a professor walks in to start up the next class.

The next day, a box of Red Hots sits on my desk. Baylor doesn't say a word or look my way, but when I get up and chuck them into the trash, he ducks his head and studies his notes. Good. Now we're clear.

Only I ruin this later, when, in the privacy of my room, I open the box of Red Hots that I bought after class and pop a handful into my mouth. Candy-sweet heat melts over my tongue, and all I can see behind my closed lids is Drew Baylor's slow perusal of my body. I go so hot and achy with need that I moan into my pillow and don't sleep for the rest of the night.

DREW

My mother once told me that the most important moment in my life wouldn't be when I won the National Championship or even the Super Bowl. It would be when I fell in love.

Life, she insisted, is how you live it and who you live it with, not what you do to make a living. Given that she told me this when I was sixteen, I basically rolled my eyes and worked on practicing my pass fakes.

But my mother was insistent.

"You'll see, Drew. One day, love will creep up and smack you upside the head. Then you'll understand."

My mom, it turns out, was wrong in one regard. Love, when it came for me, did not creep. No, it walked up to me, bold as you please, you know, just in case I wasn't paying attention. It did, however, slap me upside my head.

And while I'd be happy to tell my mom that she was right about that, she's dead. A fact that hurts even more now that I've been struck down. More like shot down. Cut off at the knees. Totally fucked. Whatever you want to call this disaster. Because the object of my affection hates me.

I am man enough to acknowledge that the cluster fuck that is my current love life is entirely my fault. I wasn't prepared for Anna Jones.

I still wince at the memory of when I first laid eyes on her at the beginning of the semester. Being late for class, I'd rushed to a seat in the back row, and was trying to remain unnoticed. I can't go anywhere on campus without getting attention. And though it sounds like an awesome thing, it gets tiring.

When the roll call reached the back row, a soft voice, rich and thick as maple syrup, slid over me.

"Anna Jones."

Just her name. That was all she'd said. It was like a hot finger stroking down my spine. My head snapped up. And there she was, so fucking pretty that I couldn't think straight. I might as well have been sacked.

Breathless, my head ringing, I could only gape. I'm not going to say it was love at first sight. I didn't know her enough for it to be that. No, it was more like oh, hell-yes–please, I'll have that. With a helping of right-the-fuck-now on the side.

Thinking maybe I was overtired and simply overreacting to something that wasn't really there, I stared at Anna Jones and tried to make sense of my extreme reaction.

As if feeling my gaze, she'd turned, and fucking hell… Her eyes were wide, almost catlike, with the corners tilting up just a bit. At first, those eyes appeared brown, but they were really bottle green. And so clear. And annoyed. She glared at me. I didn't care. One word was playing a loop in my head: *mine*.

I don't remember the rest of the class. I watched Anna Jones like a condemned man getting his last view of the setting sun. While she tried to ignore me. Admirably.

The second class ended I shot up, and so did she. We nearly

collided in the middle of the aisle. And then it all fell to shit. Because at that moment, I became a bonehead.

I've never been nervous around girls before. To be brutally honest, my life has been fairly insulated. Football, and the fame that goes with it, has wrapped me up in its loving arms and given me everything I've wanted, women included. Unfortunately, it's become crystal clear that, when it comes to my sport, Anna is not one of the converted. Poor thing.

Whatever the case, I was ill-equipped to handle her when she glared up at me, one delicately arched brow lifting imperiously, as if to say, "What the fuck do you want?"

Standing there, I became aware of myself, this big oaf, looming over her, my tongue thick in my mouth, a crazy twitch starting up on my cheek. God help me if she noticed that twitch. So I blurted out what is possibly the stupidest thing I've ever uttered in my life, "Hey, Big Red."

Yeah. Shoot me now. What the holy hell had I done? What the fuck did "Big Red" even mean? My mind screamed, *Do something, jackass! Apologize! Retreat!* I swear I could practically hear an alarm blaring, a call to activate shields and arm the photon torpedoes.

But no, I just stood there and forced a grin as heat flooded my face and a sweat broke out on my back. Yeah. I was that cool.

Her dark green eyes had flashed in outrage.

And then she let me have it.

Needless to say, I hobbled away from that encounter and remain among the walking wounded. Rejection sucks. It sucks so hard that I haven't said a word to her since. Instead, I just sit next to her during every class, silently pining. Pathetic.

Something has to be done about this. And soon. Because I'm losing my damn mind.

ONE

ANNA

HE'S LIKE THE fucking north wind.

And here he is again. Yeah, that one, the big, hulking jock striding into class like he owns this university, which he kind of does. Football is a religion around here, and he is the chosen messiah. Which sounds kind of sacrilegious considering that he's smacking a brunette on her ass as he leaves her at the classroom door. And she giggles, *giggles*, like it's a privilege to be degraded in front of thirty students. And I suppose it is to some. God knows there's a pack of girls who follow him around campus, all wanting to meet Drew Baylor, star quarterback, the phenom who will take us to the National Championship.

Their faith isn't exactly misguided. He's won it for them for the last two years. Even I remember those victories, the way the campus went wild, talk of Drew and his crew on everyone's tongue.

I fled the campus for the safety of my apartment. Not that it did much good; the whole state had been awash in football fever.

As if he knows that I have this *slight* need to look at him, his eyes find me as he ambles along. Those eyes, golden brown beneath straight, dark brows. Their focus is complete, hard. As if he can reach right down into me and pull my heart out.

God, everything just bottoms out inside of me. My thighs tighten as my pulse picks up. I can't let him see, can't let him know that one glance from him has me dry mouthed and struggling for breath.

I don't look away—that would be too easy. Instead, I hold his gaze for three seconds, counting them out in my head as his loose-limbed stride brings him closer. 6'4" if he's an inch, the guy knows how to move his body. Effortless. I'm sure he's never stumbled, bumped into a desk with his ass as he threads through the rows to get to his seat. No, not Battle Baylor.

Ridiculous name.

Apparently, a name earned because he never gives up. Thanks to the seemingly endless parade of students and professors who like to wax on about the football team, I now know far too much about Baylor's talent.

I probably sound like a snob. Maybe I am. Don't get me wrong, this is the South, I know how important football is to people. Down here, dog mascots are interred in their own mausoleum, tailgating is an art form, and women dress for games as if they're going to church. And in a way, they are. The Church of College Football.

However, my personal association with football begins and ends with my daddy shooing me out of the way whenever I stepped in front of the TV screen on Sundays. And Monday, and Thursday. Is there a day that football isn't on?

And my only personal experience with jocks was in high school. Complete ignorance of my existence comes to mind. Except that one time when a group of them managed to surround me in the hall and took turns pinching my "phat" ass. I spent a week in detention for kneeing one of them in the balls, a punishment I still find less than fair, especially since none of them had to go.

I don't understand football players. I don't understand the need to have your body bashed by some other guy while you throw a ball around. I like musicians. Wiry guys with long hair and haunted eyes. Eyes that make you want to search their depths. Not eyes that tell you something. Not eyes that say, I know who I am, and I like it, and I know who you are—I *see* you, and you cannot hide.

Baylor is getting closer. Close enough to see the way his thighs flex and shift beneath his faded jeans with every step. Close enough to see the flat slab of his belly, apparent even though his T-shirt is loose around his waist and tight across his chest. That shirt, army green with white lettering asking *How many licks does it take?* Instantly, I want to know. I imagine wrapping my fingers around him and applying myself to the test.

Okay, that's enough.

I let my eyes drop, deliberately. *You're not bothering me in any way. See? I have appraised you and moved on. Looking over my class notes is more interesting. By far.*

He slides into the desk next to mine, and his long legs stretch out into the aisle. I feel his gaze on me, watching, waiting for an acknowledgment.

He's sat next to me since that first disastrous day of class. And because I am as much of a lemming as everyone else when it comes to picking my seat, I remain where I am. It would be one thing if this were a large lecture hall, built to hold three hundred students. No one would notice a shift in seating. But those rooms are reserved for freshman classes. Like a cattle roundup, they pack in starry-eyed eighteen-year-olds and see who guts it out.

But this is History of Philosophy 401. A specialized class filled with mostly juniors, seniors, and a few grad students, all of whom are either majoring in history or padding their final semesters with advanced classes.

To move would be to admit my weakness.

Professor Lambert enters, and class begins. I don't even know what she's talking about, I'm so distracted. My neck hurts from straining *not* to turn my head and look at Baylor. It's a lost cause, I know. But I try my hardest to hold out for as long as I can. Have I mentioned that I'm screwed?

DREW

Four weeks into the semester and I still get the cold shoulder from Miss Jones. At this point, I've lost all game and have no idea how to get it back. I wish I could figure Anna out like I can football.

Football has always come easy for me. Don't get me wrong, I work my ass off to keep in top condition. What free time I have between practice and classes goes to working out or studying. I ignore physical pain and mental exhaustion on a constant basis.

But when it comes to the game? Effortless. Gripping the ball fills me with power. During a game, I don't fear the three-hundred-pound linebacker trying to take me out. I control my pocket, see paths, openings, opportunities. I talk to the ball, and it listens, going where I want it to go more often than not. If no opportunity presents itself, I find one, running the ball, avoiding the hit, until I can make a play. It's that simple.

And it's fucking fantastic. The roar of the crowds, the victories, they're addictive. But never as addictive as the need to do it all again, throw that perfect pass, trick the defense with a brilliant handoff or pass fake. Because I can always do better. So, yeah, football is my joy. And I know how lucky I am to have found it, that I have the talent to be one of the best. If there was one thing my parents hammered into me, it was to appreciate what I have.

All of which makes Anna Jones's disdain more irritating. She thinks I'm vain, a meathead. I should stay clear of her. There are tons of women who want to get to know me—kind of goes with the territory.

I still don't even know what it is about her that gets to me. She is pretty, luscious even, with the classic looks of a vintage pinup girl. Heart-shaped face, a pert little nose, dark red curls that tumble around her shoulders. But she isn't my usual type. Normally I prefer a girl who doesn't look at me as though I'm a hair that snuck into her salad.

So why can't I get Jones out of my head? All I can see these days are her eyes glaring at me, not giving a shit about the glossy veneer of my fame—hating it, in fact. And it turns me on.

So here I am, slouched in my seat, watching her arms wave and her sweet breasts bounce as she discusses philosophy's impact on society.

"Take Descartes," she's saying. "His move from trying to explain the 'why' of a question to observing the 'how' helped forge modern scientific method. In antiquity, philosophers changed our world by constantly questioning the status quo."

Because I want her to acknowledge me, I speak up. "I agree."

Anna's dark green eyes cut into me with one glare. Then, as if she realizes that glaring at me means an acknowledgment, she reins it in and gives me her profile, facing forward once more.

She clearly doesn't like it when I take her side. Hell, she doesn't like it when I join any conversation she's involved in. It's like I insult her just by speaking. Which pisses me off and makes me want to do it some more.

"Take his argument on dualism, that the mind not only controls the body but that the body can control the mind." I find myself grinning, watching Anna's tension rise, as I lower my voice, directing it toward her. "That one's passions can overtake rational thought and prompt them to act in irrational ways."

Anna's focus stays on Professor Lambert, but beneath her desk, her legs cross then uncross. Clearly, I've made an impression on her. Good. Now we're even.

"Is there a point to your mentioning dualism, Mr. Baylor?" Professor Lambert asks, her wry tone pulling my attention back to her and the class. Shit, what was I saying?

I sit up higher in my seat, clearing my throat just as a few junior girls turn their heads to stare. "Ah, just that Descartes got people thinking about the relationship between the mind and the body in a different way."

Hell, I fumbled that one. My face feels uncomfortably warm. That's it, no more talking for me. And I'm grateful when the girl in the flower skirt jumps in. Only her eyes are narrowed at Anna in annoyance.

"I wouldn't say Descartes is such a hero. His belief that animals did not possess a soul led to widespread abuse of animals." The girl's expression grows irate as her voice climbs. "Vivisection, experimentation, neglect, these atrocities to animals can be drawn back to Descartes."

Since the girl's yelling this at Anna, all eyes are now on the them. Anna doesn't cower, though. Her response is smooth as cream. "Given that my argument wasn't about Descartes, but on how philosophers changed societal beliefs, I'd say you just proved my point."

Hell, but I like this girl. I like her quick mind and her fire.

Flower Girl, on the other hand, is turning red. "So, you're just going to ignore the ill his theory brought to the world?"

"I'm not ignoring it," Anna says. "But I also don't think we need to throw the baby out with the bathwater. He was responsible for a lot of positive changes as well."

Despite my former resolve to shut the hell up, I find myself saying, "Jones is right, we can't judge the whole of a person's work based on one negative outcome. Shouldn't we give the guy a break? Maybe he had no idea the damage he'd do with a few misunderstood words."

I mentally will Anna to answer that. She stubbornly ignores me. But she's the only one.

As usual, whenever I talk, eyes turn my way. It's annoying, but I'm used to it. The fact that I'm defending Anna, however, sends curious glances her way as well.

I hear the blonde who's been trying to catch my attention for weeks now mutter in a voice meant to carry, "'Jones'? He knows *her* name?"

Anna's cheeks pink. Tension lifts her shoulders, and I could swear that she's fighting the urge to duck her head. It's strange, as if she both wants to hide yet refuses to cave. But I must be wrong. Nothing about Anna conveys shyness, and she didn't seem bothered when she was arguing with Flower Girl. Yet she drops off from the discussion and concentrates on taking notes.

Since she's no longer in the conversation, I lose interest as well. I resume watching her out of the corner of my eye and wonder if there's some sort of remedy for this kind of fascination. A smart man would give up the ghost and let her go.

Does that stop me from following her when class is over? From stalking her like some creeper as she heads to the food court at the Student Union? No. Not even a little bit.

TWO

ANNA

WHEN I STARTED COLLEGE, I loved it. I loved the freedom of choosing what classes I wanted to take and when. I loved the exchange of ideas and the notion that professors were actually interested in what I was thinking. They might not always agree with me, but an intelligent argument was valued.

And I loved the anonymity of it. No one here knew the old me. I was no longer that weird loner who everyone assumed was smoking up before class. Which is kind of ironic considering I wasn't even offered drugs until I got to college.

There weren't any obnoxious cliques in college. Not, at least, in that incestuous way of high school. Sure, you could find one, create one, but there were too many students to even notice those groups. I loved being one of thousands, not one of a hundred. Because I could start fresh, be myself without being told that being myself wasn't good enough.

But now I've grown weary of school. My brain is tired. I don't want to spend another night writing papers or cramming for exams until my eyes blur. I don't know if it's normal to be twenty-one and burnt-out, but that's how I feel. I just want it all to be over. And I still have a year left.

Of course, that fact brings its own brand of issues, as in *what the fuck am I going to do once I'm out?* I majored in European history because it interests me, not because I wanted to be a historian. The truth is, I don't know what I want to "be." Oh, I have a list of life wants: happiness, security, excitement, and making enough money that I can travel whenever I want. But shouldn't I have an idea of how I'm going to live my life? Isn't that the way it's supposed to go?

I just don't know. It's been plaguing me of late. What to do? What to do?

And because the question brings a sick lurch of fear into my gut whenever I linger on it for too long, I try to ignore it.

I'm trying now: trying to study, trying to not think about the rest of my life. Only I end up staring off into space, my pen tapping against my class notes as I sit in the Student Union dining hall.

Students come and go around me, a constant chatter of voices punctuated by random bursts of laughter. Then a familiar, and not appreciated, prickling sensation steals over my skin.

Don't react, I tell myself. *Don't do it.*

I turn my head anyway. And immediately spot him. Baylor.

How does my body know? Why does it instantly perk up when he's nearby? It's like I have internal Drew Baylor radar. I should be studied by the NSA or something. At the very least have my head examined. Because this has to stop.

My only consolation is that he's looking at me too. Maybe before I even noticed him, because our gazes instantly clash. A buzz goes through my body, a low, warm hum that has my lower belly clenching.

Maybe it is a simple matter of fascination that he keeps looking at me. And even though I know I'm not a toad, I can't help but wonder why. Why stare at me when he's surrounded by girls who are, by anyone's standards, gorgeous. God, he's probably thinking the same thing: she keeps looking at me. Only he's probably not wondering why. Everyone looks at Baylor.

They're looking now. He's at the far side of the hall with a hulking group of football players, and all heads are turned his way. I've always thought Baylor was big and tall, but one of the guys next to him looks like he eats screaming villagers for breakfast. A linebacker, if I had to guess. He even has a beard, full and bushy. Hagrid's younger brother maybe.

The guys are laughing, talking to other friends who come up to see them. A group of girls head straight for them as if they've been waiting. And their arrival is greeted with appreciation.

But not by Baylor. He's still watching me, his expression almost grim and so intent that my heartbeat speeds up. I want to look away. I should, but I just stare back.

"Do you know Drew Baylor?"

The question jumps out at me, loud and in my ear, and my pen clatters to the table.

"Jesus, Iris," I say as my best friend slips into my side of the booth. "You scared the shit out of me."

"I can see how you'd be distracted." Her dark eyes shine with an evil light that I know means trouble. "What with you eye-fucking Battle Baylor and all."

"I'm not 'eye-fucking' anyone." It's a mumble. And there is absolutely no way I'm looking back at Baylor now, even though I'm dying to.

Iris scoffs and grabs a drink of my iced coffee.

"Eye-molesting doesn't have the same ring to it, though." When I open my mouth to protest again, she waves me off. "Don't bother denying it. I know what I saw."

"How do you even know what I'm looking at anyway?" I slap my notebook closed and take back my drink. "I could have been checking the time."

There's a big clock hanging on the wall behind Baylor, so I'm hoping that excuse is believable.

Iris's smirk tells me it's not. "Because he was eye-fucking you back."

I nearly choke on my drink. "Would you please stop using that phrase?"

Iris laughs a little. "Sorry, but it was kind of hot and obvious, you know."

Hell. Was it?

Her eyes narrow. "You haven't answered my question, and it's clear that you know him in some way."

When she shifts like she's about to glance in his direction, I react like I'm five, and pinch her thigh in a panic.

"Shit, Anna!" she squeals.

"I'm sorry. But don't look at him." The last thing I want is for Baylor to know we're talking about him. I'd expire of mortification on the spot.

She glares, rubbing her thigh. "Drama Mama. I've never seen you so flustered. He's gone, by the way."

"I'm not flustered." I run a hand through my hair, which is ill advised for we curly heads. "It's just... Don't make it something that it's not. We have a class together, and we happened to make eye contact just now. That's all."

God, I feel like I'm in junior high again. I hate myself for reacting the way I do. I've worked for years to harden myself, to no longer care what others think of me, to not *need* to care. My walls cannot crumble.

Thankfully, Iris shrugs. "That's too bad. He's totally hot."

"And he knows it."

"How can he not? I mean, like, damn. That face. Those brooding eyes. Those pouty, kiss-me lips. I swear to God, he's like Captain Freaking America."

"I was always more of a Tony Stark kind of gal." I absolutely do not think of the animated gif I've had for years on my phone of Captain America's fine ass rippling as he pounds a punching bag. Over. And over.

Ignoring me, Iris fans herself in dramatic fashion. "God, that body. You just know he's cut. Like a freaking diamond."

I try not to smile, as I take another sip of coffee. "I need a nap."

"Oh, right, he's so boring to you. Or maybe you shouldn't stay up reading all night long. Which reminds me—" she slaps my thigh "—we're so going out tonight."

"No." Usually I like going out, but lately I haven't had the desire.

"Don't you 'no' me." Iris leans in, her silky black hair sliding over her shoulder. "You haven't been out in weeks. Being a home-body is one thing. Turning into a hermit is just wrong."

"You pay way too much attention to my social life."

"Kind of hard to ignore when we live together."

Freshman year, I started off living in a dorm, but that *was* a bit too much like high school for my liking, and the public bath-rooms flat-out sucked. Then I met Iris, who also had a dislike of cinderblock walls and wearing flip-flops in the shower. We decided working to pay for an apartment of our own was worth it and moved out by the end of the year. Because we got along so well, we kept the place year-round rather than going home during the summers.

Iris sighs, her slim shoulders lifting high before dropping. I bite my lip to keep from smiling, but she sees and plays on my weakness.

"Come onnn, Banana." Like a kid, she taps her feet on the ground in an impatient dance. "I don't want to go alone. I need a girlfriend with me tonight."

I narrow my eyes. "Where do you want to go anyway?"

Her white teeth flash, a sharp contrast against her bronze skin. "A party."

"No."

"Anna! You haven't even heard me out."

"You know I hate parties." With the passion of a televangelist on Sunday morning. I suck at small talk and mingling. Give me a booth in a bar and a few good friends, and I'm a happy girl. Parties suck.

Slouching back, Iris picks at the edge of my notebook. "I'm not going to leave you alone. We'll hang out."

"We can do that anywhere." I eye her with suspicion. "Why this party?"

She starts paying undue attention to the condensation on my cup, tracing patterns over it with the tip of her finger. "Well... Henry—"

"Fuck."

"You have the filthiest mouth, Anna." This isn't a new complaint. She makes it constantly. Not that she's wrong. I curse when I'm stressed. Or annoyed. Okay, I curse all the time.

"No shit?" My cussing also tends to increase when Henry Ross is mentioned.

Henry and Iris have been going out for two years, so you'd think I'd accept his presence in Iris's life. But I grit my teeth every time I see him. He's a smarmy asshole who treats Iris like window dressing. He doesn't so much talk *to* her as talk *at* her.

And though my friend is smart, funny, gorgeous, and independent, Henry is her kryptonite. He weakens her, making her oblivious to his many faults.

Sure, he's good-looking, dark-haired and dark-eyed with a nice smile. He's also the captain of the lacrosse team and makes sure everyone knows it. But I'm fairly certain he cheats on her. There are too many times when he doesn't answer her calls or has "important team meetings" on Friday nights or holidays such as Valentine's Day. Yeah, right.

As much as I wish I could tell Iris to ditch him, experience with my mom has taught me that I'd only strengthen her resolve and drive a wedge between us.

"I know you don't like Henry," Iris says now.

While I'm able to keep my mouth shut, pretending to like him is more than I can take. The sleaze always, *always*, eyes my boobs and ass. Not in the normal way a guy might make a note of them, but in a way that makes me feel covered with slime.

"He asked me to bring you," Iris continues.

Of course he did. He knows I don't like him. Which he takes as a challenge to piss me off. Henry might be a dick, but he's a wily dick. He knows I'll look like a jerk if I resist his attempts at polite interaction.

"He wants me to be happy," she pushes on. "And he knows I want to have a friend with me at his parties."

Because he'll ignore her within five minutes of getting there.

"This isn't one of his team parties, is it?"

"No." Her eyes are wide and pleading. "It's just a party, Anna. Geesh."

"Fine. I'll go."

Instantly, Iris hops up and down in her seat. "Yes! We'll have fun. And then we'll go dancing."

Iris is my opposite in all ways small. She loves reality TV, finds movies too long, and only reads when it's for an assignment. Her idea of fun involves a credit card and an open mall, and she has harbored a massive crush on Justin Bieber, despite all his WTFuckery, since her junior year of high school.

Her continuing love of The Bieb is evident by the fact that her favorite nightshirt is an ancient *My World* concert tee. And while the image of his faded face plastered over her boobs is more than creepy, I hate that she hides the shirt whenever Henry comes around. Or rather, I hate that Henry makes her feel like she should hide it for fear he'll make fun of her.

Despite myself, I glance at the spot where Baylor had been. He's gone and is probably making plans of his own. I suddenly feel restless and wrong. Like I don't know who I really am anymore. Which makes no sense. Maybe I'm coming down with something.

THREE

ANNA

AS I RARELY go to parties, I have no idea what to wear. Jeans and a T-shirt will just get me sent back to my room by Iris. She is of the "if it ain't tight you ain't wearing it right" school, especially if she's planning to hit up clubs afterward. However, I am of the "I refuse to be uncomfortable in the name of fashion" school of thought. So where does that leave me?

After forty minutes of cussing and general clothes throwing, I'm in a black camisole with a built-in bra, which is fairly daring for me, considering the size of my boobs, and a soft A-line skirt that hugs my hips but swishes around my thighs and ends a few inches above my knees.

Not wanting to leave my room, I procrastinate by peering into the mirror. My hair has a fuzz factor of three, which is acceptable, and my skin is clear. I apply a sweep of smoky-lilac shadow to make my eyes appear greener and dab a berry lip stain on my lips. So then, I've done all I can.

I tromp out to the living room for inspection time. Iris, as usual, looks fantastic. I don't even know how she does it; she's wearing tiny black leather shorts and a silky indigo top that hangs over one toned shoulder and is open in the back. If I wore something like that, I'd look horrible, but she's so lean and small, perfection on stiletto ankle boots.

Her dark eyes narrow as I stand there.

"What's with the boots?" she finally asks.

"You're wearing boots."

"Ankle boots. Totally different. Those are granny boots."

"*These* are vintage Fluevogs," I protest. "Victorias." Black-rubbed emerald green leather, they lace up to midcalf and have an ornate heel that resembles the legs of Victorian furniture. They are quirky, and the most expensive shoes I own. My mother gave them to me for my twenty-first birthday, and I kissed her for it.

Iris lets out a long-suffering sigh. "You look like you're going to a vamp ball in them."

"Watch it, Little Miss Belieber. I can still stay home."

"Sorry, sorry. You know how I get before going out."

Yeah, obsessive. Because she might disappoint Henry the Dickhead.

She strides over to me, taller now in her insane heels, and gives me a kiss on the cheek. The light, flowery scent of her perfume surrounds me. "You look gorgeous," she says. "God, I wish I had your curves."

"We can do an exchange, because I'd love to rock those shorts without terrifying the populace with my thighs."

"Fine, my thighs in exchange for your boobs."

"Deal." We both laugh, having made this deal numerous times before.

We take Iris's car because I don't trust Henry to drive me home, and I have a feeling she might go off with him later. I'll drive hers back. I'd take my Vespa, but Iris doesn't like to drive to parties alone, and frankly, I'd get helmet head if I did.

Iris taps nervously on her steering wheel as we drive along.

"Why are you so worked up?" I finally ask. "More so than usual, I mean?"

"No reason." She turns down a street.

Frat houses line the block. "Iris! You said this was an off-campus party."

But it's clearly one of Henry's horrible team bashes. Which involves beer bongs, guys pissing on the lawns—among other lovely locations—and basic asinine behavior. I was suckered into going to one once before and vowed *never again*.

"Look, I'm sorry, okay?" Her expression is desperate. "But Henry really wanted me to go, and you've been moping around the house lately."

"I have *not* been moping!"

"Staring out the window," she insists. "Like some tragic Jane Austen heroine."

"Austen's heroines aren't tragic. They are empowered."

"Says you. All those repressed feelings and prideful denials." Her snub nose wrinkles. "Pathetic. Just own your emotions already."

"Stop trying to change the subject. You kept this from me on purpose. Not cool."

She pulls up in front of a big old colonial that's lit up like summer. People spill from the open door, and a girl, laughing drunkenly, tumbles onto the lawn in a pile of limbs.

We both wince before Iris lifts her pleading eyes to me. "I just didn't think you'd come if I told you." She clutches my arm, and her hand is cold. "Forgive me, Banana?"

"You should have taken George." George is Iris's twin and my other best friend. He usually goes to these parties with her, watching over his "little" sister, while simultaneously hitting on all available women. It works for them.

"Where is he, anyway?" I grumble.

"He says he's got a headache." Iris's mouth flattens in annoyance.

"Suspect." George never gets sick. He's practically inhuman that way.

Iris pulls out her lipstick and quickly reapplies while glancing in the rearview mirror. "That's what I said." Her words are muffled as she stretches her lips to get a good coat of glossy red over them. "But what could I do?"

"Not torture me?"

With neat efficiency, she caps the lipstick and plops it into her purse. "Well, where's the fun in that?" Her eyes sparkle in the low light of the car. "Besides, maybe you'll see someone you like."

"Iris…" My warning glare is lost on her because she's already jumping out of the car with surprising sprightliness, considering her heels.

I follow, knowing I'll regret it.

DREW

It's Friday night, and I'm tired. My body hurts from a brutal practice. Not much difference from any other day, except I haven't been sleeping well, and it's wearing on me. A certain redhead occupies my thoughts to a sleep-depriving degree. When I close my eyes, I picture her. Hell, I picture her with my eyes open too.

Mostly, I picture her in profile because that's what I see when I watch her in class. The smooth arch of her graceful jaw, the rounded crest of her cheek that plumps when she smiles, the small, delicate shell of her ear. Curves. Anna is endless curves.

In my mind, I map the pale column of her neck down to where it swoops out to one of her best curves: her breasts. Large. Fuller on the bottom so they give the illusion of pointing upward, and more than enough to fill my hands. Soft. I know they will be.

I'm just enough of a shit that I long for the days when our classroom gets chilly, and she wears one of those cotton shirts that does nothing to hide the points of her nipples pushing against the fabric. Damn, but that sight never fails to make me hard. I'm fairly dying for the chance to peel off her shirt and expose those nipples that so readily stiffen. I want to know their color, their exact size and texture. She's fair-skinned, so they might be pale pink, but I've seen the shadows those sweet buds make beneath her white shirts, and I suspect they're a nice tawny rose that will go darker when sucked.

Yeah, I'm a sick bastard. But I doubt any guy would blame me. And I can't help myself. When I'm not thinking about her breasts, or the narrow dip of her waist and the rounded curve of her fine ass, I'm thinking about her voice, that syrup-thick southern drawl that makes my skin prickle.

I'm in the South now. Accents like hers surround me daily. Why her voice affects me more than others, I don't know. Nor do I care. She talks and I want to listen. Endlessly.

I've got it bad. Bad enough to be sporting semi-wood in the middle of a crowded room. And she's not even here.

I take a sip of water, not really listening to the chatter around me. What does she do on her nights off? Frequent clubs? Hang out at a coffeehouse and chastise unsuspecting men on the un-fairness of the glass ceiling? That makes me smile.

I love the way her pert nose scrunches up when she's irritated and her wide green eyes narrow into slits. Like she won't hesitate to kick someone's ass if she thinks they deserve it. Totally hot.

The water I'm drinking is warm and tastes of plastic. I set the bottle down harder than necessary. An antsy, irritable feeling grows within me. I don't want to be here. I've heard all these stories and jokes a thousand times before. And while I love my guys, I'm bored. I want to hunt down Anna Jones, rattle her cage, and see what she throws at me. But I don't know where to start looking. And it pisses me off.

I'm about to tell Gray that I'll see him tomorrow, maybe hit the sack in a vain effort to at least try to get some needed sleep, when I feel a familiar tightening in my groin and along my back.

I have no explanation for how or why I know when she's near. I just do.

Like a magnet to metal, my body swivels and my head lifts. And there she is.

Everything stops. My heart in my chest. My brain function. Fuck me sideways—someone stick a fork in me. I'm done. She isn't in her standard T-shirt and jeans, or one of her soft little sweaters. She's in a strappy top that barely contains her breasts, those creamy, beautiful breasts that bounce and jiggle with each step she takes. Those breasts are going to be the death of me. I'm afraid I've audibly groaned.

And damn if I'm not the only one who's noticed her. Too many eyes are glued to her chest. My hands clench. I'm no different than them, maybe worse, because I've made a habit of staring at her. But I'm itching to smack heads, send those eyes forward and off her. I also have the sudden archaic urge to whip off my shirt and tuck her into it.

She makes her way further into the living room, and I see the skirt. A swishy black thing that clings and sways around her pale thighs. Strong yet soft thighs that I know would feel so good parting for me, that would wrap me up and hold me tight.

Je-sus.

A frown mars her face, drawing her auburn brows close and pinching her lips. If there is anything I love more about her than her breasts, it's her lips. Deep pink and plump, those lips entrance me. Lips I've wanted to kiss since I first laid eyes on them.

Clearly, she isn't happy to be here. She scowls back at a pair of girls who look at her as if she's an intruder. I know those girls. Sports groupies. "Cock Jugglers" are what Gray calls them. And though it's crude, it's fitting. They've serviced more than half the team. Ugly experience has taught me to keep far away from them. I don't like the smirks they're giving Anna.

She shouldn't be here. *We* shouldn't. I want to take her out of here and just drive somewhere. Maybe to that coffeehouse in my imagination. I'd be happy to have her lecture me on all the ways I annoy her.

Her eyes scan the room as if seeking a way out.

Look this way, I tell her in my head. *Look at me. Give me those wide green eyes. Lock them on to me with that intensity I feel down to my bones.*

Look at me.

Look at me.

As if she hears my pleas, her pale shoulders tense, and my body seizes with hot anticipation. Her long lashes sweep upward and, *bam*, those eyes find mine.

It's like being blindsided. Except heat and breathless pleasure overwhelm me instead of pain.

Her full lips part as if she's taking a shocked breath, and I find myself doing the same. Jesus, I want her. She watches me, a mixture of anxiety and raw excitement gleaming in her eyes. I need to find a way to erase that anxiety. I need to know her better. Nothing on earth is stopping me from going to her.

Adrenaline rushes through my veins and my heart rate increases. Game on.

FOUR

ANNA

INSIDE THE HOUSE is just as I feared: packed, hot, and noisy. Guys appear to be making it their sole purpose to shout at each other as loudly as possible. Music is pulsing through the speakers and bouncing off the walls.

Eyes follow me as I walk by. I don't belong. They know it. I know it. Girls frown as if trying to figure out why I am here and who invited me, and guys take long looks at my boobs.

I'm now cursing my choice of top—and Iris, who darts like a minnow through the crowd in her quest to find Henry. The instant she does, he pulls her in and sticks his tongue down her throat. He grabs her ass to haul her in closer.

Yeah. I don't have any desire to stand next to them now. My only refuge is to find a beer and a corner to nurse it in. Because of my three-inch boot heels, I hover at 5'10". High enough to see over most other girls' heads. High enough that, when I move into another room, I instantly spot him.

Drew Baylor is looking directly at me.

His mouth hangs open slightly, as if he's shocked to see me here, which makes two of us; I'm shocked to be here. But then, as if it dawns on him that it's really me and not a nightmare, his lips quirk up at the corners and a glint comes into his eyes.

I wonder if all my happy parts are somehow connected to his smile because they flare at that expression, going warm and tingly. Which annoys the hell out of me.

Then he moves, walking away from the group of people surrounding him without a backward glance.

My uncooperative body refuses to flee, as his big body cuts through the crowd like a blade. God damn, but he looks fine, his long striding legs encased in worn and faded jeans that hug his thick thighs. His moss-brown T-shirt clings to his chest like a love song, highlighting the breadth of his shoulders and the leanness of his waist.

In a room filled with boys, Drew is a man here. Bigger, stronger, and just *more*. In an odd way, he doesn't belong here either. But the difference is they want him to belong.

His eyes stay locked with mine the whole time. It's unnerving. And enough to make my toes curl in my beloved Vogs.

He stops just before me. Way too close for a casual acquaintance. Even with my added height, I have to tip my head back a little to meet his gaze.

"Anna Jones," he drawls, "fancy meeting you here." That he appears pleased makes my insides dip.

"Not by my own volition," I manage.

His lopsided smile grows. "Who suckered you into coming?"

"Iris, my roommate and soon-to-be resident on the missing persons list."

Light laughter breaks from him, and his eyes warm. "I don't know... I'm kind of grateful to her."

"You can thank her when she stops sucking her boyfriend's face off. As for me, I'm leaving."

"Now? You just got here."

"How do you know? I might have been here for hours."

He shifts his weight onto one leg, bringing him closer. "Jones, I knew the second you walked in the door."

"Bull." I say it reflexively.

He grins. "I shit you not."

My skin is too tight, my flesh too warm. "How is that even possible?"

Another small laugh leaves him. "Seriously?"

His gaze travels down to my chest, lingering as his nostrils flare, before slowly trailing back up to my face. When my glare registers, he merely gives me a sheepish look as if to say he knows he's busted but isn't really sorry.

Not that I can totally blame him. My boobs are swelling over the edge of my top. I have the desperate urge to hike the cami up, but I resist and cross my arms under my breasts instead. The action lifts my cleavage higher.

A dare.

I think.

I'm not sure what the hell I'm doing anymore.

Color tinges the high crests of his cheeks and those hot eyes glide back down.

"Okay," he says thickly. "Now I know you're messing with me."

The fan of his lashes casts shadows on his cheeks as he peers at me. "But I'm willing to be tortured."

My arms drop. Nerves flutter in my belly. I've been with guys. And I like sex. *Love* good sex, elusive as it is. But flirting with Baylor? I can't handle it. He's too much. He makes my mouth dry and my hands twitch with wanting to run them over him.

The truth is I don't understand why he persists in talking to me. I'm nothing like his usual women. I'm not even nice to him. Something I refuse to feel guilty about.

"I wasn't offering," I say. Not precisely true. Which is why I need to leave.

I turn, ready to hunt down Iris, when he moves to touch my elbow with the tips of his fingers. Pure instinct has me evading his reach. I know without doubt that if he touches me, I'm done for.

He frowns at the action, his hand dropping. But it doesn't stop him from speaking. "Stay." His voice is a soft caress that rubs over me.

"I'd rather go." It's both a lie and the truth. I can't think straight when he's near.

"I can't believe that." He dimples. "I mean, we get along so well."

He says it with just enough dry humor that I fight a smile and shake my head. "Let me guess—you've never approached a girl who turns out to be not interested in you."

Baylor cocks his head as though taken aback, and then gives his neck a scratch.

"Well," he says slowly. "No, I haven't." A wide grin breaks over his face, all charm and dimpled hotness. "I can see that bothers you."

"Wrong. It simply reinforces my original impression of you."

"As what? Honest?"

He leans in close. Close enough to notice that his breath doesn't smell like beer, and that his eyes have a ring of deep brown around the gold irises. "Here's the thing, Jones, I don't understand how you can find that a problem."

I blink and force myself to focus on something other than his eyes. "You don't see how never being told 'no' isn't a problem?"

His smile deepens. "Stop being obtuse. You're talking about my irresistibility. I'm talking about my honesty. Two vastly different topics."

My lips twitch. Damn it. "I don't recall saying you were irresistible."

"Besides," he goes on as if I haven't spoken. "I can't see what sort of culpability I have in girls wanting to get to know me. It's not like I'm bribing them or scheming to have my 'wicked way' with them. It is what it is."

I stare at him a long moment, one in which he grins his goofy grin and I fight the goober urge to return it.

"You know what? You're right."

"Finally!" he says to no one in particular before smiling down at me.

"So let's put it this way. I could not care less about football. I don't give a shit who you are or what you do or—"

My tirade dies when he leans so close that our noses practically touch. The look in his eyes isn't angry. It's triumphant. "Exactly, Jones."

Two words and he's knocked the wind out of my sails. His not wanting me to fawn all over him is the last thing I expect. I start to frown. Maybe I even do.

"Well, hell."

He bursts out laughing. A rich, full laugh that's so infectious, I respond to it, snorting a little as I try to keep from laughing too. Our eyes meet, and the air between us abruptly shifts. Base heat swamps me so fast that I lose my next breath. Maybe he does too because he goes still. A lion about to pounce. I blink back, the gazelle caught out in full sunlight.

But then a lumbering form comes up to us, and a big hand slaps down on Baylor's shoulder.

"Battle, my man," says the hulking guy who has to be one of Baylor's linemen. "Sandra here wants to say hello."

It's like I'm not even there. Not to the Hulk, who bumps me back with his arm, as he gestures to some eighteen-year-old with a coy smile. Not when she slinks up to press herself against Baylor's arm.

"Hey, Battle," she breathes—*breathes it*, because I'm not sure I heard any actual consonants. "Will you sign my shirt?"

Of course she's wearing his jersey, the number eleven splayed across her breasts. It's no shocker when she points directly to that area, in case he wasn't sure where he should sign.

I want to roll my eyes but don't. She's not the problem here. Baylor isn't even the problem. I am.

"Well then," I say. "I'll leave you to it."

I turn and flee, hearing him call my name. But I don't look back.

I nearly reach the hall when he steps in front of me, halting my progress.

"Hold up." Baylor's lips pull in a pout, which should look petulant but simply makes him hotter. "I thought we were having a conversation."

"I think it was more like bickering," I say, and when he starts to smile, I hurry on. "And it was clearly over."

"Why? Because of that interruption?" He gives a little jerk of his head in the direction of his number one fan.

I shake my head. "Don't let me keep you, honestly."

Instead of backing off, he takes a step closer. "But I'd rather be talking to you."

My heart is beating so hard now I feel it in my fingertips. I don't know where to look or what to do. My gaze settles on the leather cord he wears around his strong neck. I've never seen him without it.

A small rectangle of polished wood hangs from the cord, dangling just below the hollow of his throat. My fingers itch to touch the pendant, to trace along the cord up to the stubble that starts just below his jaw. I lift my hand to do just that when a masculine shout snaps me out of it.

"Baylor!" Yet another one of his teammates seeking his attention. The freshman is still there, waving frantically.

"You're obviously busy," I say.

A frustrated breath escapes him. "What was I supposed to do? Tell her to get lost because I'm trying to impress another girl? Pretty counterproductive to act like an asshole, if you ask me."

I get stuck on the whole "impress another girl" part. In fact, the moment he said it, my heart stopped altogether, and heat rushed my face. Why *me*? I don't fit in here; I never did.

My throat closes, and I swallow hard. "Sorry, but you're paying attention to the wrong girl." I edge toward the hall and freedom. "I'm not interested."

A flush of color washes over his cheeks, and his eyes turn bronze. "Bullshit."

When I flinch, his voice softens and slides through my defenses like a spoon into pudding.

"Let's be honest here. I'm in danger of developing a permanent neck kink from checking you out. And if the number of times you meet my eyes is anything to go by, then you are as well."

My cheeks must be flaming red by now. I'm too shocked to reply.

His low murmur rings crystal clear in the small space between us. "Why don't you tell me what the real problem is, and we can address it?"

Address it. Like I'm something he wants to figure out and fix. Something he wants to keep. The whole idea is so foreign to me, and so terrifying, that I end up snapping. "Why don't you just let it go? Some games you aren't going to win."

He scowls, but when he opens his mouth to reply, I talk over him. "Disappointment is good for the soul, Baylor. I'm sorry, but I have to go."

This time he doesn't get a chance to stop me, or maybe he just lets me go. I head for the stairs, and some privacy, as fast as I can without actually running, and another friend approaches him. Which is all good. And maybe if I tell myself this enough, I'll believe it.

DREW

That went well. Anna Jones's gorgeous ass sways as she walks away from me. A perfect counterpoint to the swish of her little black skirt and the bounce of her red curls. I want to grab her and press her up against the nearest wall so that I can taste her tart mouth. I wouldn't even mind if she bit me, as long as her tongue soothed it afterward. Fat chance of that.

I stay where I am, defeat and disappointment—yes, thank you, Miss Jones, I'm well aware of that emotion now—crashing into me like a bad hit.

"Shit." I rub my ribs where the phantom pain spreads wide.

It's even worse when I see Gray sauntering over.

Gray is my teammate and best friend. We met when we were fifteen and attending the Manning Passing Academy. We are both from Chicago, though from different areas, and had played against each other before but had never talked until then. When my parents died, Gray was the only one I could stomach being around because he had lost his mother to breast cancer the year before. Which means he knows me better than anyone alive. This is going to suck.

His grin is obnoxious and wide. "'Crash and burn, huh, Mav?'"

I itch to punch the smile off his face. "I never should have introduced you to the glory that is *Top Gun*. You don't deserve it."

When he laughs, I roll my eyes. "How long have you been waiting to use that line on me?"

"About four and a half years, give or take."

He slings a meaty arm around my shoulder and attempts to pull my head down. I duck away and slap the side of his head lightly. I'm not in the mood.

Not that Gray cares: he's still grinning evilly.

"What's the matter? Red didn't respond to the 'Battle' cry?"

"Fuck off, Gray." There isn't much heat to my request. My mind is still on Anna, and my body is itching to follow.

Shit, I'm so screwed. Something pathetically close to a sigh lifts my chest as I stare in the direction she took—fucking fled—to get away from me. Like I was a disease she needed to stay clear of.

Which is unfortunate. Because it's still there, that insistent clamor in my head that says: *Her, her, her!*

Not so great, when she seems to have a cry in regard to me that goes: *Run, run, run!*

I don't understand it. I wasn't lying to her, and I don't think I'm deluded, when I said that we've been virtually eye-fucking each other for the past month. Fortunately, I didn't call it "eye-fucking"; she'd probably have my nuts in a clench if I had. Not that I'm entirely opposed to her touching my nuts...

"Shit." I pinch the bridge of my nose. Then pinch it harder when I realize that Gray is still there watching.

"Dude," he says, "let it go. This is getting embarrassing."

"Why? Because I have to work for it? For once?"

The masochist in me kind of likes it. I sure as hell love it when she's all snappy and taking me to task. I fantasize about her doing just that, while I suck on her neck, feeling the vibrations of her voice as she talks. Or maybe she'd wrap those creamy legs around my back, and I'd push into her heat, making her groan just a little between arguments...

I take a deep breath. And another. I'm so screwed if Gray sees me with a hard-on. Thank God for jeans—and the fact that Gray is still lecturing too much to look down.

"Sex shouldn't be work," he insists. "It should be easy. Girls come to us, give us a good time, and we send them on their way with a nice thank-you, and maybe a pat on the ass if they're extra special."

"I pity your bed partners."

"They have a good time. A great time."

"Sure. You let them do all the work while you sit back like a lazy shit. Sounds awesome for them."

He gives me a sour look. "Well, you sound like a girl."

"If I was one, I wouldn't be fucking you."

"You could do a lot worse—" His face goes red. "Damn. Would you stop that shit? I hate when you make me twist my words."

I can't help grinning.

Anna seemed to like it when I twisted her words, until she fled that is. And there's that pathetic sigh again, making me sound like a sap. Damn, but I want to talk to her.

Maybe she thinks I want what Gray's offering: a simple hook up. Maybe I ought to tell her I want more. I want *her*. The whole prickly-mouthed, sweetly curved, irresistible package.

Tracking her down to tell her wouldn't be stalking, would it? Shit, I don't even know.

Gray's right in one regard, I obviously suck at pursuing. But if there's one thing I understand, it's practice. I excel at perfecting my technique through practice.

Anna still hasn't come back down the stairs. Which means I'm going up.

"If my efforts bother you so much," I say to Gray without taking my eyes off the shadowed hallway that leads to the second floor. "I'd look away now."

I give him a light slap on the chest and head off.

FIVE

ANNA

THE HOUSE IS bigger than it looks from the outside. Upstairs is a warren of long, dark hallways, stretching out in two L-shaped wings. Several rooms are occupied, the sounds coming from within leaving little doubt as to why. The hall is empty—people going back downstairs as soon as they realize that they aren't going to get to make use of the rooms themselves.

I walk along, discreetly listening to doors to find one that's silent. I need the bathroom and do not want to walk in on anyone before I find it.

Thankfully, a small bath near the end of the hall is unoccupied. Once inside, I take a deep breath and let it out slowly. It's blessedly quiet here, the blaring bass of the music a muted thud.

My skin is hot, and my heart is still beating too hard. It's like I've run a mile in a minute. Worse, part of me wants to go back downstairs where *he* is.

Cursing, I run cold water over my hands and splash some on the back of my neck. In the reflection of the mirror, my cheeks are pink and my eyes are shining. I look excited.

"Hell."

I pat myself dry, take another calming breath, and leave the bathroom. And practically run into someone. My shoulder hits the cool wall behind me as I step back to get away.

Baylor stands there, his expression bemused as if he hadn't expected me to pop out at him. Then he moves closer, taking my air. My thoughts scatter.

His eyes, intense and determined, are all I see. We are alone. Utterly. *Finally.*

I can't look at him then. Not directly. He is the sun, burning bright.

"Why are you here?" My voice is a wisp of sound in the small space.

So is his. "I want you."

The floor dips beneath me, his confession taking up too much air. Baylor seems just as shocked by his words. But he commits to them with a squaring of his broad shoulders. "Tell me you don't want me, and I'll go."

My mouth opens, a denial on my lips. Then he reaches for me. It's barely a touch, just the tips of his fingers on my elbow, as if he's planning to guide me back downstairs. Nothing really. And yet it's everything.

The small contact burns, ripples outward along my skin with lightning-fast intensity, and my breath hitches.

His does too. A quick glance up, and he searches my face as though seeking an affirmation. Whatever he sees must tell him that he's not alone in this because he doesn't let go.

Neither of us says a word. Blood rushes hot and thick through my veins, as the backs of his fingers skim slowly, oh so slowly, up my arm. His pulse thrums, quick and visible just beneath the golden skin of his throat. I want to lick that spot, put my mouth there and suck. I want him. I want him so badly that I'm going up in flames.

A quiet, pained sound escapes me, as his knuckles drift toward my inner arm, just to the side of my breast. I'm shaking deep within myself, an increasing tremor that spreads outward, until my breath comes in choppy pants that I fight to control.

What am I doing? This is Drew Baylor. Nothing good can come of this. I need to be strong. I need to stop this. To walk away.

I lean into his touch, wanting, needing *him*.

His lips part with a sigh, as if touching me is both a relief and a source of pain.

Somehow my hand settles on his hip, the bone solid beneath his skin. He tenses, a visible clench that has his biceps bunching. The next instant, my fingers steal under his shirt.

His skin is hot, as if he's burning up from within. My palm glides along rippling muscle, smooth and toned, the cotton of his shirt tickling the back of my hand as I go.

He holds so still that when he shivers it's an earthquake. My questing thumb finds his nipple, and he stops breathing altogether. The little nub of his nipple beneath my thumb turns me on so much, I bite my lip to keep from moaning.

Oh, but it's getting to him too. He swallows audibly, those little tremors within him growing stronger.

I press down hard.

With a choked cry, he stumbles forward, his forearm hitting the wall beside my head as he braces himself. Warm breath caresses my cheek, the sound of his panting filling my ears.

Shaking, Baylor stands so close that his vivid heat envelops me. I draw in his crisp, clean scent, and grow lightheaded. Unable to resist, I flick my thumbnail over his nipple. He grunts, his hips jerking as if pulled on a string. And then he retaliates.

His long index finger curls around the strap of my top. For a moment, he simply runs his finger up and down the strap, toying with it, each pass drawing closer to my breast. Then he tugs, sliding the strap over my shoulder by agonizing degrees.

Oh, God.

My lids flutter. I want to close my eyes but can't. I'm stuck staring at his rapidly beating pulse, all of my awareness centered on the progress of my strap as it scrapes down my arm, peeling the top over the curve of my breast, which has grown heavy, aching. I don't think I've ever been more conscious of my breasts, of my body.

The top slips further, exposing more skin.

Hurry, I want to cry. I'm shaking by the time the edge of my top catches on the hard bead of my nipple. Stuck.

We both seem to hold our breaths. Beneath my palm, his heart beats fierce and strong. I can feel his stare, covetous and hot. I want him to see me. I want to be exposed to him.

The sound of laughter drifts up, and the deep bass of music has the walls buzzing. Anyone could find us here, see him pulling down my top. As if he's thinking the same thing, Baylor shifts his weight, sheltering my body from view with his own. That small gesture of consideration breaks my resistance.

Biting my lip, I arch my back at the very second he tugs again. My nipple pops free.

Baylor makes a sound that's guttural. His breath is a rasp in my ear as his big hand cups my breast. The pleasure of his touch is so acute, it's a relief, and then it's far from that. I ache for more, and so deep down, that my sex clenches.

He doesn't move, just stares at his tanned hand against the white of my breast, my pink nipple jutting out just over his fingers, as if he's trying to make sense of things. Or maybe he's just savoring the moment. His tongue darts out, and he licks his lower lip. Jesus, I want to lick it too.

The blunt tip of his thumb brushes over my nipple. Once, twice. He presses down.

A bolt of hot, sharp pleasure shoots to the empty space between my legs.

With a cry, I sag, slipping down the wall, my knees knocked out from under me. But he's there, wrapping an arm around my waist. He holds me up. Holds me still. Gentle fingertips bracket my jaw and tilt my head up. I meet his eyes. Lust there, dark like burnt sugar. His gaze settles on my lips.

He dips his head, his breath buffeting my cheeks as he comes for me. Without thinking, I wrench my head to the side.

"No. Not on the lips." It hurts to say it because the greater part of me is screaming. *Yes. Now. Please.*

But I can't. A deep, undeniable instinct tells me that if he kisses my mouth, I'll lose all resistance to him.

He hesitates, his brow furrowing. His gaze darts over my face, going from my lips and back to meet my eyes. A growl of frustration escapes him, then he swoops down.

My heart leaps, but his mouth lands on my neck, just above my shoulder. And I can't think anymore. Just his lips touching my skin has me breaking out in goose bumps. He kisses my neck the way he'd kiss my mouth, open, wet, like he's been hungering for this, waiting for this. Kisses tinged with anger. Like it's a punishment for my refusal to let him have a proper kiss. Maybe it is, but it doesn't matter because it feels so damn good that I'm not going to complain.

Hard kisses rain down over my shoulder, along my chest. He sinks to his knees as he goes. A brief, suckling kiss on my exposed nipple makes my entire body twitch, but he's moving south, his hands caressing my sides, sliding over my hips. Calloused fingers trail up the backs of my thighs, gathering my skirt, lifting it up.

Oh, God. My breath hitches, an audible sound that catches his attention. Defiance is in his eyes, but I can stop him if I want to. The knowledge is thick and heavy between us.

I don't move, much less protest. I'm so ready for him, I can't stand it. If we stop now, it might all dissolve. Illicit excitement is a drug in my veins. The wall is cold against my heated shoulder blades, and I lean into it, trying not to crumple.

He watches me pant, and inches the skirt up, and up. Until my soaking panties are exposed.

I'm so wet there the air feels cold. As if he scents my desire, his nostrils flare, and he finally looks. He groans as though in pain. "Fuck. Holy fuck."

My upper thighs are wet.

Fisting my skirt in one massive hand, he uses the other to ease my legs apart. I comply without protest. I want him to touch me so badly that I shake. My clit pulses in time with my heartbeat.

His fingers tug aside my panties before his thumb presses into my wet, swollen lips. I bite back a moan, as the world spins around me.

Baylor takes it all in, his thumb slowly stroking, slip-sliding through slick arousal. Holding my gaze, he leans closer, his lips nearly touching my aching flesh. "Stop me."

My heart is in my throat. I want this so much, my voice is as rough as sand. "Stop yourself."

He doesn't. Doesn't even try. Before I can take my next breath, his mouth is on my sex.

White lights pop beneath my lids, and I groan low and long. I can't take it. The pleasure almost hurts.

Gritting my teeth, I grab the short, silken hairs on his head as if he can anchor me, keep me from spiraling into the dark vortex of need that's pulling me down. But I can't keep still. My hips rock against his mouth, the tight seam of my wrenched-aside panties rubbing my ass in a tormenting counterpoint to his tongue.

"Yeah," he whispers against my skin. "Fuck yeah. Ride my mouth, Jones."

Crude words that make me burn hotter. Sweat trickles between my breasts. My thighs tremble, and my sex throbs. I'm whimpering, incoherent, my hips writhing.

The hall is a dark tunnel, the party loud below us. Our exposed position has my heart threatening to pound out of my chest and highlights what he's doing to me. The luscious wet sounds he makes, the little groans. The rough stubble on his jaw sanding my inner thigh, and the heat of his mouth. He's feasting on me.

His big hand holds my hips. I can't get away. I'm his. When his thick finger plunges inside of me, curling in toward some hidden, perfect spot as he sucks hard, I come with a suppressed scream that ravages my throat.

I'm falling into him, and he's sweeping me up, wrapping my legs around his waist, as he stumbles into the room behind us. I'm too far gone to care if anyone is inside. Cool, quiet greets us.

We land on a couch, Baylor knocking things from it even as he sets me down. My nails clutch at his shirt, tugging it, desperate to get the thing off. I need to see him, touch his skin. With a muffled curse, he yanks the shirt over his head in one move, his hair tufting in wild angles as it comes away.

One glimpse of his glorious chest, hard-packed with muscle and gleaming in the pale light from the outside street lamp, is all I get. Then he's on me, his mouth at my throat, licking, kissing, sucking. Zeroing in on a spot that sends pleasure and heat skittering through my flesh. Fingers rake my shoulders, grab hold of my top, and pull it to my waist. He eases back as he does this, his greedy gaze taking in everything. I lift my exposed breasts. An offering. A plea. I've become a wanton thing, needing his touch.

"Christ." It's a growl in the darkened room. "You're so…"

His head lowers, steamy breath buffeting my hard nipple, and then his hot, wet mouth draws me in. The way he goes at me. It's almost lewd, his tongue sliding and flicking over my nipple as if he's lapping up melting ice cream. I feel it to my core, as if he's licking there too. His big warm hand covers my other breast, kneading and shaping it with just enough force to have me restless and shifting beneath him.

When he plucks my throbbing nipple, I rear up, my hands finding his narrow waist, my mouth on the heated skin of his shoulder. He tastes of salt and smells of sex. My knuckles scrape on the buttons of his jeans as I tear at them. And then his cock is in my hand. I revel in the thick, satin heat of him, a pulsing living thing that twitches in my grasp, before his mouth returns to my neck, his hands grabbing for my skirt. Our heads bump, our breaths coming short. We're both too greedy, too eager to touch each other.

My panties are wrenched off and cool air hits my exposed skin. Baylor rises over me, his honed body a work of art in the weak light. His open jeans sag about strong thighs, the jut of his long cock barely visible in the shadows. He's reaching into his pocket, pulling a wallet out. His hands shake, the wallet threatening to fall as he struggles to get a condom packet free.

"Hurry." My legs tremble, my sex so swollen it aches. "Now. *Now.*"

Cursing, he tears at the battered packet. My vision blurs, and I rub a boot-clad foot over his ass. He flinches as though burned, then rolls the condom on, canting his hips and holding the root of that big cock in one hand. God, the way he moves, so confident and just a bit dirty. I can't wait any longer. I'm empty, so empty.

The hot skin of his chest presses against mine, his breath a rough, disjointed sound. Both of us groan, as the blunt head of his cock pushes into me. In, in in, working deeper. Until I'm filled with him.

We still for a moment, centered on the feel of him pulsing inside of me.

Inside me. Drew Baylor is inside me.

It's like a fever dream. Unreal, and yet it's the most present I've ever been in my own flesh. Then he moves. Pumps hard and deep. Dream or not, it no longer matters.

Every time he thrusts, he makes a little helpless grunt as if he needs more, more. I understand. The thickness of his cock filling and emptying me, the silk of his skin sliding over mine, is too much but not enough. I'm burning up, shaking with pleasure. I didn't know it could be like this.

I clutch the shifting muscles of his back, pulling him closer. He trembles, his grip moving to my ass, holding it as he does what he wants to me. And I let him, because nothing has felt better.

"Jones," he rasps in my ear. Needy. Dark.

So close. So close.

His teeth graze the sensitive area low on my neck. When he bites down, sucking hard as he grinds against my clit, I come with bright and blinding brilliance.

As if I set something off, he goes wild, bucking and thrusting. His eyes meet mine, and my breath hitches. The way he looks at me, all heat and intensity. I know exactly what he's feeling, because I need him with the same urgency.

I dig my fingers into the tight globes of his ass. His entire body goes granite hard, straining against mine as he comes with a harsh cry. Our gazes hold until the last spasm goes through him.

Lax and sated, we melt into each other, our chests lifting and falling in a shared breath.

When he talks, his voice is coarse as gravel. "God, Jones. That was…" His voice fails, but his grip on me tightens. Like he's not going to let me go.

Reality is a fall through ice into deep, dark water. I freeze in the aftermath. What the fuck have I done?

DREW

I'm still shaking when I get home. My hands are useless, fumbling with the buttons of my jeans, grasping and missing the taps before I manage to turn on the shower. Full-out cold.

I'm a wreck. My heart is beating like I've just done an hour of shuttle drills. And it doesn't seem to want to slow down.

Icy water hits my overheated skin, and I hiss.

Holy hell, what just happened?

Anna Jones has wrecked me. Utterly.

Memories assault me: the pale, undulating length of her body arching up to mine; drawing her hard, luscious nipple deep in my mouth; the soft, warm weight of her breasts cupped in my hands.

I groan. My knees go weak, and I have to lean against the tiles or risk falling over.

Water pours over my face and runs into my eyes. I squeeze them shut. But it doesn't stop those images from playing. Her rounded thighs spread wide. For me. A small thatch of curls, and plump, wet lips glistening. For me. I licked and sucked every inch of that prize. Her taste is still in my mouth.

"Shit." My voice echoes in the shower.

And though goose bumps cover my skin, I'm hot again. And hard. The tip of my randy dick presses against the cold tiles, and I find myself nudging forward just to alleviate the pressure. Shit. I want her again. Now. *Badly.*

I don't even try to stroke myself. It's not going to help. The horny bastard wants Anna, not my hand. Besides, I recoil at the thought of jacking off to memories of her now like a pathetic beggar.

God, it was humiliating to watch the realization of what she did steal over her features and the horror creep into her eyes. She couldn't get away from me fast enough. I'd sat back on my haunches in a fog of only partially satisfied lust, as she wrenched up her top and scrambled off the sofa. Her panties were a lost cause, apparently, because she simply fled the room with a mumbled "Sorry—bye" tossed my way.

She didn't even let me kiss her. That burns the most. As if kissing me was so personal that she couldn't bear it. As if she needed to relegate me to some random, meaningless fuck.

I groan again and run a hand over my face. My arms feel like lead, and I'm shivering. Slowly, I turn on the hot water and sink to the hard floor of the shower stall.

I've just experienced the hottest, most erotic, life-changing sex of my life, and I don't think I'm going to get a repeat. Tonight was obviously an ill-advised hook up for her. And I'm so screwed because it was the best thing that has ever happened to me.

SIX

ANNA

IT DIDN'T HAPPEN. That's what we'll pretend. Flashes of Baylor rising over me, of his chest sliding against mine, his thick, heavy cock sinking... My steps wobble. Okay, it *did* happen, and I'm unable to pretend otherwise. But it doesn't really count. It was a...a...cosmic blip, a slight detour from reality. It was a hook up. No more. No less. I can do this. I've had hook ups before. Wham, bam, thank you, man. Lust satisfied. Life goes on.

Taking a deep breath, I head down the hall toward class.

Shit on a Popsicle stick. Baylor lounges against the door, one long leg crossed over the other, his arms lightly folded over his broad chest. My heart pounds like a frightened rabbit gearing to spring from a fox.

He watches me, a small, smug smile tugging at the corner of his mouth.

Traitor that my body is, my heart leaps at that smile. My mouth wants to smile back. I bite the inside of my lip. It gets worse as I draw up before him. I know him now. I know the texture of his skin, what his cock feels like deep inside of me, the sounds he makes when he comes.

"Hey," he says.

God, his voice—the memory of it whispering against my wet sex. *Stop me.*

I swallow thickly. "Hey."

His smile grows. "I've been thinking about you, Jones."

"Don't strain yourself."

"Such animosity." A warm puff of air touches my cheek as he leans in, bringing that body of his way too close. "I thought we were past that stage."

I'm in my own personal hell because all I want to do is lick the side of his strong neck and dip my hand into his well-worn jeans to grab hold of what's mine.

I wrench my head back and focus on his chin because I can't look at him in the eye.

"You're right. Let's move on to the 'never mentioning it or thinking about it again' stage."

Baylor frowns. "I don't like that option."

"I don't care." I give a pointed look at the door then his big, broad chest. "Do you mind moving out of the way? I want to get to class."

He simply stands there, arms crossed in a way that does interesting things to his biceps and forearms. I still can't meet his eyes.

"Are you embarrassed?" he asks in a lowered voice.

"No. Hardly." *Yes. Completely.*

"You look embarrassed. You're all flushed here." He brushes a finger along my cheek.

I bat his hand away. "I get flushed when I'm annoyed."

His voice rumbles along my skin. "That isn't the only time you flush."

And now my knees are weak. I glance at him, see the heat and teasing light in his eyes, so I focus on his earlobe instead. A nice, innocuous earlobe. That I want to bite.

"Is this your post-hook up protocol? Bug the girl afterward?

Do you need feedback or something to stroke your ego? Are you going to ask if the earth moved for me?"

He lifts his hand and starts counting off points with his fingers. "I don't need to ask that, Jones. We both know the earth fucking melted. I don't have a post-hook up protocol. I'd make a joke about what needs stroking, but that's too easy. Frankly, I'm disappointed that you left yourself wide open for that one."

He touches the tip of my nose, and that shit-eating Baylor grin grows. "I expected more of a challenge."

"Gah!" I shove past him.

"'Gah'?" He laughs, as I wrench open the classroom door. "Is that even English—?"

"Mr. Baylor," Professor Lambert says in greeting, her pale eyes sharp with reprimand. "Miss Jones. So glad you two could make it. Would you please take your seats?"

I give her a quick nod and head for mine, utterly aware of every eye on Baylor and me as we walk down an aisle.

As for Baylor, he is a presence I cannot shake. And my traitorous body is humming as if it's at its own personal happy hour.

Class ambles along at an excruciating pace. Lambert is discussing Plato's utopian ideal, and though I try to focus, my body is too attuned to Baylor to be successful.

"What say you, Miss Jones?"

I jump at the sound of Lambert's voice.

"Could you repeat the question?" I will *not* look at Baylor, who is likely finding my flustered state hilarious.

Lambert's lips twitch. "Do you believe that Plato's utopia could work in a modern-day society?"

"No, ma'am, I do not." It's a short answer, but I'm too aggravated by Baylor's presence to give a better one.

"And why is that, Miss Jones?"

Right. I suppress a sigh and try to look unfazed. "Because, at its core, it is based on the notion of perfection. That perfection is possible. Which it is not."

"Hold up," Baylor cuts in, so fast, I wonder if he wasn't waiting for an opening that would force me to look at him. "Are you saying we shouldn't strive toward perfection?"

His eyes twinkle, and I know he's having fun egging me on. "Quite the defeatist attitude, *Miss* Jones."

"I'm saying that it isn't attainable, *Mr.* Baylor, because perfection is impossible to define."

"I agree with Baylor," a guy two rows up says.

He's wearing Baylor's team jersey, so I'm not surprised. Baylor's defender gives me an accusatory glare. "I mean if Drew didn't try to achieve perfection, we wouldn't have won two championships under his leadership."

The class cheers. I barely refrain from rolling my eyes.

"This is true," Baylor puts in helpfully.

Ass.

"There is a difference between trying to obtain a level of personal perfection versus expecting a society to unilaterally live in perfect harmony," I say. "One relies on a personal expectation. The other is based on the masses following the opinion of one. And who decides? Who dictates this utopia?"

"Plato, obviously." Baylor grins at me.

I give him a deadpan look, but it's hard to stay annoyed at his playful attitude. "Never mind the fact that we have virtually no examples of a utopian society thriving in a real world situation," I say.

One of the girls who has been mooning over Baylor since the beginning of the semester raises her hand, as if she needs permission to speak. "What about Atlantis?"

Oh, Jesus Christ in a peach tree.

I glance at Baylor, and he's biting his lip to keep from laughing. It's all I can do not to laugh too. I look away before I lose it. But I feel him beside me, and know that he's itching to let loose, which only makes it worse. It's so bad that I barely hear Lambert's response, which is good because I know it would make me laugh.

A repressed snort to my right has me turning. My gaze clashes with Baylor's and we share a look of glee, but it's short-lived. Suddenly I remember the last time I stared into his eyes. When he was deep inside me, his cock thick and pulsing with his release, and the strangled sound he made as he let go. Heat swamps me.

It must show. I don't know how to hide it. His smile slips, as his lips part. On a breath, his gaze goes molten.

Holy hell, I'm in trouble.

Vaguely, I'm aware of people standing around me. Class is breaking up. I can't look away from Baylor. Not when he slowly rises. Not when he stops in front of my desk and holds out his hand.

"Come with me."

I go, because I cannot ignore this need. But I don't touch him. The moment I do, it will be over. I'll jump on him right here and disgrace myself in public.

Maybe he knows this because he lets his hand fall and clenches it in a fist, as if he too needs to practice restraint. The corner of his mouth trembles. He's looking me over like I'm the meal and he's planning how to go about consuming me.

We turn as one and walk out of the classroom with deceptive casualness. But inside? Inside I'm burning hot. How is this happening again? My black sweater smothers me, my tight knit skirt scratching the sensitized skin on my thighs. I want these things off. I want skin to skin. I want him so badly; each step is a struggle. It's as if I'm walking through warm soap-slick water.

Though he's not touching me, Baylor is herding me along, clearly intent on someplace to go. We can't get there soon enough.

A strangled sound of impatience escapes me, and his pace increases, his hand hovering just behind my back. I quicken my strides as we head for the massive main library that sits catty-corner to the history hall.

People come and go, striding up the wide front steps and under the high-columned portico. Oblivious to us. Thick heat swirls around me, threatening to melt me the moment I come to a stop. I'm so worked up, I can barely get my student ID out and slide it through the scanner. Baylor does little better.

A quick, hot look from him, and I'm shaking again, heading toward the elevator.

God. I can have him there. Wrap myself around him. Sink my teeth into his firm flesh. Or sink to my knees and…

The door opens and we step in. And so do three other students. My teeth meet with an audible click.

Baylor stands next to me, his arm barely brushing mine. I feel it to my toes. We don't look at each other. Don't speak. He hits the button for the top floor where the rare folios are housed. Library Siberia. A haven.

Slowly people get off on other floors, and we are left alone. But neither of us dares to move. As soon as the doors open, we burst free of the elevator. We're walking as fast as we can without actually running. My throat feels raw, the space between my legs slick and my nipples tight and pushing against my bra.

Baylor's sneakers don't make a sound on the polished linoleum, but my boot heels hit with a steady hard *click, click, click*. The floor is devoid of people, and so quiet that I can hear my own breath coming out in disjointed bursts. We head for the back, to the farthest row. My knees nearly buckle, and he takes my elbow. The touch burns.

The second we reach the shadowy row, he pulls me in and whips me around to face the bookshelves. Without ceremony, he yanks up my skirt, shoving it to my waist. Rough, determined hands haul my hips back, practically lifting my ass into the air as he gets me into the position he wants me. It's all I can do not to thank him, beg him to hurry the fuck up and fuck me. My fingers grip the steel edge of the bookshelf and slip a bit from the sweat on my palms.

His breath is a raw, uncontrolled sound behind me, his heat palpable against my exposed skin. I press my lips into my sweaty wrist and arch my back, giving him a better view. The sound of his zipper going down and a foil packet tearing fills the air. My breath hitches, anticipation clutching low and tight in my belly.

My panties are wrenched to the side. One stroke of his finger to test my wetness. *Yes. Yes.* And then he thrusts. Hard. I bite the inside of my lip to hold in my cry.

So thick. So, so good. So deep that I'm on my toes, my sex pulsing. His fingers dig into my hips, pulling me back down on him, forcing himself deeper still. A ghost of a sound comes from his direction as if he too is swallowing his groan. I can't take it. He's too big. Too there.

And then he moves, a fast, frantic pumping. I close my eyes, rock into his hips, meeting him thrust for thrust. Excitement and lust run over my skin with hot bites of pleasure. All is quiet except for our muffled breaths and the wet slap of flesh against flesh that we can't control. His jeans-clad thighs press up against the backs of mine as he ruts into me. Because there's nothing smooth or polite about this. He's fucking me raw.

My fists clench, the effort to keep quiet making me shake.

His hands slide from my hips to under my shirt. His skin is so hot, his palms so wonderfully rough, that I suck in a breath. He slips under my bra, cups my breasts, and holds them as he fucks me. He's going to kill me. I'm sure of it. I nearly scream when he captures the tips of my nipples with his fingers and tweaks them, plucking in time to his thrusts.

Holy. Shit.

My orgasm hits in a series of waves, my sex convulsing and clamping down on his dick. And he loses it. His mouth finds that vulnerable spot on my neck as he wraps his body around mine. The blunt tip of his finger touches my clitoris, and I'm coming again, just as he does.

Thoughts scatter like dry leaves until only one remains: I will never get enough of him.

DREW

Thighs shaking, breath rasping, I close my eyes and try to calm. God. That was… I have no words. My legs are so weak, I might crumple to the floor at any minute.

Aftershocks of pleasure have me twitching, holding Anna tighter. I'm not allowed more than a moment to lean against her warm body and breathe her in before she jerks violently, trying to shrug me off. With her wiggling, I slip out of her and suppress a groan at the sudden loss of tight heat, but I can't seem to move away.

"Off," she hisses unnecessarily, giving me an elbow to the gut. I know she's right; we can't be seen like this. But, damn, a man needs a minute after something like that.

I stagger back, tugging the condom off—one out of the five that I'd tucked in my wallet this morning because hope springs eternal—and tie it before looking around in a daze. Where am I supposed to put it?

She's glaring at my dick, or rather, the fact that it's hanging in the wind. I make an annoyed sound as I stuff myself back into my pants and zip up. Spotting a trashcan in the far corner, I toss the condom in the empty bin—yeah, I don't care who finds it.

By the time I return to her side, she has her shirt fixed but is still adorably mussed. She smoothes her hands down her thighs to fix her rumpled skirt. Which makes me want to hike it back up. Then she gathers her hair in her hand and flips the length of it over her shoulder. "This can't happen again."

I snort. "It's going to happen again. You might as well admit it."

With a huff, she pushes a hand through her hair and glares. "No. It. Won't."

"Yes. It. Will." I don't want to be an asshole, but I'm not deluded. "I want you. You want me."

A wry laugh escapes me. "Though I think *want* is too weak a word here. *Crave*, maybe. *Am dying for*, definitely."

She goes pink, her lips, which I have yet to touch, pursing. I want to. I want to kiss her so badly, my lips actually throb with need.

Acting on instinct, I take hold of her wrist and pull her close, noting that she doesn't resist. I bring her hand to my crotch, where my hard-on is growing again—all praise the regenerative powers of a needy dick.

A deep flush works across her cheeks, and damn if she doesn't cup me, squeezing just enough to make me grunt.

"I get like this every time I think about you." I lean in, smelling the warm spice in her fragrant hair and the lingering scent of sex on her skin. "I just had you, and I'm aching to be inside you, to make you come, all over again. So don't tell me it's going to stop. Not when you're stroking me like that."

Anna snatches her roving hand away. "Okay, fine. You got me. I want you too." She ducks her head, and a tumble of curls hides her face from me, but not her words. "Badly."

She has no idea what that does to me. She couldn't possibly be that cruel. It's torture not to reach for her, tug her back to our secluded spot for another go. I probably wouldn't last two minutes, as torqued as I am. But she's moving now, striding toward the elevators with her swaying walk. I follow.

"I'm failing to see the problem here, Jones. Let's go out on a date. You know, like normal people who are into each other do?"

A sidelong glance is all I get. "Look. I don't want a relationship. Especially not with you."

I pull up short. "Why not with me?"

"We're too different." She stabs the down button and stares at the elevator doors. Dismissed.

I don't think so. "We're the same in all the ways that count." Why can't she see this?

Her back is to me, stiff and unyielding. "I don't like you. And you don't like me."

Wow. That hurts. Embarrassingly so.

I lean a shoulder against the edge of the door panel and bend down enough to bring myself into her line of sight. "There's where you're wrong. I do like you. A lot." I glance away, trying not to wince, then force myself to face her again. "I'm sorry if you don't like me."

She ducks her head, another flush hitting her pale cheeks. "Sorry." She shakes her head then clears her throat. "That was a shitty thing to say. I do like you. I just..." She lifts her hands up in a helpless gesture. "I don't want a relationship right now."

Disappointment tumbles into my gut like an unmoored boulder.

"Fine. Then we just fuck." I give her a level look as a bell dings and the doors to the elevator open. "Because any chance you give me, I'm taking it."

SEVEN

ANNA

I'M LATE MEETING Iris and George for lunch. Call it reluctance to face the firing squad. I'm under no illusion that they won't figure out I've had sex with Baylor. I'm horrible at hiding things, and Iris is already suspicious of my sudden disappearance at the party the other night.

Part of me wants to talk about it. Not about Baylor precisely, because the idea of him discussing details with his friends makes me cringe, and I won't be a hypocrite. But I need to process this *craving* that's got a hold of me. I cannot believe I had sex with him again. And in the library of all places. Anyone might have seen. The irony that I'm afraid to be seen with him yet let him fuck me in a public space, twice now, isn't lost on me.

Without warning, I think of him kneeling in front of me, his head buried between my legs. My cheeks burn and dark heat licks up the back of my thighs as I walk into the fifties-style diner that sits just outside of campus. Good God, I want to turn around, find Drew Baylor, and do it again.

I now know that it isn't the thrill of possible discovery that makes having sex with him better than anything I've experienced. It is him, the way I react to his body, his touch, his voice. And that scares the hell out of me.

I like you. A lot.

Damn it. If only he was someone else. Something else. A regular guy. A nobody like me. But he's not and never will be. When I think of the public scrutiny he, and by default anyone he's with, endures, I want to hide away, run for the hills.

I take a deep breath instead and tell myself to chill. It's over. It's done.

Iris and George already occupy a booth. George is facing my way and spots me first. He raises a brow in reproach.

"Sorry," I say as I slide in next to Iris. "I lost track of time."

"We ordered you a vanilla milkshake, and fries are on the way," says George. "But you choose the rest."

Six feet to Iris's five foot three, George towers over her, but they share similar features, their Mexican heritage showing in their dark eyes framed by thick lashes, honey-gold skin, and glossy raven black hair.

The waitress comes with our drinks and fries, her gaze lingering on George. "You know what you want?"

"Always," he answers with cheeky confidence that makes the waitress beam, and Iris and I roll our eyes. Not that I can fault the waitress's taste. George is incredibly good-looking. And while I appreciate that on an aesthetic level, I've never felt a glimmer of sexual attraction to him. Which is a good thing, as I'd rather have his friendship than a brief physical release.

We order our burgers and, once alone, Iris turns in her seat to study me. "So…you gonna tell us where you got that exceptionally large hickey decorating your neck?"

Shit. As if her notice has activated it, a spot where my neck curves to meet my collarbone starts to throb. Memories assault me, of Baylor's mouth there, his tongue sliding over my skin just before he sucked hard. I don't want to know how bad it looks.

George's eyes glint as he leans forward. "That's a beauty. Who's the guy? Or is it a girl? God—" he puts a hand over his heart "—please say it's a girl."

I toss my napkin at his head.

"It's Drew Baylor," Iris says. "Isn't it?"

I occupy my mouth by drawing a deep pull of milkshake.

"Get the fuck out," cries George with a laugh. "Seriously, 'Ris, stop playing."

The icy glass in my hand lands on the table with a thud. "Why is that so hilarious? Am I such a hag that the idea of me being with Drew Baylor is laughable?"

A gurgle dies in George's throat, and he straightens. "Are you kidding me? You're gorgeous. Baylor would be lucky to get near you."

"Well, thanks," I say, somewhat mollified, and at the same time completely shaken.

It's happening already. The disbelief. The questioning. Why would Baylor pick me? Even I want to know. Which both stings my pride and makes me want to disappear.

George shifts in his seat, looking irritable at his sudden burst of sentiment. "He's just not even near your type. And you aren't exactly his."

Tell me something I don't know, George.

"Opposites attract," sings Iris. Then she all but pounces on me. "It was Baylor, wasn't it? Oh my God, was he as hot as I think? Do the size of the shorts match the shoes?"

George's nose wrinkles like he scents something foul. "Can we not go there, 'Ris? I'm a guy."

"Oh, are you?" She shrugs. "I must have forgotten."

He makes a face. "Does that mean you want details of my hook ups?"

"God no," Iris and I say as one.

George laughs, but he's not deterred. "Well? Was it Battle?"

I pick up a fry, stabbing it in a pool of ketchup. "Does it really matter who it was?"

"Yes," George and Iris say as one.

"Jinx!"

"Ha! You lose, 'Ris. No talking until I say your name. Which will be in one hour."

"I'm not playing that tired game, boy."

"You called 'jinx.' That constitutes playing."

When they get together, Iris and George act like they are still in the fourth grade. I sink further into my chair. Maybe they'll forget all about me if I refrain from making sudden moves.

No such luck. Iris's dark eyes home in on me like a hunting hawk's. "You might as well tell us. Better we know the truth than speculate."

She has a point.

I swirl my fry.

"Spill it, Anna."

"It was."

"Say that again?" George puts his hand to his ear, but he's grinning wide.

"You heard me." I'm sure as hell not saying it again. I'm mad that I said it at all. What happened was... I don't even know how to describe it, but I know it belongs solely to me. And to Baylor. No one else is getting details. At least not on my end. Hell, is he telling his friends? I try not to squirm in my seat.

Iris squeals. "Was it good? What am I talking about? Of course it was. You two are obviously hot for each other. Oh, this is so awesome!"

At the sound of Iris's enthusiasm, a few eyes glance our way. Suddenly I can't breathe properly. Iron hands of fear grip my spine, push down on my lungs. My hands go numb.

"Okay, stop." My tone is deadly serious, and both Iris and George gape. I tried to remain calm but can't. The cold within me is making me quake. "This goes no further than this table. No one can know. No one. Ever."

I can't handle it if people know. I just can't. Not with the speculation that would arise. Drew Baylor banged *that*? It's bad enough that I've been waiting for the realization to creep into his eyes, that he's made a mistake in pursuing me.

A growl works its way up my throat. What the fuck am I talking about? I'm better than this. I'm not some hag. I shouldn't be ashamed. Cursing myself for my panicked knee-jerk reaction, I press the hot tips of my fingers against my eyelids until stars dance in the darkness. Shit, I haven't thought this badly of myself since I was fifteen.

And I can't go there again. Despite the fantastical thoughts of us dating that are running through Baylor's head, there's no chance of a girl like me being with a guy like him. I've spent too many years and dealt with too much pain while climbing out of that pit of doubt and insecurity for me to be pulled back down now. My overeager libido is just going to have to take a cold shower.

My friends are looking at me as if I've grown two heads.

I take an unsteady breath, feeling ridiculous close to crying. "Are we clear?"

"Crystal," George says, frowning. "But you should already know that."

A twinge of remorse plucks at my insides, but not enough to make me regret my words.

Iris appears just as thoughtful. "I won't tell. I wasn't going to…" She stops as if pinched and looks at me closer. "Oh my God, you did it twice!"

So much for calming her down. And what the hell? Is she psychic?

Iris laughs at the obvious horror in my face. "That hickey is fresh. And I *know* you hooked up with him during the party. You both went upstairs at the same time. And—" she points an accusatory finger at me "—you both did the walk of shame back down them."

"I didn't realize you paid so much attention," I reply. "What with having your tongue down Henry's throat all night."

George makes a noise of disgust. "Why do I hang out with you two? Can we *please* stop with the details?"

"Fine by me," I say. "I'd love it if we talked about something else."

Rolling her eyes, Iris snags a fry. "Of course I paid attention. I was waiting for it to happen."

I sit up straight, my hands slapping down on the cheap Formica table. "Wait. What? Did you...? You knew he'd be there, didn't you?"

Unrepentant, Iris grins. "Well, duh. It gets around what parties the football team plans to attend. And for as much as you denied it, I knew you were into him. You just needed a little push in his direction."

"You little weasel." I'm half-pissed, and more than a little impressed. She has Machiavellian depths that I never considered.

She shrugs and grabs another fry. "Pretend to be outraged if you want, but you obviously liked hooking up with the boy if you did it *twice*."

"Do me a favor," I say scowling, "and restrain yourself the next time you feel the need to help me out."

"Fine. My work here is done anyway." She pops a fry into her mouth and chews with exaggerated vigor.

I'm tempted to chuck a fry at her head, but they're too good, and I'm hungry.

"Two times," George says after a moment. "In less than a week? That's like a relationship for you, Banana."

I nearly choke on my food. "It is not."

"It is," says Iris. "And you know it."

All right, hook ups to alleviate occasional and unavoidable horniness is more my style lately. Since my breakup with Hayden sophomore year, I have made it a point not to see any guy more than once.

Hayden. Ugh. I don't want to think about Mr. Haunted Poet and Quiet Angst. I thought we were kindred spirits. It turns out he thought Amber, vegan and professional protester, was his soul mate. They found each other one dark and stormy protest night and dropped out of school to tour the country in a van. I never saw him again.

Unfortunate, as my last vision of him was that of his pasty butt pumping between Amber's skinny legs when I caught him cheating.

Hayden was supposed to be the safe choice, and he didn't have anything close to the potency of Drew Baylor. I cannot fall for Baylor. I will not.

"So it was more than one time." I shrug. "But it isn't a relationship."

"Would a relationship be so bad?" Iris asks gently.

Jesus. First Drew, now Iris. Whatever happened to the carefree and innocent college days of kinky sex experimentation?

"I don't need or want a relationship. They're emotionally exhausting. I'm lucky if I can muster the energy just to go to class these days. And what's the point of risking getting close to someone when we're going to graduate and move on in less than a year?"

"It might last longer," Iris begins.

I shake my head and take another pull on my straw. "It isn't worth the risk. Nor do two random hook ups a relationship make."

It's going to happen again. You might as well admit it.

"It's a start," Iris says.

"It is *not*." I shove my shake away. "I just… He's… We're…"

"You conjugating here?" George asks, his lips twitching.

"Ha." I expel a breath. "I don't know what's going on. There's something between us that's like…" My hand lifts helplessly.

"A fat zit that needs to be popped?" George puts in helpfully. "You know, all hot and throbbing and dying to be touched. The pressure to give it a squeeze builds and builds until you give in and, bam!" George taps his fists together. "Eruption."

"George!" Iris tosses a balled-up napkin at him, and I chuck a fry. He's too busy cracking up to defend himself. "You're going to make me sick."

"That's totally gross," I add with a laugh.

"Seriously," Iris huffs. "Did Mami drop you on your head when you were a baby or something?"

"Come on—" he's still laughing "—you know it's true."

"I do *not* want to think of any guy I'm…"

"Fucking?" George offers.

"I'm *whatever*," I grind out, "in terms of a zit."

"Yeah, well—" George steals one of my fries "—it would definitely kill the buzz if you did."

"I'm going to think of you as a pimple," Iris snaps. "You know, those deep-seated ones that make your life hell and always show up right when they will embarrass you the most."

"Ah, you love me, sis." George blows her an air kiss.

Iris rolls her eyes before turning back to me. "I think you're making a mistake."

"Agreed," I say succinctly, purposely misinterpreting her words. "It was a mistake that won't happen again."

DREW

Gray and Diaz are in my kitchen when I get home for the day. My mood is so rotten, I almost regret giving Gray a key, but then I smell something drifting from the big pot on the stove that makes my mouth water and decide his occasional invasions are worth it.

I would have asked him to be my roommate, but every time we go to an away game, I have to room with him, which is more than enough socializing for me. Besides, I like living alone.

When my parents died, I was handed a life insurance payout check for two million dollars, along with two death certificates. I promptly threw up the contents of my stomach and didn't get out of bed for a week. I couldn't even touch the money. I wanted my parents, not some fucking check.

Eventually, Coach convinced me that my parents took out those life insurance policies because they wanted to provide for me. Not the best comfort, but I bucked up and called a financial advisor who put the money in various accounts.

Last year, when I learned the true value of privacy the hard way, I bought a small bungalow-style house. I don't plan to live here permanently, but I bought it with cash and, over the summer, I had the master bath and kitchen redone. When I'm ready, I'll sell it at a profit and put the savings away. For now, however, it's my haven.

Tossing my keys on the hall table, I make my way through the open concept great room. I kept a few things when my parents died: the dining and living room furniture, my mother's beloved wedding china, and some childhood mementoes and pictures. Giving the rest away was a nightmare that still haunts me from time to time.

Maybe some people might think I'm not letting go by keeping the furniture, but there's something soothing about seeing my mom's carefully selected leather couch and chair set from Pottery Barn, the coffee table they bought on a weekend getaway, or the dining table that came from my dad's parents' home.

Gray and Diaz give me a nod as I walk past them and into my room. After a quick shower, I join them.

"What's cooking, honey?" I ask Gray, who tosses a dishtowel at my head in annoyance.

Unlike me, Gray can actually cook. His mother was Norwegian, and apparently Norwegian women believe in equality for all domestic tasks. He's been cooking since he was in the seventh grade.

"Stew, sweet cheeks," Gray answers with sarcasm. "Now fetch me a beer, will you?"

Diaz simply grunts with amusement. He's one of the best fullbacks I've played with, but he doesn't say much. Ever. He does, however, know how to find a good, free meal, which explains his presence here.

I reach into the fridge and then toss Gray a beer. A raised eyebrow to Diaz, and he finally speaks. "Got Gatorade?"

The thirty-two-ounce bottle of berry flavor goes to him. I know he'll drink the whole thing.

As for me, I forego alcohol for the season, so I'm having water. I'm beginning to get sick of water. I'm sick of a lot of things, actually.

We're silent as we settle in the living room to eat while watching TV. Something I'm grateful for. I don't really want to talk. The stew is good. Better than anything I've had all week. Damn, I'm going to have to ask Gray to teach me how to cook one day, because this beats carryout and frozen meals by yards.

My mouth is full of stew when Gray attacks.

"So, what's the deal with you and the redhead? Did you tap that?"

Though I don't say a word, Gray knows me too well, and when the corner of my mouth tightens in annoyance, he grins.

"Booyah for you, man. It's about fucking time. Rubbing the chub just isn't the same as fucking."

He shakes his head in exaggerated horror as I roll my eyes.

Gray has despaired of me foregoing casual sex for the past year. I've despaired of me too—having become way too acquainted with my right hand, as Gray so thoughtfully pointed out—but the risks haven't been worth it until now.

I don't want a relationship. Especially not with you.

Yep. That still hurts.

Gray gives my arm a smack. "I'm thinking she's more than a handful, eh? Man, she has an ass on her."

"She has a name. It's Anna. Use it." I stare at Gray. Hard. "And if I catch you talking about her body again, I'll rip a piece of yours off."

Mistake number one: giving a name to your tormentor. Mistake number two: becoming visibly protective.

Gray's grin stretches. "You like her."

He has no idea.

I take another bite of stew.

"You're into her, yet you're moping around like a sad sack. What's the deal?"

Fucking pest.

"There is no 'deal.'" I gesture to the TV with my fork. "I'd like to watch *Pardon the Interruption*, if you don't mind."

"And I'd like a blow job every night before I go to bed. Disappointment's a bitch."

"Man…" Diaz shakes his head before attacking his food again.

Sighing, I put down my now empty bowl. What's the deal? Where to start? I think I've become fuck buddies with the girl I'm falling for. And while the sex is phenomenal, the fact that she views me as little else is killing me. Yeah, that wouldn't crush my pride to say out loud.

"She's…" I frown at the TV. "I don't know…hesitant."

"Let me get this straight. She'll let you bang her but doesn't want anything to do with you otherwise?" Gray snorts a laugh, covering his mouth to keep in his stew. "Oh, the irony."

Gray is too smart for his own good.

"Asshole," I mutter then give him a glare. "And we're adding an addendum to the rules. You don't get to discuss Anna in terms of sex, in any shape or form."

He wipes his mouth and takes a swig of beer. "Look, man, I'm not trying to be a dick—"

"Right."

"I'm just kind of…shit…shocked. I thought she was into you."

He gets up to refill his bowl, and I slouch further into the couch. "I wish."

A movement at my side has me tensing. I forgot Diaz was there he's so quiet.

Warily, I look over, and he regards me for a moment before giving a small shrug. "She don't belong, that's all."

"Want to run that by me again, D?" I sit up, my fists clenching. I don't need my teammates trying to make Anna an outsider.

He shrugs again. "Don't mean anything bad by it, but she

knows she doesn't fit with our crew. I saw her at the party. She wasn't comfortable there."

I squeeze the back of my stiff neck. This is the most Diaz has said to me in weeks, so the words take a while to sink in.

"This is true," Gray says as he plops back into his seat. "She looked antsy as all hell."

I pinch the bridge of my nose. A headache is coming on. "Yeah."

They're right. I know this. I've just ignored it in favor of feeling sorry for myself.

"If you want her," says Diaz, "you better take it slow." His teeth are white against the dark bronze of his skin. "Slow, as in wooing her, cuz you're clearly her bitch if that glazed look and drunken-ass walk you got goin' on mean anything."

"I can kick your ass too, D."

"Boy, please."

"So," Gray asks Diaz, "how do you woo a chick, D?"

"Poetry."

"Poetry? Are you fucking kidding me?"

"No, you philistine. It's cool and women love it."

Gray presses a hand to his chest as if he's pained. "I...have no words."

"Because you're a punk player." Diaz stabs into his stew with his spoon.

"That hurts, D. Deep inside my soft gooey center."

"Man..."

"I bet you read 'em haikus. Can't imagine you saying more than seventeen syllables at once."

"You best be imagining my foot up your ass, cuz it's about to be there."

They continue to talk shit, but my mind drifts elsewhere. I think about my father and the time we worked on changing the carburetor of my old car. The rusty piece wouldn't budge.

"Never force something, Drew. A bolt, a pass, a game, whatever." His dark brown eyes hold mine. *"Force it and you'll lose. Patience and*

persistence is how you win in life. Take your time, look for the solution, and if it doesn't come to you, fall back, reassess, and try again."

I know the true Anna. I've seen glimpses of her. When she's not thinking up reasons for us not to be together, that girl looks at me as if I'm worth something to her. She's the Anna that makes my heart beat faster, enjoy each second I'm with her. If she thinks she can hide behind sex, then I'll let her hide until she realizes I'm safe, that actually being together could be something transcendent. And damn if I won't have a good time doing it. Because while I might be patient, I'm no saint.

EIGHT

ANNA

IT'S A PERFECT SUNDAY. The weather is cool, and the sun is shining. There are things I could do, assignments to finish, books to read. I could go shopping or into town to watch a movie. But no, I'm sitting on the balcony watching the scant street traffic. My stomach aches and my skin feels too tight. I know what's wrong. I'm infected with want of Baylor.

It's going to happen again.

Addiction is best defeated with abstinence. So I'm going to be strong. I'm not going to reach out to him. I just need to get off my ass and do something.

On the table beside me, my phone dings.

I'm hoping it's Iris telling me where she is so I can join her. But it's not.

Unknown: Hey. It's Drew. You busy?

I stare down at the screen, my mind trying to make the letters form comprehensible words. Drew? Texting me? I glance over my shoulder, as if he might be behind me or something. Which is completely juvenile. I'm still pretty sure he's made me a little insane. There is a part of me, however, that gives a little leap of excitement. The lower part of me, I think darkly as I text him back.

Me: How did you get my number?

I head into the apartment, the feeling of being watched still riding strong.

Unknown: Class study roster. ☺

Me: Damn study roster.

Unknown: Highly grateful for it myself.

"Yeah well, you would be," I mutter, but, who am I trying to kid? I am too. The phone dings again.

Unknown: Where are you now?

My cheeks start to hurt from my repressed smile.

Me: Home.

Unknown: Where's that?

I pause, my heart now giving a little leap as well. I shouldn't do this. He'll hurt me. Without even trying. I have to protect myself. The thought barely forms, and yet I find myself responding.

Me: Why?

Unknown: I want to know, obviously.

Me: Is this a booty call?

Damn if all my happy parts aren't perking up now. Traitors.

Unknown: In the spirit of the brutal honesty in which we interact, yes. Yes, it is.

I laugh, too shocked not to. And a grin pulls at my cheeks when I respond.

Me: Brownie points for that honesty, Baylor.

Unknown: Then give me the address, Jones. My list of semipublic places has grown thin. I've come up with janitors' closets and bathroom stalls. Both unsavory. And I don't want someone other than me seeing your gorgeous butt. I'd like to refrain from punching people, if possible.

I have to agree about the lack of privacy, although my brain's stalled out on his reference to my butt. He thinks it's gorgeous? Okay. I can do this. I can keep it about sex. Only sex. Awesome, hot, perfect…

Before I can talk myself out of it, I tap out my address. Sweat blooms along my skin the second I hit Send.

My phone is quiet. For too long. When the text signal chimes again, my heart skips a beat.

Unknown: I'm on my way.

My heart promptly begins to race. And so do I.

I practically slam down my phone as I fly into action, grabbing strewn clothes, trash, a sock, my ratty comfort bra, and a variety of other junk that's cluttering the place. It all goes into the closet. Okay, I shouldn't care what my place looks like. If I'm a slob, I'm a slob.

But I'm also a girl, and I'm not letting him see my place in any other condition than pristine.

I don't know how far away he is; why didn't I ask where he was? Skidding into the bathroom, I look myself over in the mirror. At least I don't have a zit or anything. Which makes me think of George and his zit analogy. Fucking George.

I look all right, but Drew's coming here for one thing, and I'm now slightly sweaty. I don't have time to wash my hair so make do with washing my body, shaving all pertinent areas in record time before dashing butt-naked out of the shower and into my room. I stub my toe on the dresser.

"Fuck!" I'm hopping around on one foot as I tug on some yoga pants. The doorbell rings and I'm still half dressed. "Fuck, fuck, fuck!"

Grabbing a sweater hanging over my desk chair, I shove it over my head. A quick, frantic look down to check for stains—please don't let there be stains—calms me somewhat; the sweater is a nice one, deep green and silk wool knit.

One second before I open the door, I pull out my hair tie and fling it into a far, shadowy corner of the living room.

And then Baylor's standing before me, hands shoved in his pockets, short hair tousled as if he's run his fingers through it. Golden eyes under straight dark brows, a little dimple on his left cheek, body to kill or die for. He makes my knees weak. Every damn time.

We stare at each other, him grinning, and me with my heart

pounding like a kettledrum. Do we talk? Are we just supposed to go at it?

"Hey." My stunningly witty opener.

"Hey, yourself." His gaze runs over me. "You look pretty. Flushed," he adds, his grin deepening. "But pretty."

"Yeah well—" I stand back and wave him inside. "I've just run all over the house cleaning it so…" I shrug.

He laughs a little, walking into the center of the living room. God, but he's tall. Without heels on, I'm an elf next to him.

"I'd say you were joking with me, Jones." He turns and catches my eye. "But I know how honest you are."

I bite back a smile and close the door. "You say that like it's a bad thing."

"Funny, I thought I was giving you a compliment."

"Have we drifted into the compliment stage?" I'm a little too breathless, and I have no idea what to do except babble.

"Jones, I've been giving you compliments since day one." His voice is low and easy, and it makes my toes curl into the carpet. "You just haven't been paying attention."

Taking a breath, I ask him the important question. "You want a drink?" Or do we just start fucking like bunnies?

I don't even know what answer I'd prefer until he says, "A drink's good." Something in me eases a bit, when really I ought to be more agitated.

He follows me into the open kitchen, his eyes taking in everything, from the decorating by IKEA and secondhand furniture to Iris's hot firemen of NYC calendar hanging on the dividing wall to the kitchen.

"Nice place," he says kindly. Because it isn't that nice.

"We did what we could with my mom's castoffs. Though some of it has seen better days." I glance at the big brown sofa. "I think Mom got that thing when I was ten."

"I did the same. When my parents…" He trails off, looking pained.

"When they what?"

He clears his throat, ducking his head as he gives the back of his neck a scratch. "Ah, when they died."

My insides lurch on a jolt of prickly heat. "Your parents are dead?" *Of course they are, he just said that.* "I mean... Hell, Drew, I'm sorry. I didn't know."

The corner of his mouth lifts in a weak attempt at a smile. "How could you be expected to know?"

"This is probably one of those common knowledge things about you, isn't it?"

"Maybe. But then we both know you don't follow football or my life." He sounds oddly relieved about that.

"Did you—" I fight to keep my voice from wavering "—go live with your grandparents or relatives?"

He clutches the back of his neck again. "Naw. I don't have any. It was just me and my parents left at the time."

Jesus. All I can think is that he's an orphan. Alone in life. And look at what he's accomplished. It isn't my business to feel it, but pride and admiration swell within me. Not that I can tell him that without it sounding patronizing.

"Drew, I am sorry. That sucks."

"Yeah. It does." He doesn't look at me.

"How..." I wince. "Never mind."

"Nothing wrong with being curious either." A small, wry noise leaves him. "It happened the summer after I graduated high school. They were hiking in Colorado. A flash flood came and... It was... I don't know. I mean, who the fuck expects something like that?"

No one. I want to hug him so badly that my arms ache. But I don't think he'd appreciate the gesture. If it were me, I'd take it as pity. As if he's worried about that very thing, he glances toward the kitchen. "Can I still have a drink?"

"Sure." I snap out of my daze and move to the fridge. "Right."

Baylor leans a hip against my breakfast bar.

"We've got—" I open the fridge and peer in "—one Blue Moon, water, white wine, and orange juice."

"I'll take a water." His stomach gives a loud and impatient gurgle. Color tints his cheeks, and his mouth tips wryly. "Sorry."

"Hungry?" I ask, pouring him a glass of filtered water.

"Almost always." He doesn't even try to make it sound like an innuendo. And yet somehow it does. Probably because I can't be in the same room with Drew Baylor and not think about sex. But I behave as I open the fridge again and rummage through it.

"Okay, there's cheesecake, two pieces of chicken satay, yogurt, though we really shouldn't touch that, or Iris will kill us..."

Behind me, Baylor takes his water and has a long drink before peering over my shoulder. "Iris? Your roommate, right?"

"The very one." Every muscle in my body twitches at the close proximity of his. "She's on a Greek yogurt kick."

"Ah."

"There's also..." I peek under an aluminum lid. "Ooh, kebobs."

"Did you have a party or something?" His arms rest on the edges of the door, bracketing my shoulders, and I feel oddly sheltered.

"They're from catering gigs. The right to bring home leftover food trays is one of the main reasons I took a job in the catering department. Iris and I save a boatload on our food budget."

Baylor's eyes crinkle at the corners. "I'm pretty sure you are every athlete's dream roommate."

I do not ask if that includes him, but turn back to the food. "Well? What will it be?"

"You're really going to feed me?" He sounds surprised.

"Of course I am." I shift uncomfortably from one foot to the other. "Or don't you want me to?"

Because I can take it back. I can simply lead him into my room and—

"No, I mean, yeah. I want it." Baylor full-on blushes now. "Shit. Food. I mean—"

I laugh. "I know what you meant."

He groans and pinches the bridge of his nose. "Just make the kebobs."

Still laughing, I pull out the container and a pack of eggs. "Okay, but I don't do reheats. I like to think of leftovers more as raw material for new meals."

His self-deprecation melts away, and he leans back against the counter. "What are you making me, Jones?"

"A frittata." I grab a small hunk of Gouda that actually was left over from a party. "With cheese."

"Sounds awesome."

It's surprisingly easy and fun with Baylor in the kitchen. He helps me free the meat and veggies from their skewers, and then I chop it all up into smaller sizes, while he grates the cheese for me.

"You know how to cook," he observes as I begin refrying the kabob pieces. The scent of onions and beef perfume the air.

"I'm proficient." I whisk a bowl of eggs and pour it into the frying pan. "Growing up, it was just my mom and me, so I helped where I could."

Four generations back, my mother's family immigrated, not to New York with the rest of their Italian brethren, but to Georgia. But my father is pure Irish, and here for a visit when he met my mother. Pictures of him as a young man paint him in tones of milk white and vivid orange.

I ended up a physical blend of them with pale ivory skin that tans but also freckles, dark green eyes, and dark red hair.

I really don't remember much of my dad now. Time has a way of fading the sharp edges of a person's image. Unfortunately, it also has a way of letting a wound fester and burrow deep beneath the skin.

"Iris is the real cook here," I babble on. "She's like a fifth-generation Mexican American, and her family owns this kick-ass Mexican restaurant in Tucson."

Drew watches me push the eggs around. "What happened to your dad?"

It's a quiet question. Because he knows firsthand that my answer might be bad.

Is it? I'm fairly numb to the whole dad thing. Until I have to talk about it. A familiar lump of pain settles at the back of my throat. I ignore it and shrug. "Out of the picture since I was seven."

Baylor is looking at me now. I focus on scattering the cheese over the half-cooked eggs and tossing the whole pan under the broiler. "There," I say. "In a minute we'll have a frittata."

My voice is overbright and too brittle. I shouldn't have talked. I shouldn't have cooked for him. This is a hook up, not some after-school tell-all. But it's too late now. And he's still watching me with eyes that are too knowing.

"Why is he out of the picture?" he asks softly.

I pull out two dishes and get the forks. "It's a shitty story."

"I told you my shitty story." He sets the plates and forks out, one set next to the other. "Besides, I'm a great listener."

While his job is to give orders and think fast, something about his calm demeanor and quiet strength makes me want to confide in him.

"When I was seven, my father told my mother that he couldn't handle parenthood, that I was too much of a pain in the ass, always whining for attention." My smile is weak and wobbly. "His words."

I turn and pull out the frittata, setting it down to cool on the stove. It's golden brown and the cheese bubbles. I pick up a knife and hack at the frittata. "So, he went back to Ireland, and my mom raised me."

Sometimes I wonder if my dad would have stayed if I hadn't begged him not to leave. But I had. And he'd merely looked pained. After he left, I'd curled up under my bed. And my mother had done much the same. Only she had cried. I never did. I wouldn't let myself.

A warm hand covers mine, and I still. Gently, Baylor relieves me of the knife before cupping the back of my neck.

"You're right," he says. "That was a shitty story. And your father is an undeserving asshole."

I study the floor. "What? No 'you're better off without him'?"

Baylor's thumb strokes along my hairline. "But you know that already."

"Yeah, I do." I risk a glance at him. His expression is so serious, as if he's hurting for me, when he's the one who has no family left. Something deep within my heart clenches.

The gentle exploration of my neck doesn't stop, and his voice drops low and tender. "Some people never understand the gift they have." A light pressure on the back of my neck eases me closer to his warmth. "And some people wait a lifetime to have someone to love."

Emotion wells up within me, and it's warm, but dizzying. I want to burrow in and let him take my pain. He's strong, maybe he can weather it. Oddly, I want to pull him close and hold him as if he is the one in pain. I don't understand it. This isn't light or fun. This is consuming me. A steady, relentless attack.

As we stare at each other, his lids lower and his head dips toward mine. My lips part and ache with the need to touch his. I want his taste, to draw his breath into me and let it fill my lungs.

His whisper brushes my cheeks. "Anna..."

The front door opens, and I spring back, nearly knocking the damn frittata off the stove. Drew puts a hand out to steady me, but I'm already turning toward Iris as she saunters into the apartment.

She stops short as she sees us, and George, who is following close behind, slams into her. "Damn, woman, give a little warning—" Abruptly, he stops talking, and they both gape at Drew.

Iris I could have handled. George is another task entirely. And I know I'm going to pay when an obnoxious light gleams in his eyes.

His voice is just shy of singsong when he says, "Hey, Baylor. I'd say you were the last person I expected to see in Anna's kitchen, but I'd be lying."

Drew raises a brow at me, and I glare at George, who just smiles and steps forward, offering Drew a hand. "George Cruz."

They shake hands in that hard, abrupt way guys do when they're sizing each other up, and I roll my eyes.

"And this is Iris," I say, for my friend is simply standing there grinning like the Cheshire Cat.

Drew offers his hand to her. "The roommate who has excellent taste in parties."

And Iris fucking titters. God, this is too weird. Baylor is too big for the kitchen, towering over all of us.

"Oh, hey, is that food?" George makes a grab for the pan, and I slap his hand. He snatches it back, holding it to his chest. "Ay, woman! Share the love, eh?"

"Get your own." I split the big frittata down the center and spoon half onto Drew's plate. "Eat," I tell him.

George is far from done whining. "But I'm hungry too. Why does he get some and I don't?"

Iris coughs in her hand, going red. "You have to ask?"

Drew laughs, though his cheeks go a bit red too. He's smart, however, and promptly tucks into his food.

George on the other hand, pouts. "Seriously, Banana? No food?"

Drew's head snaps up, a smile spreading over his face. "Banana?"

"Yup." Iris helps herself to a yogurt. "Anna Banana."

"Her mom calls her that," George puts in helpfully. "Anna has a ratty old stuffed banana hiding in her closet—"

I smack his head.

"Ow, damn!"

I cut a small slice of the remaining half of the frittata, take it for myself then pass the rest to George, the ass. "Just take your ill-gotten gains and flee."

He makes a happy sound and steals my fork.

Drew's soaking it all in, and though his smile is large, there are shadows in his eyes. "You guys know Anna well."

Fishing.

Iris helps. "We've been together since freshman year."

"Roommates," George says around his mouthful of food.

Drew's brows rise at that. "All of you?"

"Until George moved out last year for fear of 'being overrun by estrogen.'" Iris makes a face. "His words, not mine."

George nods to confirm, his expression lofty. "A man can only take so many feminine supplies in his bathroom before it's time to cut and run."

"I have my own bathroom, you tool," I say.

"Yes. And you give me food. Now I'm wondering why I moved out." Quick as a flash, George leans forward and lands a smacking kiss on my cheek. He's fucking with Drew, seeing if he'll care.

And it's working. Drew's expression goes completely neutral. He picks at his frittata before setting his fork down. "So... you guys...?"

He looks from George to me. Iris makes a horrified face, and George laughs. He's a stinker, but he isn't a jerk, and he puts Drew out of his misery.

"This might be hard to believe, cuz you're obviously into our girl, but the thought of doing anything with Anna kind of turns my stomach."

"Ditto," I snap back dryly, noticing that Drew looks way too pleased.

George grins at me. "She's like the sister I never had."

"Hey!" Iris gives his arm a punch. "I'm your sister!"

"No, you're my twin. Totally different, 'Ris."

"Whatever."

As George and Iris debate whether there is a distinction between "twin" and "sister," I lean in close to Drew. "Their constant bickering may have factored into George moving out."

He chuckles and takes another bite. "This is good, by the way." He glances at my plate. "You sure you have enough?"

I stop his move to offer me some of his with a touch to his hand. He's warm, and I want entirely too much to twine my fingers with his and tug him out of here. I pull back.

"That's sweet, but this is fine. I cooked this more for you."

His expression goes soft. "Thank you, Anna."

The space between us grows close, quiet, as if Iris and George aren't squabbling, as if we're alone. His large thigh presses against my smaller one and heat blooms along the connection.

When he speaks, it's low and just for me. "So, 'Banana,' huh?"

I give him a look. "If you call me that, you'll lose a finger."

A little dimple forms along his left cheek. "Why a finger?"

"Isn't that where the bad guys always start? Lose a finger, then an eye, maybe an ear..." I shrug. "Seemed appropriately threatening."

"Oh, very. Don't worry, Jones. I've learned my lesson. No cutsey nicknames for you." His index finger taps the tip of my nose. "Our relationship is special that way."

There it is again. That *R*-word. I take a bite of frittata. The eggs have gone cold.

"Well, I'm out of here," announces George.

Iris's face scrunches up. "You said you were going with Henry and me to the movies."

"You don't need me being a third wheel, 'Ris." George wears the same expression I'm sure I do when talking about Henry: valiantly trying to hide disgust. "And I'm not in the mood to be one."

Iris plunks her fist on her hip. "Hasn't stopped you from going out with us before. Besides, it was your idea to go to the movies."

George simply shrugs. "Changed my mind. It happens." He turns to Drew. "Good to meet you, Baylor. I gotta say, you do some impressive work on the field, man."

Et tu, George?

Drew takes the praise in stride and simply smiles. It's a polite smile, not like the ones he gives me when his eyes light up and a dimple graces his cheek.

"Thanks. I try my best. Good to meet you too."

George isn't gone for more than a few minutes when the lock to the apartment door turns and Henry walks in, key in hand.

"You gave him a key," I hiss at Iris. There is no way I'm letting Henry have open access to our house.

She has the grace to wince. "Not permanently. I'll get it back."

"Now," I insist in a low voice. Beside me, Drew is frowning, having heard the exchange.

Henry saunters up to the breakfast bar. "Sweetness." He gives Iris a messy kiss, but his eyes are on the rest of us. Mainly Drew. He does a double take as recognition sets in.

"Battle Baylor." He sets a hand on Iris's hip. "I thought I was seeing things."

"Nope." Drew's tone is bland, but his eyes are watchful.

Henry laughs, as if they know each other. I'm not sure that they do. I've never seen them exchange any words. Henry ends my suspicion by saying, "Henry Ross. I play midfield on the lacrosse team."

His gaze shifts from Drew to me. "And here I was, beginning to think you didn't like guys, Anna."

"No," I say lightly, "you got that wrong. I don't like assholes."

Henry leans his forearms on the bar and gives me a nasty smile. "I figured you were too uptight to put out."

Before I can say a word, Drew's warm hand lands on my nape. It engulfs me, a comforting weight and a support. "Careful."

He's not speaking to me. His eyes are on Henry. There's nothing overtly threatening about his pose, with his other hand resting casually on the counter and his shoulders relaxed. And yet the message is clear. Should Henry make a wrong move, Drew would take him down in an instant.

I don't need to be protected. But it feels nice knowing that he's willing.

Henry's frown is as contrived as his tone. "Careful?"

"Do I need to spell it out for you?" Drew doesn't raise his voice. The authority of his presence is enough for Henry to look away first.

"You all need to relax. I'm just messing around."

Aware that Iris is embarrassed, I refrain from calling him on that lie. Drew does as well, but he doesn't drop his hard gaze from Henry.

"We going out?" Henry snaps at Iris.

"Yes." She gives us an apologetic look as she takes Henry's arm and all but tugs him to the door.

"Leave the key," I say before they get there.

Henry stops, his shoulders stiffening, and turns his head to glare at me. But his gaze clashes with Drew's, and he simply shrugs before reaching into his pocket and pulling out the spare set of keys. Henry tosses them onto the counter where they land with a loud clang.

As soon as they leave, I lean against the counter with a sigh. "He's such an asshole."

"I'm guessing Iris doesn't see that." There's a knowing tone in Drew's voice.

"I'd like to believe that she's living in ignorant bliss rather than choosing to be with him with eyes wide open."

I move to take Drew's plate, but he reacts first, picking up both his and mine and taking them to the sink.

"Whatever the case," I say as he rinses off the dishes and I open the dishwasher to tuck them away. "She hasn't kicked him to the curb."

Drew leans a hip against the counter. "It happens sometimes to guys on the team. They'll go out with a girl who is bad news, manipulative, caring only about the fame. Every now and then someone will try to warn the poor sap."

"It's sweet that you guys watch out for each other."

His teeth flash in a quick but tight smile. "Well, it isn't entirely altruistic. A team is only as strong as its weakest link. None of us like to see a guy laid low by head games."

Drew's broad shoulders lift on a shrug. "Not that it matters. Warning a guy about a girl only pisses him off and drives him closer to her."

"Which is why I grit my teeth and try to steer clear of Henry."

"I saw him at the party. Is that why you didn't want to go?"

"I didn't want to go, because I don't like parties." I toss the hand towel into the sink. "Henry being there merely made it that much worse."

"I'm still glad you were there." His eyes are liquid caramel, and all thought of Henry melts away in a rush of heat and longing. As if feeling the same rush, Drew's chest lifts on a breath, and his voice lowers to a rumble. "Show me your room, Jones."

NINE

ANNA

DESPITE THE HEATED promise in his voice, and despite the fact that he came to my apartment for only one reason, when we get to my room, Drew doesn't touch me. We lie side by side on the bed, both of us staring up at the ceiling. Our shoulders brush, but that is the extent of our contact. My hands are safely folded over my stomach and so are his. We aren't fucking. I'm not trying to climb him like a tree or lick him like a Tootsie Pop. Though I want to do those things. Part of me always does.

I still can't believe I have Baylor in my room. His presence fills every inch. He's so expansive with his charisma that I can't get enough air, or when I do, it makes my blood fizz and my head spin.

When he finally talks, my skin jumps at the rich, deep sound.

"What's your thing with old Siouxsie there?"

I don't need to see him to know he's gesturing with his chin toward the framed poster of Siouxsie Sioux, lead singer for Siouxsie and the Banshees, that hangs over my bed. With her exaggerated straight black brows, wild black bob, and tiny red bow mouth she looks like a deranged Betty Boop, a goth flapper girl. She screams timeless beauty and "fuck off" all at once. I love her style.

"She's not old," I protest. Up there, on my wall, she's immortal.

"You didn't answer me." A soft rustle of noise, and I know he's turned his head to look at me. I keep my eyes on Siouxsie. This doesn't deter Baylor. "You seem to have a thing for her."

We're listening to her now, her haunting voice singing a cover of "Dear Prudence."

"Just look at her. She didn't give a fuck. She led an all-male band, was part of a sound revolution." I shrug. "And she's fucking cool."

He chuckles. It's a good laugh. Deep and infectious. Just hearing it makes me smile.

His laughter dies down, and we're silent for a moment, just listening to music and lying there. His legs are so long that his bent knees rise at least five inches higher than mine. They are dusky blue hills beneath the backdrop of Siouxsie's haunted eyes. I'm relaxed, I realize. And at the same time, the ever-present tension when he is near, simmers low in my stomach.

"So you like old music, huh?" he asks.

I turn my head just enough to see his arm. His biceps is so big that I wonder if I can get my two hands around it. I'm tempted to try.

"Yeah," I say, my voice far too husky. "I guess I do."

He nods, and his square chin comes into view. And his mouth. I'm in love with his mouth, and I've never even tasted it. The lower lip is wide yet full, a gentle curve that I want to follow with my tongue. But I won't.

His upper lip is almost a bow, a cruel little sneer of a lip, and yet the effect is ruined because Drew is almost always smiling. He isn't now, though. His lips are relaxed, fuller.

They move when he speaks. "I like Zeppelin, Queen, The Doors, Nirvana, Pearl Jam." He says this like it's a confession.

Like I'm going to sit up and point and shout, *Ah-ha! Closet classic rock junkie!* When he ought to know that I won't, not when I listen to Brit-punk albums older than I am.

It's his turn to shrug, as if my silence is agitating to him. "My dad used to listen to that stuff." His body tilts toward mine as he reaches in his back pocket and pulls out his wallet. The picture held between his thumb and his forefinger shakes only a little as he hands it to me. "My parents."

His parents are young in the photo. They're hanging on to each other, arms slung over their shoulders as they ham it up for the camera. His dad is tall, dark, and handsome, in a fashion victim sort of way, with flowing shoulder length brown hair, and wearing torn jeans, and a beat-up flannel shirt over what looks like a ratty concert t-shirt. But his grin is wide, and a dimple graces his cheek.

Drew's mom is kissing his other cheek, but she's sort of smearing her lips over him as she turns to the camera, and she's clearly laughing about her antics. She's her own fashion victim, maybe more so than his dad, but she looks awesome doing it. Her hair is pinned back from her forehead with multiple butterfly clips and brushes her shoulders in a brilliant blond nimbus of curls. She's got on an honest-to-God black lace bustier and a ruffled plaid mini-skirt, paired with combat boots that I kind of covet when I see them.

"Your mom was a nonconformist, I take it?" I grin over at Drew, and he laughs lightly.

"Yeah, for a few months, the way she'd tell it." His expression turns soft. "They called this their Hall of Shame picture."

I'm smiling as I study the picture. But my heart aches. I can almost feel their joy, and their absence.

"They look so young and happy. Beautiful too." Because they are. Drew has his mom's nose and eyes, and his dad's sharp jawline and smile.

I give him back the picture, handling it with the care that it deserves. He doesn't look at it as he tucks it away.

"They met in college." His voice goes quiet, and he turns to stare up at the ceiling. "And they were happy."

His profile is tight, the corners of his mouth hard. "I don't know, I guess... I guess I feel closer to them by listening to what they listened to."

The pain, that sharp, dark pain, buried deep in his words, the pain that he's fighting to hide, hits me straight through the middle.

I clear my throat, find my voice. "And who doesn't love Queen?" I give him a little nudge, just the barest move of my elbow against his arm. "I mean, isn't 'We Will Rock You' like every jock's anthem?"

My reward is his grin, and the way the corners of his eyes crinkle. A soft laugh leaves him. "Yeah," he says quietly, and then with more lightness, "Yeah, suppose it is."

I don't know what else to say. I'm comforting Drew Baylor when I'm supposed to be fucking him. An uncomfortable knot begins to writhe in my stomach. I don't deserve to hear about his parents. To even look upon their smiling faces. Suddenly I want him out of here. I can't breathe.

I'm about to ask him to go when he talks again.

"I guess you like those emo type of guys." He turns his head slightly, and our eyes meet. There it is, that low, hot hum within me that happens every time, as if his eyes have some freaking superpower with a direct line to my sex.

The bed groans beneath him as he rolls to his side. He props a hand under his head, and now he's looming over me.

His voice slows, gets richer, lower, as if he too feels the hum. "Guys who dress in vintage and pluck out half-ass tunes on their guitars to show their inner torment."

There's a guitar in my room. A Gibson acoustic that my mom gave me on my eighteenth birthday. His gaze had landed on it when he first entered my room.

"Maybe I'm the one who plucks half-assed tunes."

Baylor's grin is lazy, and those little lines that bracket his mouth deepen. There's a knowing look in his eyes, as if he can read my mind. And maybe he can. Because his next words are, "I bet it pisses you off that you can't play a whole song."

I affect an affronted look, but I can't be properly pissed off. He's right, after all. I wanted so badly to play, but I suck. My fingers are like drunken frat boys stumbling all over each other on the frets. A disgrace. "It does."

As if my honesty needs a reward, his smile grows wider. That smile. It takes my breath, then gives it back. But now my breath is too fast and too light.

His golden gaze slides down to where my breasts are rising and falling in sudden agitation, and his expression turns serious, almost stern, as if he's contemplating doing dark things to them. I'm up for it. I'm pretty sure he could bite me there, and I'd like it.

But he slowly looks back up at me. Color darkens his high cheeks, and though his voice is a bit rougher, he's still in control. The bastard.

"I can play," he says. It isn't a brag. It's a statement.

"You? The guitar?" Skepticism stretches out my words.

White teeth flash. "Me. The big, dumb jock."

He says it mockingly, but not in anger. As if he knows that's what most people assume, but he doesn't really give a fuck.

"I think you're incredibly smart," I blurt out. It's as close to a real compliment as I've ever given him. And we both know it.

He stills. And then his massive body, all that flat-packed muscle leans into me, pausing close enough to feel the heat of his breath against my cheek when he whispers, "I think you're incredibly smart too."

Then, in that quick, effortless way of his, he rolls away and goes for the guitar.

I sit up, curling my feet under me, as he settles on my bedroom chair and fiddles with the strings to tune the guitar. It looks good in his hand.

No, he isn't reed thin or wearing skinny jeans—the mere idea of which makes me want to laugh; Drew Baylor was made for low-slung Levis and T-shirts that strain against defined muscles. But he holds the Gibson with authority.

"Mom said that I couldn't just be about sports. So, if I wanted to play them, I had to learn an instrument too."

"What a slave driver," I tease.

"That was the gist of my protest."

When he gets the guitar the way he wants it, he begins to play. The melody is complex and familiar. It takes me a moment to place it. "Norwegian Wood."

A flush rises to my face. After all, it's a song about a woman using a man for sex. Did he pick it specifically for me? Or was it just to show off his skill? I'm not going to ask.

"Now my mom," he says as he plays, his attention on the strings. "She freaking loved The Beatles."

His eyes meet mine, and there's a playful glint in his. "Or maybe an old open mic standard?" He eases into Dave Matthews's "Crash Into Me."

"Emo guys love playing this one."

Hayden, my old boyfriend, used to play this song. On open mic night. All the fucking time. But he never achieved the quick, flowing ease with which Drew's fingers coax the melody from the guitar.

Half laughing, Drew sings. He isn't perfect, his voice drifts off-key and is rough, but it doesn't matter because he sells the song. I can hear my Grandpa Joe's voice in my head telling me that this boy could sell ice in Antarctica.

Drew doesn't finish the song, and I know it isn't because he can't, it's because he's not trying to show off. He's just messing around. He proves this when he catches my eye and grins wide. I'm in his thrall.

I grin when he stops and begins to thump on the side of the guitar and belt out the words to "We Will Rock You."

And then I laugh. Because he gives it his all. Makes an ass of himself, and clearly doesn't care. And suddenly I don't care either. I join him, shouting out the words along with him.

"You dork," I say when we finish.

"Look who's talking."

Drew begins to laugh, and I lose it again. We feed off each other, laughing until I'm holding my side. It isn't really that funny, what we're laughing over. Maybe it's just a way to break the tension that always pulls tight between us. Or maybe it's because he, like me, hasn't really laughed just for the hell of it in a long time. I don't know. I don't even care. It's good not to care about anything for a while.

As if by some silent, mutual agreement our laughter dies down as one. And we're left staring at each other, both a little breathless. His gaze goes molten. It's like he's flicked a switch, leaving me in the dark, and he's my light. He's all I can see.

The chair creaks beneath him as he slowly lowers the guitar. I can't move. I can't catch my breath. I'm so hot my skin hurts. There's an ache between my legs and in my breasts. A throbbing beat that matches my heart. I can only pant and watch him rise.

His mouth is hard, his eyes glittering darkly beneath half-lowered lids as he comes for me. I find myself leaning back, like I'm afraid of him, when really, it's all I can do not to beg him to hurry up and touch me. He stops at the foot of the bed and looks me over, an insolent, languid perusal that I should find insulting but only makes me burn hotter.

When he speaks, his voice is rough, quick, sharp. It scrapes against my heightened nerves, shouts in the quiet room, even though it's a murmur. "Lift your top."

Oh, God. My head goes light and then heavy, my breath chuffing out in strangled half gasps. I fumble with the bottom of my sweater. Cool air kisses my skin as I expose my belly.

He merely watches, waiting. My breasts ache so bad that when I ease my sweater over them, I whimper. I'm not wearing a bra. He had to have expected as much; my breasts are too big to hide the fact. Even so, his nostrils flare on a sharp breath.

And then he's coming for me, the slow, rolling stride of a lion. He crawls over me, a veritable mountain of testosterone and intent. One thick thigh shoves between my legs, pressing there, giving me sweet relief and soft agony. When his hot, wet mouth closes over my nipple, I groan so loud it scares me a little. Not him. He sucks me harder, and we fall back into the bed. I don't have another coherent thought.

DREW

Anna's tits, naked and in the full light of day, drive me out of my mind. I can barely think, I'm shaking so badly. Her tight nipple fills my mouth, and I flick my tongue over it, loving the way she arches into me, her breath coming in quick pants. I let her go with a loud pop, then lean back to look at her again.

Holy hell, she's perfect to me. Firm and teardrop-shaped breasts so full they spill over a bit on the sides of her narrow frame. A smooth, luminous cream color, they quiver with each breath she takes. Her nipples, one of which I've sucked to a wet peak, are a dark, rosy brown. Brown sugar topping vanilla ice cream. I want to eat her up.

With a grunt of impatience, I tug off the sweater that's bunched around her neck, and her wild red curls tumble about her face. Then I tear off my shirt; I'm too hot to breathe with it on.

She laughs a little, until I sit back on my haunches and pull off her pants and panties in one swift move. Then she simply watches me with her big green eyes. But I see the way her fingers curl into the covers and her beautiful tits lift with each breath she takes.

Lust flares through my veins like fire. It gets worse as my gaze travels over her body.

Jesus. Her waist is tiny compared to the rounded swells of her hips that ease into full, smooth thighs, and long calves. Freckles cover her shoulders, even a few on her hips. Endless cream sprinkled with sugar, and laid out on her bed like an offering of everything I've ever wanted.

My attention settles on the place I need to sink into. That small triangle of curls, so dark red it's like a valentine between her sweet thighs. Lots of girls wax themselves bare. It's always creeped me out, like I'm with a preteen. Not Anna. She's perfect for me.

Suddenly I can't breathe right. My voice comes out rough and strangled. "Spread your legs and let me see that gorgeous pussy."

Her entire body tightens, her soft mouth parting on an agitated breath. Oh, but her eyes gleam bright. She likes my words raw and unfiltered. I've never talked much during sex before, never thought to do it. I don't know why it's different with Anna. Maybe it's because I want her so bad, I don't think about anything but the blinding, gut-wrenching lust and the need to bring her along for the ride. That she seems to get off on it as much as I do has me shaking again. In this way, at least, she is all mine.

Her trembling thighs part. She glistens there, her pink lips plump and wet.

"You're so beautiful," I rasp. "So beau—"

I can't talk.

The air between us goes thick. She spreads wider, without shame, without artifice. She's not even looking at my face, but at the bulge of my crotch where my hard-on is desperately trying to punch through my jeans. With an unsteady hand, I snap the button and pull down my zipper, the sound loud in the quiet room. I'm so fucking hard, my dick springs straight up, pulsing in time with my heartbeat.

Her breath hitches, her teeth catching the plump curve of her lip. I hold her gaze as I reach down and give myself a light stroke, enough to make my dick surge, but not nearly enough to satisfy me. She watches the movement, and her breath becomes agitated.

"Do you want this in you, Anna?"

Her gaze flicks up to mine. She's panting now, licking her lips wet in a greedy way. I nearly groan.

"Do you want me to fuck your pussy?"

Her abdomen clenches.

"Tell me, Anna," I whisper, leaning over so I can run my lips from her bent knee, down her soft thigh.

She trembles, her flesh jumping beneath my touch. I smell her musk, the faint scent of shower gel lingering in her soft curls, and feel the heat of her core. Up close, she's all shades of rose. Beautiful.

I give the crease at the top of her thigh a slow lick.

"Drew..."

God, I love hearing her say my name. I reward her and kiss the pink wet lips quivering before me. "Or maybe you want me to suck you," I say before I do just that.

She arches off the bed, and I place a hand on the gentle curve of her belly to hold her still.

I love doing this to her. Licking, nuzzling, fucking her with my tongue, letting myself take deep tastes of her sex.

I feel the heat of my own breath as I manage to ask, "What do you want, baby?"

And then I hear her. "I want it all."

I'm lost. My fingers fumble with the condom, nearly tearing it in my haste to put it on. I surge up, hooking her legs over my arms as I go. My dick sinks into her with one thrust, and she groans so loud and hard that I nearly come right then. But I find her shoulder and hold it steady with my teeth as I pump into her. Her ass clenches against my palms with each thrust.

Strong legs wrap around me, her heels digging into my back to spur me on. I'm going out of my mind.

Sliding my hands up to her back, I swing her up into my lap. Her arms come around me as if they belong there. I fill my hands back up with her plump, irresistible ass, squeezing as I find the sweet spot on her neck with my mouth. She's fragrant here, smelling of spice and Anna.

"Take me," I demand against her damp skin, my tongue slicking over the silky surface before I suck. "Take me."

Her hands grasp my shoulders, and then she's riding me, her hot pussy clasping my dick so hard I shake. I clench her ass, trying not to hold her too tightly for fear of hurting her. But it's a struggle. I want her too much, and my hips surge up to meet her on the down stroke. She makes those noises, those little whimpers that get me so hot I'm sweating, my breath a rasp against her neck. Her full breasts jiggle and slide against my chest with every thrust. I'm in heaven, and I don't want it to end. It can't end.

TEN

ANNA

MAYBE I'VE MADE a mistake letting Baylor into my home. It's a personal thing, showing that part of myself, exchanging stories about our families. Maybe it was too much for him too. Or maybe the novelty has worn off, and he remembered that he dates perfect-looking jock groupies.

I don't know. I miss decisive me, when it was easy to walk away. Now I'm stuck in class trying not to look over at Drew Baylor, who has been hunched in his seat for the past forty-five minutes.

Okay, so I might have been the one to send him packing after we had sex in my bed. But it had been intense, too intense, and I'd needed to collect myself in private. And, yes, I was the one who made it clear that I wouldn't see him until our next philosophy class.

And though it's probably safer if we don't look at each other during class, his behavior now is odd. He's withdrawn, not talking. By the time class is over, I'm convinced that we are too. It's shocking how much this hurts.

Drew leaves first. I find myself following. I might be overreacting. How would I know anymore? My inner radar has gone AWOL. But I buck the fuck up and decide to find out.

He's already out of the lecture hall and descending the wide front stairs.

"Baylor." I don't say it loud, but he hears.

His long stride stutters, and then he turns. And because I'm following him down the stairs, we both come to a halt at the same moment, face-to-face. I'm a step above him, which makes us almost even in height now. I hadn't noticed it before, being a paranoid freak and all, but now that I get a good look, he's pale beneath his tan, and his mouth is pinched and white around the edges.

"Are you okay?" I ask. "You look terrible."

His mouth flattens further. "I'm fine." He glances toward the quad as if to find safety. And I go cold. He's never looked to get away from me before.

"All right." I move past him. "See you."

I don't get to take another step before he grabs my hand. "Anna…"

He lets me go when I look down at our hands, and instantly I want his back.

"I have a headache," he grumbles.

My lips twitch, a strange aching relief pushing through my veins. "And big, strong men don't admit to weakness?"

The corner of his mouth curls, but he won't meet my eyes. "Something like that." Then he goes so pale that I move closer.

"Hey," I say softly, as I search his face. "It's really bad, isn't it?"

He gives a bare nod. "Migraines. I get them."

"I do too." And they suck. I touch his arm, and the skin under his forearm is like silk. "You need to lie down. You shouldn't have come to class."

"I can't skip class," he says with a sigh. "And I can't go home. I've got practice in an hour."

"Practice? Drew—"

"It's what I do." He presses his fingers to his eyes. "Sometimes it sucks. But that's part of the job. I've downed about ten ibuprofen, I'll be okay."

"You're going to have guys slamming into you while you have a migraine?" I need to let this go, but my head hurts for him.

Instead of being annoyed, he gives me weak smile. "Feeling sorry for me yet? Because I think I can manage a tear or two."

"Stop trying to deflect." I take hold of his elbow. "Come with me."

"I don't know, Jones. As much as I want to, I don't think I can perform at top level—"

"Drew, shut up."

Meekly, he complies.

I could take him back to my place but there isn't enough time. So I lead him toward the Student Union. The sun is high and bright as we walk across the quad.

"Put your sunglasses on," I tell him as we walk.

"You want me incognito?" He's already pulling them out and putting them on. And looking way too good wearing them.

"No, it's for your eyes—" I shut up as I catch his grin. "Stop fucking with me."

He laughs. "But fucking with you is fun, Jones."

"Did you seriously just double entendre me?"

Another laugh. "I don't think that question was grammatically correct, Jones, but yeah." He slings an arm around my shoulders, hugging me close, and kisses my temple. I'm engulfed in his warmth, feel his affection.

Flustered, I pull free to open the door to the dining hall.

"What are we going to do here?" Drew asks, holding the door for me.

I don't even need to duck under his outstretched arm. "Getting supplies."

Despite his paleness, he wags his brows. "You've got my complete attention now."

No. I'm not going to smile. Not even a little.

I smile. "You have a one-track mind."

"Not true, Jones," he says in a voice only for me. "I have a few choice tracks in regards to you. But yeah, they eventually lead to the same place." The wicked look in his eyes tells me exactly where that place is. Not that I have any doubt.

Fighting a grin, I head toward the food court. Only to get inundated by people. That is, people swarm Drew. Honestly, I don't know how he stands it. Sweat immediately prickles my lower back and my shoulders hunch. I'm jostled about as guys come up to slap Drew on the shoulder or give him a high five.

The brush of Drew's fingers against mine tells me he's trying to grab my hand. I evade him and step away. He doesn't look happy about that, and I point toward the salad bar. "I'll be there."

I leave him frowning before he turns and talks to his fans.

At the salad bar, I find a small condiment container and fill it with olive oil.

"What's with the olive oil?"

I almost drop the container at Drew's question.

"For someone so big, you can sneak up on a person surprisingly well." Now that he's here, I feel the warmth and energy of him at my back. I pop on a lid. "And you'll have to wait and see."

He leans his head over my shoulder to peer down at me. "Your protests of innocence are wearing very thin at this point." He says this lightly, but I hear the strain in his voice. Is he upset that I left him behind?

Those people didn't come to see me. The back of my neck grows tighter. "All right. I've earned your skepticism. But you'll soon be sorry for it."

With slow care, he eases a lock of my hair back from where it dangles over my forehead. "I trust you, Jones."

"Come on," I say a bit too thickly. "We're headed to the second floor."

Drew's expression goes flat and distant. And my heart skips a pained beat, but then I realize it's not for me. He's not even looking my way. He's putting on a game face to get us out of here quickly. He strides forward, his hand just touching the small of my back, and not a soul comes forward. In truth, they part for him like the Red Sea.

"How do you do that?" I ask out of the side of my mouth. "It's like a superpower."

"You learn fairly quickly how to broadcast 'back off' when you need to."

Unfortunately, some people are always going to be oblivious. And to my horror, a familiar face breaks from the crowd. I haven't seen Whitney Summers since graduating high school. In truth, I didn't know she went to this university. Not that I'd have cause to keep track of her whereabouts—we hate each other.

Thin, toned, and tan, with long blond hair that hangs in a thick sheet down the middle of her back, she's always reminded me of Barbie. An unfortunate stereotype, but there you go. She beelines straight for Drew.

Having no option other than walking into her, Drew stops.

Whitney's big blue eyes blink up at him. "Drew Baylor. I thought it was you."

"You were correct," Drew says.

She ignores me completely. Not surprising. She'd been a world-class bitch to me for years. Smiling wide, she offers Drew her hand. "Whitney Summers. I know your friend Thompson." Her smile grows. "And Rolondo." A giggle now. "And Simms."

Jesus. Is she implying what I think she is? Drew and I exchange a look, and it's clear he's wondering the same thing. His mouth twitches. "Um. Yeah. Well, nice to meet you."

He moves his weight onto the balls of his feet, as if he intends to walk around her, when she leans closer to him. "I just thought I'd introduce myself," she says. "You know. Say hi."

"Okay. Hi."

Whitney flips a long length of her hair behind her shoulder and continues to smile at him. "Maybe we can grab a cup of coffee sometime."

Great. Perfect. I get to witness Drew being propositioned in living color. I don't dare look up at him. I don't want to see his expression. I just can't react. Not when Whitney treats me as though I'm not here.

Looking at her, I feel the same impotent rage as I did in high school. How was it that someone like this, someone petty, shallow, and boring could hold the student body in the palm of her hand? And what was so lacking in me that I had been shunned? I was never unattractive or a jerk.

In truth, I don't understand how the world works the way it does. Grandpa Joe used to tell me that meanness never pays off. But I'm pretty sure whoever made up that saying never went to high school.

Standing next to Drew, I grit my teeth and fight the urge to run away. Or smash my fist into Whitney's nose. Maybe he's aware of my annoyance, because he touches the small of my back. I feel it like a brand of heat along my spine.

"If you'll excuse us," he says to Whitney. "We have somewhere to be."

Her smile falls flat. She catches my eyes, and a calculating look twists her face. "I know you." Her head tilts as she peers at me. "I think."

Oh, very nice. "You do. We went to high school together." And junior high, and grade school, but whatever.

"Oh. Ann, right?" She laughs a little, like she's embarrassed by her gaffe, but she isn't fooling me. And she's looking up at Drew, not me. "Some people aren't as memorable as others."

I tense, ready to lay into her. But Drew halts my response by draping an arm over my shoulder. The hold is proprietary and clearly marks us as a unit.

"Well, I don't think I'll forget you now." His tone is not at all nice.

Not that Whitney notices his sarcasm. No, she beams.

Although I know Drew means well, I never wanted him to

witness something like this. The way people react to us are as polar as true north and south.

Humiliating or not, this is my battle to fight. Heart hurting, I stand rigid in his embrace and stare down Whitney. "Considering you've called me Anna Banana–pants since the third grade," I add coolly, "you're either extremely dense or a liar."

Her mouth falls open as color works over her face. She hadn't expected honesty.

Drew gives my shoulder a light squeeze as he looks at me. "Weren't we going somewhere?"

"Yep."

He guides me around Whitney, neither of us saying good-bye to her. A muttered "bitch" follows us as we walk away, and Drew leans close, his breath buffeting my ear. "Kind of the pot calling the kettle, eh?"

A reluctant smile pulls at my lips, even as I step away from his hold. "You'd never convince her of that."

"I'm sorry she was rude to you." He frowns, concern darkening his eyes.

I shrug, as though I don't feel too tight for my own skin. "Likely, she was flustered by your grand presence."

His scowl grows. "Making excuses for her, Jones? She doesn't deserve it."

No, she doesn't, but the alternative of telling him that she and everyone else I've known for most of my life behaved that way on a constant basis is unthinkable.

"Whitney was a cheerleader at my high school. She's nuts for all things football." I have no doubt she would have had her claws in Drew had he gone to our school.

Drew gives me a look, as if he knows all too well what I am thinking.

"I take it you don't like cheerleaders?" he asks.

We sidestep a group of girls, all of whom eye Drew. Quiet giggles rise up as we walk by.

"Oh, I don't know," I say. "Last year, in my study group, there was a girl who is on the squad here. Laney. She was nice. Worked her ass off to succeed at her sport, and I admired her for it."

"I know Laney. She goes out with my friend Marshall."

Drew opens the door to the stairwell for me.

"Then there are cheerleaders like Whitney," I go on, "who seem to have studied the handbook for stereotypical bitches everywhere." I shrug, pulling free a thick lock of hair that's caught beneath my bag strap. "Why they feel the need to act accordingly, I'll never know."

Drew's eyes, bleary as they are, crinkle at the corners with tired humor. "You'd be surprised how easy it is to play a part." He pauses, his hand on the banister. "Or maybe not. Nonconformist that you are."

Praise never sits well with me. I make a face and force my voice to be light. "Bah. Nonconformity is a role too."

"Maybe, but..." Drew flashes a quick smile, genuine but tight with pain, "'Whoso would be a man must be a nonconformist.'"

"Throwing Emerson at me?" I shake my head as we make our way up the stairs. "Now you're just showing off."

"What can I say? My mom was an English lit professor. Emerson was her favorite. Other kids got *Goodnight Moon* before bed. I got that *and* an Emerson quote."

"Leave it to you to pick the chauvinistic one out of the bunch."

"What?" His brows rise in outrage. "There's nothing chauvinistic about that quote."

I repress a grin. He's too easy. And if teasing distracts him from his pain, more the better. "Right. Whatever. 'Whoso would be a *man*.'" I make quote gestures with my fingers for emphasis. "Why not 'human'?"

Unfortunately, Drew is too quick. His growing scowl suddenly breaks into a knowing smile. "'Man' is generic, and you know it."

"It is also sexist," I retort, having way too much fun.

"I highly doubt they viewed it as such in 1841, Jones."

I'm about to rib him further, but then I take a good look at

Drew. He's getting paler, a light sweat breaking out on his high forehead. A pang centers in my chest.

"Come on." I take him by the elbow and guide him down the hall. "Let's get you settled, before you fall on your face."

Upstairs we head for the campus radio station booth. It's a large glassed-in area, manned by Floyd Hopkins most afternoons. He's there now, taking a break by the looks of the sandwich and soda he has on the desk outside the inner DJ booth.

He sees me coming and breaks into a smile. Tall, thin, with a bushy dark blond halo of curls and a scraggly goatee, he's a modern day Shaggy. But there's no denying his charisma. There's always been something charming about the way he carries himself. A lazy confidence.

Floyd was the guy who introduced me to weed sophomore year. We got high and had sex. It was that eventful. But we remained friends. Well, 'friends' is kind of stretching it. More like acquaintances with carnal knowledge. Not that this stops him from hugging me for a bit too long. Or maybe he does so because of Drew standing next to me; Floyd's eyes stay on him for too long as well.

"Anna Jones, how you doing?"

I break free of Floyd. This was a bad idea. One of many. "Fine."

"Yeah…" Floyd looks between Drew and me as if waiting for an explanation. Drew appears ready to flee.

"Look," I say, "can I use your back room…" Horror has my voice fleeing, as Floyd's instant creepy grin and Drew's raised brows hit me like a brick, and it fully registers how my request sounds.

"Get your mind out of the gutter," I snap, flushed and wanting to die.

Thankfully Floyd laughs. "I'm just messing with you, Anna. I know you'd be the last girl to ask to borrow my couch for sex." He glances at Drew. "Even with Battle Baylor here. She's too discreet, you know?"

Drew merely looks at him, and Floyd kind of deflates like a day-old balloon. As for me, I want to hit something. Floyd runs a finger along his hairy chin. "It's cool. Go on and take your seven minutes."

"We really need more like an hour…" Again, my voice dies on a gurgle.

Floyd's grin erupts full force. At my side, Drew makes a smothered sound like he's choking.

"God, just…" I tug Drew past Floyd and storm into the lounge, shutting the door on Floyd's amusement.

Not on Drew's. He bursts out laughing, even as he clutches his head. "Ow, shit." He laughs again. "God, you should have seen your face."

"Funny." I'm pleased to find the lava lamp is already on. Yes, the room boasts one, which I found cheesy the time I visited, but it serves a purpose now.

"I mean, that was not very subtle, Jones." His eyes are both bleary and twinkling. Bastard even looks good in pain.

"You're going to be sorry you teased me." I turn off the overhead light and plunge us into a darkened world of dreamy blue moving shadows. "And if you make a crack about sex one more time…"

"You'll get *very* angry?" Drew asks as he plops down onto the couch. A sigh leaves him as he leans his head against the padded back. He's hurting but he seems pleased. "Thank you for finding me a place to lie down. I needed this."

Carefully, I sit next to him. "I'm just happy he didn't notice the oil."

Drew bursts out laughing again, but it ends with a groan. "Anna."

The underlying emotion in the way he says my name makes my grip unsteady as I uncap the oil and rub a bit between my palms. "Give me your hand."

Drew's brows rise but he complies. Usually, his hands are warm, but his skin is now cold and clammy.

"Most people think a neck rub is the best thing for a headache," I say, holding his hand between mine for a moment to warm it. "But we carry an enormous amount of tension in our hands. They have pressure points that link directly to headache pain."

His big hand is almost too much to manage. I concentrate at first on his wide palm, kneading my knuckles down the center of it. And Drew groans, letting his head fall to the side. His long fingers loosely curl, engulfing my smaller hand.

"My mom used to do this for me when I had migraines," I say. "Aside from a shot, targeting pressure points is the fastest way to alleviate the pain."

"You are a goddess," he says on another groan. "A hand-rubbing goddess."

"Flatterer."

His forearm is carved oak beneath my fingers, his skin smooth and rapidly warming. "Only to you, babe."

We're quiet then.

"So, Floyd?" he says out of the blue.

My hands still for a second. "I'm supposed to answer that?"

He tilts his head, eyeing me. "Old boyfriend?"

I tug gently on one of his long fingers, squeezing at the end. "Not really."

"You just leave a string of hook ups in your wake?"

Though it's dark in here, he clearly sees too well. I stop and look him in the eye. "Like you can talk."

His fingers thread through mine a second before I can pull away, and he holds firm.

"I'm jealous." The light of the lava lamp casts his face in undulating blue. Lines deepen around his eyes, but he doesn't look away. "Okay? I..." His lashes lower. "I don't like seeing you with a guy who knows you that way."

"Do you know how many girls I've seen hanging on you?" My heart is pounding far too hard. "How many ass slaps you've given outside our class?"

He frowns. "I'm a jock. We slap asses by way of affection. And just because I'm friendly to those girls doesn't mean I'm having sex with them, you know."

I make an unflattering sound of disbelief, and he gives my hand a small tug. "Fine, don't believe me. The question is, did it bother you to see that?"

Trapped. By my own big mouth. I fiddle with the tip of his thumb, running the pad of my finger along his trimmed nail. "I wouldn't like it now."

He doesn't say anything. Not for a long, excruciating minute. But I feel his gaze like a heated blanket. Then his thumb runs over my knuckles. "Well then," he says gruff and stilted, "you can sympathize."

A pang much like guilt shoots through me. "He was just a hook up."

Drew waits a beat before answering softly, "So am I."

I swallow hard. "Yeah, but you're the hook up that doesn't seem to end."

He smiles, but his grip tightens for a second. I ease it by pinching the fat pad between his thumb and forefinger where a world of tension hides. He grunts and slides further down on the couch, closing his eyes. "That's good."

"I know. Your hands are too tight."

"Funny," Drew murmurs. "That's what Coach Johnson, my offensive coordinator, says. He's always after me to stretch them more."

The lines of his face are still tired and pinched, but there's a smile hovering around his mouth. I set his hand gently down on his thigh and take his other one.

"You really love it, don't you?" I ask.

His hand in mine jerks a little before he opens his eyes. "Football? Of course. I wouldn't do it if I didn't."

"I don't know—" I shrug "—some people would. To please their parents, to fit in, for the attention. There's plenty of reasons."

"Yeah, well they aren't going to get very far if they don't love it. The pressure will topple you otherwise."

"Does it get to you," I ask softly. "The pressure?"

He goes so silent that I know he doesn't want to answer. Though his reticence shouldn't hurt me, it does.

"You don't have to—"

"Sometimes it does," he says in a low voice. "Sometimes..." He takes a deep breath. "I wake up on the verge of a scream. Like it's all trying to bubble out of me when I let my guard down to sleep."

I don't know what to say, so I simply press the ball of my thumb deep into his palm and rub it in a small circle. The tension in his hand eases, as does his voice. "But you have to accept that as part of the life. Let it ride, then let it go.

"Every year, before the start of the season, my dad would ask, do you still want this?" Drew turns toward me. "Because he knew how hard it would be if I didn't. He warned me that it would get to me, and that I'd have to find a way to deal with it."

"Did your dad play?" I'm dying of curiosity about his parents.

He blinks, a slow sweep of his lashes. Maybe the ibuprofen and massage are kicking in. Or maybe I've hurt him with the questions. I hope it's the former. I keep rubbing his hand, stroking up to his wrist then along the hard plank of his forearm.

"Not football," Drew answers, watching my fingers. "He played baseball. Pitcher. Was recruited by MLB straight out of college. A torn rotator cuff during his last season kept him from going pro." He flashes a smile. "Dad was my little league coach."

"And yet you chose football? What, no good at baseball?"

His eyes flutter closed. "I kick ass in baseball, Jones. I could have played that instead. But football was always the one."

"If you were good at both, how did you know?"

Drew's long fingers twine with mine, holding me in a warm, engulfing clasp. He doesn't open his eyes as he speaks. "Some things are like that. You just know."

I clear my throat. "I envy you. I've never been totally sure of anything."

Other than wanting Drew from the moment I laid eyes on him.

I untangle my hand from his, and he lets go as if he knows I need to get free.

"Don't be too envious," he says wryly. "Knowing what you want and having it are two different things."

His eyes lock onto mine with a punch that I feel deep in my belly. "I'd rather have what I want than just know."

I look away first, then shift over to the end of the couch and turn to sit cross-legged. "Lie down."

He squints at me with a slight frown as if he doesn't really want to move. "There's more?"

Grabbing my coat, I bunch it on my lap and slap the spot. "Head here."

Drew's brows rise, his expression a mixture of confusion and weariness, and I laugh. "What do think I'm going to do to you?"

"I don't know," he says, as he eases down, unfolding his long length on the couch. "But I'm hoping for the best."

"Where's the trust?" I say with a dramatic sigh.

His head settles in the lee of my crossed legs. "I just told you something about me that no one else alive knows, Jones. I don't think my trust in you could be more clear."

I lean over him, our faces upside down from each other's. He's humbled me. My palms settle on his shoulders, pressing there gently to warm him, and my fingers find the leather cord he wears around his neck. I trace it, watching his skin prickle as I go. When I get to the pendant, I run a thumb over the polished wood.

He's watching me, his gaze guarded, vulnerable. But when he speaks, it's as if he's leaving himself wide-open. "It's a chunk of wood from the lintel on the front door of my parent's house." His lashes sweep down. "Figured that way I'd always carry a piece of my old home with me."

Ah, Drew. He's slowly carving his name into my heart. And it hurts. I want to curl over him and shelter him with my body. But his cheeks are flushed and his neck grows stiffer by the second, as if he's regretting his confession.

I rest my palm over the pendant, holding the wood against the hard wall of his chest.

When I can speak without emotion clogging my words, I tell him, "I'm going to massage your face now."

"My face?" he repeats as if I've offered to stick my finger up his nose.

I smother a laugh. "We hold even more tension in our face."

Keeping my hands on him, I rub the tops of his shoulders before doing the same to his neck. He likes this and sinks down further into the couch.

His eyes flutter as if he wants to shut them. My hands ease up to his jaw then settle on his brow. "It's okay. Close your eyes."

When he does, I simply run my fingertips over his face, taking in his strong, clean bone structure. Strangely, I've always attributed Drew's attractiveness to his inner light, the way he carries himself, and how his emotions shine through. But, God, he really is beautifully made.

Whereas my face is all curves, his is like a diamond, made up of dramatic angles and cut lines. His nose is high and straight, widening a bit in the middle, which only gives him more character. Prominent cheekbones veer down sharply toward his mouth, that gloriously mobile mouth that is always quick to smile. Relaxed now, it's as if he's pouting. His jawline is defined and in perfect symmetry with his cheeks.

With steady, firm pressure, my fingers ride over the ridges of his sweeping brows, following the tension. The slow, undulating light of the lava lamp casts deep blues and grays over his skin.

"Keep talking to me," he whispers.

I pause. "Doesn't noise hurt your head?"

Thick lashes cast shadows at the tops of his cheeks. "Your voice isn't noise. It's a song I want to hear over and over."

Oh. My.

Taking a deep breath, I pinch along the underside of his brows, moving outward. Drew groans low.

"Is your full name Andrew?" Not the most brilliant of conversational openings, but I'm curious.

The full curve of his lips lifts a little. "Nope. I'm just Drew." He talks low, barely over a murmur. "Mom didn't like nicknames. She figured they would name me what they wanted to call me. So just Drew Baylor. No middle name either."

"I kind of love your mom for that," I say softly.

His eyes open and lock onto me. Pain still lingers in them, but there's also a warmth that has me blushing. "She would have loved you too."

No, she wouldn't have. What mother would like a girl that uses her precious son for sex? None. I palm his face, effectively blocking his view, and run my thumbs down the sides of his nose and over his cheeks, digging in deep.

"Christ," he breathes out. "That's good."

"I know." I smile a little.

"What about you?" he asks. "You have a middle name?"

"Marie." I stroke along his jaw. So much tension there.

"Anna Marie," he intones. "I like that."

He goes silent, and I gently hum, not a song, really, just a lilt that fills the silence. He sighs, his body easing more under my touch.

"When's your birthday, Anna Marie?"

"You're going to make me regret telling you my middle name."

His smile is wobbly, as if weakened by pain. "Just answer the question."

"Why?" I slip my hands under his neck, finding the base of his skull. His muscles are so dense here that my fingers barely make a dent. "You going to give me a present?"

"You put it that way...oh, God, that's a spot..." His brows furrow on a wince. "God, do that some more, Jones."

Heat flushes my skin, but I comply. He shudders, his long body twitching as it releases pain.

"You put it that way," he says returning to the topic of presents, "and I kind of have to, now don't I?"

"Stop tensing," I murmur, running my fingers along the back of his skull, before answering him. "You set me up for that one, Baylor. When's your birthday, then?"

Drew lets out a breath and moans as I find the tension spots plaguing him. He's now lax, lying heavy on the couch. I've had my hands all over his fine body, and yet touching him to take his pain away is a gratification that I never expected.

His voice slurs with drowsiness. "November nineteenth."

I pause. "It is not."

He cracks open one eye. "Why would I lie?" Both eyes open. "When's yours?"

I bite my lip. "November twentieth."

Drew grins, his whole expression lightening. "We're birthday buddies." His smile turns smug. "Only I'm older."

A small laugh escapes me. "You can keep that victory. I don't know any girl who wants to be older than her—" My voice dies.

But it's too late, because it's obvious what I was going to say. *Her boyfriend.*

Satisfaction steals over his expression, but there's something more. Something that has my heart racing in my chest, and my mouth going dry. An acknowledgment. As if he's been waiting for this very slip.

His lashes are long and thick, framing his light brown eyes. Beneath my fingertips, his throat lifts on a swallow. "Anna."

My chest tightens to the point of pain.

My mother always accused me of having an excess of pride. People think pride is something you should be able to control, that it's something sinful, best used in small doses. And they're right. But for most of my life, pride has been the only thing that's kept my head up. Now it's holding me back from Drew. I know this. Hell, I *feel* its hard hands upon me, clutching with a tightness that speaks of desperation. I know this, and yet I can't break free. I'm not ready.

I snuggle back into its familiar hold. Safe there. And instead of acknowledging this growing *thing* between us, my hands move up to cup Drew's cheeks.

"Sleep," I say, running a thumb along his bottom lip. "You need it."

Protest darkens his expression.

"Sleep," I insist as if my throat isn't closing in on itself. "I'll wake you."

He resists for a moment, watching me with those eyes that reveal too much. But then he does as I ask, putting himself in my keeping. I run my fingers through his silky hair and watch over him.

ELEVEN

ANNA

IT'S GETTING WORSE, this addiction. I need Drew with greater frequency and with more urgency. At least there are rules. Rules to keep myself under control, safe. Rules that are somehow agreed upon and understood without having to say a word. We always meet at my place, never so late as to warrant a sleepover, never stay together more than an hour—or three if we are particularly…needy. And still no kissing on the mouth, though I'm starting to see more and more shadows of discontent from Drew regarding this rule. But he's yet to vocalize it. And I do an admirable job of telling myself that it's for the best. I need to protect myself. Because I'm never getting left behind again.

Now we're naked and on my bed, my favorite fleece throw covering our bodies. I draw the line at getting under the covers with him. That's too personal, too much like making love versus hooking up. Not that getting under the sheets is an issue when, from the instant we close the door to my room, we think of nothing else but being skin to skin.

Even more concerning is that now that we've finished, he isn't leaving. Nor am I hurrying him out. Sweat gives his golden skin a fine sheen, and he's panting lightly as if he's run miles.

The light is fading outside, the rays of the setting sun stealing through my blinds and spilling into my room until we are painted in glowing stripes of deep orange.

One of his hands rests lightly on the rippled wall of his abdomen. I focus on that as I sprawl half on my side, one hand caught beneath his shoulder, the other hand still gripping the bedpost. I'd held on so tight to that post when he pounded into me that I wonder if he'll have to help pry my fingers free from the wood.

A luscious, little shiver runs over me. The things he does to me. The thoroughness in which he takes his pleasure and gives me mine.

Drew turns away to take long gulps of water from the bottle sitting on the bedside table. And that's when I see it. The room is shadowed but not enough to hide some things.

"You have a tattoo." There's a singsong quality about my observation that I can't hide and don't want to. Because I'm grinning. An evil grin.

He turns back to glare at me properly. "Yeah."

"It's a battle axe," I add with glee. A cute little cartoon-style battle axe about the size of my thumb on the crest of his left butt cheek. Like something Papa Smurf might wield. How could I not have seen this before? Right, because normally he'd have hauled his pants up and would be headed out the door about now.

Drew's high-cut cheeks go pink. "Fucking Cancún. Spring break, my sophomore year, I got so wasted one night. I vaguely remember a burning sensation on my butt cheek while my teammates chanted 'Battle, Battle.' That's about it. I woke up naked in a bed full of…" The blush returns with force, and he runs a hand through his hair, which makes it stand up on end on the right side. It's kind of adorable. So is his embarrassment. "Full of girls *and* guys."

I laugh, a crackling mad witch laugh that earns a pillow tossed at my face.

"It's not funny," he insists, though there's a hint of humor in his voice. "I was in an orgy and don't remember a thing. Imagine the horrors." He mocks a shudder.

This only makes me laugh harder.

"With the mother of all hangovers," Drew adds bitterly, though now he's fully smiling. "And this fucking tattoo."

He cranes his neck to glare down at his ass. "Fucking, stupid battle axe."

"Battle Butt Baylor." I'm dying now. And give a small screech when he dives for me. There's a bit of a tussle, mainly involving Drew cramming another pillow in my face while I howl with laughter. But then he ends up half over me, his thick thigh pushed in between mine and his chest pressed against my torso. We're still laughing a little, though, and he smiles down at me.

"I swore off drinking to excess that very moment and got myself checked for every disease known to man the second I returned home."

His smile dims a little, and his gaze searches mine. "I'm clear, you know. I get regular checks." The seriousness of his tone and the way he says this makes me believe he's suddenly worried I'll bar him from further play due to his checkered past.

"I am too," I say. "The day I turned sixteen, my mom put me on the pill and started me on a biannual STD check."

Drew's brows rise. "That's kind of..."

"Paranoid?" Lord knows I didn't need to be on the pill back then.

A little shiver of sensation travels along my scalp, and I realize that he's playing with a lock of my hair, curling it around his finger.

His voice is low between us. "I was thinking more like 'untrusting.'"

I don't want to explain just how wrong he is, because then I'd have to tell him that not a single boy even looked in my direction for the whole of high school.

Instead, I lift a shoulder. "My mom's an ob-gyn. For her, it's a sign of love. You know, like how a dentist's kid will be forced to brush and floss three times daily before she's two."

Drew grins, but then his expression goes quiet and intense. I feel it down in my heart, as though he reached through my ribs and gave it a squeeze. He's looking at me as though he likes me far too much. As though he likes this intimacy.

"Let me see it again," I say. Because I need to move out from under him. And because I truly do want to look at his little mark of shame again.

"No," he whispers with a small smile. He leans in, the tip of his nose almost touching mine. I note the individual lashes curling thick and dark around his eyes. His irises are polished amber and alight with amusement.

"Yes," I say, breathless.

"No." His lips brush my jaw, my chin. He's too close to my mouth. Too close to me.

"Yes." I push a thumb between his ribs, and he yelps.

"Jones," he warns, skittering away when I do it again.

"Baylor," I intone. "Let me see."

"Easy with the thumbs of evil, woman."

"Then let me see."

"Okay, okay. The things I do for you." He huffs, as he rolls over with a mutter.

Oh, but his body is a work of art. Long, lean, muscular. Perfect in proportion. His back is narrow and straight, the valley of his spine deep between slabs of tight muscle. It dips then sweeps up to the rounded globes of his fine ass. An ass so strong that his butt cheeks indent on the sides. His long legs are covered in a down of light brown hair and are as sculpted as the rest of him, with thick thighs and well-defined calves.

I want to lick him from neck to heel. And take my time about it in between. But he's waiting for me. His butt is twitching as if he's feeling my stare. Chin propped on his bent arms, he turns his head to give me a sidelong glare. "Well?"

"Just enjoying the view," I say with a leer that makes him snicker.

"Turnabout, Jones. Don't forget it. Wait, not the light— Gah!" He squints when I flick on the bedside light. "Are you trying to blind me?"

"The room was too dark, and I want to see this sucker properly..." My breath hitches. "Jesus, Drew, your side."

"Hmmm?" He cocks a brow and then glances over his shoulder. "Oh, right."

"Right?" I can't hold back from leaning down and running a hand along his lower side. He's covered in bruises. Big ugly bruises like berry stains over his golden skin. Blackberry, blueberry, raspberry. They're a mottled landscape of pain. And I'd been poking him there. Jesus.

"I had a game yesterday," he reminds me. As if it's nothing that his body has been pummeled.

"Is it always like this?" I'm curled at his side, my hand slowly running over the smooth skin of his back and along his flank. He's paler here, and on his upper thighs where his shorts have blocked the sun. He shivers a bit, his skin prickling.

"Some games are tougher than others. This one was a bitch."

My throat hurts. There's a black bruise just above his hipbone. I touch it with the tip of my finger, and he shivers again.

Instantly, I draw back. "Does it hurt?" Of course it does. How can it not?

Drew turns to look down at me, his hips lifting a bit and revealing the shadow of his cock against the bed. The extent of my distress is great, because I'm not even distracted. My palm comes to rest on the warm rise of his butt when he waggles his brows.

"If I say yes," he asks, "will you kiss it and make it better?"

He is teasing me, but he doesn't know that kissing his battered flesh is something I ache to do. I lean forward. He looks almost vulnerable, the way his body tightens, and his eyes follow my movement.

Inches from him, I hover, waiting, my heart pounding as I look up.

"Yes," he whispers.

My lips touch his skin, and his breath catches.

"Yes," he says again, more urgent.

Another kiss, soft, gentle. My lips map his pain with each *yes*, *yes*, *yes*, my hair sliding over his skin like a bloodred river.

Everything becomes languid heat. The bed sheets rustle as he turns onto his back and I crawl over him, my lips traveling along the blooming bruises upon his rock-hard belly. I trace the grooves between his muscles with my tongue, and he makes little noises of contentment. And I do too. God, he's beautiful, his skin taut, his body so honed it looks like it's been cast from bronze.

The silken heat of his cock, now hard and erect, brushes my cheek, and I still. He's watching me beneath half-closed lids, his breath light and quick.

I stare up at him as my lips graze the tender head, and he croaks a weak "Yes."

Yes.

I've wanted to taste Drew's cock since the moment I saw it. He's glorious here, thick and long and straight. He smells of musk and warmth, and he's trembling as if he's trying to hold himself still.

The round, swollen head is satin smooth and hot against the roof of my mouth as I draw him in and give a soft suck.

Drew groans loud, his hips bucking, which shoves him in deeper. I wrap my hand around him and suck again.

"Yes," he groans. His trembling fingers thread through my hair. He holds me there, making helpless little sounds as he lightly pumps in and out of my mouth. The sight of him, head thrown back, lips parted and brows furrowed as though in pain, the way his muscles stand out in sharp relief because they're clenched so tight: all of it makes me so hot that I begin to sweat.

My thighs tremble and my sex pulses as I flick my tongue over his head, suck him hard then light, take as much of him as I can into my mouth before pulling back out in a slow glide.

I want to drive him out of his mind. The way he does me.

I love it when he fists my hair harder, drives himself into my mouth, his free hand clutching the bedspread like he might soon become unmoored.

"Anna..." My name is a plea on his lips as he writhes. "Baby... Please, I'm going to..."

I run my palm along the armor-plate of muscle that is his belly, and he releases with a sharp cry.

It's warm and viscous and salty sweet. I've never done this before, staying with a guy to the very end. But with Drew, I drink him down. Until he goes soft and helpless in my mouth. And I know that I am in deep, dark waters. Because, although this feels like addiction, I'm not so sure it is anymore.

TWELVE

ANNA

I NEED PERSPECTIVE. I need to remember why keeping my resolve is a good plan. I need to go home. Mom's off on Mondays. Fuck it; I'm skipping class.

I give her a call to let her know I'm coming. It's a perfect autumn morning when I climb on my Vespa and head toward my mother's house. The scooter isn't very practical; I can't use the highway and must stick to back roads. I know I'll catch hell from my mom yet again for driving it to her house. But I love the feel of air rushing over me, and the ability to weave in and out of traffic.

Even so, it would be smart to trade my scooter in and buy a car. I don't like driving the Vespa in rain, and the winter months flat-out suck. I have some savings—hell, my mom would buy a car for me, she hates the scooter so much.

Indecision regarding my scooter fills my thoughts, and I'm

happy about that. It keeps me from thinking about other things, other people. Soon enough, I'm pulling up in front of the house I grew up in. It's a 1920s colonial made of Georgia red brick.

I love this house, with its five windows along the top floor and four windows, two each flanking the red center door, on the ground floor. I love that somehow it managed to escape the dreaded Tara-style front porch that so many southern homes try to emulate.

It's a simple, unpretentious house. And though the front walk has always been clean and inviting, I've never really used it, choosing to go in through the side door instead.

I pull up into the carport, parking next to my mother's ancient blue Mercedes. She's had the car as long as she's had me. Just looking at it fills me with a sense of homecoming, as does the smell of old brick and decaying crepe myrtle flowers.

Through the window, I spot Mom at the stove. It's been months since I've seen her, but she hasn't aged. Then again, my mom never seems to age. She's magically preserved. Slim and fit, she wears sky blue silk lounge pants and a thin cream cashmere sweater. Her glossy black hair tumbles artfully around her shoulders, and she gives it an impatient flick as she pulls the old battered moka pot off the stove.

Although my mother is a southern lady, she's also a doctor and second-generation Italian, which means I'm getting a cappuccino and fruit for breakfast instead of biscuits and gravy. Her one concession might be some fresh low-fat scones.

She turns as I open the door, and her heart-shaped face brightens. "Banana!"

Mom hurries over to me and gives me a kiss on the cheek. I'm surrounded by the scent of lavender that she favors. "How has my baby been?"

"Good." It's the only answer I can think to give.

With a nod, she sways back to the moka pot and proceeds to pour thick, rich coffee into a waiting cup half filled with heated milk. The scent is homey and mouthwatering. If I could just once achieve my mother's coffee perfection, I'd be a happy girl indeed.

"Come," she urges. "Let's sit and talk."

She places the cup next to a set place, complete with linen napkin. Freshly cut melons, strawberries, and raspberries wait in a crystal bowl. This is my mom at her finest. Warning bells ring in my mind. More so when she turns and pulls a tray of hot scones from the oven. Those do not look low-fat.

"So," she says as she serves me a scone and doles out some fruit. "Anything new going on?"

This is standard fare. Mom doesn't like to pry, but at least she's interested in my life. I think she'd be less gracious about it, however, if I told her that I've been fucking the star quarterback in my bedroom. My cheeks heat as I take a sip of coffee. God, that's good.

I close my eyes and savor the flavor. "I've missed you, Mom." I don't know where that came from, but it's the truth.

Silence falls over me, and I open my eyes. Her eyes, so like mine in shape but a deep, dark brown, stare at me. "Is something wrong, Banana?"

I shrug and take another needed sip. "Can't a girl miss her mother?"

"Of course she can." She cups my cheek with her cool hand. My mom's skin is always cool. "Only, I know my baby and something's upsetting you."

Sighing, I start in on my scone. I was right. This is not low-fat, and it's my favorite orange and lemon flavor. There's even fresh butter on the table, soft and waiting for me to dive in. I slather some on a section of scone before popping it into my mouth. *Heaven.*

"I'm fine. Happy." And though doubt assails me on a constant basis, I *am* happy.

The truth slaps so hard that I flinch in my seat. I'm happy. I awake filled with anticipation. Fight sleep to keep the feeling close to me. Why can't I enjoy it? Accept it? God, what a fucked-up mess I am.

"Mom—"

The back door opens again, and Terrance, my mom's boyfriend of the hour, walks in. I should say "of the year" because that's about as long as these guys last. I've hated every one of them. And while that might sound petulant, it's always been with good reason.

There was Marcus, who called her trash to her face, spat in her food, and then cried that she didn't love him enough. All in front of me.

There was Oliver, a thin spaced-out professor who ended up stealing ten grand out of her bank account. And Jeremy, who criticized her so much that she gained twenty pounds and forgot to wear makeup to work one day, which is the equivalent of a mental breakdown for my mother.

At least none of them hit her. Not that I know of, anyway.

Terrance owns a used bookstore and pinches pennies by collecting packets of salt, pepper, ketchup, and whatnot from various fast-food restaurants around the area. I can't make this shit up. He also generally loathes being left out of any of Mom's business.

"Hello, Anna," he says as he comes further into the kitchen and stares at my boobs. Intently.

He takes a seat next to my mom and immediately drapes an arm around her shoulder, leaving his long, pale fingers to dangle right over her breast. Because, while he might stare at my boobs, he takes any opportunity he can to touch my mom's when I'm around.

My stomach turns. "Hello, Terrance." I keep my eyes on his greasy hair, parted severely down the middle. Like Hitler's. When my stomach turns again, I look at my mother, who is trying to appear casual and calm, even though some creep is stroking her like she's a lapdog.

I don't bother giving my mother a dirty look even though he's here on my day with her. He does it every time.

If I live a hundred years, I'll never understand my mother. She's smart, *brilliant*, beautiful, and talented. And she has the self-esteem of a gnat. I cannot fathom why she'd rather not be alone than settle for these... I don't even want to call them *men*.

"Did you tell Anna the good news, Cecelia?"

Mom has the grace to flinch, and I know it will be bad. God, please don't let it be marriage. I've feared that since I was ten and finally realized that one of these jerks might become a permanent fixture if Mom actually married one of them. Luckily, the relationships ended before then.

"Well, dear—" She neatly shrugs out of Terrance's grasp as she leans forward. "I'm getting older now."

She's fifty-five. Hardly old.

"And there's so much to see in this world."

Okay, true.

Terrance's hand lands on her hip, and he strokes her butt. I'm now officially ill.

"So I've decided to retire," Mom says with forced excitement.

"That's..." I struggle. "Well, that's great, if that's what you want, Mom." I'm happy to think of Mom relaxing, even though I suspect she'll be bored within months.

But she's not done. She shifts in her seat, and my heart plummets. God, please not the marriage thing.

"What?" I ask.

"I've also decided to sell the house."

The words set off a bomb within my skull. I just sit there, my brain scrambled, leaving me unable to speak.

"We're going on a world cruise," Terrance puts in, grinning at me with his gray teeth.

"Are you selling *your* house?" I ask him. "Oh, right, I forgot. You rent." Because I'm beginning to get the idea.

Terrance's beady eyes narrow. "I don't think that's any of your business."

"Yet you're here, when this conversation is really between me and my mom."

"Anna," Mom begins.

"Don't." I hold up a hand. Then take a deep breath. "Can I say anything to change your mind?"

"You should be happy for your mother, young lady." Terrance is turning an ugly shade of red. "Not making her feel bad."

"Do not fucking call me *young lady* again. And I'm not talking to you."

"Anna, language." Mom eases closer to me, like she might reach out and pat my hand.

I place my hands in my lap.

"Can I talk you out of it?" I ask again.

Her expression turns sad, regretful. "You don't live here anymore, and I thought I'd buy something smaller when I return."

"Never mind that your parents gave you this house. That it's the only home I've ever known."

Terrance all but crows. "I told you she'd covet the house, Cecelia."

"Like you are, Terry?" I snap back.

"Anna." It's a plea from my mom.

"Cece, don't baby her," Terrance cuts in, rising to glare at me. "She can take care of herself."

"All evidence to the contrary." I stare down his looming figure. "And if you come any closer to me, you'll see how easily I can take care of myself."

Mom jumps up then. "Anna, Terrance, stop this now." She places a hand on the sleaze. "Let me handle this."

I can't watch anymore. In truth, I should have left long ago. I know the drill. She might love me, but she always chooses her boyfriend's side.

"I have to go."

Mom's mouth falls open, as if this is a shock to her. "But you just got here. You haven't even eaten."

If I eat now, I'll throw up.

"I'll talk to you later." I grab my purse and leave. And she doesn't try to stop me again.

★ ★ ★

Hurt, anger, and disgust is an ugly cocktail in my veins. Well, I think ruefully, I wanted a reminder, and I sure as hell got one.

I drive around until my arms are tired and I'm nearly out of gas. I don't want to go back to my apartment. I don't want to talk to Iris or George about it; they've both heard the saga of my mom many times before, and whatever they say is not going to help. Nothing is going to change the situation. Which only makes my agitation burn stronger.

The beautiful fall day is totally incongruent with my mood. Fluffy clouds bump around in a blue sky. The air is just this shade of cool, and the sun shines hot on my head as I walk across the campus parking lot, leaving my Vespa behind.

The stadium looms over me, and my heartbeat picks up. The closer I get, the easier it is to hear the sounds of play, the errant trill of a whistle, and the grunts and thuds of young men throwing themselves against each other or those padded training contraptions, the name of which I cannot recall.

Scattered about the stadium seats like birds alighting for feed are people watching the football team practice. Heads crane forward to see Drew throw a pass. The ball spirals through the air, fast and sure, and lands with perfect precision in a wide receiver's hand. The player laughs and jogs lightly back to Drew, tossing him the ball before one of the coaches makes a comment to them. I'm too far away to hear it, and I like it that way.

Sitting a few feet from a couple of younger guys who wax on about the awesomeness that is Battle Baylor, I feel anonymous. Safe. The sun has slipped behind the line of the stadium, and my spot falls into shadows. Sweet relief from the heat.

Drew makes a few more throws, each one farther, each in a different direction, with a different approach. He's wearing a helmet, loose basketball shorts that hit him at the knees, and his jersey without the extra bulk of pads. And every time he throws, a swath of tawny skin shows along the bottom of his jersey—a sight that makes all my happy places clench sweetly.

I shouldn't be here, mooning like some groupie. It's a clamor in my head, which grows as people slip away and I become more exposed sitting alone on the bench. But I can't find it in myself to leave. I like watching him move, like seeing the way his team and coaches interact with him. They love him. It's clear to see. As is the joy he feels. He's lit up from within. And this is only a practice. I envy him. Never in my life have I felt that way about something I've done.

The team breaks up again, moving into clusters, and Drew starts some strange squat-then-jump-into-a-lunge exercise with a group of guys who must be backup quarterbacks, because they're all holding footballs and pretending to throw them with each lunge. It should look ridiculous, but it's more like a dance: graceful, powerful. None more than Drew.

God, he's fast. My thigh muscles would rip away from my bones if I tried to move that quickly. But he just keeps going, as if it's effortless.

My butt goes numb from sitting, but on the inside, a calm settles over me. I take a deep breath, drawing in the scent of grass, the metal seats, and a faint trace of clean, male sweat. A loud whistle rings, and they're jogging off, leaving the field.

All but Drew. He's pulling his helmet off, his eyes on me, as if he's known all along that I was there. Maybe he has. I don't know. My breath surges, as my heart rate increases. I find myself rising, my legs taking me down the concrete steps while he walks my way, his stride long and confident.

By the time I reach the emerald green field, he's grinning. And though part of me wants to grin back, suddenly I am nearly in tears. Shit.

He draws close, still holding a football in his hand as if it's an extension of himself.

"Miss Jones." His voice is light with teasing. "For a while, I thought you were a mirage."

I can't quite look him in the eyes. Not when mine are burning. Inside, I'm shaking. Drew is so near, I could reach out and touch him with ease. I could press my cold palms to the dense muscles of his chest, where I know it will be warm.

I need you. I need you so badly...

I think of smug, fucking Terrance groping my mother's ass, and I shove my hands deep into the pockets of my light jacket. "And here I thought I was being stealthy."

"I thought I told you, Jones. I always notice when you're around." His smile wavers as he sees my expression. "Something wrong?"

I blink hard and look away.

"There is." He takes a step closer, the ball dropping at his feet. "Are you okay?"

"No." *Shit, shit, shit.* I'm going to lose it. "I, ah... No."

On the next breath, his arms are wrapped around me, holding me against his lean body. For a moment, I tense, feeling exposed in too many ways. I've never been held like this by a man. Not one of my supposed boyfriends or hook ups has ever really hugged me. And I certainly haven't been hugged by my father. The knowledge is a shock, as is the all-encompassing comfort I feel in Drew's embrace.

I burrow my nose into the center of his chest as I wrap my arms around his lean waist. He's damp with sweat, reeks of it. I don't care. He feels so freaking good, his hard body solid and warm against mine, that I want to stay this way until he has the sense to let me go.

But he doesn't. He holds me. Not weaving or speaking, just holding me strong and secure, his lips pressed into the crown of my head. I'm tucked into the shelter of his body. Safe from the entire world.

When I fully sink into Drew's embrace, my body relaxing, he speaks. "Want to talk about it?"

I love this particular tone of his voice. I've never heard him use it with anyone but me. But I ease away from him. I can't talk about this and cling to him at the same time. Not if I want to maintain any dignity.

Thankfully, he lets me go, but his expression is fierce, as if he'll go kick someone's ass if I ask him. Were I not so drained I'd smile. "I went to visit my mom."

Fear, stark and deep fills his eyes, and I curse myself. "She's fine," I say quickly. "It was... She just... Ah..." Shit-fuck, how can I be complaining about my mother's antics to him when I know he'd do anything to have his mother back?

He reads me too well, and a wry look comes into his eyes. "You're allowed to be in a fight with your mother, Anna. I promise, it's not going to upset me."

My shoulders fall on a sigh. "It just seems petty when..." I trail off again, strangled with frustration.

He touches my cheek, brushing back a lock of my hair. "What happened?"

I rock back on my heels as I stare down at the fresh-cut grass. There's a bit of chalk on the toe of my boot.

"She's selling the house." Bitterness fills my mouth. "So she can go on a world cruise with Terrance-The-Ass-Fuck."

Drew braces his hands low on his narrow hips. "Shit, Anna. I'm sorry."

Yeah, because he knows how it feels to lose his childhood home. Again, I wince. I shouldn't be complaining, but he doesn't seem upset. In fact, his nose wrinkles a bit along the high bridge.

"Er... Who is Terrance-The-Ass-Fuck?"

Despite myself, I fight a smile. "Her boyfriend of the moment. I wasn't being literal, thank God." My smile falls flat. "Though I really should call him 'He of the Roving Hands.'"

Drew's brows snap together, his nostrils flaring as he straightens. "He hasn't touched you, has he?"

I can see old Terrance in a hospital bed if I say yes, but I shake my head and Drew relaxes.

"No. But he feels up my mom in front of me."

Drew's scowl returns. "I think I'd lose it if I'd had to see some guy grope my mom."

"He does it to bother me. It's because of him that she's selling our house. Old Terry doesn't have the funds to pay his way." I curse again. "There is nothing I can do. She won't hear me, no matter what I say."

I blink rapidly, try to calm myself.

"I know I'm being a baby about this. It isn't like I live there, or plan to anymore. But it's like that final safety net is gone. And now I'll never be able to go..." My words die, horror invading me, as I realize what I've said.

But Drew finishes my sentence for me. "Go home again? Don't hold back your words out of pity, Anna. I don't need that."

I want to shrivel into the grass. "I think there's a difference between pity and sympathy, don't you?"

He slowly nods. "Sometimes, without warning, I'll catch the scents of my old home. I don't know what it will be exactly, maybe a mix of old books and coffee, or laundry detergent and cool air." His gaze turns inward. "But it smells just like home. And I'll miss mine so fucking badly that I can't breathe."

"I wish you could go home again," I say, wanting to cry.

Drew's eyes lock onto me. "I do too. But I think we have to make our own homes."

Looking at him, gilded by sunlight, his expression tight with weariness but earnest as he watches me, I think that I could love this man. I could love him forever. My breath grows short.

"When I do find my own home," I say, "I'm never letting it go."

His throat moves on a swallow. "Good plan." He takes a step closer to me. "I'm sorry, Anna."

I know he's speaking of my mother, my loss of safe harbor. "Me too." But I'm talking about him. Because Drew should never have lost his family. He shouldn't have to wear a piece of his childhood home around his neck because that's all he has left.

The tight, antsy feeling has returned. I shift on my feet, my gaze roving the field.

Drew takes an audible breath and runs a hand along his sweat-damp hair. His eyes squint as the setting sun's rays fall full on his face. "You want to try something?"

I raise a brow, and he laughs. "Such a dirty mind, Jones."

"Why would you assume that?" I cross my arms in front of my chest. But I'm smiling too. Smiling is better. "Unless you have a dirty mind as well."

"Of course I do." He touches the tip of my nose with a finger, making me bat him off in annoyance. He only grins. "Why do you think we're so perfect together?"

My breath gets a little unsteady, and the light in his eyes dims a bit. But he simply picks up his football.

"However, this time, I was just going to ask if you'd like to toss around the ball."

"Throw a football?"

"Such a sour face," Drew observes way too happily. "It isn't going to blow up in your hand."

"Says you. I suck at sports."

He rolls his eyes. "No one is asking you to be good. Just throw it." He tosses the ball high and catches it without looking. Show off. "Trust me, Jones. It's an excellent stress reliever."

Drew proceeds to show me how to hold the ball, placing my fingers on the laces, and my thumb positioned beneath the ball. "Hold it lightly with your fingertips. Finger control is very important."

"Oh, believe me, bud, I'm a big proponent of finger control," I say, just this side of saucy.

Oh, but it's a mistake to joke, because I'm remembering those long fingers of his pushing inside of me, curling just so to find that spot that drives me wild.

Sunlight gilds the tips of his long lashes as he blinks down at me. "Stop trying to distract me, Jones. Your cheap seduction tactics won't work on this hallowed field." The roughness in his voice tells me otherwise, but I decide to be good.

"Can I throw now?" I fight a grin. "Or do you have any more deluded fantasies running through your brain?"

"I have tons of fantasies. But you only get to hear them when we have a place to act them out. Now do as you're told, Miss Jones."

I submit and place myself in his capable hands as he rattles off instructions—*step back this way, hold the ball up by your ear, wind up your arm like so, throw it here, step thusly.* I'll be surprised if I retain half of it.

"Remember." He steps back to give me space. "Let the ball roll off your fingers. Your power comes from your core and your legs. It's all about momentum and confidence."

"Right." I'm going to mess this up royally.

Drew grins wide. "Yes, the first throw is going to suck."

"Get out of my head," I mutter.

He just laughs. "More like reading your expression. Now stop stalling."

I go through the motions, feeling like an uncoordinated goober. And the ball wobbles through the air to land with a dull thud some ten feet away. Awesome.

"*Welp.*" I dust off my hands. "That was fun."

I turn to go, when he grabs my arm, still laughing. The jerk. "Nice try, Anna. But I don't think so." He slaps the ball back in my hand. "Again."

"So bossy."

"You like it." His eyes are gold now, glinting in the sun.

Yeah, I do. I grumble and try again. And again. Drew stops me every once in a while to give pointers. Suddenly, it's fun. Not spectacular fun, but kind of addictive.

I say this to Drew, and he positively shines.

"Exactly," he says. "Why do you think I do this? It's the need to do better every time."

"To do better?" I stare up at him, shocked. "But you're already perfect."

His expression turns soft, warm. "You think so, huh?"

I know that tone too. And when his lids lower, his gaze going to my mouth, my heart kicks in my chest. I grip the ball between my hands.

"Show me," I blurt out.

He blinks, and a furrow wrinkles between his brows. "What do you mean?"

"Show me how far you can throw the ball."

One corner of his mouth kicks up. "You want me to show off for you?"

"If I'm asking, it isn't showing off. But, yeah, I want to see what you can do."

Drew studies me for a moment, the soft breeze lifting the ends of his hair. "Okay, but you're going to have to snap the ball to me."

"Snap the ball?" I make a face. "Like bend over…"

His grin is evil. "And I put my hands between your legs. Don't give me that look. Dex does this for me every game."

"Is this the point where I launch into a diatribe about the blatant homoeroticism found in football?"

"I'd be disappointed if you didn't. But since we're talking about me putting my hands on you, I don't think it applies here."

He leans close to my cheek, and his deep voice rumbles in my ear. "I promise to let you know the next time the team hits the showers."

"Oh my—" I wave a hand as if to cool myself off, which is only half in jest. "That's a pretty picture you're painting, Baylor."

Drew gives me a nudge with the football. "Just snap the ball, Jones, before I change my mind." But he's grinning as he steps back.

"Fine." I sigh and get into the position I've seen players assume.

Drew moves in closer than I think is strictly necessary. His size and strength is a wall over me.

"Mmm, spread those legs wider and get that sweet butt up higher, babe."

Despite our teasing, heat floods my belly. But I give him a dirty look over my shoulder. "You're enjoying this way too much."

He winks. "You know it. Snap count on three."

"What does that mean?"

"Third sound I make, you hand me the ball." He gives my butt a light slap. "Keep up, Jones."

And then his voice rolls over me like thunder. "Hut, hut, hut!"

Jesus. My nipples tighten, and a thrill courses through me as I obey and toss. He manages to catch the bobbling ball. I turn to watch him, and it's gorgeous. He's gorgeous. Up close, his body is poetry. His muscles ripple along his torso and up his arm as he throws, his expression fierce and focused. I want to tackle him, throw myself on his body and devour him bite by delicious bite.

I'm so caught up in gaping at him that I nearly forget to watch the ball, but I keep it together and look.

"Damn," I say. The ball is a rocket, hurtling through the air in a high arc. It keeps going. Until finally it comes down from space to land with a hard bounce in the end zone.

Drew's lips curl up at the corners. "Good throw." He says this to himself, not exactly as praise, but satisfied, and I wonder if he always appraises his work.

My curiosity is drowned out by a long, appreciative male whistle.

The tall blond guy I often see hanging with Drew jogs down the stairs. "Beautiful, fucking bomb, man. But you missed me by a mile."

Drew laughs. "And we know how hard it is to miss that big head of yours."

"You best be thinking about connecting with my hands and not my head, dude."

The blond holds a hand up against the sun's glare to study the field. "What was that, anyway? Sixty-five yards?"

He whistles in appreciation again and then lopes across the grass, moving as though walking is never an option when he can run.

"Seventy-one," Drew answers. "But who's counting?"

Drew's shoulder brushes mine as the guy stops before us. He

is massive, an inch or two taller than Drew and easily twenty pounds of muscle heavier. The guy eyes me with caution, but he puts on a polite smile. "Hey."

"Hey." I'm pretty sure Drew's talked about me, *us*, and his friend doesn't approve.

"Anna," Drew says, "this is Gray Grayson. He plays tight end."

"Ass jokes are welcome and encouraged," Gray adds with a wag of his brows. Like Drew, he's extremely good-looking, but in a California surfer way, with his mop of sun-streaked blond hair flopping over his tanned forehead.

"Gray Grayson?" I shouldn't repeat his name that way, but I can't help myself. What were his parents thinking?

Gray winces. But beneath dark blond brows, his blue eyes show no hint of annoyance. "I know, right?" he says to my un-answered question, which he must get a lot. "My mom had a total crush on Gray Grantham, a character from this John Grisham book, *The Pelican Brief.*"

"She named you after a character in a book?" I blurt out. At-ticus Finch is one thing. Hell, I'm pretty sure the South is pep-pered with Atticuses and Rhetts for that very reason. But this is a new one to me.

"She was reading it during the end of her pregnancy. Anyway—" Gray shrugs "—she thought Gray Grayson would be 'just so cute.'"

He makes a face, but there's no real anger behind it, only fond-ness, and a slight wince as if it pains him to think of his mother. "So that's what I got stuck with."

"Sometimes we call him 'Gray-Gray,'" Drew puts in helpfully and earns a punch on the arm from Gray.

"And sometimes I call him—" Gray nods toward Drew "—'QB with my foot up his ass.'"

Gray eyes the ball waiting in the end zone then looks at Drew. "You ready, man?"

Because Drew is standing so close, I feel the tension in his arm.

"Yep." Drew glances as me. "It's Gray's birthday."

I give Gray a polite smile, because I'm still pretty sure he doesn't like me. "Happy Birthday."

Gray's answering smile turns more genuine. "Thanks. Though I don't know about turning twenty-two. It's like the beginning of the end."

"I don't know what he's crying about," Drew says to me. "He's the baby of the bunch."

Gray sighs loud and long. "Feels like yesterday when I retired my fake ID."

The corners of Drew's eyes crinkle. "The way you carried on over that damn thing, you'd think it was your baby."

"Hey, it gave me years of service, devoted to finding me pleasure."

I smile at their interplay, but then catch on to what Drew says. "You're already twenty-two?"

"I told you I was older, Jones."

"I thought you meant by a day." I glance between him and Gray. "How is it you're both twenty-two?" Hell, Drew's almost twenty-three.

"We redshirted our freshman year," Gray says, as if this is obvious.

Drew understands that I have no idea what the hell Gray's talking about. "Basically, we spent our freshman year on the sidelines, taking classes but not playing. It's called a redshirt."

"Think of it this way," Gray puts in. "We're aged like wine. The longer we're here, the bigger, stronger, and better we get. Why should a program lose out on playing us when we're reedy little eighteen-year-olds instead of waiting until we've reached maximum efficiency?"

It all sounds kind of mercenary, but smart, I suppose. And because there's a hesitancy in Drew's eyes, like he expects me to think less of him because of the redshirt, I tell him this, watching as he visibly relaxes.

"College football is nothing if not mercenary," he says lightly.

Gray gives Drew's arm a slap. "The guys are waiting. Let's get a move on."

But Drew hesitates. "You want to go, Anna? We're just hitting a couple of bars."

It's sweet the way he's visibly conflicted, as if he doesn't want to leave me but wants to go out with his friends too. I smile and shake my head. "Thanks, but I've got a paper due."

"I'll walk you to your car." His fingertips graze my elbow, and my insides flutter. Jesus, I've got it bad.

While Gray runs off to gather the other guys, Drew and I leave the stadium. The air between us is subdued, as if both of us are too aware that we don't hang out like this. And it's just as clear to anyone who'd bother to look that we aren't just friends. Not by the way we walk so close, our arms nearly touching. His hand brushes against mine, and I wonder if he'll hold it if I reached for him. But we're already at my scooter, and I reach in my bag for my keys instead.

Drew sizes up my ride with a quirked brow.

"You ride a red Vespa. With a basket on the front?" His dimple is showing. "God." He clutches his chest. "The urge to make a Red Riding Hood joke is killing me." An exaggerated groan of frustration leaves him.

I roll my eyes as I crouch down to unlock my chain. "I knew it."

He's unrepentant. "It's fucking adorable, Jones." Warm brown eyes look me over. "You're adorable."

"And you're about to lose valuable equipment, Baylor."

He gives me that shit-eating Drew Baylor grin. "I'd be worried if I didn't know you have a vested interest in my equipment."

"God, I walked right into that one, didn't I?"

For a moment we just grin at each other, then something changes. My heart begins to beat faster and another wave of warmth washes over me. I think I'll want him always. And by the way his eyes darken and his body tightens, leaning closer to mine, he wants me too.

But he's looking at my mouth, his lids lowering, his own

mouth going soft. I stand and abruptly smash on my helmet. My hair springs out around my neck like red tentacles.

"Well," I say with false brightness. "Have fun tonight."

Drew's quiet as he steps up to me. Everything inside me seizes, but he simply lowers my visor with a gentle hand. "See you, Jones," he says. "Take care."

I straddle my bike and start it, but I pause and lift the visor.

"Drew..." I take a small, unsteady breath. "Thanks for listening, for making me feel better."

He rests his hands low on his lean hips, and when he speaks, it comes out just a bit rough. "Thanks for trusting me enough to share."

My throat aches as I leave him standing in the parking lot, my neck tight with the knowledge that he's watching as I drive away.

THIRTEEN

DREW

FOR THE FIRST time since I've been with Anna, I'm relieved that she doesn't want to be with me tonight. I don't want her to see the spectacle that is Gray's birthday celebration.

We hit a few bars, staying only long enough for the crowd to shout its appreciation, for Gray to have a drink, maybe play a game of pool or darts, and then move on. It might seem tame, but even now, there are rules. No binge drinking, no public spectacles, and absolutely no taking home random girls. Right now, we're ranked number one across the board, and every team wants to take us down. There's no room for mistakes. Maybe other teams play it differently, but it works for us. Dex and I are in charge of keeping the guys in line. We're the sober sentinels standing on either side of the ever-moving group of our guys.

Ordinarily, this is a suck-ass job, but I don't mind it tonight. Though I love hanging with my guys, the whole scene tires me.

A few months ago, this might have had me worried, but now I recognize it for what it is: my idea of fun has changed. It no longer includes anticipating how many different sets of tits are flashed at me or how many girls I can fuck. I don't care if people recognize me or slap me on the back and offer to buy me a drink. I'd rather they not notice me at all. That sort of attention means dick-all to me now.

Life has more color, flavor, and heat in the few hours I'm with Anna, than I've experienced in all the years I've partied. Because that type of fun always felt like I was searching, pushing for some ineffable satisfaction that constantly eluded me. With Anna, I feel like I've landed right where I want to be.

Exhaustion weighs down my shoulders and my eyelids are gritty as we head back to my house. Normally, I wouldn't agree to a party here. But it's Gray's birthday, and he deserves to have his fun. My house is safe from the public eye and events can be contained there. Because Gray has been adamant about one birthday request.

With a suppressed sigh, I lean back against my living room wall and watch four half-naked women give Gray a lap dance. There are so many naked limbs, it looks like a female hydra writhing around him. Tits bounce in his face, an ass grinds on his crotch, hands run over his head and shoulders.

He's loving it, as are our teammates. Hoots and catcalls ring out. Especially when the women fan out, each of them headed for a guy. Music thumps in time to writhing and sleek female flesh.

I eye the clock on my phone and grit my teeth. Yeah, I'm officially a grumpy old man. I just want to go to bed.

Across from me, Dex leans against the kitchen counter nursing a bottled water. With his bulky frame, shaggy brown hair, and full beard that he insists on wearing, women often call him Bear, something I'm fairly certain he gets off on.

Ethan Dexter, or Dex as everyone calls him, plays center, my right hand, ultimate lookout, and the last man standing between me being flattened by hungry linemen. I love this guy and am not ashamed to admit it.

I make my way to him, stepping over the legs of the woman now kneeling before Gray, her head bobbing up and down in rhythmic fashion. Holy hell, I do not want to witness that. Some things can never be unseen.

"Who the fuck arranged for a full-service performance?" I ask Dex, as I stand next to him. "That was not part of the deal."

Dex crosses his beefy arms over his chest. "Simms. The little fucker."

Simms, who is a massive defensive end, is also getting some personalized service.

I turn away and fish a water out of the fridge. "Let them finish off, and then the girls are out of here." I take a long swallow before grimacing. "I don't give a shit if it's Gray's birthday, I don't need to see all of that." Never mind that if we get caught, we're in deep shit.

Not by the police; it's a sad truth that we're so revered by this town, this state, that we can get away with anything short of murder. And some days, I wonder about even that. No, I'm talking about Coach. Who doesn't put up with any shit.

Dex grunts. His face is ruddy, and his mouth pinched. If there's one thing that I know about Dex, it's his intense dislike of exhibitionism. He's never gone for casual sex. For all I know, he might be pulling a Tebow and is still a virgin.

"Why not stop them now?" he asks.

"Seems cruel to stop a guy in mid…" I shrug, not wanting to finish that statement.

But I've made Dex blush harder.

"You can go if you want," I offer. "I can clear them out on my own."

Dex shakes his head and grabs his own water, chugging it in two gulps. He slams the empty bottle down and wipes his mouth with the back of his hand. "Naw, I'm not doing that to you, man. Can you imagine any girlfriend being okay with this?"

Despite my foul mood, a smile tugs at my mouth. Anna would probably go into a tirade about the objectification of women and how such paid services dehumanize both sexes. She'd be right, but then she's never had to deal with a whiny Gray before.

Pride washes over me with warm satisfaction when I think of Anna. And then it promptly flushes away, leaving me cold, because I want Anna to meet Dex and the rest of them. I don't know if it will ever happen. She'd balk at the idea. Then again, she came to my practice today. She sought me out for basic comfort.

The warmth returns. Strange how much satisfaction I got just from taking the hurt out of her eyes and replacing it with happiness. When I think of her fuckhead absentee father, who I'd personally like to pound into a stain on the turf, or her mother's roving hands boyfriend, Anna's reluctance to make a deeper connection becomes clearer. Whereas I grew up seeing firsthand what a loving, committed relationship can be, she likely hasn't got a clue.

"You got a woman, Dex?"

Dex studies the cabinets before him as though they hold the secret of life. "I was just thinking out loud."

"Doesn't sound like it." I take a drink and try to hide my smile. "Sounds like you're afraid of what a specific girl might think." Which would make two of us.

"There was a girl." The corners of Dex's eyes crease, like he's caught between a regretful smile and a grimace. "She didn't like football. And what could I say to that?"

I sympathize.

"Said we were just boys in oversized bodies."

"Well, sometimes we are," I mutter. "But, isn't every guy at some point or another?"

"You know it's going to be worse when we go Prime Time. Take all of this—" Dex jerks his chin toward the living room "—add a shit-ton of money to it, and see what mess comes out."

Money. The way most of us are playing, we'll be making bank by this time next year. It isn't a pipe dream; it's a fact. And it will come with the expectation of excellence. Against guys who are tougher, faster, stronger, and far more experienced.

After gaining national recognition, I've had the privilege to talk to some of my heroes: quarterbacks who've won the Super Bowl. They make no bones about the unrelenting pressure. *In college, you have what feels like ten minutes in the pocket. In the NFL? It's ten seconds. And you better believe they'll hit you hard. You aren't looking down the barrel of a gun but a fucking cannon, kid.*

Does it scare me?

It makes me antsy as all hell. I want that life to happen now.

I shrug and set my now empty bottle down too. "We'll be all right. And by 'we' I mean you, a few others, and me. I don't know about some of these boneheads."

Dex just watches me as if I haven't answered the way he wants. "You think it's smart to fall for a girl now when you know what's out there in the near future?"

"What do you mean by that?" Does he think a guy can simply cut off his feelings?

Dex's massive shoulders lift and fall. "I'm thinking a girl's got to love the life as much as she loves you to put up with the shit we'll be dealing with, is all."

The scowl on my face seems to sink down into my bones. I want to roll my neck just to throw off the ugly feeling settling over me. Love the life? Shit, I don't even know how to get Anna to consider the possibility of loving *me*.

One girl decides to lose the G-string and hop on Gray's lap, and I've had enough.

"All right, that's it," I say, "I'm calling this game."

"About time," Dex rumbles.

"Listen up," I boom out in my play voice. "Party's over."

"What?" shouts Simms. "We just got started."

"And now you're going to end it." Dex plants his feet wide and crosses his thick arms over his chest. "We're coming down to the wire. Coach hears about this shit and it's lights out."

"Damn, man, that's just wrong," grumbles another guy.

But they're listening; Dex and I are co-captains, and they're used to obeying us. Besides, they've committed too much to the season to mess up now.

The women, on the other hand, are pouting at Dex and me in clear disappointment. Which makes my guys slow their feet.

"Come on." I clap my hands together. "Let's go."

"Yes, Mom."

"That's right," I say to the group. "Mom and Dad have spoken, so be good little fuckers and go to bed."

Someone halfheartedly throws a cheese puff at me, but they're going, grumbling their way to the door with Dex herding them out. As for the girls, all but one of them scurry off into my bathroom to put their clothes back on, freshen up, or whatever; I don't want to know.

It's the one who's stayed behind that worries me. She's eyeing me like I'm ice cream on a cone as she strides over, clad only in black heels, her breasts bouncing with every step.

Hell.

I busy myself with collecting empty bottles, praying she's simply heading for a drink.

No such luck.

"Battle Baylor. God, but you're hot." She edges nearer, her nipples grazing my arm as she moves around to face me. "Even better looking in person than you are on TV."

Life-sized too. I refuse to edge back, but I want to. I keep my eyes on her face. "I've got cleanup to do here. You and your friends all set with payment?"

The smile she gives me is tight, her lips shining with a layer of pink gloss that would probably taste like stale wax. "Don't you worry about payment. I'm off the clock for this. I've been dying to get my hands on you."

Blue eyes rimmed in dark kohl gaze up at me. She's all but thrusting her bare tits under my nose. Something my baser self can appreciate—a naked woman is a naked woman, after all. The rest of me, however, is embarrassed for both of us.

When I was in high school, I had fantasies of being serviced by multiple women at once, of receiving this exact type of proposition. Young me had thought it would be sexy as all hell. The reality, I'd soon come to realize, is seedy and awkward.

"Sorry to disappoint, but I'm not interested." Not even a little. The need to hurry her out of my house presses on the back of my neck. More so when she leans into me and her breasts brush against my shirt.

She smells of beer and deodorant, and she had my best friend's dick in her mouth not ten minutes ago. The thought makes me wonder how she kept her lip gloss so pristine.

"Ah, now, Battle—" She rubs her hand over my chest while looking up at me. "I think you'll change your mind when you see what I can do with my mouth."

I don't want anything to do with her mouth. I'm fairly certain I'll never be able to look at pink lip gloss the same way again.

Gently, I take hold of her wrist and lift her hand from me. "Honey, you could suck the center out of a Tootsie Pop, and I'd still say no. Not that I don't appreciate your offer."

She pouts, but steps back. "You've a funny way of showing your appreciation."

"So I've been told. Time to go. Drive safely."

It's almost amusing the way she appears so nonplussed. As if she's never entertained the thought of being turned down.

She takes one long look at me, and then collects her things, pulling a T-shirt and tight pants from her bag to toss on. "Why are the really hot ones always gay?" she says as she hoists her bag over her shoulder. With a flip of her hair, she's out the door.

I want to sag in relief. Only Gray is busy glaring at me in disgust. I hadn't noticed him standing close by.

"I cannot believe you turned that down."

"I cannot believe you'd think I'd take her up on the offer."

Gray shakes his head. "Fine, you don't cheat. But some of us haven't lost our dicks to a girl. I had plans, you know? And they did not include you sending those women home."

Yeah. I don't like to think of what those plans might be. Especially when Gray's eyes are glassy and he's slurring his words.

"Look, if you want to get laid, call one of your girlfriends." Which is a very loose use of the word for Gray. "Don't take women like that home."

Gray scoffs loudly through his lips. "You think there's a difference for me?"

"There's a world of difference, and you know it." At least one of his hook ups—and I'm beginning to fucking hate that term—wouldn't expect payment.

Darkness lurks in his expression, and it hits me that his family hasn't called him. "Want to crash here? We can hang out."

He waves me off, wobbling on his feet as he does it. "Naw. Not ready to call it a night."

"I'll go with you."

"No way. Not when you're in Mother Hen mode. Go to bed. It's all good."

Over his shoulder, I meet Dex's eyes, and he gives me a nod. He's got this.

"Fine." I'm not happy about it, but pushing would only piss Gray off. Not something I want to do any more of tonight. As long as I know he'll get home, and stay there, then I've got to respect his wishes.

I squeeze Gray's shoulder. "Happy Birthday, man."

He glares at me for a moment, pissed, but then the clouds break and he's suddenly pulling me into a bear hug. We give each other a punch on the back, and I find myself relieved.

Alone in my room, however, I can't sleep. The bedside clock says 1:00 a.m. Part of me is now sorry I kicked the guys out so early. I lie back against a pile of pillows, my bent leg slowly rocking side to side as I stare in the darkness. My phone rests heavy in my hand. Anna has confessed to being a night owl, mostly due to staying up reading. I could be reading as well. My playbook rests on the far side of the bed, and there's a Jack Reacher novel collecting dust on the nightstand. Instead, I run my thumb along the edge of my phone, and my leg swings with greater agitation.

"Fuck it."

My thumb is swiping the screen and tapping Call before I can talk myself out of it.

She answers with a husky, "Hello?"

The sound courses along my skin in little licks of pleasure.

"Hey." I settled down further into my bed. "I didn't wake you, did I?"

"No. I was just—"

"Reading?" I offer with a smile.

"Yeah." She sounds vaguely pissed off that I guessed correctly, and my smile grows. She makes a small noise like a stifled sigh. "It's too late for a booty call, Baylor."

"Is sex the only thing you think about, Jones?" I rest my head on my bent arm and stare up at the ceiling. "I mean, what if I just want to hear about your night?"

"If anyone has had a memorable night, it'd be you. Speaking of which, why are you calling me now? Shouldn't you be, I don't know, getting smashed?"

"I don't drink during the season."

"Seriously?"

"As a history lecture." I run a hand over the bare skin of my abdomen and wish it was Anna touching me. "It messes with my performance, and I don't need the hassle that comes with partying that way. Tonight, I was the designated driver and all-around wet blanket."

"The guys must have loved you." There's a dry smile in her voice.

The darkness surrounding me is warm and close now. "There may have been some grumbles."

"Poor baby," she croons without any sympathy whatsoever. "Not getting to have any fun."

"Depends on your concept of 'fun.'" I like her ribbing and want more.

She laughs, a soft, rolling chuckle that makes my gut tighten. "So, what *did* you do tonight? Or shouldn't I ask?"

"I'd tell you, but maybe you don't want to hear."

"Pfft. That just makes me more curious. And you know it, Baylor."

I grin before turning on my side. "All right. Some of the guys bought Gray a group of strippers."

"They any good?"

It's then I admit to myself that I want her jealousy. Which is petty of me. And petty to be disappointed when she isn't. I shrug, but then realize she can't see me. "Gray seemed to think so."

"But not you?" A world of skepticism lives in her tone.

"No."

"Right." I can almost hear her rolling her eyes. "So a bunch of naked, gyrating women do nothing for you. Nice try, Drew."

"You want to know what it made me feel?" My response is sharper than I want it to be, but I can't rein it in. "Empty. Like the world is full of lonely people who don't know what the fuck they're doing with their lives."

It isn't until I say the words that I realize how lonely my life has been. Until her.

Until I understood how life could be if she'd just let me in.

Anna is silent for a moment. "Maybe that's true. But you can't fix other people. Only yourself."

She sounds so sad, I feel like a heel for snapping at her.

"Besides." I make my tone lighter and teasing, because it's easier for both of us. "There's this girl who I can't stop thinking about. She takes up all my attention, even when I'm not with her."

Her voice is playful, falling in line with mine. "Are you sure this isn't a booty call?"

Do you want it to be?

I almost ask, but I'm too tired, so I tell her the truth instead. "It's about me not being able to sleep and wanting to hear your voice."

Her breath catches, a gratifying sound if ever I've heard one, and then comes the sound of her moving about, like she too is sinking beneath her covers.

"Iris and I went out for burgers tonight," she says softly, a conversational opening that both surprises me and sends a pang through my chest. "George usually comes with us, but he's been begging off lately. Which is kind of odd."

Maybe I should be jealous of George. It's clear he's Anna's closest friend. Except they really do treat each other like siblings.

Tucking my arm beneath my pillow, I close my eyes so there's only her and me. "What do you think is going on?"

"I'd say it was a girl, only George has a tell when he's into someone, and he isn't doing it."

"A tell?" I'm laughing at the idea.

"Yeah. He'll start singing 'Ain't No Rest for the Wicked' by Cage the Elephant under his breath at all hours."

"That's...interesting?"

"It's freaking weird, is what it is. Especially since he sounds like Mickey Mouse when he sings it."

And then we're both laughing.

I don't know how long we talk about inconsequential things before I nod off to sleep. When I wake in the morning, the phone is still cradled in my hand.

FOURTEEN

DREW

WHEN I ENTERED college my choice of major wasn't a pressing issue. Truthfully, I could have coasted by on a general education track, doing the minimum requirements, and no one would have batted an eye. Not that I asked; the point was made extremely clear to me. And I made it extremely clear that I didn't want that kind of ride. It went against everything my parents taught me. Granted, I chose English lit because I'd been raised on it, and I knew it would be easier for me. Football is a full-time job, and I needed every advantage to hold my head above water when it came to academics.

But I work my ass off and manage to maintain a 4.0 grade point average. I am proud of that. Even so, I am looking forward to graduation. Endless studying and too little sleep are getting to me.

In fact, my eyelids grow heavy, and my head wants to fall forward as my Literature in Film professor drones on about the differences between *A Room with a View* the movie and the novel. I take deep breaths, try to clear my head, but the stuffy room isn't helping.

The end of class can't come soon enough. I eye the clock as Professor Gephard hands back the quiz we had last week. An honest-to-God quiz. Like we're still in high school. I'd wanted to laugh when he gave it to us.

"Good work, Mr. Baylor," Gephard says as the quiz lands on my desk. 100 points.

Perfect score.

I've been acing this class. Frankly, it's easy and I like the material.

I give him a nod, my eyes scanning the quiz for lack of anything better to do, when I see a mistake. Rubbing my eyes, I read it over again. Yep, I'd answered question number 10 incorrectly.

Hanging back until everyone clears out, I head to Gephard's desk. He looks up as I approach.

"How can I help you, Mr. Baylor?"

"There's a mistake on my quiz, Professor. I have the wrong answer for number 10." I point to the question. "It should be Charlotte Bartlett, not Freddy Honeychurch."

Gephard doesn't even glance at the paper but blinks up at me as though I'm speaking gibberish. The back of my neck goes hot. It's just one stupid question. I shouldn't push it. But it bothers me all the same.

I point to the page again. "I wrote that Freddy told Mr. Emerson about Lucy breaking off her engagement with Cecil. But it was Charlotte."

Smiling, Gephard puts his palm over the quiz and slides it back to me. "It was obvious you'd read the work thoroughly, Mr. Baylor. I saw no reason to mark you down for a simple mistake."

Something thick and ugly bolts through my gut. "But I got it wrong."

"Yes. However, it was clear you knew the answer. The fact that you were able to discover the error tells me as much." He smiles again. "Excellent game last week, by the way. Took my granddaughter to see you play."

A pulse starts throbbing at the base of my neck. "That's great…" I look down at the big red 100 scrawled over the top of my quiz. "Are you telling me that when a student answers a question incorrectly, you ignore it if you know they've 'read the work thoroughly'?"

His smile slips a little. "You are an A student. Top of this class."

Bile burns up my throat. I swallow it down but can't control the way my heart is now pounding. "Did I get there on my own, or did I have help?"

Gephard sits up straight, his mouth thinning into a purple line. "Just what are you implying, Mr. Baylor?"

"I'm not implying anything," I say evenly, as though I don't want to grab hold of his lumpy wool sweater and shake him until his dentures rattle. "I am asking if you make the same allowances for the rest of my classmates."

His watery gaze flickers away from mine. "My colleagues and I are aware that you have more responsibilities than your classmates."

"You have got to be kidding me." It takes everything I have not to smash my fist into the desk. "I never asked for your help. I don't want it. Ever."

"Oh, for God's sake…" Gephard snatches the paper and makes a slash through the question with his red pen. His knobby knuckles tremble as he writes a spindly 99 on the top of the page. He shoves the paper back in my direction. "There. One whole point deduction. You now have a slightly less perfect A, Mr. Baylor. Are you happy?"

Rage pushes its fist against my breastbone. "Don't you dare try to shame me."

Gephard's wispy brows rise, but I don't give him a chance to speak.

"I have just as much a right to ask questions as any other student." Holding the test up between us, I glare at him. "Apparently more."

His face turns magenta. "You are overreacting."

Bracing my fists on the desk, I lean my weight on them, bringing my face level with his. Fear widens his eyes, and part of me wants to laugh. He thinks I'm a thug. Lovely.

I keep my voice level and enunciate so he can hear every word distinctly. "I beg to differ."

Snatching the quiz up, I turn and leave the classroom.

I manage to walk out on Gephard without screaming, but I'm far from calm. I can barely see straight as I leave campus and head home. My head is throbbing. There is a buzzing sound in my ears.

On the seat of my car, my quiz lies face up, mocking me with its false score. Yeah, I still received an A. But how many other times have I been helped out by my professors?

For the most part, English lit is subjective, the bulk of my grades coming from how well my professors believe I've handled the topic. I think of the hours I've spent hunched over my computer, trying to put my thoughts down in words. And the pride I felt when I got high marks on those papers.

My sweaty hands grip the steering wheel as a wave of humiliation slaps down on me. Was it all a joke? A fucking joke on me?

I don't know. And it burns me. I have to know.

At home, I run through my house until I reach my office.

Lies. It could all be lies. Years of it.

Hands shaking, I tear open my filing cabinets, intent on ripping out old tests and essays. Papers flap, slap, and flutter to the floor. I grab an old test, ready to pick it apart, when I stop, my breath coming out in hard pants.

The page wavers before my eyes, the sound of my heart pounding in my ears. And then I crumple the test in my fist. I can't look.

"Fuck!" I chuck the balled-up paper as hard as I can. It hits the wall with an ineffectual tap. "Fuck!"

Sinking to the floor, I grab the ends of my hair and blink hard. I'm shaking, and I can't stop. I want to vomit. I want to kick my desk apart.

I'm a coward, because I can't bring myself to know the truth. If they've all helped me, I can't live with the humiliation. But the doubt is already seeded, and I know it will never go away. I can try to be the best person I can be, but the world only wants to see one side of me. And I feel sick to my bones.

FIFTEEN

DREW

ANOTHER GAME, another win. We're undefeated. The play-offs, a first for college football, are closing in, and the championship is ours to lose. The guys are jubilant as the bus rolls back onto campus.

Rain comes down in thick, hard sheets that pound the top of the bus like gunfire. It doesn't stop us from running out into it, or laughing as Marshall slips in the mud, falls on his ass, and curses.

I stop to get my bag, waiting my turn as the driver sorts through the luggage. Seems the sensible thing would have been to stay on the bus.

Across the way, Harrison's girl is waiting under a massive umbrella, her butt leaning against a gleaming black Range Rover.

"Wooo." Rolondo Johnson, our star wideout, whistles under his breath as he comes up beside me. "That's one sweet ride."

"Whose car is it?" I ask, frowning as Harrison runs over to

greet his girl. Because we both know it was either an overly supportive booster or an agent who handed him that car. Agents are particularly aggressive in their pursuit of us. They can't outright give us things, but they are masters of finding gray areas—lend a luxury car indefinitely, buy a guy's destitute parents a mansion, buy his childhood friends gifts in exchange for putting in a good word for them, and a dozen other shining carrots dangled in our faces if we just sign with them.

"Garrity's."

One of the sleazier agents. Oh, there are some who are subtler. They show up at games with company reps, promising massive advertisement deals they can work for you. Or they arrange for girls to take personal care of you. I touched my first pair of fake tits courtesy of an agent's special room delivery. Lesson learned? Plastic is never as good as real flesh.

Rolondo shakes his head, sending water scattering from the ends of his dreads. "Harrison better not get hurt or he's gonna miss that ride."

"He shouldn't have taken it at all. It's risky. Not to mention he's playing Russian roulette with the Committee on Infractions." Who have brought down bigger and better players for lesser violations.

Hearing my tone, Rolondo glances at me, and his expression goes tight, rain bouncing on his shoulders. "You think it's so easy? You already have money." He frowns. "You didn't share a shithole room with two siblings or search your sheets for roaches at night."

His words wrap around my neck, choking me. Should I feel guilty? Maybe I should. Maybe I should nod and shut up. Not like he'd notice; he's still laying into me.

"You didn't have to deal with any of that. You had a family who—" Rolondo stops short, his eyes wide with horror, and worse, pity. "Damn, man, I didn't mean that."

"No, you're right, I had it good." I *refuse* to be pitied about the loss of it. "And you can call me a patronizing bitch if you want. But Harrison, you, me, we've got the talent to do it all on our own. Not suck some agent's dick cuz he's got fancy toys."

Rolondo's nostrils flare, his mouth hard, but then he breaks out into a wide grin and laughs. "Shit, you don't need to go all After-School Special on me, Battle."

"Me?" I snort. "You're the one expounding the disparities of our upbringing."

His feathery brows lift, and he gives me the amused look he always does when I fall into what he calls "Professor Mode."

Heat spreads over my cheeks and intensifies when Rolondo says, "And here I thought I was pointing out the impact of our divergent socio-economic status when faced with potential agent-induced incentives."

We both look at each other for a second then laugh again.

"Fucking sociology major," I mutter.

"Henry-muthafucka-Higgins. You gonna Eliza Doolittle me?"

"There you go again, trying to get me to do you. Let the dream die, man."

'Londo puckers up, blowing me the finger, and then he sobers. "Besides, you got it turned around. They're sucking our dicks."

"Who's sucking dick?" Gray comes between us and slaps a hand on both our shoulders.

"Harrison," we say together.

"Sounds about right." Gray gives us another pat. "We going? Or are you two going to sit in the rain and wax lyrical about dicks?"

There's talk of heading out for a pizza. Others are going to watch NFL games at Dino's Bar.

I don't want to do either. "I'm going home to get dry and take a nap."

"Wimp."

"One that's going to get some sleep." I sling my bag over my shoulder and head for my car. I'm soaked through, and my body aches with a general tiredness that never truly goes. But it's the emptiness centered just behind my ribs that bothers me the most. It's getting worse these days. Growing.

I don't really want to go home. There's no one waiting for me, no one to talk to.

The guys are like brothers to me. I'll have fun hanging with them. But lately I find myself wanting to just...be. No shit-talking, no expectations, just be me. Which makes dick-all of sense. But the need is there all the same.

Running a cold hand over my wet face, I fish out my keys and flop into my car as soon as the door is open. Inside, the sound of rain is louder, the interior dim and musty. A lump swells in my throat. I hate this feeling of isolation. Rubbing my aching chest, I move to turn the ignition when my phone buzzes.

A smile breaks hard over my face at the sight of the name on the screen. Anna.

It grows when I read the text.

> This message is brought to you by the BCBS [Booty Call Broadcasting System]. If you are back in town, get your wet ass over here.

Only Anna can make me laugh and get me hard in one fell swoop. I turn on the car and peel out, my day suddenly brighter than the desert at high noon.

ANNA

Rain taps with hard nails against the window as I hug the bed. Drew has just taken me from behind and, after taking care of the condom, is now a comforting weight against my back, his arms bracketing mine, our fingers linked. We breathe as one, lightly panting as we come down from the high sex took us to. My face is smashed in my pillow, but I don't care. I'm a boneless mass of well-pleasured flesh. And so warm with him on me that I want to beg him not to move. Ever. We could just lie like this and listen to the rain. Never get up.

Only I'm the one who is supposed to be kicking him out. A knot gathers just below my breastbone as I try to gather the will to say the words. And then he does it: his lips press against my shoulder in a gentle, reverent kiss.

Instantly, I tense. And so does he. I can feel him growing tight along the length of my body. But he doesn't move off. No, he tenses further and then deliberately kisses me again, as if daring me to protest. Another loving kiss upon my shoulder. Then another one.

My heart turns over in my chest.

"What are you doing?" I can barely get the question out, and it sounds too soft, too weak.

He pauses for only a moment, his lips just touching my shoulder. "Kissing your freckles." The tip of his tongue flickers on my skin, the barest taste, and something deep within me melts.

"But why?" I ask as he keeps on doing it. Slow. Steady. Exploratory.

It's the tenderness behind it all that makes my heart beat fast and my breath catch.

"Because I've been dying to do it."

God, his voice. It's so low and gentle, a caress of sound. It unravels me. Combined with his kisses, I'll soon be a quivering mess. His big warm hands cup my upper arms, as if I might run. Which I might.

"You have so many here," he continues in lazy fashion, his lips brushing along my skin. "Like golden sugar on cream."

I huff. "They're orange spots."

He makes a rumbling sound deep within his throat. "Potato-po-tah-toh. Now quiet, I'm busy here."

It's not like I can move. His heavy thigh lies across mine, and the warm weight of his chest presses against my ass.

He's moving, nipping and tasting his way over my shoulders. A gentle touch sweeps my hair off my neck so he can kiss my nape.

I shiver. A full-body shake that feels as delicious as it is terrifying. It's too much.

Too intimate. He surrounds me, all heat and strength, every touch like adoration.

He presses an open-mouthed kiss on my shoulder blade and a

small groan comes from him. "I dreamed of doing this the other day."

"What?" I've fallen into a haze, but this stirs me enough to lift my head.

I can see him grin, but his attention is on my freckles.

"In class," he says. "I lost track of time thinking about peeling off that white sweater you were wearing and licking my way across your shoulders."

As if to emphasize this little confession, he licks a path from my nape to the tip of my shoulder blade.

"You can't be thinking about that in class." God, he *can't* because then I'll be thinking of him doing it, and I won't remember another freaking word our professor utters.

Unfortunately, Drew shakes his head as he proceeds to kiss his way down my spine. "Sorry, Jones, but you don't have a say over my fantasies."

"Shithead."

He laughs outright at that, but doesn't stop. "Take your breasts, for example. Those play a starring role in so many." He's conversational now as he slides his way down my back, his hands holding my ribs, his mouth destroying me. "God, I almost lost it during a footage review, thinking about your nipples, the way they go stiff when I suck them, and how you make those little whimpers when I do."

I may have whimpered again because he stops for a moment, his lips hovering. "Yeah," he whispers. "Like that."

"Jesus." It's all I can say.

"Or your pussy. Your sweet, pink—" he kisses the dip in my waist "—pussy. Always so wet for me."

The tip of his tongue glides downward, scattering pleasure in its wake. "I think about that every time I drive over here." He sucks the tender skin at the small of my back. "How tight and wet you'll be for me."

His words are crude. I should protest. I can't. He's turned my body against me. It has become this languid thing, stretching and undulating into his touch like a cat to sunlight. I'm so hot my skin shivers. But he doesn't stop. Of course not.

The truth is, I don't want him to. Nothing has felt better than this.

"And then there's your ass." He lets out a long appreciative groan that makes me blush. Not that he's noticed. He's too busy molding me. "This ass." His big hands palm either side of my butt and squeeze.

"Drew!"

"Shh." He gives my butt a light slap, and I blush harder at the resulting wiggle of flesh. While he merely hums. "I'm having a moment." His voice goes husky. "With this fucking perfect ass."

"It is not!" Though I'm mostly happy with my body, I know what it is and what it isn't.

"Ah, Jones," he tuts. "You're just fishing for compliments now." He gives my left butt cheek a featherlight kiss.

"I'm simply being honest, you goober."

Another kiss lands on my skin. "You're deluded. Your ass. Jesus, your whole body…" He pauses, his mouth just touching the point where my back swoops up to meet my butt. "Nothing compares, Jones."

I'm struck breathless. He's the one who is incomparable.

"I've seen the girls you've been with, Baylor." As soon as the words are out of my mouth, I wince. It only hurts me to call them to mind. But I've said it, so I've got to finish. "You cannot claim that my body is…"

I was wrong; I can't finish.

And if the way his hands tighten on my waist is any indication, I don't think he wants me to either.

When he speaks, it's quiet but insistent. "The fact that I'm finding it hard to even recall another woman should tell you something."

"Yeah, well… Shit."

Slowly, he laughs. "You're never going to win this argument."

"Oh, no?"

"No. Because you're begging the question." His palm slides down my hip and then back up. "It is my opinion that your ass is perfect. Ergo, your ass is perfect to me."

I can't help laughing. "I cannot believe you're pulling out philosophical constructs now."

"Believe it, baby." Happiness and a certain smugness lighten his voice. "I like debating with you."

I like it too. I like *him*. "You realize I can use the same argument? Seeing as you've made the state of my ass a question of personal preference rather than a discussion of empirical facts."

He chuckles, the laugh muffled by his lips pressed to my skin.

"And, anyway," I add just a bit strangled. "You're cheating."

"How?" He sounds like he knows perfectly well how. He just doesn't care.

"You attack only after putting me in this weakened condition."

I'm proven correct when he grins. "I'm a competitor. What did you expect?"

"Not your face in my butt," I mutter. But, in truth, his attention and care feel so damn good that I don't want it to end. Ever. I want to lie here and let him do what he wants to me until I can't remember my name. Or his. So of course, I tense up further.

"Relax, Jones," he whispers, his fingers lightly tickling me as they drift along. "You can handle it."

"Easy for you to say. You're not having your ass inspected at close range."

Another chuckle rumbles. "You can inspect my ass. I won't mind."

"Baylor…" I warn.

"Jones…" he mocks. And then his tongue licks the curve of my butt cheek.

A pathetic whimper escapes me, and my head hits the mattress. He simply laughs in that husky, satisfied way again.

"If you can't handle it, call this a boon," he suggests before giving me a small nip.

"A boon?" It comes out way too close to a squeak.

"Yeah." His breath is warm. "Like a reward for hauling my ass out here in the pouring rain for a booty call."

"Oh, I see." My breath hitches as he hits a sensitive spot. "So it's a chore?"

I'm teasing now, and he knows it.

"Never said that." He nuzzles, *fucking nuzzles*, my butt. "I said you could call it that if it makes you feel better. Me? I'd be here every day if you'd let me."

I'm not going to get into that. But I can't help but smile against my forearm. "And what boon do I get the next time you're the one to call?"

He gives me another soft kiss. "Anything."

The quick, yet steady way he answers sends a little thrill through me. He might have backpedaled or given me conditions, but instead it's a promise more than an answer. I press my lips harder into the flesh of my arm. "Careful, Baylor, you might regret that."

He makes a humming noise. Content. Amused. "Possibly. But something tells me I'll enjoy it too." Lightly, he traces his fingertips over my hips, raising gooseflesh in his wake.

"What if it's an hour-long foot rub?"

"Maybe I have a secret foot fetish." I know he's smiling. I can feel it along my skin. "Maybe I get off on foot rubs."

I laugh just a bit. "If you think that's going to scare me, you're wrong." He probably gives great foot rubs. Strong fingers. Intense concentration. I'm tempted to beg for one now.

"Damn." His sigh tickles my back. "Then what?" Another kiss. "Come on, hit me with it."

I tilt my head and snuggle down into the cradle of my arms. "Maybe I'll have you edit my class paper."

He goes so still, I can hear my own heartbeat, and then he rests his cheek on my butt. I want to squirm, but he slips his arms under me and holds tight.

"Edit it?" His voice is a vibration through my skin.

Absently, I nod. "Mmm. You know, point out all the flaws

of logic like you do in class. Which I hate to admit, you're right more than you're wrong. Not surprising, smart as you are."

I'm basically babbling, but his hold on me clenches, and he takes a sharp breath.

The sheets rustle as I crane my neck to look down at him. From my vantage point I can only see his profile from above, the gold streaks in his hair at the crown of his head and the darker brown along his temples, the high bridge of his nose, and the thick curve of his lashes against his cheeks.

With his head resting on my ass, his body is half off the bed, he's so damn long. Lean yet strong, muscular yet graceful. I could look at him forever. But his shoulders are so tight now that every sinew and curve stand out.

"You don't think you're smart?" My voice is a rasp in the quiet.

His answer is just as rough, but there's a hint of bitter laughter in it. "Oh, I know I'm smart."

He glances up, and when our eyes meet, that familiar, sweet punch hits me straight in the heart. His eyes are dark and shining in the low light. "It's just that, outside of my team, not many people give a shit if I am or not."

No, most care about that arm of his. The one now wrapped around my waist, giving me a little squeeze as if he needs to bring me closer. Or his hand, which is tenderly pressed into my lower belly, so warm and secure that contentment spreads over me.

I want to keep this moment. Keep this part of him, like a secret. But he's not mine to keep, and even though it might hurt him that people only see his surface, he still loves that life. And why shouldn't he? His talent is immense, and he works his ass off. I don't want to change that. It would change him.

Watching me, his expression turns pinched and pained. "I caught one of my professors grading a test in my favor." He almost chokes on the words, as if it's killing him to admit this to me. "I don't know how many times it's happened without my knowledge, or if they've all done things like that."

He holds himself so tightly, the pain and humiliation he feels so evident that I see red.

"Fuck him, Drew." Never have I wanted to punch someone as much as I want to hit his professor. "Fuck anyone who does that."

Drew's cheek presses harder into my flesh. "I know. I just don't like thinking my academic career has been a lie." His voice drops to barely a whisper. "It means something to me."

My fingers dig into my forearms as I glare at the herringbone-patterned bedspread. "You did the work, and you have the intelligence. No one can take that away from you." I swallow past the thickness in my throat. "And if you never even went to one class, you'd still be one of the smartest people I know. The most dedicated."

Silence follows my statement, and the soft caress of Drew's breathing tickles my skin. When he finally speaks, his voice is rough. "You always make me feel better. Like myself again."

A pang shoots through my heart, sweet and aching. Drew doesn't make me feel like myself. He makes me feel *better* than myself. As if there is a little broken part in me, rattling and loose, and whenever he's near it falls into place and tightens. The thought has me withdrawing, sinking into that cold, thick place that chokes me. I'm beginning to need him too much.

And because he *is* smart, and knows me now, knows my debilitating fear of intimacy, his hold suddenly shifts. One hand eases up to cup my breast while the other hand drifts down. Long, calloused fingers slide between my legs, and I close my eyes, my muscles clenching in that delicious way that makes me feel like an addict, wanting to beg for more and more. Always more.

"Again?" I ask as if half-exasperated, but I'm not. I'm grateful. And my heart falls that much further into his keeping. Which terrifies me.

I don't get a chance to plummet into terror. Drew is turning me over, his lips following the path of his hand. "Just proving my earlier point of your irresistibility." It's a murmur against my skin.

I close my eyes. *Don't think. Just feel.* And he lets me, because we both are excellent liars now.

SIXTEEN

DREW

AS QB, I lead my team. I set the tone of the game, lighting a fire under my guys' asses or making them fall flat if I'm not on top of things. I never really felt the pressure of that responsibility because it isn't in me to sit back and be subordinate in a game. I love leading my team. But it can get lonely.

The backs and receivers, the linemen, both defensive and offensive, form their own close-knit groups. They can talk strategy and technique among themselves and often hang out together. Quarterbacks? I don't hang out or commiserate with the backups. There's only one QB who gets the job, while the others warm the bench and wait for a chance to take over.

I'm lucky in the fact that our team is close. Coach makes sure we are. But as I sit alone on the bus to Florida, surrounded by the deep rumble of my guys chatting it up, the gulf between them and me stretches wide. Which is fucking maudlin and untrue.

I have no reason to feel lonely. Any second now, Gray will be tossing his ass into the seat next to me to talk my ear off. And if not Gray, someone else will. I know this. Only it isn't enough right now.

Outside my window, the landscape blurs by in streaks of brown grass, blue sky, and gray road. All I want to do is turn the bus around. I want it so badly that my stomach hurts.

"Fuck me," I mutter, rubbing my hand over the afflicted area.

The seat next to me dips with a squeak. "You're not my type, Baylor," says Dex.

I push myself out of my slouch. "Good thing," I quip, "you'd snap me like a twig."

He chuckles. "You know it."

Three hundred pounds of pure muscle and quick speed, he really could snap me in two. But he's the least aggressive guy I know.

He offers me a stick of beef jerky out of the bag he's demolishing, and I shake my head.

"What's doin', Battle?" His gray eyes scan my face as if he's seeing under my skin. "You seem…subdued."

Keen powers of observation and constant awareness of his surroundings are what make Dex an excellent center. But I'm not appreciating those skills now. I'm thinking of Anna, who kissed my bruises with a tenderness that made my heart flip over in my chest before she sucked my cock until I lost my mind. Anna who, with her plain speaking and fierce declarations, gave me back a piece of my pride. Anna, who still won't kiss me on the mouth or let me kiss hers.

I want to be with her so badly right now, to claim that mouth once and for all, it takes effort to respond with a calm voice. "As compared to who? Rolondo?" I glance at the man in question, who is currently showing off his new touchdown victory dance in the aisle.

"Or maybe Lloyd?" I give a nod toward the massive defensive end sleeping in the seat across from us. A line of drool hangs from his lips, and Marshall—running back and all around knucklehead—is leaning over him, dangling a dirty shoelace before Lloyd's nose. That won't end well.

Dex snorts at the antics but isn't deterred. "I mean subdued for you."

During the games, it's his job to watch over not only my ass but also every man on the field. He can read an impending blitz, call a play change if he senses a shift in defense. His instincts have been honed like a blade, which means he notices anomalies before, during, or after any game.

"Headache," I say with a shrug. This is a major concession, because no one wants to admit to physical pain. But I prefer that over the truth, which will lead to endless hounding.

Dex takes a bite of jerky, his big teeth grinding down the toughened meat like it was a dinner roll. "So not chick problems, then?" His grin is knowing.

Fucking Gray. Fucking blabbermouthed, soon to be dead, pain in my ass Gray.

"Cuz I've heard you've got yourself a cute little redhead—"

"You guys are worse than girls, you know that?" I mutter then slouch against the window. "A bunch of gossiping girls."

He just shrugs. "I ain't the one staring all hangdog out the window. Like a love-struck *girl*. I thought we talked about this. Not smart, man. Especially for you."

It's all I can do not to fist my hands, show any sort of reaction. After the fiasco that was known as Jenny, I suppose getting involved is a bad idea. Dex's dig is unfair, however, seeing as after the breakup, I was so focused on kicking ass, we won the National Championship. Again.

Unfortunately, thanks to Jenny's bitter lies, Dex's job of keeping me healthy on the field was that much harder at the time. I might as well have had a "Pummel Baylor" sign on my chest after the dirt she slung about me got out.

"You ask Battle about his new girl yet, big D?" Rolondo's now hanging over my seat, his grin wide and fucking evil. He laughs, a low, easy chuckle, before giving my head a playful slap. "You think you're hidin' anything, man?"

"Seriously?" I groan at them. "You all haven't got anything better to do?"

"Yeah." Rolondo's grin is still in place, shining brighter than the diamond in his ear. "Doesn't beat seeing you squirm in your seat. Damn, boy, you blushing?"

I pinch the bridge of my nose and pray for a bus crash.

"He's got it bad," observes Diaz from behind me. Which is when I realize that they're all fucking looking at me. The whole goddamn bus.

I am going to kill Gray, who is conspicuously quiet in his seat at the front, trying to appear innocent as he flips through *Sports Illustrated*.

"Who is it, yo?" asks Marshall from across the way.

"I heard she's the girl from that lacrosse team party about a month back," Dex says. "The redhead wearing that killer black tank top."

At this, all the guys who were there instantly nod in understanding. Hell, Anna's top obviously made an impression.

Dex looks around at his now captive audience. "The way Baylor was watching her, you'd think she was the championship trophy."

"Naw, Dex," says Diaz. "You can't eat no trophy. And Battle most definitely looked hungry."

Snickers break out. Jesus, was everyone watching me make a fool of myself at that party?

Rolondo whistles low. "Must be one fine girl to get Battle worked up."

"She looks like Christina Hendricks," Dex adds helpfully.

Rolondo shakes his head. "Man, ain't no one on campus got tits that big. Believe me, I'd know."

"Watch your mouths," I snap. I don't care if I have to take down the whole bus. No one is discussing Anna that way. Even if Rolondo is technically correct, Anna is nowhere near that big... Shit. I officially hate these guys.

Rolondo holds up his hands in defense. "Hey, man, I didn't mean no disrespect." Because if there is one golden rule among men, it's that you do not talk smack about a guy's girl or his mom. "I'm just sayin', you mention Christina Hendricks, and I'm thinking about one thing."

"And I didn't say anything about your girl's ti—*breasts*," Dex insists. "I said she kind of looked like the lady. As in has a noticeable resemblance. *Facial* resemblance."

Pinching the bridge of my nose is clearly useless against this burgeoning headache.

"Yo, don't you think she looks more like the Black Widow in *The Avengers*?"

A round of appreciative agreement rumbles through the bus.

"That movie was tight," Simms interjects. "Remember when the Hulk smashed the shit out of Loki like he was some rag doll? Damn, I'd kill to do that on the field. Take some running back and *bam, bam, bam!*"

"Bet you sorry you ain't green too." Rolondo throws an empty Pringles can at the Hulk-loving defensive end, which he bats away with a scowl before retaliating with a half-full water bottle.

"Whatever she looks like, our boy Drew is whipped." That from Marshall. Bastards. All of them.

"Why don't you just call her, man?" someone shouts from behind. Jenkins. I compile a mental list for revenge purposes.

"Oh, honey," intones Thompson—another smart-ass, "I miss you soo muuuch!"

When they start making kissing noises, I do the only thing I can. "Marshall's girl gave him a pink teddy bear, and he carries it around in his bag," I shout.

"Betraying bastard!" bellows poor Marshall. But it's too late for him. He goes down in a tackle of guys as he tries to defend his backpack.

Chaos ensues until the assistant defensive team's coach stands up at the front of the bus and settles everyone down with the threat of extra drills. Yeah, I love these guys. I'm smug and satisfied until Dex leans in, speaking only to me. "If you're really into this girl, lock that shit up. Lock it up tight and concentrate on your game."

And like that, my bubble bursts. What the fuck am I doing with Anna?

ANNA

He's not here. He's at an away game. Florida. This is how far I've sunk. I know his schedule. And I'm sitting in my room at ten o'clock on a Saturday night instead of going out with Iris and George. I'd begged off, using a need-to-read excuse. I love curling up with a good book. Except tonight it was a lie. My eReader is off and sits on the end of my bed where I tossed it earlier in a huff of irritation. A girl can only read the same line so many times before giving up the ghost.

I'm so restless my legs twitch, which only adds to my annoyance when my bare legs slide over the comforter and little zings of feeling run along my sensitized skin. Thoughts of the things Drew has done to me on this very bed invade my mind and make me flop back with a groan. Shit.

Shoving my face into a pillow doesn't help. Nothing does.

I should do something, something physical, go for a walk—because I hate running—or try those core-strengthening vids that Iris is addicted to. A thousand sit-ups sounds about right. I'm rummaging for a sports bra when my phone dings. And my whole body freezes. But not my heart. That pounds with want and glee.

I walk with admirable calm and leisure to my bedside table where my phone lies.

The message, with its little green symbol shines up at me on the dark screen. Drew.

A grin splits my face. My hand shakes only a little when I slide the screen and read.

Baylor: Hey. You there?

Should I answer? Maybe I shouldn't be "there" because I know what he means. Not am I by my phone. What person on this campus doesn't have a phone on hand at all times? He means am I free to talk. Am I sitting around on a Saturday night pining for... I pause. If he's asking then he too must be free.

I nibble the corner of my lip as I answer.

Me: I'm here

It only takes him a second to reply.

Baylor: What are you up to?

And then:

Baylor: I'm in my hotel room.

Like he needs me to know that he isn't just checking on my whereabouts, but that he wants to chat. I am absolutely not grinning as I settle down on my bed and get comfortable.

Me: I'm in my room too.

Baylor: On the bed?

Me: Beats sitting on the floor.

Baylor: I love that bed.☺

The pig. I'm never having sex with him on this bed again. Maybe his bed—let *him* have memories haunting him every time he tries to sleep.

Me: Pig.

Baylor: I'm a guy. Porcine thoughts are indicative of our sex.

Only Drew would use words like *porcine* and *indicative* in a text.

Me: Knowing is half the battle. Why aren't you out?

There. I asked. And it nearly killed me. It kills me more when he takes a few seconds before answering.

Baylor: Didn't want to go out.

Me: Why not?

Stop. Stop now, you masochistic fool!

My phone remains still, accusatory. You had to ask, it seems to say to me. I jump when it dings again.

Baylor: Tired of it. Going out. The scene. The guys want to party.

He doesn't say the rest. He doesn't need to. No one on his team really drinks, which means there's only one party option available. My stomach threatens to do an ugly, green slide into jealousy when I think of all the girls that would be hanging all over him were he out tonight. But he's not. He's texting with me. He sends another.

> **Baylor:** And you're not here.

My throat closes. Honest to God closes. I can't swallow. I stare at the phone lying limp in my clammy hand. An insidious voice in my head shouts *Danger, I'd Turn Back If I Were You!* This is too close to a relationship. I don't want one.

The worst part is, I'm lying to myself. He isn't the arrogant jerk I thought he was. I want him. Constantly. I want to talk to him, laugh with him. A few texts and my whole night is brighter, the color and textures of my room richer, deeper. I can smell my body lotion, grapefruit and vanilla, when it had been a muted muddle before. And I can taste the sourness of fear in my mouth. It sharpens when my phone rings in my hand.

Drew.

He's onto me. He knows I'm about to freak. My heartbeat is a relentless, *thud*, *thud*, *thud* that I'm certain he hears when I slowly slide the bar and answer. "Break a finger over there or something?"

"I decided I wanted to hear your voice instead," he says with a little laugh.

Because he isn't in front of me, because I'm not distracted by his golden glow, his voice has that much more power over me. It sinks through dense flesh and slides along bone, nestling deep into that hard-pumping organ that used to be my heart. It doesn't feel like mine anymore.

"And I hate texting," he continues. He's unsure. I can hear it in the way he tries to force a light, joking tone. And because I know this is hard for him, the guy for whom everything comes easy, I clear my throat and dive in.

"It's impersonal," I add.

There's a real smile in his voice now. "Yeah. Most people don't get that."

"Are you tired?" My tongue feels bigger than normal, like I'm going to soon trip on my words, tell him something I'm not ready to admit.

"Yeah." The sound of him shifting around comes through the phone, and I immediately wonder if he's in bed. Does he sleep naked? "Can't sleep though," he says, thankfully unaware of my devolving thoughts.

"Happen a lot?" I know it does. We've already talked each other to sleep before.

"More so now." He pauses. "I keep thinking about you."

Shit on a pretzel stick.

The pillow is soft against my back, but my skin is still too warm. "I think about you too."

He sighs. It's soft and gusty, and I lean toward it, pressing my cheek to the phone.

"I wish I were there," he says.

I do too. So much it hurts. It hurts deep in my chest and along my stomach. I slide farther down the bed, as if I can run away from the feeling.

When I don't say a word, he just keeps talking. Maybe he knows I'm hiding under the covers now. Maybe he knows I've lost my voice.

"You ever wonder if who you are is the person you're supposed to be?" He speaks low now, as if he's lying beside me on the bed, as if we're having the kind of drowsy chat you use at a sleepover, just before you nod off.

"Like should I be trying to change who I am?" I ask him.

"Not exactly. More like…" He laughs softly. "Hell, I'm not even sure. I just… I've always wanted to play football. I can't even fathom an existence that doesn't include it."

"At least you know. I have no idea what I want to do. I don't want it to be drudge work. I don't want it to be boring. I want a life outside the ordinary. But how do you get that when you've no clue?" *When all you are is ordinary.*

I've opened more of my soul to him. But it doesn't hurt, because he gives me glimpses of his in return.

"You think knowing is better? All I know how to be is a quarterback. And every moment of it revolves around winning. Or losing." He pauses as if struggling. "Think of it, a whole life constantly focusing on the next game. So does that make me who I am? An endless roster of victories and losses?"

For a moment I feel the weight of every one of those eyes that constantly bear down on Drew. And it's crushing. My fingers tighten around the phone. "Are you afraid to lose?"

At first, I think he won't answer, but he does, and his voice carries a strange, almost secretive tone. "You want to know what winning really is?"

"Tell me."

"It isn't about talent. Not at the top level. That's almost equal. And it's not even about who wants it more. It's about who believes with the most conviction they can take it. Fear, doubt, hesitation, that's what kills you."

"Are you afraid?"

"In the dark, late at night? Yeah. Sometimes. On the field? No. Hell no. It's just in me. Knowing I can do it."

I smile at that. "Yet you sound…low. Did you lose the game today?"

"We won." There's a hint of amused censure in his tone. "Do you ever watch my games, Anna?"

Anna. The sound of my name on his lips feels more personal than when I bare my skin to him.

I burrow further under the covers. "Once." It had been a beautiful and agonizing thing to watch. My stomach had clenched every time he took the field. "I didn't like seeing you get hit."

I'd hated it, hurt for him. And yet every time he made a play, I'd felt such pride, such awe of his skills that my breath had grown short and my heart had ached.

The silence between us is pregnant and swelling. I rush on. "And I think how you see yourself makes you who you are. Your soul doesn't have a title or an occupation. It's just you. The rest of the world can go fuck themselves."

That brings a dry chuckle from him. But he soon goes quiet again.

"And how do you see me?" he finally asks. So carefully.

"You're just Drew."

A coward's answer. But also the truth. He's too much for simple words and too much to be cut into categories by them.

"I think you're beautiful," he says softly.

"Beauty fades," I choke out.

"Not when it comes from inside."

Jesus. My eyes flutter closed, and I'm curling into myself. We don't talk. His breathing is a light noise that mingles with the sound of my own.

When he speaks again, his voice has gone even lower, a caress along my cheek. "I want to kiss you, Anna."

My breath hitches. I'm all the way under the covers now, in a dark, heated world. And there's nothing but his voice.

"I think about it all the time. How soft will your lips be? What will they taste like? Will you make those sweet little noises like you do when we make love?"

Make love. Not fuck. I shiver. *Drew.*

I don't even know if I've said his name aloud. It doesn't matter because he just keeps talking, a confession that grows more urgent even as it slows down. "I want to kiss you so badly, I'd forgo the sex for a chance at your mouth. I love your mouth, Anna. The way your upper lip is like a bottom one, a plump, smooth curve that puffs out like a pout. I love your soft, pink, upside-down mouth."

His whisper is rough and thick. And I'm so hot I'm sweating. My hand glides down my chest, to the swells of my heavy, aching breasts, and stops over my heart. I press against it as if to keep it from breaking free of my body.

"But you won't let me kiss you," he says to me in the dark. "Why won't you let me kiss you, Anna?"

I can't breathe.

"Why, Anna?"

"It's too much," I rasp.

"Not when I want everything." He says it so deep and strong, a staking of a claim. "And I want everything with you, Anna."

I think he says my name now because he knows what it does to me. He must, using it that way, over and over, like he's saying something far more important than just my name. He says it with reverence. With intention.

Tears prickle behind my eyes. What the fuck is wrong with me? I *care* about him.

He's my lover, but he's my friend too. The one I find myself turning to first and foremost. Why can't I just give in? Why can't I let myself have him?

In my mind, I see Drew Baylor, microphones shoved under his face as he hollers in victory after winning the National Championship. One hundred thousand screaming fans are in the background. Drew Baylor, who personally brings millions of dollars in revenue to this university, who is interviewed by ESPN, who has agents crawling around him, promising the world. Drew, who will go to New York for the draft and sign a multimillion-dollar contract by this time next year.

I've lied to him. I don't just see Drew. I see the star too. And I'm just Anna. I don't like the light. I need the dark.

He's too smart not to understand that he's pushed me to my limit, and his tone turns gentle, tender. Which is infinitely worse. "I just thought you should know. Good night, Anna."

I don't say a word. I hold on to my phone long after he's hung up.

SEVENTEEN

ANNA

THE SANCTITY OF my morning is broken by Iris and Henry. Who are not quiet about what they're doing. I'm sure I've been guilty of the same. Though I do try to contain myself when I know Iris is here. Not so for them. Especially not for Henry. I have my suspicions that the asshole is being loud on purpose; he'd be the type to get off on something like that. When he starts to grunt "yeah, yeah, yeah," I don't care what his motivation is, I need to get out of here.

I pick up the phone and dial. "You want to go for a bike ride?" I ask as soon as he answers. I'm desperate now, practically hopping around my room as I get dressed. "Iris and Henry are going at it like rabbits."

Thank God he says yes.

"Do me a favor, will you, Anna?"

My bike hits a rut, and the whole frame rattles, and me along with it. "What's that?" I say when the danger of biting my tongue passes.

George gives me a quick glare before swerving around another pothole. "Do *not* tell me that my sister is going at it with that sleazy little bitch again."

Instantly, I cringe. "Shit. I'm sorry. That was so wrong of me. I wasn't thinking."

He falls into a nice, quick pace. "Yeah, well, be forewarned. Do it again, and I'm bringing Sylvester to our next dinner out."

"Ew, no! I'll behave, I swear!" Sylvester is Iris and George's creepy handsy cousin who I'm convinced is a serial killer. Years from now, I'll see George and Iris being interviewed on CNN. "We always had our suspicions about Sly, but our mother made us hang out with him."

Having sufficiently terrified me into compliance, George gives me a reassuring smile and speeds up. We pace each other as we ride along the bike trail. Early morning light peeks through the gold leaves and the air is crisp. I draw it in and let it cool me.

After a couple of miles, we reach a clearing, and George nods toward it. We roll over to a large elm and leave our bikes resting on the ground as we sit. Silence surrounds us. Despite the good weather, the path is basically deserted. It's early Saturday morning, so I'm guessing most people are still sleeping off Friday night.

After taking a long drink of water, I nudge George. "So what's going on with you?"

George finishes his own drink before answering. "That's what I was going to ask you."

"Tough. I asked first, so spill."

"Damn, woman." But George smiles. His smile gets bigger, but he's obviously trying to maintain an air of cool, and my curiosity skyrockets. He doesn't leave me hanging for long. "I got an internship with Jackson and Goldman in New York."

"Georgie!" I nudge him again. "That's great!" After years of hearing George drone on about finance, I know that Jackson and

Goldman is the best investment banking firm in New York, and George's idea of Nirvana.

"Fuck yeah it is." He grins wide as he ducks his head. "A couple professors put in a good word and..." He shrugs.

"And they recognized the brilliance that is you?" I add, making George laugh.

"Yeah, and that."

We both grin wide and happy.

"You are so inviting me to your Hamptons' beach house." If there is one thing George and I have in common, it's our desire to live in New York when we graduate.

"Extended stay, Banana?"

"You know it. I can do the dishes."

"No thanks. You suck at doing dishes."

I shove him with my shoulder, and he chuckles, but shadows linger in his eyes.

"So," I say when we've grown quiet again, "what's the problem? Are you worried about doing well?"

George chuffs, amused. "I'm going to kick ass. It seems like I've been waiting my whole life just to get this chance."

"But...?" Because it's there, something dark and heavy weighing on him.

Tension gathers along the corners of his eyes, and he studies his hands that dangle over his bent knees. "It's Iris." His shoulders lift on a sigh. "We've always been together. And now..."

They won't be. Iris hates New York City with a passion. And she's already been accepted into Arizona State's archeology graduate program.

"You haven't told her, have you?"

"No. I've been trying to work up to it." George shifts as if his shirt is too tight. "I mean what guy whines about leaving his sister behind? But she's also my twin."

"I know." And I do. Despite their occasional bickering, they are as close as any siblings I've met. They often finish each other's thoughts. And they are almost always together.

George could have gone to an Ivy League school where he might have gained valuable contacts. He had the grades and the offers. But he chose to follow Iris to State.

As if he's thinking the same thing, he says, "I promised my ma that I'd watch after 'Ris. I wanted to do it." A weak huff leaves him. "Now everything feels so real. We'll be going our separate ways and, shit, it's a fucked-up thing to realize that maybe I really needed her to look after me."

George blinks rapidly and fiercely, and I let him have a moment. I have no words of comfort. How can I? My future is a dark, empty hole now. If I look too hard at it, I'll scream.

A biker rides by, breaking the silence. And I take a deep breath. "So we let Iris do the dishes all summer."

A laugh bursts from George. "She'll bitch, but you know she'll love it." Iris is a complete neat freak.

We both smile as we finish our waters.

"What's the deal with you and Baylor?" George gives me a searching look. "For serious now. No bullshitting." He knows me well enough to understand that this version of me isn't normal.

"Are we still sharing?"

George glares. "I spilled my guts, so yeah, we are."

I sigh and rest my arms on my raised knees. Green grass tickles my ankles as a breeze dances over the lane. I pick up a brown leaf and twist it around by its brittle stem. "We're having sex. A lot of it."

God, it ought to be easier, but then confessions never are. And I'm afraid if I open my mouth to purge, the flow might never stop.

"Is he stringing you along, Banana?" The implicit threat of George hunting down Drew and making him pay is clear.

A huff of laughter escapes me. "More like the other way around." Shame creeps up my neck and makes it tight. "He wants…" *Everything.* I shudder. "It's just supposed to be sex."

George hums in his throat. "Who do you think you're fooling with that one?"

"No one but me, apparently." I frown down at the ground.

After a long moment, George stirs. "This isn't like you. Not this weird limbo shit you've got going with him. What's the deal?"

Because it's either a hook up or casual dating for me. Drew doesn't fit in either category. He never really did.

"He's… He's my mirror." It sounds absurd when I say it but also rings true inside of me. "When I'm with him, I can't hide. All the bullshit, all the fucked-up issues I think I've overcome are reflected back at me in perfect clarity, telling me that I'm full of it."

"Shit," says George.

The leaf spins round faster. "You know the most fucked-up thing of all? Even though I see all of my flaws, when I'm with him, I'm…"

I toss the leaf away and shrug as a helpless sound comes out of me. "God, it's going to sound so sappy, George, but I feel… everything."

I press the heels of my hands into my eyes so I don't have to see my friend. Because it is sappy. So freaking sappy, but undeniable. "I'm so happy that I'm afraid to take the next breath because it might end."

I might not be able to see him, but I can feel George's presence. And the weight of his stare.

"If it's that good," he finally says, "why are you keeping him at a distance?"

It takes several swallows to find the strength to answer. "Because it has to end. He's going to go out there and have the world in his palm, while I'll struggle just to find a nine-to-five job. And when it does end, I won't recover."

Silence greets me. Filled with the chirp of late fall crickets and the distant motor traffic. I want to crawl away and die. Especially when George sighs.

"Shit, Anna."

"Yeah," I say, knowing what he really means: I'm screwed.

He puts an arm around me and tugs me against his sweaty

shoulder. I lean into him, registering even now that his comfort isn't half as relieving as Drew's. Which just makes it worse.

I don't see Drew all week. He texts me to say that, thanks to his away game, he's behind on his classwork and has to catch up. No one I know has a schedule as intense as Drew's. Up at dawn to work out with his team, classes afterward, then practice, then meetings, then classwork and studying. Frankly, I'm shocked he ever finds the time to see me.

When Drew finally is available to hook up, I'm the one stuck working. As if the universe is conspiring against us, our one class together is canceled when Professor Lambert sends an email telling us that she's got the flu.

But late at night, when I'm in my bed and he's in his, he calls me. We talk of nothing too deep, just small things. I now long to hear his voice as much as I need to feel his body against mine. All of which winds me up and makes me twitchy. But maybe a little space is for the best.

EIGHTEEN

DREW

HOME GAME. Seconds on the clock, and we're sixty yards from the end zone. One touchdown and the game is ours. The noise of the crowd is a jet engine revving up for liftoff. It rushes down the sides of the stadium and washes over me with a power that vibrates my bones. The hairs on my skin lift. My balls draw up tight. *Go time.*

Heart in my throat, I bend close to my guys to call the play. I can barely hear my own voice and use hand signals as well to make myself clear.

"Crabapple Betty. One."

"Hut," they shout in tandem. A clap of the hands and they break and get into formation.

A sea of fans in red surround us, cresting high like a breaking wave. Many swing plastic battle axes back and forth, their chant a rhythmic pulsing: *Battle, Battle, Battle.*

Before me is a stretch of endless green and a wall of hulking linemen twitching with the need to crush me. Grunts and stamping feet. Under the lights, it's brighter than midday and hot as hell.

Adrenaline surges, and I tamp it down. Quick check toward Coach. Good to go.

"Hut!"

Dex snaps me the ball. Players burst into action. The thuds of flesh against flesh ripple through the air. Handoff fake to Gray, then I step back into the pocket. Footsteps pound. Linemen rush in when they realize the fake. My boys hold them off.

Rolondo is going deep, but a safety and a cornerback are all over his ass. I duck a tackle, cut right, duck again. Gray's covered. Diaz worse. Energy pulses, the crowd screams. I check Rolondo again. He's pulling clear with a burst of speed.

Everything slows down inside me. It's just me and the spot 'Londo needs to be in. Breathe deep, pump my arm back. *Fly!*

An arm hooks my middle, I crash into the turf with a bone-jarring thud. My eyes following the ball as it arcs through the air. And it's damn beautiful when my baby drops from the sky to land in the cradle of Rolondo's fingertips like I'd personally placed her there.

Right in the end zone. Perfect.

The victorious roar is deafening.

"Yeah," I shout, my voice lost in the chaos.

My guys swarm in, pulling me up, bouncing me around like a pinball.

"That's what I'm talking about!"

My head rattles in my helmet from all the slaps.

"That's right, bitches. Whoo!"

I jump high, punch the sky, then run toward 'Londo. He meets me halfway, bumping his chest to mine.

"That's how you do it!" I slap his helmet, grinning wide. "Fucking beautiful, man."

"Cuz my boy threw me a mutha-fucking rocket on a string,"

he shouts back laughing and grabbing my jersey to hug me. "We own this!"

Stumbling back to the sidelines, we're surrounded once again by the team. The band plays a victory song. The crowd screams for us. For me. And there is nothing like it. It's like flying and falling all at once. Only one other thing in this world makes me feel a high like this, one person. And I'm going after her.

NINETEEN

ANNA

SATURDAY FINDS ME working a mixer for the engineering department's alumni fund, held at the Student Union. It's a big party with a full dinner service, which means my back is aching from hauling around massive trays laden with dinner plates. Attendance is fairly low, something my manager, Dave, blames on holding the dinner at the same time as the football game. I think of Drew playing and a strange twinge of guilt pricks my gut. I ought to be there. Watching. Cheering for him. I shake it off and concentrate on my job.

It takes us a good hour to clean up the back kitchen, load the sheet pans into the washer, and lock up the remaining wine. When the rest of the staff leaves, I stay behind with Dave, because someone should and no one else is volunteering.

As manager, Dave is responsible for returning the key to the main office. Once he's done here, I'm done for the night.

He walks out with me, which is nice since the building has gone dark, and screams "ideal slasher film location." When I tell Dave that, we have a laugh over the idea, even though a shiver crawls along my spine. I'm creeping myself out.

"Though, really," Dave says lightly, "every venue we work is ideal for murder. Just think of what could go down in the architecture hall. All that unrelenting glass." His blond brows wag. "There's no place to hide."

I laugh again. "Stop. Or I'll never work another night shift again."

He mocks a terrible Bela Lugosi accent. "Do not resist. Your nights are mine, Anna Jones."

"Goof."

We're almost to my scooter when I see him. My steps slow to a crawl.

Bathed in the brightness of a parking lot light, he's leaning against the side of a cherry red classic muscle car with thick white racing stripes running down its center. I know enough about cars to identify that it's a Camaro and it's in mint condition. Not that it really matters. My eyes are on Drew. And, God, he looks good.

Faded jeans hang low on his lean hips. He's got one leg crossed over the other and his hands stuffed in his pockets, pulling the jeans lower. A pale gray Henley hugs his broad chest and gorgeous arms.

He's watching me, has been since I noticed him, and that one dimple on his cheek deepens when our eyes meet.

"Oh man, that's pretty," breathes Dave at my side.

I'm fairly certain he isn't talking about the car. I roll my eyes. "Night, Dave."

He ambles off, muttering under his breath about lucky bitches, as I walk toward Drew. A casual stroll, as if my heart isn't going ten miles a minute, as if I don't want to run and jump on him.

A wicked smile curls his lips as I get closer. I'm smiling too. I can't contain it. He just looks so fucking good. There's a strange buoyancy in my chest. *Happiness.* I'm so happy to see him, my legs want to go faster. I force a steady pace.

When I'm five feet away, Drew pushes off the car and stands tall. He's still grinning when I stop in front of him, and his eyes travel over me. I feel that look down to my bones. God, he's sexy. I don't usually think of guys in those terms. Sexy sounds false, an adjective better left for advertisers' use. But Drew is sex on a spoon. I want to slide him into my mouth and savor him.

"He's gay, you know," Drew says by way of greeting.

It's a minor miracle that I know what he's talking about because I can feel the warmth of his body, and it's making me dizzy.

"Considering I've met more than a few of Dave's boyfriends, I'd say, yeah, I know. You're warning me, why?"

Drew huffs out a short laugh. "Petty jealousy, Jones. He's a good guy for walking you out."

"Mmm." I look him over. "You win tonight, Baylor?"

I'm guessing he did. Even here, far away from the stadium, the faint strains of the school band and laughter drift through the air.

His whole face lights up. "Yeah."

I can't help but grin. "Good on you."

Drew shrugs as though it's nothing, but he isn't fooling me. Happiness bounces around him, a bubbly fizz in the dark night. "I did my part." His gaze roams down my body. "Nice outfit, Jones."

I'm still in my catering clothes, a white oxford shirt, black knee-length skirt, and ballerina flats. I probably look all of twelve.

"You have your uniform. I have mine. Why are you smiling like that?"

There's a gleam in his eyes that's so dirty it makes my heart skip a beat.

"I'm picturing you in my uniform."

"Because those massive shoulder pads would look sooo sexy." I make a goofy face.

His tongue runs over the edge of his teeth. "Actually, I was thinking more along the lines of my jersey. God, you'd look hot in my jersey."

"A jock's wet dream, I suppose?" I quip, but my breath is a little too fast now. It's as if I can feel the silky texture of Drew's big jersey sliding over my bare skin.

"You bet, baby."

"God." I roll my eyes and shake my head.

He's laughing again, a low, rolling sound that warms me inside. Suddenly we're closer, less than a foot apart. I don't know if he moved or if I did. I can't think. He's so close that heat surges between my legs, and my breasts grow heavy. I'm surrounded by Drew. Again.

"I've missed you." His voice is soft, that special tone that I've come to think of as mine. A low intimate sound that fills the space between us. Like we're in our own world. All I can think about is the last time he used that voice on me. *I want to kiss you, Anna.*

From the way he's looking at me, his focus going to my lips and his brows drawing tight with intent, I'm guessing he's thinking about that too. He hasn't yet touched me, but his body leans closer to mine.

A gust of icy wind rushes over the lot, and I shiver. "I don't know how you can stand it out here without a coat. Aren't you cold?"

Drew reaches out and grasps the lapels of my secondhand pea coat that's hanging open to the breeze. His touch is so gentle as he pulls the ends together, that I stand there, throat closed, mouth dry.

"I just played football for hours." He doesn't let my coat go, but holds it, his thumbs slowly rubbing over the wool, his forearms an inch away from my breasts. "If I could get away with it, I wouldn't be wearing a shirt at all."

"That would—" Be wonderful? Yes, please? With sugar on top? "—give the campus police something to talk about over donuts in the morning."

"Mmm," he agrees with a lazy rumble, while he tugs just the slightest bit on my coat. I drift closer, and his voice drops to a murmur. "The press would have a ball. Drew Baylor shocks all by revealing his nipples."

He shouldn't be allowed to say words like *nipples* in public. As if called, mine instantly perk up. His lashes lower, and I know he's noticed. I hear his slow inhale.

A steady throb joins the heat between my legs. My chest is so tight now that when he dips his head to graze his lips across my ear, I can't breathe.

"Did you miss me, Anna?" he whispers.

My hands find their way to his chest, and I press my palms against the dense muscles there. He smells clean, like the shower gel he uses and, underneath it, his natural scent. It's so familiar to me now, I can no longer describe it. I only know I want to draw it deep into my lungs. I want to close my eyes and lean into him. But I keep them open and focus on the golden skin of his throat.

I love that part of his body, the vulnerability of his sensitive skin. I love the little hollows just above his collarbones where his neck dips down to meet his shoulders, and I know that if I press my mouth to that tender spot and suckle it, he'll give me a helpless, near whimper of sound that he always does when I kiss him there. I almost whimper myself.

Did I miss him?

"Yes."

I can feel him smile against my cheek. "Good." The tips of his fingers graze under my jaw, just over my racing pulse.

"Is this your car?" I blurt out. Smooth. Either Drew likes to lean on strangers' cars or I'm Captain Obvious.

Drew draws back a little and glances at it. "Yep."

"It's gorgeous." I'm a wimp. Taking the coward's way out of Dodge.

His tilted smile is wry. He knows I'm trying to distract him, and it clearly amuses him. But he plays along. Drew turns and lovingly runs his palm over the glossy hood of the car. "This here is Little Red."

"Little Red," I repeat. It makes me think of what he called me the first time we talked: Big Red. The moment I decided to hate him. And I wonder how it is that I'm here now. How has this happened? Me wanting him more than my next breath. Me needing him more than I've ever needed anyone.

Perhaps he feels my tension, because he eyes me carefully. "It's a term of affection, you know," he says in a low voice. "Anyway, I didn't name her."

"Her?"

"All cars are ladies, Jones." He winks.

It should be cheesy, winking like that, but it's not. It makes me want to kiss his cheek. He's not only sexy, he's fucking adorable. And he's completely ignorant of my moony expression because he's back to stroking his car.

"She's a 1971 Chevy Camaro Z28." His expression dims a little, becoming almost bittersweet. "She was my dad's. He got her at a junkyard and restored her from the frame out."

His pride rings clear, and he gives the car another pat. "It drove my mom nuts when he spent his weekends tinkering with Little Red, but she knew how much he loved it so…" He shrugs.

"Did you ever work on it?"

"Mostly it's only tune-ups and belt changes now, but, yeah, I know how to fix a car, if that's what you're asking." A little mischief brews in his dark eyes. "Want to go for a ride?"

"Now?"

"No. Three hours from now," he deadpans. "I figure you can get in your pj's, maybe sleep for a while, then we'll go out."

"Smart-ass."

He's already opening the passenger door. "Come on, Jones, ride with me."

I hesitate.

"It'll be nice and warm with the heat on," he adds.

The Camaro's dark interior gleams in the yellow glow of the parking lot light.

Drew is waiting. He wants to kiss me. He wants everything.

I take a little breath. "Okay, but this thing had better go fast."

"She'll set your hair straight." He gives one of my curls a playful tug before closing the door behind me.

Inside, the car smells of old leather and a bit of Drew's shaving cream. It's that subtle scent of Drew that makes me sink into my seat and inhale deeply. Then he's getting into the car. His grin is like a kid's when he turns the key and the car rumbles to life with a growl.

"Oh, yeah, baby," he says to her, "purr for me."

"Would you like a little time alone?" I ask, but I love the way he appreciates his car.

His dimple deepens. "This is a shared experience, Jones. Get with the program. Now buckle up."

I do as ordered, and happily sit back as he pulls out of the lot. He goes slow through the campus, turning on the heat and fiddling with the radio. Soon I'm warm enough to pull off my coat, and Led Zeppelin's "Kashmir" fills the silence.

"You weren't kidding about the classic rock," I say, taking a look around the dash. "I'm surprised there isn't an 8-track in here."

"I'm surprised you know what an 8-track is."

"Likewise."

He laughs. "Dad put in a new stereo the year before he—"

He stops talking and turns out onto the main road. The car springs forward with a throaty little rumble.

"It's a beautiful car," I say to fill the pained silence. I hate that he hurts, that he misses his parents. "I'm glad you have it."

"I am too." He's quiet for a moment, then smiles softly. "When I finally made straight A's, he let me use it on dates. It became my personal quest to get laid in here."

"Nice." I wrinkle my nose. "And you've just put the kibosh on getting any from me in here."

"Damn, there goes my plan." He sighs in exaggerated disappointment. "Actually, the back seat is ridiculously small for a muscle car. Can't do anything back there but get a leg cramp."

Much to his amusement, I glance over my shoulder. The seat is small. Annoyed that I fell for his trick, and at Drew's smug chuckle, I pull out my phone. We're heading for a large stretch of empty road now, and I know he'll let the car go then. "This radio work with my phone?" I ask.

"I like old cars, but I have my standards." He reaches down and hands me an input wire as I download a song.

It's my turn to smile. "I think you'll like this one." I hit Play.

His expression is priceless, his nose wrinkled in confusion at the twangy plucking of a guitar and two guys conversing in a beatnik style. "What the hell?"

"Just listen."

He does and his mouth twitches. The guys are making fun of The Doors now, and Drew snorts in amusement.

"It's the Dead Milkmen," I say.

One guy asks the other what car dude's dad got him. My gaze catches Drew's and we're both grinning.

"Don't tell me," Drew says.

Just as the band launches into a hard and fast punk rock riff about a Camaro. It's chaotic, all drums and guitars and screaming singers.

"'Bitchin' Camaro,' man," I say with a laugh.

And Drew takes off. We're flying, my back presses against the seat, and I'm laughing so hard my sides hurt. Drew's laughing with me. We're mad on speed and ridiculous lyrics. And I don't want it to end. Little Red eats up the road, gray asphalt is a blur. I ought to be afraid, but I feel alive.

We race along until the song ends and then Drew slows. "That was excellent."

"So's the car." I rest my head on the seat and smile at him. I'm sore from laughter, little aftershocks of giddiness quake though my belly.

Everything is quiet except the steady hum of the engine, and that's okay. The realization steals over me. We can sit together in silence and feel comfortable. When had it happened? Before I can wonder any longer, Drew's stomach growls. With insistence.

"Why do I get the feeling that your stomach likes talking to me?" I ask him.

The corner of his mouth quirks. "Kind of your fault."

"Oh, really?"

"You fed it once. Naturally it's going to come asking for more."

"Naturally." I grab my bag. "I don't know if I should be enabling this development, but I happen to have a sub—"

"Hand it over, Jones."

"You sure? You'd let us eat in Little Red? I mean this interior is pretty pristine."

Drew looks at me sidelong. He's fighting a grin, but he manages to look pseudo threatening. "Hand over the food and no one gets hurt."

I pull out a twelve-inch-long section of the party sub I'd taken from the catering kitchen, and he makes an exaggerated groan. "Oh, baby, it's so big."

"That's my line."

"Yes, it is."

Smiling, I help myself to a small section of sandwich then hand him the rest.

His groan is real and appreciative as he starts to devour the sub, one hand on the wheel the other lovingly holding his food. "Italian," he says between bites. "Bless you."

"You must be really hungry because this sub is mediocre at best." The sandwich is soggy on the bottom and overly salty.

"I'm starved. I haven't eaten since before the game." Drew gives me a quick, guilty look.

It's harder to swallow my bite. "Thanks for taking me for a ride." My words are soft in the dark car, and when silence falls, it's less easy now.

Drew shrugs and finishes off his last bite. "Wasn't anywhere else I wanted to be."

Which makes the ache inside of me stronger.

He peers down at my bag. "I don't suppose you have any—"

I have my water bottle out and to him before he can finish, and I am rewarded with another one of his grins.

"You're a goddess, Anna Jones."

I affect a casual tone, as if my heart isn't bruised and bewildered. "Well, since you're feeling nice and indebted. Can I drive Little Red?" I need something to do, something to calm me before I fling myself at him and offer my undying adoration.

And I have to admire the way he struggles not to react with the horror that's so clearly stealing over him. I figure no one except Drew drives this car. It must be the case, because he's almost squirming in his seat. I'm about to let him off the hook, tell him it's okay, I get it, I understand it's a guy thing, when he suddenly pulls over to the side of the road.

"Okay, but—"

"If you make some lame crack about my ability to handle a stick, I will end you," I quip, just to break his tension.

"I want to live," he teases. Then looks at me hard, but there's a gleam in his eyes beneath the scowl. "Seriously, I want to live so..."

"Ass." I give his pec a light punch before I wrench open the heavy car door and get out. We meet in the middle, the car's headlights illuminating us. Or rather, I run by him and jump into the driver's seat, slamming the door behind me. "It's freaking freezing out there now," I tell him as he gets into the passenger seat.

My legs hover somewhere in no-man's land. He's so tall; the pedals are at least a foot away from me. Muttering about giants, I roll the seat forward.

And he shakes his head. "More like redheaded pixies who need to pull the seat up to the steering wheel."

"I do not, in any way, resemble a pixie." The very idea is laughable.

His fleeting gaze travels over my breasts and hips, and it's hot. "You might be right."

I'm only a little flustered when I start the car.

I don't punch it. I drive fast and smooth, learning the feel of the car and its tics.

Drew studies me, his body angled in the seat a little. "I thought you'd floor it."

I shrug as we glide around a soft curve. "I'm getting to know her first."

The way he looks at me, as if I've said something special. I don't understand that look, it makes me twitchy deep in my belly, so I ignore it and drive.

We're quiet, lulled by the gentle purr of the motor. And it's nice. The old car, with its soft leather and warm heat, is cozy.

The road is really a big loop, bringing us back into town. I can see the lights of the campus coming up upon us in the distance.

A mile later, I spot an abandoned lot, and put on my blinker. Which is ridiculous considering we're the only ones out here, but habit is habit.

When Drew speaks, his steady voice is so deep it's soothing. "You can drive us back. It's up to you."

I don't think I can take the feel of his gaze on me any longer. It's doing strange things to my heart, speeding it up, slowing it down. I'm beginning to think he knows exactly how much he affects me.

"It's okay," I say as I pull in. The tires crunch over gravel and the car rocks over a small bump. I ease it to a stop, turn the engine off, and promptly realize the error of my plan. We're alone in the dark, warm cocoon of the car. And while I've never shirked from the chance to jump on Drew, everything feels different now. Somehow, without my permission, we've grown closer, and I know a decision must be made.

Drew seems twitchy as well, his biceps bunching beneath his shirt as he taps on his knee.

"Let's change seats then," I say, not quite looking him in the eye.

It's clear that neither of us wants to go outside, which means only one option. We've got to climb over each other. Or maybe it's the excuse we both need to touch.

As soon as we spring into action, the reality of it isn't the sexy situation I'd envisioned. Not when our knees bash into each other at the same time as my chin collides with Drew's massive shoulder.

"Ow!"

"Oof!"

I rear back, hitting my head on the roof as Drew awkwardly falls to the side, his ass connecting with the steering wheel. The Camaro's horn is a bellow in the dark night. Muttering a curse, Drew tries to get his leg over the console the same time as I do, and we tangle again.

"Move your butt, you big mountain," I grumble.

He starts to snicker, which sets me off. We both laugh and curse as Drew slides by me and I half crawl to the passenger seat, only to feel a tug on my skirt.

"Shit! I'm stuck on the stick."

Drew laughs harder.

"Don't you dare make stick jokes," I warn through a laugh.

"I'm too busy trying to get my ass out of the steering wheel." His shoulder crushes my chest as he wiggles, laughing so hard—he's as clumsy as I am. "Fuck, did you not put the seat back?"

"No. Ow. Would you move?" I yank at my skirt but his thigh is pinning my calf to the driver's seat. "I wasn't thinking that far ahead."

"Obviously. Hold up." His ribs shove in my face as he bends over the driver's seat. There's a loud click and then we're falling as the seat zips back. Drew twists, landing on the seat, his arm wrapping about my waist and pulling me with him.

I end up on his lap with a thud, and Drew's pained grunt. My bent leg is awkwardly braced on his chest and putting me off balance.

"Seriously, Jones," he says, still a bit breathless from our laughing fit. "If you wanted to get in my lap, you only had to ask."

He puts a hand to my back, keeping the steering wheel from digging into my spine.

My cheeks hurt from grinning. "You caught me. It was all part of an evil plan to turn us into a human pretzel. Watch your head. Leg incoming."

He ducks his chin, as I lift my leg up and over his head, effectively straddling his lap with my knees tucked under his arms in the tight space. Not very comfortable, but who am I kidding? I like where I am.

The position, however, bunches my skirt around my hips. Instantly, his free hand lands on my exposed thigh.

"You cold?" he asks quietly, as he begins to rub it to keep me warm.

I shake my head, my voice having fled. How can I be cold with his firm, heated torso this close to mine? His heartbeat is steady and hard beneath my palm.

"Did I hurt you anywhere?" He eases me closer still, until my breasts pillow his chest.

"No."

Face-to-face, all I can see is Drew colored pale blue by moonlight, his eyes gleaming and dark as they study me. His gaze lowers to my lips and stays there, as his grip becomes firmer, laden with intent. Heat invades me swift and strong.

His mouth. So close. Close enough that our breath mingles. I love his mouth, the lush shape of it, and I don't even know what it tastes like, how it feels. His fingers press into the flesh of my thigh, as though he needs to hold on to something, and my gaze flicks up to meet his.

A pained expression there, and a plea.

Drew will never take from me. Not unless he knows I want it too. Tenderness mixes with the pervasive heat inside of me, a heady stew that has me sinking further into his embrace. Carefully, I trace his jaw, the texture like fine sandpaper against my fingertips.

"Anna." It's a whisper of sound.

Holding his gaze, I lean in. My lips brush his. So gently it's barely a touch. But it's everything. I feel it down to my toes. Drew sucks in a sharp breath, his body going tight. So I do it again. Stronger. More sure. Clinging just a bit to his lower lip.

And then he groans. His fingers thread into my hair, clutching tight as he tilts his head and kisses me back. It isn't hard or frantic. It's a warm, melting exploration, as if we've fallen into the middle of a kiss, tongues sliding, lips melding and parting in a slow rhythm. And I ignite, burning brighter than the sun. Sensation, want, need, surge through me on a moan that's lost in his mouth.

Drew shivers. His fingertips run along my neck, my cheek, and back down again, as his lips nuzzle and suck on mine. Going deeper, having more of me every time. And every time my heart clenches just a bit harder within my chest.

Dizziness swamps me. There is no up or down, just Drew. Drew's mouth. His taste and his heat. I want to sink into him, drown in his touch. I tremble, whimpering in frustration as I rock against his erection and open my mouth wider for his kiss. He holds me tighter. Grounding me.

"It's better," he says inside a kiss.

"Better?" My hands roam the plains of his chest, the rounded swells of his shoulders. I've missed the feel of him against me.

"Kissing you. It's better than I imagined."

I hadn't let myself imagine. I touch his cheek, and our gazes collide. My breath grows short. My heart actually hurts. "Drew." I don't know what else to say. But it seems enough for him right now.

He holds me like I'm precious to him, like he wants to fuse us together.

"Come home with me," he whispers between kisses that are growing more urgent, fierce. His skin is damp, his body shaking as hard as mine. "I need you, Anna. I need you in my bed."

I can barely keep my eyes open. My clothes smother me. Sweat trickles down my back, and my thighs tremble with need. And I can't stop kissing him. Deep, light, hard, soft. It's too much. I knew it would be. I am lost in him.

"Anna…" His voice is weak now, and rough as his breathing.

"Yes," I manage. "Yes."

Pressing his forehead to mine, he nods once, his fingertips still roaming over my face as if he needs to memorize it by touch. "Okay." Another seeking kiss. "Okay."

TWENTY

ANNA

I STAY IN his lap as he drives us home. It's dangerous but neither of us is thinking very clearly now. It's not an option to move off him, to let him go. Drew's arm remains wrapped around my waist, his big hand clamped on my hip as if he's afraid I might change my mind, try to escape.

I don't. I won't. I'm too far gone now. I'm weak and needy for him. So he drives, and my head rests on his shoulder as my fingers trace his neck, touch the spot where his pulse is a rapid tattoo. He holds me tighter, presses his cheek against the top of my head, as he maneuvers the car down darkened neighborhood streets.

His heart beats as fast as my own. We're almost humming with anxious anticipation. If we don't get there soon, I know he'll pull over and take me in the back seat, cramped or not. I almost make the suggestion, I'm so achy for him, but the car swerves into a driveway and then lurches to a halt.

He's got the car turned off and the parking brake on in seconds. The door wrenches open, and somehow, we're out. I'm in his arms. I don't even know how he's accomplished swinging both himself and my body weight out of the car with such ease, nor do I protest that he's carrying me. I'm pretty sure if he puts me down right now, we'd both fall.

His house is a small Craftsman-style bungalow with a peaked roof that creates a wide front porch. Drew makes short work of the front steps. I burrow my nose into his neck and cling with my legs around his waist as he fumbles with his keys before the glass-pained door. Then we're stumbling inside.

I get a glimpse of white walls, high ceilings, and dark floors. A retro '30s metal dome table lamp casts a warm haze over a leather couch and chair and teak credenza. This isn't a college guy's hangout. It's a home. Framed and matted photos hang from the walls. That's all I see of it. Drew captures my mouth with his once more, his grip on my ass tight and sure as he strides across the room.

His room is cool, quiet, the mellow glow of another table lamp limning everything in golden light. Drew sets me down at the foot of his bed before attacking my buttons, his fingers fumbling and desperate, his mouth never leaving mine.

My knuckles press into his abdomen as I rip open his jeans, shoving them down in my haste. The waistband of his boxer briefs snags over his hard cock, and he curses. He frees himself then reaches for me. Everything becomes a blur of flying, discarded clothes and messy kisses. And then the world lifts away. In his arms one second, and sinking into a cool, thick down comforter the next.

Drew climbs over me. Hot, smooth skin slides over mine. Hard muscles. Heavy, dense flesh. And everywhere he touches, I ignite.

We don't stop kissing. I don't think I'm capable of stopping. I'm starved for his mouth.

He moves between my legs, and I tilt my hips to give him better access. *Now.* I want him now. Hard. Fast. But suddenly he slows us down, suckling my lower lip before he raises his head. Arms bracketing me, he looks into my eyes, his fingers playing with my hair.

His lids lower a fraction, but he doesn't close his eyes. "Every night," he says. "Every single night I've thought about you being here. Just like this."

I shiver. Every single night I've feared being here. Like this. Because I wanted it so very much.

Skin to skin, we lie, trembling and sweating. Between our pressed bellies, his cock throbs hot and firm. I struggle to breathe. My palms skim over his narrow, tight waist. "Now that you have me here, what are you going to do to me?"

Drew's lips curl into a slow, satisfied smile. "Keep you here."

Promise?

Just when I fear emotion might cripple me, he moves, canting his hips until the rounded tip of his cock nudges against my opening. My attention zeroes in on it, that spot where everything has gone so hot and needy that my sex clenches. Holding my gaze, he slides the tip in. Then the bastard stills.

"Drew." Squirming, I try to take more.

He only smiles and holds steady, a solid plank of unyielding muscle. "Do you want me?"

"You know I do." Every substantial inch. But that's not what he's asking, and we both know it.

"All of me?" His expression turns serious, his voice a ghost in the silence. Oh, but he rocks his hips, pushing in just a bit more, an inducement designed to make me come apart. "Do you want all of me, Anna?"

I can feel my heart beating against his. Twin steady, quick thrums that match pace. I could lie and say no. Retreat to safety. And it would end the best thing that has ever happened to me. With a shaking hand, I reach out and skim my fingers along the damp hair at his temple. "Yes."

He swallows audibly, his body trembling with something that feels like relief against my skin. "Glad we've got that settled."

He moves to thrust but halts again. This time with a curse that mingles with mine.

"Now you're just being cruel," I wail.

"I'm not... Fuck." He pants. "I left the condoms in the car."

"In the car?" I squirm, barely able to think. "What the hell are they doing in there?"

His breath gusts over my cheeks on a pained laugh. "It's not like I need them in here, Jones." He tilts his head and kisses me at a different angle, all open mouth and wet. When he talks again, it's a thick whisper. "I'd have left them at your house, but it seemed presumptuous."

God, I even love the way he murmurs *presumptuous* against my mouth. My lips vibrate with it, and I lick them, before licking his. I'm so hot, so turned on, I can't stand it. I'm so empty it hurts. "Forget the condom," I say in a strangled voice. "Just... just fuck me."

A tremor lights over him, and I feel the head of his cock twitch. Honey-brown eyes stare down at me. "You sure?"

We both know it's a matter of believing each other when we say we're STI free, and trusting that we're exclusive, of Drew trusting me when I say that I'm on the pill. Do I trust him? Yes. Am I nervous? Hell yes.

I swallow hard, resisting the temptation to move. "Unless you don't want to?" I won't hold it against him if he wants a condom. Never. I start to tell him that when he replies.

His answer is a kiss, a dirty-sexy, wet fuck of my mouth, as he thrusts his cock in deep. That thick invasion, it fills me up, makes me gasp.

"Holy hell." He groans. "You feel so good." And then he's pumping, groaning low as he moves. My focus narrows to the smell of his skin, the feel of him pushing in and pulling out of my swollen sex, the near helpless sounds he makes with each thrust.

His thumb finds the tight bead of my nipple and rolls it. Combined with the way he licks along the inside of my upper lip, the simple action is almost indecent. It shakes me to the core.

"Oh, fuck," I gasp into his mouth.

An orgasm steals over me, not with violence, but a slow, swelling wash of heat that has me shivering and whimpering into his open mouth. I'm weak with it, my arms falling limp at my sides as it takes me.

"That's it," he whispers against my lips. "Let it ride." He cups my cheek, his hand big, warm, solid, as he watches me come undone, his eyes burning.

Helpless, I grab hold of his hair, as another roll of sensation hits me.

"Drew. I…" I can't breathe. "I need…"

You.

"I know," he says as if hearing my silent plea. "I know."

He captures my hand, forcing me to stay with him as he plucks my nipple and grinds his hips. I'm at the precipice when he loses control. A shudder runs over him and then he levers himself up on his arms and pounds into me. Flesh slaps against flesh. The impact makes my hipbones ache. I'm so wet, so messy wet, that every sound is magnified. And I love it.

"You're so fucking perfect," he rasps, moving his hips with a swivel, raw and greedy, like he's rutting against me, and my world goes dark and violent with lust. I'm coming again, the sensation punching into me, making me arch up, my hips chasing his, my hands clawing at the hard swells of his shoulders.

Drew lets go with a long, low groan, and a flood of warmth fills me up.

For a moment we lie quiet, Drew curled around me, his cheek against mine, the corners of our lips touching as we pant. Slowly, I come back to myself, aware of his fingers stroking my shoulder and the pulse of his cock within me.

It's so quiet that when he whispers in my ear, my whole body shivers from the sound. "You've destroyed me, Anna Jones."

I know exactly what he means, because he's destroyed me too.

TWENTY-ONE

ANNA

BENEATH THE COVERS where it's warm and quiet, we can't stop touching each other. Nothing obvious, just small caresses. A stroke of a finger along a shoulder, a tickle down an arm, a brush of lips across a temple.

We're face-to-face. Drew's arm snakes under my neck and wraps around my shoulders, holding me close enough that we share the same air, our legs threaded together in a hot tangle. I don't want to move. I want to keep my hand where it rests upon his sweat-damp chest and feel his heart's steady rhythm. I want rest. I feel like I've been running forever.

"Congratulations again on your win tonight." I speak in hushed tones, not wanting to rupture the fragile little world we've co-cooned ourselves in.

Drew's answering smile is one of lazy satisfaction. His big, warm hand curls protectively around my neck and his thumb traces my jaw. "It was the sweetest win ever."

Slowly he pulls me in. His smile grows, even as he gives me an easy, butter-soft kiss. He hums and does it again before easing back. "I finally got Anna Jones to let me kiss her."

His words take a second to sink in, and then I snort. "Dork."

Drew chuckles low, but he's kissing me again, soft, seeking little kisses, like he's memorizing my lips with his.

"Am not," he murmurs against them. "You think winning a football game compares to that victory? Please." The tip of his tongue touches the corner of my smiling mouth before his lips follow. "You must be crazy, Jones."

His hard cock is a silken weight brushing against my side. And then he's rolling over onto me, slipping his hips between my spreading thighs. I wrap my arms around his shoulders and sigh. "Well, someone's crazy," I say. "That's for sure."

"Mmm." Drew kisses my neck, my jaw. "Someone is," he says at my ear, making me shiver and hold on tighter, as his hips rock gently, sliding along the wetness of my sex.

He'll soon sink into me. But not yet. He likes to tease. And I love it when he does.

In the lambent light of the lone bedroom lamp, his eyes are dark gold. His touch is achingly tender as he brushes a knuckle along my cheek. "Kiss me, Anna," he whispers, his lips inches from mine.

And I'm lost. My hand feels too heavy, shaky as I reach out to thread my fingers through his silky hair and pull him down. My mouth moves over his, slow, searching, pouring everything I am into him.

He responds with a little moan, his hips lifting, and then he's sinking back into me. Filling me up.

"Again," he demands as soon as the kiss breaks.

So I do. I kiss him as he works me, until we're both too weak to do anything more than hold each other, reduced to a shivering pile of exhausted limbs and mouths.

And when he threads his fingers through mine and whispers "Stay."

I do.

DREW

I'm exhausted. Long into the night, Anna and I reached for each other. I'd drift off to sleep, only to slip out of it when smooth hands slid over my ass or a hot tongue licked along my neck before traveling down. Anna, once satisfied, would sigh and fall asleep, all warm and soft against me, my hand cupping her full breast. I'd be unable to resist playing with her nipple, flicking and gently pinching it until she squirmed and turned in my arms with a murmured, "Again?"

Yes, again. Until we couldn't move anymore.

In the early morning hours, I slept with her warm weight against my side, her hand upon my chest as if keeping my heart guarded and safe. The simple act of sleeping has never been so good.

When we had to wake, I greeted her with kisses. Anna rewarded me with a wide smile and wrapped her legs around my waist to hold me there as we shared lazy kisses.

Now, after leaving her sleeping under my covers and taking a long, hot shower, I'm in the kitchen, knees weak and cock sore, my hands mildly shaking as I attempt to make scrambled eggs. I am failing miserably. When they turn brown and clump together in hard balls, I curse and shove the pan off the burner.

"Toast," I mumble to myself. "I can do toast."

"What's that awful smell?" Anna walks out of my room, wearing one of my T-shirts, which engulfs her to midthigh, and a pair of black yoga pants. My heart flips over in my chest.

"Hey." I shift over to block the evidence of my egg debacle. But she isn't looking my way. She wanders over to the mantel where my Heisman trophy sits. The swell of pride I feel over the fact that she notices it is probably ridiculous, but it's there all the same.

Her slim finger runs along the base where my name is etched.

"Got that my sophomore year," I say. "When we won our first championship."

She glances at me, her eyes bright. "This is kind of a big deal, isn't it?"

"Ah, yeah." The biggest in my career so far.

She isn't fooled by my humble act. "You're amazing, Drew."

So are you. I don't voice that, however. I'm in danger of dropping to my knees and confessing all at this point. Instead, I keep a casual slouch, as she walks toward me.

"Where'd you get the pants?" I ask, pleased that my voice doesn't crack.

She glances around the kitchen, her nose wrinkling as if she's scenting out the crime. But then she stops, runs a hand through her tangled curls, and smiles. "Stuffed in my bag in case of emergencies."

"Emergencies?" Like unplanned overnights with guys? I'm *not* going to be jealous.

"After Dave crashed into me with three gallons' worth of fruit punch during an alumni picnic, I've never gone into work without backup clothing."

But she's wearing my shirt.

Anna's curls tumble about as she shakes her head. "Unfortunately, no hair products, so I couldn't wash my damn hair."

It's then I notice her skin is pink from a shower. "In case you failed to notice, I do have shampoo."

She gives me a look as if I've just said a dirty word. "I'll wear secondhand clothes, buy cheap T-shirts from Target, but I am *not* using drugstore shampoo on this hair. Not if I want to walk among the living."

I can't hide my grin. "Oh, well, don't sugarcoat your distaste."

"It's fine for you. You're a guy. You could probably use soap on your hair and it'd look good. Annoying, tend-to-fuzz-out-of-control curls are a whole other story." She walks further into the kitchen and sees the eggs.

I cross my hands over my chest, feeling distinctly flustered. "I tried to cook."

Her lips twitch. "I can see that."

I shift my weight onto my other foot. "Not sure what happened."

A small laugh escapes her. I find myself laughing too.

"Too-high heat would be my guess." Her hand lands on my chest, right over my heart, as she goes up on her toes and gives me a kiss that makes my breath hitch. Instantly, my arms wrap around her. She feels warmer in the morning, softer. I kiss her back, exploring deep, and taste my toothpaste on her tongue.

Anna's voice drifts up between kisses. "You got practice today?"

I hold her just a bit tighter. "Yes. Damn it."

And she laughs, a slow, contented sound.

For the first time in my life, I want to skip practice. I don't want to do anything other than spend the day with Anna and convince her to stay another night.

I'm seriously considering letting her talk me back into the bedroom right now, but she pulls back and gives my chest a friendly pat.

"Then let's get some food in you. Eggs, I can make us," she says. "I just need some coffee first." She glances around my countertops.

"Uh…" I scratch the back of my head. "I don't have any."

It's like I've slapped her. She gasps, her face going pale. "What?"

"I don't have coffee, or a coffeemaker, for that matter."

I give her what I hope is an apologetic, peacemaking smile, because Anna starts to bristle. Like a fricking hedgehog getting ready to attack.

"How on earth do you not have a coffeemaker in your house?" Pacing the length of my kitchen, she lifts her hands up in appalled outrage. "In this gorgeous kitchen?"

"I suck at making it and get my coffee at a shop?" I offer helpfully.

Her nostrils flare in a huff. "You can't make coffee? Oh, come on, Drew. It's just grinds and water! Gah!"

"Believe me," I say as I pour her a glass of orange juice, "coffee can be royally fucked up."

Her lips quirk as she glances at the mess that used to be eggs. "Oh, I believe you."

It takes me two strides to reach her. She squeals when I clasp her waist and lift her onto the counter. But her thighs instantly part to make room for me, and I step in closer, setting my hands on the full curve of her hips, as she clutches my shoulders.

"So." I nip her upper lip, then her bottom one. "Now that we've established that you turn into a raging beast without your morning coffee—"

"I wouldn't say 'raging beast'…" She pauses with a grin and a blush. "Okay, fine, I'm a raging beast."

"A cute one, though." I kiss her once. Twice. "If you had your choice of coffee, what would it be?"

Her legs wrap around my hips, drawing me in as she explores my neck with soft lips. When she hits that spot, that damn spot that I feel down to my balls, I groan.

Her smile imprints on my skin. "Espresso," she murmurs, still busy with that spot. "Most mornings, though, I like lattes or a cappuccino."

"I could be wrong—" I lift a section of her heavy curls and kiss behind her ear "—but I don't think a simple coffeemaker would do the trick."

"You're right. You'd need a moka pot."

"What the heck is that?" I kiss my way to her jaw.

Humor warms her voice when she answers. "It's a pot for making espresso." Anna pulls back with a slight frown. "Sadly, I can't make it nearly as well as my mom. I really need one of those fancy espresso machines to achieve perfection. But I can't afford that."

"Well then," I say, "let's go get you some coffee."

"We're doing carryout," Anna says against my shoulder. "I'm a freaking hair catastrophe."

"What? You're perfect."

"Drew," she says in exasperation, "my hair looks as if I've been wind tunnel testing."

I lean back to inspect her, and she crosses her arms over her chest, her chin lifting in defiance. Okay, so her hair is a bit wild, swarming around her delicate face in a dark red, angry cloud. But that only makes her look like she's spent hours in my bed. I approve.

Wrapping my arms around her shoulders, I pull her in close, because, really, I can't keep my hands or mouth off her. "You're beautiful."

I'm not surprised when Anna rolls her eyes. My prickly girl.

"Beautiful." She says the word like it's a disease. "Typical."

"Why typical?" I fight a smile. She thinks I don't know her. But I do. And I know exactly where she'll go with this.

Her nose wrinkles, which makes her cheeks plump. Though I've caged her in with my arms, she manages to lift a hand and tick off her points on her fingers. "Why not funny, or smart, or interesting?"

I grab a finger with my lips and suck it in my mouth, making her shiver. Slowly, I draw back releasing her finger with care.

"You know you're all of that." I run my thumb along the crest of her cheek. "But I don't think you know how beautiful you are. So that's what I chose to tell you."

A slow smile curls the corners of her pouty lips. She's fighting it, though, which means I've touched a nerve. "Because I need to know I'm beautiful?"

"Yeah." I press a slow, lazy kiss on her mouth. "Yeah, you do."

Anna has confidence and has never hidden her body from me, which is a huge turn-on. But I don't think she's been appreciated for all that she is.

Her green eyes shine up at me with pleasure, and my heart clenches. Then her long lashes flutter closed as she kisses me back with gentle, languid attention, and my head spins. A small hum rumbles in her throat.

"And what do you need to know?" she asks, running her fingers through my hair. God, that feels good.

I sag into her, nuzzling the warm, fragrant spot on her neck where it curves toward her collarbone. My words come out muffled. "It's not my place to tell you."

"A challenge?" She sounds way too pleased about that.

"Maybe." I lick a path across her collarbone.

"Hmm…" Her hands cup my cheeks. She lifts my head and looks into my eyes as if she's searching for some hidden secret. "Well then, you're funny. Smart. Interesting."

While I'm happy she thinks that, it isn't what I need to hear from her. I'm beginning to regret challenging her. Because I can't tell her what I need without exposing my underbelly. So I resort to the safety of quips. "Not beautiful?"

"You are." Her grin turns cheeky. "But you know that already, don't you?"

"Maybe."

"You do."

I nip the tip of her nose. "Not as important to guys as it is to girls, I'm afraid."

"You're probably right." She snuggles closer, wrapping her arms around my neck, her hands playing with my hair again. I love the glint in her eyes. "Oh," she says lightly. "There's one other thing."

"What?"

Her expression eases into something soft. "I like you just the way you are, Drew Baylor."

Poleaxed. Again. My throat closes too tight to find my voice. I swallow convulsively.

"I like you just the way you are too, Anna Jones." *I'm crazy for you. I fucking adore you.* "Go put your damn hair up," I tell her instead. "And we'll get you some coffee."

TWENTY-TWO

ANNA

SLINKING INTO MY apartment in the middle of the morning, I feel like an intruder. I don't want to be here anymore. I want Drew. Disconcerting, as I'm more needy than I've ever been in my life. About anything. Though I'm pretty sure Drew is just as needy. It took twenty minutes of making out in his car before he let me go with a sigh and a promise to meet me after practice.

Practice and team meetings are not a choice but an obligation. I honestly don't know how Drew will manage, seeing as he barely slept. But his body is a machine—a gorgeous, perfect machine—and he knows how to operate it.

Despite his protests to wait for him at his house, which were varied and persuasive, I came home. It would be too strange waiting around in his house alone. Too much of an opportunity to think. And Lord knows I'm an expert at overthinking things.

So here I am, lips swollen, hair wild, holding tight to my keys to keep them from jangling, and tiptoeing past the living room on the way to my room. When the couch squeaks and a dark shape lifts from it, I do the sensible thing and shriek like a poked banshee.

The keys fly across the room, and Iris barely ducks in time to avoid them hitting her head.

"What the fuck, Anna?"

"Sorry." I sag against the living room wall. "You scared the ever-loving shit out of me."

"Must have been preoccupied, what with doing the walk of shame," Iris grumps before bursting into tears.

"'Ris!" I drop my bag and hurry to the couch. Only then do I realize she's a mess, her makeup smeared, her hair standing up on one end. Her clothes are rumpled and creased as if she slept in them. And judging by the dents in the couch cushions, she probably has. "What's going on?"

"Henry," she wails as I sit next to her. "He fucking...fucking..."

"What?" I grab her arm. If he hurt her...

"Cheated." She gets out.

Expecting the worst, this actually fills me with relief, but my heart aches for Iris. I'm not the touchy-feely type, but Iris is. I pull her into my arms, and she leans heavily against me.

"Oh, God, Anna, it was so embarrassing." She sniffles and reaches for the half-empty box of tissues by her feet. There's a snowstorm's worth of used ones littering the floor. "I went over there to surprise him, you know?" Her dark, wet eyes blink up at me and all I can do is nod, not liking where this is going.

"His roommate let me in, and I...and I..." She shudders. "I was wearing this slinky teddy..."

Hell.

"And waiting on his bed, when he...he... He fucking burst into the room with his tongue down some bitch's throat!"

Ouch.

A keening noise pierces the air as she leans forward, pressing her hands against her face. "They didn't even notice me until they were right on top of me!"

"Oh, 'Rissy." I stroke her hair. "I'm so sorry."

She rears up, her palms hitting her thighs with a slap. A wild anger lights her eyes. "And that piece of shit, *puta madre*, fuckhead had the nerve to shout at me." She stabs a thumb to her chest. "Because I came over without asking."

Her laugh is pained. "He was all, 'Shit, Iris? What'd you expect? We aren't married or anything.'"

She breaks into a rapid-fire string of Spanglish cursing that I appreciate if only for its inventiveness.

"I cannot believe he didn't even try to apologize!" I say when she calms enough to get a word in.

Iris whips around to face me. "Well, why should he? When Henry is *never* wrong." Her fists tighten on her thighs, and then she's crying again.

I can't do anything more than rub her back. "Do you want me to call George—"

"No!" She looks horrified. "He'll just make it worse by going over there and kicking Henry's ass."

And George would do a good job of it too. While he might be happy-go-lucky and obsessed with finance, George likes to keep in shape by practicing mixed martial arts.

"This is a problem, why?"

Iris scowls. "I don't want Henry thinking he's worth it." She scrunches down in her seat and scowls. "Besides, George will be all, 'I told you so, 'Ris.' Which I do *not* want to hear."

Mental note: bite back any and all urges to say "I told you so."

"He'll find out sooner or later." I hold up a hand when she looks ready to tear my head off. "But I'll keep quiet for now. Why don't you go take a shower, and I'll get us hooked up with some truly terrible and truly good munchies, and we'll have some quality veg time on the couch."

Iris smiles and leans in for a quick kiss on my cheek. "Thanks, Banana. That sounds good."

It takes me no time to run down to the corner store and fill my bags with goodies. I'm just getting back into the apartment when my phone dings.

Baylor: Hey, beautiful. Had a quick break between drills. What are you up to?

I smile wide. I am so gone on him. I want to dance in place. I want to run and hide. I settle for answering him back.

Me: My armpits in drama. Iris discovered Henry with another girl last night. It's bad over here.

Baylor: Damn. Sorry for Iris, but that guy is a POS

Me: The biggest. Iris was with Henry for two years. She's a wreck.

Baylor: I'm guessing you'll have your hands full?

Disappointment tugs with both hands on my breastbone.

Me: Epic girl time is imminent. Movies ordered. Junk food acquired. Dart board w/Henry's pic attached is being hung at this moment.

Baylor: Lol. I guess I'll be seeing you in class then.

Me: That's probably a good guess. ☹ Sorry.

Baylor: I'll console myself by hugging the pillow you slept on. Maybe the guys will come over & watch Snakes on a Plane with me. Sigh...

Me: Funny. 😜

Baylor: 😊 I'd call you at some point, but I want to live.

Me: I knew you were smarter than you look.

Baylor: See you, Jones.

Me: Later, Baylor.

Damn, I already miss him. An age-old panic tries to claw its way up my chest. Exposure. I feel it rip through my skin, and I rub the backs of my arms to prevent it from spreading further. It's just habit. Everything is fine. Everything is *wonderful*.

Iris shuffles back into the living room, her damp hair spreading wet spots on her Bieber shirt. His goofy, clean-teen smile mocks me. But Iris seems diminished, her shoulders curling in on themselves. I shove my phone into my purse and meet Iris on the couch to give her a big hug.

"I'm sorry, 'Ris." I kiss the top her head.

"Yeah, me too."

★ ★ ★

One tray of brownies and five Kahlúa and vodkas later, Iris and I have watched *The Hangover* (1, 2, and 3), *Bridesmaids*, and *Wedding Crashers*. When we realized the unfortunate wedding-based theme running through our DVD selections, we moved on to a TV rerun of *Die Hard*. Not that it helps.

When Bruce kisses his wife at the end of the movie, Iris throws a chip at the TV.

"God," snarls Iris from her sprawl on the couch, "is there any movie that does not have a romantic element in it?" She flops a pillow over her head and groans.

I'm not feeling much better, having consumed my weight in sugar. I ease to a sitting position, the room spinning slightly. "'Fraid not, butter bean."

She lifts the corner of her pillow and her dark eyes narrow. "Butter bean?"

We stare at each other for a moment before bursting out laughing.

"He wasn't even that great in bed," Iris says between chortles.

I don't want to know. But Iris is in a sharing mood. "Had like one mode. Fast, jerky, and oblivious. I swear to God, there were times my teeth would rattle."

"Iris!"

She glances at me with an evil grin. "It's true! He was like a wind-up fuck toy, you know? All…" Sticking her lip under her teeth, she bobbles her head as she thrusts her hips in rapid fashion.

We both laugh then, giddy giggles that are designed to drive out Iris's pain. But it only makes the room spin faster. Our laughter dies down on a gurgle, Iris's or mine, I can't tell.

"You know what the worst thing is?" Iris says to the ceiling. Her voice is suddenly somber, strained.

"What?"

"I knew he was cheating. I swear, I *knew*." Her nose reddens. "I just made myself believe it didn't matter. Shit, I am such a fool."

I turn to my side to fully face her. "You just wanted it to be okay. And he's the fool, not you."

Her attention remains on the ceiling as she expels a long sigh. "I can't blame him entirely."

"What the hell do you mean by that?" I lurch up. Not a good idea.

She glances at me, her dark eyes glistening. "Just that he isn't exactly in an easy position."

"I'm not getting you, 'Ris."

Iris shrugs, then hugs the throw pillow to her chest. "He's hot. He's the captain of the lacrosse team. A lot of girls throw themselves at him. And I don't know…" Another shrug. "How would I react to the same temptation?"

My mouth opens and closes as I try to speak. Is she serious?

"Iris, unless they're naked and landing on his dick when they throw themselves at him, Henry has no excuse screwing them when he's supposed to be committed to you."

The couch creaks as she turns to look at me. Her mouth is a flat line of protest. "Are you saying that if you constantly had guys hitting on you, you'd ignore them for Drew?"

Again, is she serious? Has she seen Drew? Nothing compares.

"Yeah, I'd ignore them."

Dark eyes bore into me. "And you think he'd do the same? That he isn't tempted on a constant basis?"

An afternoon's worth of junk food threatens to rise up my throat. I want to say that Drew would never do that. My whole soul cries it. But my jaw seems to have locked.

Iris's voice is low yet clear. "I mean, he's a star, way more than Henry ever could be. He's got his own Wiki page, TikTok and Instagram fan accounts devoted to him. He's his own character in a football video game, for crying out loud. He's met the freaking president. Of the United States. Did you know that?"

Dully, I shake my head.

"His last girlfriend was like a beauty queen."

Seriously? Now she's just being cruel. Does she think I want to know that Drew had a fucking *beauty queen* girlfriend?

An ugly too-close-to-raging-jealous feeling weighs down my

gut as I glare at her. "This is the South. Any halfway pretty girl with an ambitious mama has at least one crown on her mantel."

Iris scoffs as if I'm full of shit, and I swear to God if she tells me this old girlfriend rescued baby yaks in Tibet, I'm going to punch her.

But she simply shakes her head. "Do you have any idea how many women would kill to be in your place? How many of them are probably waiting for the opportunity to take it? Or maybe they have. As you keep pointing out, you're just hooking up."

My throat feels scratchy. "Why are you saying this to me?"

Her slim shoulder lifts. So nonchalant, as if, with a few well-placed reality points, she hasn't destroyed the contentment I've finally managed to achieve. I want to hit her. But I just sit there as she stares at me with sad eyes.

"I'm only pointing out that you never know. You think it's all good. You think he wants only you. But if you're with someone like that, you never know."

I rub the back of my arms and resist the urge to cower.

She doesn't even see me. "Maybe it's a good thing you've kept it casual. Save yourself the pain."

TWENTY-THREE

DREW

I STAND IN front of shelves lined with small cast-iron casserole pots in a rainbow of colors. "What the hell do you use these for?" I ask Gray.

In the act of crouching down to inspect a much larger pumpkin-colored pot, Gray glances up. "Individual servings."

"For who? Barbie and Ken?"

Gray snorts and stands. "Probably. I don't know, I guess you'd use it for an appetizer. Soup, maybe?" And now the little doll pots are the center of his attention.

When Gray picks up a bright blue individual pot, his hand nearly engulfs it. He frowns and sets it back on the shelf. "Yep. It's fucking useless. I don't even want a soup serving that small."

With assured authority, he moves on, and I follow with all the awkwardness of a guy who is in foreign territory. I roll my stiff shoulders, feeling like an ox in a dollhouse.

Women cast wary glances our way. We're not the only guys in the kitchen supply store, but we are the youngest, biggest, and scruffiest with our battered sneakers and worn jeans.

Gray's irritated expression shifts to thoughtful. "Man, wherever I get drafted, it had better be to a city that gets cold enough for soup."

"Soup? That's your criteria?" I don't know if Gray has an actual team or city in mind. It's an unwritten rule that you do not say what team you want to play on. The disappointment would be too harsh if it didn't happen, and chances are it won't. For that reason alone, I've never stuck my hopes on any one team.

"Never underestimate the power of soup." Gray shrugs. "I like cold weather. Fall. Winter. I don't want some tropical shit. Even if it means freezing my ass off playing in the snow."

"So you won't say 'no' to Green Bay then?"

"Let's not go crazy now. I'd like to refrain from freezing my balls off too."

"Man, please. We're from Chicago. It's a miracle we got through puberty without freezing our balls off."

We both snicker.

"What about you?" Gray sounds almost melancholy. I get that. We're so close to it now. Early on, when the NFL was more of a distant fantasy, we would entertain ourselves by lying around and talking about what we wanted from our careers: Super Bowl, MVP, passing records, yardage records. In short, the obvious stuff. Now it's only months away. And though we've both been courted by scouts from just about every team, in all likelihood, we'll no longer be playing together. Which sucks.

"Honestly? I want the team dynamic. I want the same synergy."

"Dude, I wouldn't hold my breath on that."

"Not going to." Because we both know that the NFL is a hard-ass business. The best get paid un-godly amounts to keep it going. Not many teams are going to be able to shell out for top talent in all positions. Not to mention the egos involved, which always adds another level of shit that you have to deal with.

I rub my sternum and pick up a spatula that resembles a Mickey Mouse head before dropping it back in the bin. "I want a big city that has diehard fans, coaches that don't suck, and a GM that doesn't have his head in his ass."

"An owner that doesn't want to play back seat coach would be cherry too." Gray's grin is wide and wry.

We make our way toward the opposite side of the store.

"So, Anna...?" Gray waves a hand in lazy fashion, as if asking me to fill in the blanks. "What's going on with you two? Something's changed, that's for damn sure."

A goofy grin pulls at my mouth. I can't hide it.

He rolls his eyes. "That bad?"

"Nothing bad about it." In fact, it's so good, I wonder if a person can die from pleasure. I'm willing to test the theory. As soon as I can get her to myself again.

We stop before a row of the gleaming steel appliances.

"I don't understand you, Drew. Putting this much effort into a girl? It's like you've lost it."

I finger a price tag. $1,500 dollars. As a rule, I don't spend much on myself. On Anna? I wouldn't balk at $15,000. Have I lost it? I don't care. Making Anna happy makes me happy.

"Can you explain to me how it feels to take the ball down the field for a TD?" I ask.

"You're trying to equate the perfection of playing football to getting laid?" He gapes. "Are you shitting me? Seriously?"

I smile then, partly because I'm thinking of Anna, but mostly because I know I'm going to freak Gray out, which is always fun. "No. I'm explaining the perfection of being with Anna to playing football."

"I'm going to be sick. All over you," he adds with a sour look.

"That's your problem, Gray. You don't know what it feels like to fall for a girl. If you did, you wouldn't question it." I slap his shoulder. "Now, help me pick this shit out, will you?"

ANNA

Funny thing about life, it's so easy to view it from the outside in. We can see the exact point where our friends fuck up, do the wrong thing, are blind to what's right in front of them. As in, why the fuck won't they just listen to us and take our advice instead of bumbling all over the place?

We watch horror movies and know when to shout at the clueless girl who goes in the basement to investigate that noise; we revel in her stupidity, feel superior to it. If it were us, we assure ourselves, we would do everything right.

Sure we would; we just wouldn't realize the danger. Because the truth is, we're all blundering through life like automatons half of the time. And even though I can tell myself this afterward, after I fuck up, it doesn't make me feel any better. Because I'm about to do a fuck-up *royale*. With cheese. I feel it in my bones, like an inevitable death I can't escape, but I do it anyway. And part of me knows this even as I hurdle down the path toward destruction. The bigger part of me, in fact. Does that make me dig in my heels and try to stop? Of course not. I'm the girl walking down those dark stairs into the basement. The truth is, I've been her since this all began.

TWENTY-FOUR

ANNA

FROM THE WINDOW, the quad is a carpet of green, ringed by copper and gold-tipped trees. Branches sway in the gentle breeze and the golden leaves dance. A pretty picture. Students stroll past on their way to one of the many red brick buildings that line the square. It's all so silent, this vibrant life teeming just outside the window.

Inside, however, I'm facing the firing squad.

"Anything interesting out there, Miss Jones?" Professor Lambert taps her notepad with the tip of her pen.

I give her a half-guilty smile. "I love the fall. It's my favorite season." I'm pretty sure, from now on, I'll always equate Drew with crisp air and gilded sunshine.

The fine lines around Lambert's eyes deepen. "I prefer spring. The flowers and new green leaves." Evidently tired of dancing around her intended mission, she takes a small breath, and her focus tightens. "Tell me, Miss Jones, have you given any thought to what you might do upon graduation this spring?"

I knew the question was coming. It's why I'm here. Evaluation of my progress thus far and prodding into my future plans. As head of the department, Professor Lambert has met with me for similar discussions throughout my college career.

I lean back and cross one leg over the other. "I've given it thought." When I'm not thinking about Drew, I'm thinking about that. "But it hasn't gotten me very far."

Understanding softens her expression. "Don't let it worry you too much. For most of us, it takes a lifetime to truly figure out who we are and what we want. I'm merely trying to help you take a step in the right direction."

I had thought college would be that step but, apparently, not so much. It's only made me an intellectual dilettante.

"Have you considered graduate school?" she asks. "With your grade point average, I imagine plenty of programs would be interested in having you."

Having a 4.0 opens doors, true. It also kind of makes you think that academia is the only safe place for you.

"No. Honestly, Professor, I have no desire to continue with school right now." The thought makes me shudder. I study because it's my current job, but I don't have any passion for it. I'm freaking burnt-out on school as it is. And even though it scares the hell out of me, I want to be out in the world, a little fish in a big blue sea.

Lambert studies me, her head tilted to the side, as if by looking at me from another angle, she might unlock a clue of who I'm supposed to be. Well good luck to her. I've stared in the mirror for hours at this point and still haven't got a clue.

When she speaks it's cautious. "I understand you are involved with Mr. Baylor."

My body turns to lead in my chair while my heart begins to pound. "What makes you say that?"

This time, her smile is soft and wry. "Come now, Miss Jones. You two are in class with me. Give me a little credit, will you?"

I resist the urge to squirm like a child in my seat. Were we that obvious? Likely we were. It takes all my willpower not to look at Drew, not to reach out and touch him when he sits a foot away from me. And Drew has always been less circumspect. Every class, I feel the heat and power of his gaze on me like the rays of the sun.

"I'm not sure how this pertains to our conversation," I say.

She bites the corner of her lip, and in that moment, she appears much younger than her sixty-odd years. She leans forward, bracing her arms upon her desk, and her silver bobbed hair swings over her ears. "I realize this is none of my business—" an intro that never bodes well "—but it's easy to become lost in the fervor of love."

There's that *L*-word again.

"Which is understandable," she goes on. "But when it comes to someone like Mr. Baylor—"

"You fear I'll waste my potential on a football player," I finish for her. "And here I thought I knew better than that."

Her mouth purses at my sarcasm. "Mr. Baylor possesses a powerful personality, one that easily overshadows others. And while most of my fellow faculty members would be urging you to keep him happy, I'm more concerned about your life."

I lean forward as well. "You're right. It's none of your business. However, I can appreciate your concern."

The corners of her eyes tighten as she peers at me. "All I ask of you is that you consider yourself first. It is all I ask of any student, by the way. Even Mr. Baylor."

But we both know that Drew doesn't have to worry about being lost in me. His life is mapped out in glowing pinpoints of light.

A dark chasm opens up beneath me, threatening to suck me down. Because she is right, I have no idea who I am supposed to be, or what the hell I'm going to do once college is over and Drew's gone on to fame and fortune.

★ ★ ★

The edgy, disheartened feeling does not abate as I follow Professor Lambert into our class. I just want to go home and crawl under the covers. The room is too cold, and the tips of my icy fingers begin to throb as I take my seat and pull out my laptop. Due to the meeting, I'm early and Drew isn't here. But he will be soon.

I'd been looking forward to seeing him for days. Missing him and wanting him with a force that ties me in knots and robs me of sleep. Now anxiety roils within my stomach.

And then he's here. As always, I sense him before I see him. But when I do, I am breathless.

Drew stops at the entrance to the room and simply looks at me. Then smiles. His entire body seems to light up. Like he's plugged into me. And that energy bounces back over me, lifting the little hairs along my skin, tripping up the steady beat of my heart. Lost. I know that now. I've lost myself to him. Utterly.

His grin grows as he strides forward. He's so lit up, people stare as he walks by. And my pulse races faster. I'm practically bouncing in my seat with the need to jump up and wrap myself around him. But then I catch Professor Lambert's knowing gaze and tense. Fucking busybody Professor.

Drew stops before my desk. "Hey." Oh, that soft, for-me-only voice, it melts me every time.

Before I can say anything back, he leans down and captures my mouth with his. I feel it down to my core. The kiss is possessive, tender, and just enough to have me wanting to chase after him as he pulls away. But we're in class, so I brace my fists against the desk and keep still.

The glint of affection in his eyes tells me he knows exactly how affected I am. His warm hand cups my cold cheek, and I shiver.

"I missed you," he whispers before brushing a kiss over the tip of my nose and then slipping into his seat.

I start to give him a sidelong smile but notice the sets of eyes on us. Jesus. Everybody stares. They stop as soon as Drew notices them. But he doesn't seem to care. He simply moves his desk closer to mine, until our arms brush, sparking off more tingles of feeling over my skin.

When his fingers twine through mine, I lean into him. "Do you really have to give them more to gawk at?"

He snorts softly under his breath. "I'll never understand why they care what I do."

"I think it's more about who you do," I mutter darkly.

He laughs, his thumb caressing the back of my hand. "Well, I care about that too."

Another glance from Lambert, and I draw my hand from Drew's to open my laptop. He does the same, but he remains close to my side, touching me in small ways every chance he gets. And I feel suffocated, as if wrapped up in thick, hot wool. Not by Drew, but by the rest of the world, watching us from the corners of their eyes the whole time.

Notice of us doesn't let up after class. It follows us as we walk out of the lecture hall and onto the grass. Drew, as usual, is oblivious. He's more concerned about putting his arm around me and nuzzling my hair.

"God, you smell good," he says. "What is it that makes you smell so good, Jones?"

I can't help but laugh. "A liberal application of Moroccan oil to keep my hair from frizzing out of control is the likely culprit."

"Ah," he says with a small smile. "The expensive stuff that kicks my dime-store shampoo's ass, right?"

"You know it, babe."

I think it's the "babe" that gets to him, because as soon as I say it, I'm surrounded by Drew. One hand slides to my nape while his arm wraps around me to gather me close.

Part of me wants to melt into him and never leave. The other part feels as exposed as an open nerve. The better half of me wins as he kisses his way down my neck, heading for that spot that makes me his. I shudder, pressing my hand to his taut side.

"Call me babe again," he murmurs, his breath hot against my skin.

"Why?" I can't resist running my fingers through his hair.

His teeth graze a particularly sensitive spot. "Because I like hearing it."

My lips twitch, as warmth floods between my legs. "Babe."

"Mmm." He holds me closer. "Again."

"Goof." I laugh softly.

"Lay it on me, Jones," he insists, his own husky laugh lost in my curls.

"Babe. Babe. *Baby...*" The last one comes out far more tenderly than I intended.

I can feel him grin against my neck. "Come home with me tonight. I have something for you."

"I bet."

"That's my dirty girl," he teases.

Then I hear them, the voices of two girls who aren't trying to hide their disdain. "Oh my God, that cannot be who he's with."

"Her? Why her?" says the other. "Because I could so rock his world better than that."

"Look at the size of her ass. Just no."

The comments come at me like rapid gunfire, ripping through my skin and shredding my insides. I don't think Drew hears them. He doesn't tense or even flinch as he nips and nips the curve of my neck, his hands going to my ass to squeeze it. My ass that currently feels five sizes larger than usual.

I jerk back, bracing my hand on his chest to keep him from following.

His eyes are hazy, confused, and he gives a slow blink as if to clear his thoughts. "Does it tickle?" He looks far too pleased at the prospect.

"Not here." I refuse to look at our audience.

"What about here?" A crooked smile tilts his lush mouth as his warm palm skims up the back of my neck to cup the base of my head.

His lips capture mine, soft, searching, and it's easy to forget the world. He hums in the back of his throat, an irresistible sound that makes my knees weak. I can't help but grip the front of his shirt, if only to hold on.

A muffled, evil giggle, breaks through my fog. "Slumming much, Baylor?"

"Maybe he lost a bet."

I can't stand it any longer. I tear free.

"No," I say to Drew. "Not *here*."

Out of the corner of my eye, I can see the two girls, now joined by a third, watching. And it's humiliating.

"Anna," Drew says, oblivious and confused. "What are you talking about?"

He makes a furtive gesture to touch my cheek but pauses when I tense, he glances in the direction of my fleeting gaze. Dark color floods his cheeks and his brows snap together. "Are you kidding me?"

His voice carries across the quad, and I stiffen further. My gaze darts around. A few people are slowing down. Watching. I can see it in their expressions: What's Baylor doing with that girl?

"Keep your voice down," I say. I hate scenes. *Hate* them. My face burns in mortification.

Drew looks like he wants to punch something. "Why? Because someone might know that we're together?"

"That's not—"

"Right," he snaps, cutting me off. "We're just fucking." He's really yelling now. "How could I forget?"

I want to die on the spot. More people have drifted to a stop. Drew sees me looking, and scowls over his shoulder at the girls watching with wide eyes.

On a curse, he grabs my elbow. His grip is firm but doesn't hurt as he marches me over to a stand of trees at the edge of the quad. It gives us a bit of privacy, but we're still exposed. *I'm* still exposed. I have to stop this, to explain. But I can't seem to say a word. I don't have to. Drew's going at me again.

Hurt and anger color his words as he leans over me. "So I can put my dick in you. You can suck me off—" I wince. "I can go down on you until you scream my name," he adds with a sneer. "But the very idea that I might try to kiss you in public is so horrific to you that you actually fucking flinch away."

My lip trembles, and I bite it. God, I've hurt him. I'm hurting him now. I need to fix this, but my mind and body are shutting down. "I just…"

"Just what?" he presses. "Just don't want people to know that you're…" His mouth works, but no words come, and his jaw bunches, his eyes going bright with frustration.

"I'm what?" I can't help but ask. A coward? Yeah, I know that. I know it well.

But he doesn't say that. He says something much more painful.

"Mine!" he shouts. "That you are mine!"

The ground beneath me sways, tilts back. My head hits the trunk of the tree. *His.* I can't even fathom a world in which I belong to someone. It's never happened to me. No one has ever wanted me that completely. He'll see that. Eventually he'll see what the others see.

"We. I." I take a breath. "We were never supposed to…"

"Yeah, I got that." He rakes a hand through his hair. "You made it quite clear what we are and what we aren't." The corners of his eyes are creased. Pain there. Disappointment.

I'm not worth it. I want to shout it to him. I'm not worth his pain. He has the world in his palm. He doesn't need the burden of me. But I can't move. I'm frozen.

It's his turn to look away, his fist going to his hips, his head ducking as he presses his lips together. A lock of hair drops over his forehead.

His voice turns low and bitter. "I mean, God forbid that perfect, classy Anna Jones be seen with Drew the man-whore, right?"

What? He's got it all wrong.

He shakes his head on a snort. "You don't even know how

fucking ironic that is." His gaze catches mine then, and his is burning. "You haven't got a fucking clue."

I can't stop myself then. "Drew. I don't want to hurt your feelings."

"Says the girl who doesn't have any feelings."

I blink rapidly, wanting to cave in on myself. I don't even know what I can say. I knew this would end sooner, rather than later. I wasn't meant to be his. Even as I think the words, I know I'm fucking up in the worst possible way.

Helpless, I reach out. My fingers graze his forearm. And he explodes like I've sliced into him.

His arm flies up and he takes a huge step back.

"No!" He grips his hair at the back of his head as if he might pull it out. "I tried to give you space, give you time. I thought that you were just scared, shy— Fuck, I don't know what, *something*."

God, he knows me so well, I want to cry. But he's not done. "But I was just fucking kidding myself. You just didn't want me the way I wanted you."

"No, Drew, it was—"

"Tell me I'm wrong then," he insists, his voice raw. "Tell me that this whole hooking up bullshit hasn't been about who I am."

My throat hurts so badly that the words feel like broken glass. "It was."

His expression goes blank, his gaze going right through me. And my heart plummets. I've done this. I've made him look at me like I'm a stranger.

"You know what? I don't need this." He's backing away. "I don't need any of this." Even though I know what's coming, it still plunges in like a knife when he finally says it. "I'm done. We're done."

And then he walks away.

TWENTY-FIVE

ANNA

I'M DEAD INSIDE. My emotions have locked down so tight, I hardly feel a thing, just the dense weight of my body as it moves me along. Like I'm pushing through thick, cold sludge. I don't even know how I end up at the local coffee shop. I must have walked. Must have ordered; there's an untouched latte sitting by my laptop. I'm writing…something. My midterm on Queen Elizabeth and the use of virginity as a means of political power.

Perfect. I don't even want to look at what I've written. If it's any reflection of my thoughts, I've said something along the lines of: Remain a virgin. Do not engage. Run away while you can.

Not that refraining from sex would have protected me from Drew. He'd burrowed beneath my skin before he'd laid a finger on me.

People come and go, and a few glance at me, as if they know me. I don't get it, but I also don't really care.

I'm about to leave when Iris finds me. Her smile is the overly bright one she uses when she wants to cheer me up.

"I guess you had a rough day," she says, as she sits in the chair opposite me.

"What are you talking about?" We both know. But I don't know *how* she knows.

"It's all over social media that Battle Baylor had a 'lover's tiff with some foxy redhead' on campus today."

Foxy? Wait, what?

"People fucking talk about that?" is all I can blurt out. Holy shit. It's on social media? Who the hell are these people? Don't they have a life?

Iris looks at me as if I'm ignorant. "Of course they talk about it! He's Drew Baylor, girl."

"And how the hell did you even see this?"

Iris shrugs. "There's several hashtags. #BattleBaylor, #BaylorsBootieCalls, #BattleBaylorWorksOut, #BestOfBaylor. I follow them."

"You follow them? Are you kidding me?"

"Me and thousands other people. I started to follow them when you hooked up with him."

I groan and press the cold heels of my hands against my aching eyes.

"Don't worry, sweetie." Iris gives me a sympathetic pat on the shoulder. "At least there's no video. Not yet anyway. Though I haven't checked Instagram or TikTok in a while. We'll do that later."

"Oh, God." I hadn't even considered videos. I want to die. Just die. I think I might if there is photographic evidence of Drew shouting at me. My chances are nil. I officially hate fucking social media. I'm banning myself from it. For life.

"So." Iris picks up my coffee, finds it cold and sets it back down with a frown. "What happened? You get tired of all that endless sex?"

The question punches into me like a fist. She's grinning as if my heart hasn't just been ripped out of my chest. Apparently, I've been too effective in my protest that Drew and I were nothing serious. Either that, or misery loves company. Whatever it is, I want her gone.

"I don't want to talk about it."

"Did you ask for exclusivity, and he gave you the brush-off?" There's a hard glint in her eyes. "Because I'll kick his ass if he hurt my Anna Banana."

"I don't know what's worse," I say dully. "The fact that you think I was part of some harem or that you think I would be begging."

I don't address the laughable idea of Iris kicking Drew's ass. That part is kind of sweet. Even if the twerp just called me desperate.

"I know." Iris snaps her fingers. "You fell in love with him and blurted it out. And now he's running scared."

That is it. I'm done. I collect my laptop and shove it into my bag.

"No," I say in a falsely bright voice. "It was because he wanted to kiss me in public, and I treated him like he had the fucking plague. And when he said he wanted me to be his, I was too worried about what other people thought of me to say yes."

I stand and shoulder my bag as she gapes up at me. "Don't you know? I'm incapable of falling in love and all that emotional shit."

Night finds me alone, listening to Trent Reznor sing "Closer," the volume so loud that poor Siouxsie's picture vibrates against my wall, in danger of falling to her doom.

At least I'm not wallowing on the floor, hugging a pillow like the poster child for broken hearts everywhere. No, I'm beating the shit out of the punching bag George set up for me on my twenty-first birthday. Because, as he said, I ought to be able to beat the shit out of something now and then.

But the only person I want to beat up now is myself. My knuckles hurt as I pummel the hard bag. It isn't enough. I hit it again and again. Sweat pours down my face, burns my eyes. I don't hear the door open or his footsteps as he crosses the room.

I don't even notice him until he stands next to me. My breath saws in and out as I halt, resting my gloved hands on my hips.

George's dark eyes take everything in. Sadness and sympathy dwell in those eyes of his, but he does his best. "Nine Inch Nails?" he asks. "Really, Banana?"

Poor Trent, so misunderstood in this song. It's not about fucking. It's about need, desperation for salvation. My eyes burn and I fight for a breath.

"Seemed appropriate," I say. And then burst out crying.

George pulls me in and hugs me tight. A few seconds later, Iris comes into the room. The three of us huddle together, but they're the ones holding me up.

DREW

My feet hit the pavement with a loud *thump, thump, thump* that pounds right into my head. I don't know where I am or where I'm going. I just run. My shins burn and my throat is raw, but that's nothing compared to the yawning chasm spreading over my chest. Pain. It pushes out from my heart and through my bones, my veins, my skin like a thick, ugly sludge. Holy fuck, it hurts.

I pick up my pace, trying to outrun the pain. It only grows.

What have I done? What have I done?

The ugly scene replays itself. I remember my words, the way they flowed from my mouth as if I was outside of myself, unable to control them. But I didn't stop, and she didn't contradict me. She didn't make one protest when I walked away.

Defeat has never sat well with me. But this isn't a game. Games come and go. You win some, you lose some. There isn't anyone else like Anna. I can't simply go out and replace her. And I've just lost her.

My gut clenches hard. I'm going to be sick. I've pushed it too far. My knees hit the pavement a second before I throw up in the grass. It's violent, but it doesn't purge me. No, that sick feeling simply returns, filling me back up.

I sit on my ass, panting, sweat trickling into my eyes. Birds chirp. Someone's starting a car. In the distance, a woman calls for her kid to come inside. I wipe my mouth and hug my knees to my chest.

I miss my parents. I miss them so badly that the hole Anna left in my chest when she ripped out my heart grows so large that I fear I might fall apart. I want to talk to them. Which is ironic, considering that when they were alive, I never discussed my love life with them. Were they still alive, I probably wouldn't talk now either. But I would have gone home, had dinner at their house, and let their idle conversation wash over me until I felt some semblance of normalcy. Instead, I feel more alone than I've ever been.

It's enough to make me want to shout. I force my legs to lift me up and keep moving.

Hobbling home, stomach aching, pain spreading, I don't think of anything other than putting one foot in front of the other.

The house is quiet when I let myself in. It's always quiet. But now the silence scrapes along my skin. I just might hate silence now.

My hand shakes as I help myself to a bottle of sports drink. It tastes foul to me, bitter and off, but I gulp it down. Rivulets of sticky drink run down my chin.

Then I spy it, sitting on my counter like a fucking mockery. The brand-new shiny chrome espresso machine. My vision goes red as something hot surges up through my body. The bottle in my hand flies through the air, smashing in an explosion of bright orange on my cabinets. And then I'm reaching for the machine, ripping the cord from the socket with enough force to crack the socket cover.

Sharp steel pokes my arms as I kick my door open and hunt down the garbage can.

With a shout, I slam the stupid machine into the bin. I want to stomp on the thing, fucking punch the hell out of something, but I catch sight of my elderly neighbor Mrs. Hutchinson gaping at me. The tiny woman appears ready to keel over. Shit.

Clamping my mouth shut, I turn and slam back into the house. I stand in the empty hall, clutching the back of my neck and struggling for deep breaths as rage runs rampant through me. My chest lifts and falls, my teeth aching where I grind them together. And then the rage simply flees. Only it leaves me with something worse, an insidious pain that nearly brings me to my knees.

I stagger to the shower and stay there a long time. By the time I can stand again, my throat is swollen and my body is weak. I don't want to think about anything.

When Gray arrives, I'm sitting on the couch, playing *Call of Duty* in the dark.

As usual, he barges into my house and flicks on the lamp next to the couch. "I'm going to assume you meant to cram that thousand-dollar espresso machine into your garbage."

I grunt and continue to annihilate targets without mercy.

"I took it," he adds, as if I'll care.

"Knock yourself out." It hurts to speak, so I decide to refrain from doing any more of it.

Gray sighs and comes further into the living room. I catch the scent of some smoked meat product but don't bother to look. I don't want anything to eat anyway. But my attention shifts when he sets a six-pack on the coffee table with a plunk. The bright green bottles seem to glow against the dark wood. A lump gathers in my throat. Green River soda pop. I loved that shit as a kid. My dad used to let me have them during summer barbecues.

"Where…" I clear my throat. "Where'd you get that?"

You can only really find them in Chicago.

"Special order. I meant to give it to you on your birthday," Gray admits, settling on the couch beside me after he puts down the other bag, the one containing food by the smell of it. "But I figured you'd appreciated it more now."

No need to ask how Gray knows; this fucking campus spews gossip with the power and efficiency of a fire hose.

"They've been sitting in my fridge," he continues. "Because if we're going to drink what looks like toxic waste, it ought to be cold."

The lump in my throat grows to epic proportions. The controller hangs heavy in my hand as I blink down at it.

Gray is silent for a moment then hands me a pop and pulls a hot dog from the other bag. "Now, I realize these aren't as good as a Chicago dog, but we'll have to make do. Because none of those bitches deliver."

I hold the ice-cold drink in my hand. "Thanks." Shit, if I say any more, I'll be bawling and embarrassing us both.

Thankfully, he doesn't say any more. We sit together, drinking lime soda, eating subpar hot dogs, and playing video games until it's dark out.

TWENTY-SIX

ANNA

THE NEXT FEW weeks are an exercise in perpetual misery. My state of comfortable numbness thaws. In its place an aching chasm opens. It is so big that I'm surprised when I look down at myself and don't find a gaping hole. All my effort goes into not curling over into myself, to remain upright each time I enter our shared class and see him. Not that my false front of calm matters. Drew won't even look at me.

Worse? He's changed seats. He selects a desk as far from me as possible, all the way at the opposite end of the room where I'd have to crane my neck to see him. Everyone notices, of course. He's their sun. Anytime he shifts position, their worlds go out of orbit. Mine most of all. I feel off-center, as if I might topple over in between the desks.

Every time he speaks up in class, my skin twitches and my heart does a little leap like it's trying to return to its owner.

I might have tried to apologize, but he leaves me no opening. He's out the door as soon as the professor gives the okay. Short of chasing him down, I'm not getting near him with any ease. I could do it, but my feet won't propel me forward. I just want it all to end.

What could I say to him, anyway?

I'm sorry, Drew, but I can't let go of my stupid old insecurity. You remember high school? And that chubby, awkward girl? There is one in every school. The one that everyone knows, but no one really sees? My school? Well, she had frizzy red hair and braces. She was too pale, too quiet. She never got asked to a dance. Never went to prom or made out in some guy's car. She never even experienced a kiss until she got to college.

And no matter what she tells herself now, that insidious fucking shame, those icy cold years of isolation, don't seem to leave her. It doesn't matter that she knows she attracts guys now. It doesn't matter that she knows she's smart, or that she has friends. Deep down, she's still that girl. Even when she fights to cut the line.

And she can't fucking breathe with the spotlight turned on her. Because they'll see. They'll all see that she's still that chubby girl who didn't fit in. And you're a spotlight, Drew. You dazzle her.

Yeah. Pathetic. Because I ought to be over it. I hate that I'm not. I hate my weakness. And I'd rather Drew hate me for the wrong reasons than feel sorry for me for the right ones.

Which only makes me hate myself more.

And so the pain continues as I follow him out of class the next week, only to stop dead when he meets up with another girl. She has cheerleader-sorority girl written all over her, from her size-four jeans to her bone-straight hair, falling like a shining sheet to her tiny ass. And maybe she carries a wealth of insecurities deep within her skin, but I hate her on sight anyway.

He gives her his bright smile, the one that used to make my knees give way, and she tucks her arm in his. And they look so good together that I stop. Maybe it's for the best. He deserves to be happy. Deserves someone who isn't a mess.

On the heels of that charitable thought comes a stronger one: Fuck. That.

I'm about to go tell him the truth. That I do care. I care too much. Then he turns his head, as if he feels me watching. Our eyes meet, and he cocks a brow as if to say, what the fuck are you looking at? As if to say, your chance is gone.

I turn around and leave without another glance.

DREW

The locker room reeks of mud, sweat, and defeat. I sit alone on the bench in front of my locker and stare down at my hands. Hands that managed to perform the three fumbles, four incompletions, and the interception that lost the game. Worst fucking game of my life.

Each breath I take sends shards of agony along my bruised back and hips. My head pounds so hard I fear my eyes will pop out. Low murmurs bump about on the air, but no one talks to me. I don't blame them. I am their leader, and I've let them down.

It's worse when Rolondo gives me a quick pat on the shoulder. "Happens, man," he says low and just to me. "It's in the past now."

I want to shrink down inside myself then. I'm the one who threw him the shitty passes, making *him* look bad on that field. That he knows why I've fucked up and isn't killing me over it has my throat closing.

Sweat trickles along my temples and burns in my eyes. But I don't move to wipe it away. I wait, quiet until the guys shower and change. Until they leave me.

I shower alone, standing under the hot water as a lump fills my throat, and then I turn off the taps. I'm dressed and zipping up my bag when Gray comes back in.

He looks at me for a long moment, his brows bunched together in a scowl. Yeah, I've fucked him over too. "Sorry" seems too trite.

His voice cuts through the silence. "Look, man, you've got to know I love you like a brother."

"Your brothers are all dicks." It's an old joke, said many times before, but my voice sounds like gravel and feels like glass against my throat. Humiliation crawls over me. Everyone loses now and then. But not like this, not by being a fucking bonehead and throwing away a game. One game is all it takes to lose a championship.

A small smile cracks his face. "Total dicks." He ambles in further. "More than a brother, then."

I want to smile, want to pretend it's all good. But I can't even look him in the eyes. I know I've got whatever it is he's going to say coming to me. God knows I heard more than an earful from my coaches.

"I don't want to bust your balls," Gray continues. "So I'll just say this once. Get your head out of your ass and get over this chick."

Easier said than done.

"We need your head on right, Drew. I appreciate you being upset for a while, but enough is enough. A piece of ass is not worth this shit."

My head jerks up. I glare at Gray, not daring to open my mouth. But he simply shakes his head and steps closer. "She's just some heartless bitch—"

I don't remember moving. A red haze fogs my vision as I slam him into the wall, my fists clutching his shirt. "Don't you ever..." I grind out through my teeth before my jaw locks.

Gray's mouth falls open. "What the fuck?"

Shit. Gray has been shoved around enough by people who are supposed to care about him. I step back, abruptly letting him go, and he sags a second before pushing upright, getting into my face.

"You'd fucking attack me over her?"

Taking a deep breath, I back away. "I didn't mean to do that. Just don't... Don't talk about her that way. She's not a bitch."

"I cannot believe this." Gray looks me over as if I'm a stranger. "Are you kidding me?"

I grab my bag and sling it over my shoulder. "You want someone to blame? Then blame me. I'm the one who lost the game, not..." I can't say her name.

"She dumped all over you!" His face is red.

I run a hand over my head where it aches so bad that my vision blurs. "She never lied. I did that to myself."

His eyes narrow as he stares at me, and then his brows lift high. "You're in love with her."

Fucking headache. My eyes are filling now. I blink once, hard and desperate.

Gray looks away, as if he's embarrassed for me.

Heat prickles over my skin. "I'm sorry I let you down." I head for the door. "It won't happen again."

ANNA

Iris has disappeared. She didn't come home on Friday night. Or on Saturday. Since she's currently "without boyfriend," I worry. Iris doesn't do hook ups. It took her six months just to have sex with Henry for the first time. So the fact that she isn't here bothers me. As does the fact that she isn't answering her phone or the ten texts I've sent her.

My worry grows, and I call George to ask if he knows where she is, which is the wrong thing to do because George goes deadly quiet on the other side of the line.

"You mean to tell me Friday is the last time you've seen her, and you're just calling me now?" George replies in a voice I've never heard before.

I grimace, my grip on the phone tightening. "I'm sorry. I was distracted."

"Shit." George lets out a heavy breath.

Cold sweat breaks out along my back. "I thought she was with you. She *said* she was with you."

George explodes. *"Puta mierda! Pendejo, cullo…"*

That he's cussing in Spanish makes me more afraid. Like Iris, George never does that unless he's beside himself.

He takes another audible breath before speaking again. "She fucking said she was going out with you!"

"You don't think she's with—"

"Yeah, I fucking do," George snaps. "I swear to God, I want to kick that little *pendejo* bitch's ass for touching my sister again."

Because if she's put both of us off with lies, we know she's with Henry. And I want to kill her. Death by pillow bludgeoning. Maybe if I beat her on the head enough with one, I'll knock some sense into her.

"I'm going over there," George says.

"If you kill him," I say, "make it look like an accident." I'm only half kidding.

George snorts before hanging up.

I'm making myself a frozen waffle and coffee when she finally answers my text-athon.

> **Iris:** Chill. I'm fine. And did you have to go and freak out George?

Though relief swamps me, I want to hit her in the head. My thumbnail taps hard against the screen.

> **Me:** Damn right I did. You scared the hell out of us, 'Ris!

> **Iris:** Okay, okay, I'm sorry. It was shitty of me to not call.

Scowling down at the phone, I tap out another message.

> **Me:** Where are you, anyway?

Though I know, I need written confirmation before I kill her.

> **Iris:** With Henry.

Me: WTF, Iris? He CHEATED ON U!

I can practically feel her fuming. The silent phone is a testament to it.

The ding sounds overloud in the kitchen.

Iris: Yeah, Anna, I know. I was there.

I roll my eyes and take a bite of my waffle, which has gone cold and hard. Another ding.

Iris: He had his reasons.

I toss the waffle aside and respond.

Me: Was it the falling into an unsuspecting vagina thing?

Yeah, I'm being a shithead, but I can't help it. How could she have gone back to him? Has she a freaking clue? He'll do it again. They always do it again. We've discussed this.

Iris: Funny. He was scared, ok?

I'd laugh, but she wouldn't hear it.

Iris: Things were just getting too intense for him.

Me: So he thought he'd simplify it by fucking some girl?

Or girls? Who knows with that assmunch.

> **Iris:** Look, people do stupid things when they're scared. And you should talk. You totally pushed Drew away because you're scared.

My face heats and my fingers fly.

> **Me:** I didn't cheat on Drew! We weren't even an official couple!!

> **Iris:** Yeah & why is that, A? Because you were ashamed to be seen with him? You treated him like your personal boy toy. How is that better?

Heat swamps my entire body now. It prickles behind my lids, and I want to chuck the phone across the room, see it shatter into a thousand pieces.

> **Iris:** Admit it, we always treat the ones we love the shittiest.

There's a rushing sound in my head. Bitch. That total bitch.

> **Me:** I don't love Drew.

> **Iris:** Right. Whatever you say.

I'm punching out letters so hard now that my nail hurts.

Me: We're not talking about me right now. We're talking about you.

Iris: And why can't we talk about you? Why can't we ever talk about you? Because you have it all figured out? That shit don't fly, A.

I slam the phone down on the counter. She doesn't want my help. Fine. Let her screw up her life. I'm done. Except I pick up the phone, ready to tell her exactly that. But she's sent another text.

Iris: That's right. It's my life. My mistakes to make. And at least I'm trying. What R U doing about your mistake?

I'm not going to cry. Even if the tip of my nose feels numb and there's a lump in my throat the size of an apple.

Me: There's nothing to do.

Iris: Call him? Say you're sorry?

My hand shakes as I suck in big breaths of air.

Me: He's MOVED ON! OK!?! He moved the fuck on. End of story.

And so did I. I'm fine. I'm *fine*.

When the phone rings, I pick it up out of habit. I don't even say a word, just accept the call.

Iris's voice comes through soft and hesitant. "Hey, girl. I'm sorry. That was harsh of me."

"It's okay," I mumble. I'd rather run naked through campus than talk to her right now, but hanging up would just make it worse. Iris would hunt me down eventually.

Iris sighs. "Look, I know you're just trying to protect me, okay? And I love you for it."

Kind of hate you right now, Iris.

Which she must know, because she keeps pushing. "And what I said about you and Drew..." She pauses. "I'm sorry. I've been an insensitive bitch about the whole thing. I didn't realize... Just. Just take it easy this weekend, Banana. Okay?"

"Yeah." I clear my throat. "Sure."

"I gotta go," she says. "Henry's up and—"

"Right." I toy with the handle of my mug. "Okay, then."

We hang up with awkward mumbles of goodbye.

TWENTY-SEVEN

ANNA

FOR THE FIRST TIME, I am not happy that it's my birthday. I'm not in the mood to celebrate. Drew's birthday was yesterday. And though I'm the jerk who pushed him away with both hands, somewhere in the back of my mind, I'd planned to celebrate our birthdays together. At the very least, I'd have found a way to be with him on one day or the other. Who did he celebrate it with? Will he think of me today?

Sitting on my bed in the empty apartment, I curl over on myself, pressing a hand to my chest. When is the pain supposed to end? I feel so hollow, yet so heavy with hurt that I can barely move. Sleep is no longer a comfort. Every moment I've spent with Drew plays in a loop in my head. When I wake, my pillow is damp, and my cheeks are tight with dried tears.

I'm walking out to meet George downstairs when I trip over the box on my doormat. It's a present, large and square, and done up in plain white paper and a black ribbon. An envelope is tucked under the ribbon. I can't see any writing on it, but instantly my heart is thumping so loud I hear its thud in my ears. I'm almost afraid to pick the present up.

From outside, a horn blares. Grabbing the package with clumsy fingers, I run out to the car.

"You aren't supposed to get yourself presents, Anna," George jokes when he sees the package in my hand.

"Ha." I tried to laugh, but I can't.

We drive off, the present cool beneath my sweaty palm. Staring out the window, I press my fingertip against the hard corner of the card until it bends. Should I open it now? At least see who it's from? I think I know. But I might be wrong. I'm not sure what would crush me more, if I'm right or if I'm wrong.

Only one way to know. And I can't wait until I get home. My fingers tremble as I pull the envelope free and rip it open. It's a plain white card with "Anna" printed on it in hard, masculine script.

My breath seizes at the sight and a wounded sort of wheeze escapes. I don't even know if it's Drew's writing. I'm only guessing. How sad is that?

Fumbling, I open the card.

> *I bought this before—*
> *Seemed petulant to waste it.*
> *Happy Birthday.*
>
> *—Drew*

I haven't cried in weeks. I won't let myself. But staring down at the wrapped present, I feel a familiar burn and tickle behind my lids. My throat constricts so hard that I struggle to swallow. I can't bear to rip into Drew's present. I want to keep it just as it is, in the precise way he last touched it. But something waits inside for me, and I have to know what it is.

The car speeds along the highway as I carefully pull the ribbon free and attempt to open the present without tearing the paper.

Inside is a box, and when I lift my present free, a sob wrenches out of my chest. It's a framed Siouxsie and the Banshees album cover—*JuJu*, circa 1981. And it's signed by the entire band. A rare and wonderful thing that I don't think anyone else in the world would know that I'd love.

Like that, I'm a veritable fountain of tears, snot, and heaving sobs as I clutch the frame to my chest.

George casts me a horrified look. "What the hell? Anna, talk to me."

I can't. Not without dying a little more inside. "I'm sorry. I'm PMSing."

While George's look of horror grows, I sniffle and search for a tissue in my bag. I find a crumpled cocktail napkin that scratches my face when I use it. "The present is from my mom," I lie. "I guess I'm homesick."

He doesn't look convinced. In fact, I'm sure he knows I'm lying. But he lets it go with a shrug. "I guess it's good you're going home for break soon."

But my home isn't a place anymore. I've realized too late that it's a person. And I've torn him from my life.

DREW

I turned twenty-three yesterday. Ever since my parents died, I've hated my birthday. It only serves to remind me that my family is gone, and I am essentially alone. Gray is clearly doing Anna damage control. He managed to talk me into seeing a movie yesterday—a sad sack way to celebrate, in his opinion. Now he wants to drag me out to do a birthday celebration with the guys, who aren't taking no for an answer. I'd rather pretend birthdays didn't exist.

I think about the present I left on Anna's doormat. Since the album cover arrived, I'd been wanting to see her expression when she opened it. Now I can only try to imagine. Did she smile in that quick and bright way of hers when she's surprised? Or did she smile with slow, blooming reluctance, like she's losing the fight with her emotions?

Did she even like it? Am I pathetic for giving it to her? Hell, if she ever found out how much I paid for it, I'd certainly look like a sap. But it wasn't as if I could return it; I'd bought it at auction.

Why am I torturing myself with this? I can't go back and beg for another chance. I have some pride. And I don't know how to fight for her and still keep it. Giving her the present was the last thing I could do. I can only hope she understands: I'm here, if she wants me.

"Take the L," I mutter to myself.

A knock on my bedroom door has me sitting straighter. "Be out in a sec," I call to Gray, who is waiting for me to get my ass in gear. Shit, I really don't want to go out. But a guy cannot tell another guy that he'd rather mope around the house. Not if he wants to survive the ribbing.

"You got a package." Gray's voice is muffled by the barrier of the door, but there's something about his overly neutral tone that has my chest clenching.

In two steps, I'm at the door, wrenching it open. He just stands there, a bland look on his face, holding out a wrapped present. For a moment, I frown. Is he being funny? It is from him?

But I can't imagine Gray using silver paper or an elaborate white silk bow. It's too feminine.

I have to clear my throat to speak. "Where'd you get it?"

Gray does a piss-poor job of hiding his wariness. "I thought I heard something on the porch. Found this leaning against the front door."

My entire body tenses against the need to run out of the house and search the street. It had to be Anna. Why didn't she knock? Hell, I hadn't knocked, maybe she thought that's the way I wanted to play it. Not really. I'd just chickened out like a total puss.

"Well?" Gray wags the box. "Are you going to take it? Or should I toss the thing?"

Before he can move to do just that, I grab the present from his hand. I don't look at it but hold the box down and slightly away from my body as if it might burn me. But my fingers dig into it.

Gray and I stare at each other while I remain immobile with indecision and doubt. Maybe it isn't from Anna. And why am I dithering like some old lady? I give Gray a dirty look, because he's starting to smirk, and shut the door in his face. No way in hell am I opening this potential bomb in front of him.

Going for the bandage approach, I rip open the package with one swipe. A card falls to the floor. With a shaking hand I grab it as I study the leather book the torn wrapping paper has revealed. *Emerson's Essays.* Gold-lined pages. Pristine condition. I sink to the floor, my back leaning against the bed for support. I smooth a hand over the cover and then open the card.

> *What do you get the guy who doesn't*
> *seem to want anything?*
> *I figured a bit of the past might be good.*
> *Happy Birthday, Drew.*
>
> *—Anna*

My fingers clench the book so hard I hear the spine creak. Pressing my forehead into my raised knees, I take deep breaths to keep it together. Doesn't want anything? Is she serious? I want to tear out of the house and hunt her down. Just so I can take her by the shoulders and shout, *"You! I want you, you stubborn, deluded pain in my ass!"*

At the same time, I pull the book closer to my chest. *Emerson's Essays.* She remembered. And she's given me back a piece of my parents. Did she know I'd be missing them on my birthday? I blink rapidly. Of course she did. Her note all but said it. Suddenly, I find it hard to breathe.

Another knock on my door echoes through my room. "Drew, man... You ready?"

Swallowing several times, I press my fingers against my too-hot eyes and find my voice. "Yeah."

I put the book and card in my bedside drawer and leave the room. Life goes on. Even if you don't want it to.

TWENTY-EIGHT

ANNA

IT'S 10:00 P.M. on a Friday night, and I'm at a club. On a date.

When Iris insisted I needed to get out of my funk and go on a date, everything in me recoiled at the idea. But then I pictured Drew's cold eyes meeting mine as he walked away with another girl. True, he gave me a birthday present, but his card said it all—he couldn't return it so it might as well have gone to me.

We are over, and I have to accept it and move on.

Cameron is perfect. He's lithe and dark. His black jeans hug his legs as they disappear into his vintage Pumas. His lean chest is covered by a tattered Mr. Yuck T-shirt, which frowns at me as he leans back and takes a pull of his beer. We've been discussing the places we'd like to visit in London, and I'm having fun.

Well, as much fun as a girl can have with a goddamn hole in her chest. A fucking empty hole that won't go away. But maybe tonight will be the trick and I'll find a way to fill it back up. I absolutely don't surreptitiously rub a hand along my breastbone when Cameron turns his attention toward the stage.

A band is about to perform, and the stage lights cast a halo of blue light over Cameron's black hair. Those glossy locks swing over his shoulders when he leans toward me, his breath holding a hint of beer as he talks in my ear. "I heard these guys are great."

I nod. I really don't know a thing about the band, but I'll take Cameron's word for it. He really is beautiful. Thick black lashes frame his blue eyes, and when he puts an arm around my shoulders?

I feel nothing.

I'm not willing to concede defeat. I don't move away when his warm fingers rest on the back of my neck. Pretty bold, considering we met about an hour before.

"So, how long have you known Iris?" he asks me.

Cameron works at the Juice Shop with Iris. She'd been trying to hook Cameron up with me for months. I resisted because of Drew—who I will *not* think about tonight.

"We met freshman year." I take a sip of my beer. It's gone flat. "Orientation."

"Cool." He tosses back a lock of hair.

It's such a perfect move, highlighting his sinewy muscles and showing off his glossy hair, that I wonder if he practices in the mirror. An unwelcome impulse tempts me to ask if he plucks out half-assed versions of "Crash Into Me" on the guitar.

I'm blinking rapidly into the stage lights when I see *him*. He's standing at the bar, and he's brought a friend. Although, by the way she rests her hand on his ass, I'm guessing *friend* isn't the word I should use. He doesn't seem to mind her groping. His smile is slow and easy as he hands her a beer and leans in to hear whatever it is she needs to whisper in his ear. He laughs a little, the broad expanse of his shoulders shaking.

I should look away. But as usual, my neck doesn't want to obey. No, I just sit and watch as they chat and her hand becomes more familiar with his ass. It barely registers that Cameron is still play-

ing with the edge of my shirt collar, the tips of his fingers glid-
ing along my skin, or that he's talking about his favorite bands.

I need to make an effort to drag my attention back to my date.
It would suck if Drew saw me staring. I'm almost in the clear
when Drew turns, his gaze scanning the crowd in a lazy fashion,
and his eyes lock onto me.

Caught, I can only stare back. He's more than twenty feet away.
The air is hazy and dim. Heads bob and weave between us as
people walk past the bar. And yet it's as if he's right in front of me.

Did he like the book?

Just as Drew had, I'd bought it long ago. But, unlike Drew, I
was too chicken to give it to him. Until he'd given me my gift.
I should have sucked it up and handed it to him in person, but I
didn't have the guts to face him.

The ache in my chest digs in, and my palms tingle. I can't
move, locked in his gaze as I am. I want to go to him so badly
that my thighs tense, as if I might rise. But then the connection
is broken.

He turns his attention to Cameron. Or rather, to Cameron's
hand. Even from this far away, I know that's what he's looking
at: Cameron touching me.

Drew's eyes narrow. His expression isn't pretty, and it's so
intent that I wonder if it's what a linebacker sees just before he
throws a touchdown pass right over their head.

Suddenly, I'm angry. He has no right to scowl like that when
he's got some groupie taking hand measurements of his ass. And
that lovely thought draws me right into queasiness. Especially
when I see Miss Cop-A-Feel wrap her arm about his waist. Now
she's stroking his stomach. *My* spot.

"Excuse me," I say to Cameron. "I'll be back."

Luckily Cameron doesn't ask why I need to get away. I don't
look in Drew's direction as I make my way to the bathroom.

Inside, I run cool water over my wrists. Always go for cool-
ing down the wrists. Splash water on your face, and it's a given
that someone will enter the bathroom. And they'll know you're

upset. Best, they'll look at you with pity. Worst, they'll ask you if you're okay while looking at you with pity.

The wrists, however? You can easily pretend you're just washing your hands.

I stand there until my fingers grow numb. I don't look into the mirror. I don't know if I'll like what I see. A few drops of water hit my belly and I flinch, breaking out of my fog. My black T-shirt is riding up, exposing a strip of skin over my jeans. The damn shirt is too tight. This is Iris's brilliant addition to tonight's wardrobe choice. Because, in her words, "if you have boobs like yours, you got to display them properly." Low-cut tops, Iris insists, are cheap and uninspired.

"But remain fully covered in something that hugs your assets and guys can't help but want to see what's underneath. It's like the ultimate tease." Ladies and Gentlemen, the world according to Iris.

Right now, I'd be satisfied with a floppy tee and pajama pants. I want to go home.

Drying my hands, I tug one last time at the bottom of my shirt and then exit the bathroom. Only to walk directly into Drew's path.

He's leaning against the wall of the restroom hallway. It reminds me so much of the first time we touched each other that my knees go weak. Beyond him, the club is dark, and the music has started. Here, it's too bright. Every line on his face, the deep gold color of his eyes, the little hint of a dimple on his left cheek, is illuminated. And utterly familiar to me. It's like history repeating itself, and I wonder how my life would be right now had I simply walked away from him the first time we collided in a dark hall. But I didn't. And here we are. Here I am, broken.

Seeing him so close is pain. Having his attention, so long denied, now fully focused on me is both a warm blanket and a sharp blade.

He talks first, and his butter-rich voice sounds so good I press my palms against the grainy wall to keep from touching him.

"Thanks for the book." His expression is blank, showing no

emotion, except for the creases at the corners of his eyes, as if looking at me burns.

It certainly burns to look at him. "Thanks for the album cover. It was… Well, I love it."

Hell. Now I'm gushing.

He frowns a bit, but then nods his head. "Same for the book." His eyes meet mine, and his words come out stilted. "I love it too."

Heat invades me. I can't do this. I can't stand this close to him and not touch him. I glance toward the bar, wondering if Cameron can see me, wondering if the girl Drew's with will come looking for him. This all feels wrong as if the world has flipped over on its head.

Drew notices the direction of my glance, and he stands taller, his shoulders stiff. "I see you found your emo boy."

I affect a careless shrug. "If we're going for accuracy, he's more hipster than emo."

When Drew glares, I continue sharply. "Isn't your date going to wonder where you are?"

The corners of his mouth curl. It is not a smile. "That's right, a date. I see you are familiar with the concept, despite all evidence to the contrary."

"I don't serial date like some, but I try to get out."

What am I doing? I don't want to hurt him. I just want to get away.

"Are you keeping track of who I date, Anna?" he asks softly, a smirk on his mouth.

I want to hit that smirk. I want to shout at him for plowing through what amounts to sorority row when less than a month ago he claimed that I was his.

"No, Drew," I say, suddenly weary. "I just know your MO."

He pushes off the wall and is in front of me in a fluid move. And some sick part of me loves when he crowds me. I love being surrounded by his strength and his heat. The familiar scent of him makes my heart ache and my body perk up. *Yes, please*, it says to me.

He leans in closer, his nose almost touching mine. "I never looked at another girl when I was with you. Never even thought about one. Not once."

I force myself to meet his eyes. "I didn't look at anyone either. Only you."

"Then why—" He cuts himself off with a curse, and his fist slams into the wall.

I jump, ready to escape, but he's boxed me in, his forehead pressing against the wall as he breathes in and out. He's so close to me that his chest brushes mine with each inhale. And I shiver with the need to hold him. But I don't.

I can feel his anger. He vibrates with it.

"We could have been so good," he says.

Before I can answer, he launches away from me with those quick reflexes that make him a star athlete. He's backing up. Returning to his date.

I move to go the other way, when he grabs me. One hand cups my neck, the other splays against my back, slipping under my shirt to touch my bare skin.

His mouth crashes into mine on the next breath. And my body goes supernova. His tongue slides deep, his lips bruise, and it feels so good that I moan behind it all.

It's always like this. I can't get enough of him. I devour his mouth, play with his tongue. My breasts crush against the hard wall of his chest. Sweet relief.

Drew.

But then he's pushing me away, and I'm staggering back. His eyes are dull, filled with pain, regret, and worst of all, disgust.

"So fucking good." He leaves me there slumped against the wall.

DREW

As far as mistakes go, that was fairly colossal. Fucking stupid is what it was. Damn, I shouldn't have followed Anna to the bathroom. And I sure as shit shouldn't have kissed her.

My ribs compress painfully at the thought. Holding her, feeling her soft, plump lips once more was both agony and ecstasy. I still taste her in my mouth. I haven't taken another drink since I kissed her, some desperate part of me reluctant to wash her away. In short, I am undone.

Unfortunately, rationality left the building the second I saw Mr. Yuck put his fucking hands on Anna. It was all I could do not to trample through the crowd and smash Emo Boy's face in. Holy hell, watching his fingers stoke Anna's neck while knowing exactly how her skin feels, knowing that I'd never get to do the same, gutted me. Nothing could stop me from seeking her out, from touching her and letting her remember just what she was missing.

Great plan. Now I remember with perfect clarity what I am missing too.

Having just experienced true jealousy, I can safely say that the emotion is insidious, and I never want to feel it again. But it lingers like a plague, eating through my insides with dull, thick teeth.

I rub the hollow spot in the center of my chest and then pull my head out of the fog I've been wallowing in. Christ, I'm out with another girl. I shouldn't be thinking about the one who didn't want me.

I take a breath and face… Shit. What is her name?

In the darkness of my car's interior, her eyes shine as she looks at me. She's pretty. They all are: these girls I ask out with no intention of letting things go any further than one date. Hell, they all look vaguely similar, same general features, same body type, taste in clothes. All-American, perky sorority girls. Why hadn't I noticed this before Anna? And I accused her of only wanting one type.

Bitterness fills my mouth.

My date smiles, hesitant. "That was…nice."

Nice. Right. We'd been at the club for all of ten minutes before I disappeared, stuck my tongue down another girl's throat, and then promptly came back to haul ass out of there like the place was on fire. Really nice of me.

"Yeah." I clear my throat. "Sorry, I'm tired tonight. We've been practicing a lot."

Lie. But one most girls seem to appreciate.

She's no different. She smiles again, sympathetic. "That's okay. Your dedication is admirable."

Tell that to the guys, most of whom want to kill me about now.

"Thanks…" *Fuck. What* is *her name?* Stacy? No. Shannon! "Shannon."

I brace for impact just in case I've gotten it wrong, but she smiles as if I've just given her some great reward.

Having nothing more to say, I turn my attention back to the road. Why did I go out with her? It was thoughtless. Suffocating. I can't get her home soon enough. I turn on the radio in a desperate attempt to fill the silence. Jack White is singing about falling in love with a ghost he's not brave enough to kiss. I stab the Off button with more force than necessary.

Thank God we're now in front of her sorority house because I don't think I can drive anymore. I pull over and brake hard enough to send us both rocking forward.

As if she's been waiting for this moment, Shannon turns in her seat and gives me an expectant look. Her body language is crystal clear, from the way she leans in toward me, to her gaze flitting from my mouth to my eyes. She wants me to kiss her.

My fingers tighten around the steering wheel, and the leather creaks.

I'm not kissing her in this car. Not where I first got my mouth on Anna's. Just seeing another girl sitting in the passenger seat is a slap in the face. It's wrong. Anna should be there. In a way, she is. Haunting me with each breath. The fact my safe haven is now effectively ruined makes me want to punch something.

With a snap of the seatbelt, I wrench open my door and stumble into the cold night air. I suck in a deep breath, as I round the car and open the door for my date.

Not deterred, she manages to slide her body against mine when she rises out of the car. Hell.

"So," she murmurs, resting a hand on my chest. "Thanks for taking me out tonight."

I edge back, shutting the car door with my hip. She follows, and her hand finds my neck.

"Yeah, sure." I sound like a robot. Why did I go out tonight?

Her eyes stare up at me. Waiting.

No. Not going to happen. I can't even stir up a bit of enthusiasm. But then I think of Anna going home with Mr. Yuck. She's moved on. Frowning, I bend my head closer to the girl who is willing. Rosy lips part in invitation. I stall out.

Just do it. Do it and move on too. Kiss the damn girl, already.

She takes the decision out of my hands. Her lips mash into mine. They feel wrong, not the right shape. She smells wrong, of sweet flowers instead of warm spices.

Wrong, wrong, wrong.

My entire body recoils. I rear back, breaking out of her hold in an awkward fumble. Jesus. My dick feels like it's shriveled in my shorts.

"Sorry," I say just as she does.

Heat floods my face. I ought to have been able to at least go with the kiss. She's cute, after all. And willing. Instead, my flesh crawls. And it pisses me off. I'm infected with Anna. I want to punch a hole through the roof of my car.

Giving Shannon an unsteady laugh, I step farther away, my ass hitting the car door. "I'm, ah—" *completely fucked* "—tired."

"Yeah…" Her wrong-shaped mouth twists in a half smile. "You said that."

"Right." God, just get me out of here.

But before I can make an escape, she talks again, her tone strangely neutral. "Is it because of her?"

I jerk so hard that my elbow hits the car window. "Her?"

Shannon blinks back at me. "You know, the redhead in the

bar." So much for me being subtle. "Is she the one you had that blowout with? Is she Red Hen?"

"Red Hen?" I repeat, my head buzzing. What. The. Hell?

She gives me a look designed to reassure, though I'm far from it. But there's a gleam in her eyes like she's dying for gossip. Does she honestly think I want to talk about Anna with her?

And, again: *Red Hen?* Oh, hell no.

"You know," she says. "The one that they're talking about on TikTok and Instagram."

An ugly, sick feeling trickles over my shoulders. For a moment I can only stare at this girl as the buzzing in my ears grows louder. "What the hell are they saying?"

Oblivious of my growing anger, she answers eagerly. "That you dumped some redhead in the middle of the quad."

That day haunts me still. Hearing someone else talk about it hurts my chest.

"Why are they calling her Red Hen?" I sound like I'm talking through a long tunnel. Does Anna know this? She'd hate that. *Hate* it.

"I don't know who came up with that."

"What does it mean?" My heart is thudding so hard it hurts. As a rule, I stay far away from social media. Obviously, the guys were keeping something from me, because they'd usually tell me about any nonsense.

Shannon shifts from one foot to the other. "I guess it's because she tried to trap you into a relationship. You know, by getting pregnant."

The ground seems to sway beneath me, and a cold sweat breaks over my skin. Holy shit. Is Anna pregnant? She didn't look… Hell, what does early pregnancy even look like? But she would have told me tonight, wouldn't she? Then again, I'd pretty much gone on the offensive with her, which didn't exactly make for an easy opening to a topic like that. Holy fucking shit, but if she is…

I'm going to hurl. Right here on Shannon's sidewalk. Yet behind the instant terror is a strange sort of elation. If Anna is pregnant, I'm going to her and am sticking. Screw pride.

Somehow, I find the ability to talk. It's a miracle that I can form a sentence. "Why do people think she's pregnant?"

Maybe Shannon finally notices that I'm about to lose my shit because she clamps up.

"Why!" My shout rings out in the night.

Shannon visibly swallows, her eyes growing round. "Well, in the videos, you, ah… yell at her about your relationship being just a hook up, and, well, she walks away all hunched over, clutching her stomach, so…"

So, no proof of Anna being pregnant. Just fools jumping to the wrong conclusion and sticking their noses in places they have no business being. Even though relief swamps me, the ringing in my ears grows to a clamor. "So, you all think that I would get a girl pregnant, then publicly dump her when she tells me?"

"Ah…well…"

"And believing this, you still wanted to go out with me?"

Okay, I might be yelling. Shit, it's a miracle that I'm not shouting to the clouds at this point. That's what people think of me?

Shannon backs away a step. "I didn't blame *you*." As if this supposed pregnancy was all Anna's doing.

"Well, you should," I snap. "If it were true. You should stay far away from any asshole who would do something like that."

She just stares at me like I've gone insane, and the rage within me surges. What the hell is wrong with this girl?

I take a breath, not wanting to scare her any further. I'm much bigger than her, and even if I can't wait to get away, it isn't cool to make her afraid.

"Look," I say with forced calm. "Whatever you've heard, it's wrong. Yes, that was the girl, and yes we broke up. But it was a mutual decision."

I wince a bit with that one, but it isn't really a lie. Anna didn't want a relationship, and I couldn't pretend that it wasn't the only thing I wanted.

"She's a nice girl. And it makes me sick that people would think otherwise."

Wide-eyed Shannon nods as if her life depends on it. She's clutching her arms over her chest. I put that fear in her, and guilt clenches my stomach.

"I've got to go. Sorry." I'm not sure what else I can say. I just need to get out of here.

By the time I get home and manage to turn on my laptop, my hands are shaking. Nausea rolls around in my stomach as a TikTok search for my name pulls up millions of views. And there they are in endless posts of malicious glee. Speculation on why I was arguing with a curvaceous redhead. Hate-filled comments about Anna that make my heart ache and my blood boil. But it is nothing compared to the videos.

There I am, looming over Anna, who looks so tiny in comparison. I'm a monster with muscles bulging and a vein sticking out on my temple.

I've never felt so ashamed. Anna's pale, her chin lifting in defiance. That I remember. But I never saw the aftermath. There's one of me walking away, humiliating because it captures my own pain. My face is twisted with it. And then one of Anna.

She's leaning against the tree, clutching her arms around her middle, her gorgeous eyes looking up toward the sky as if it holds some answer. Pain etches her features.

With shaking fingers, I nearly touch the screen. Pain that mirrors my own.

Have I done the wrong thing by ending it with Anna? Does it matter? She's currently on a date with Mr. Yuck. And I can't overlook the fact that she was right. One public argument with me has brought the ugliness of public opinion down upon her head. I never wanted that for her. After reading through the hateful comments, how can I blame her reluctance to be seen with me?

For the first time in my life, I dread going out on the field and playing again. Because they're all watching for the wrong reasons.

TWENTY-NINE

ANNA

I'M SO GRATEFUL for the fall break I could cry. Not only will it spare me from having to face Drew in class, but I need to get away. For the first time in years, my mother's home is a haven to which I want to run as fast as I can.

Better still, I won't have to see Terrance when I get there. Last month, when my mom voiced second thoughts on selling her childhood home, Terrance went ballistic, telling her that she had no right to keep them from their dream by being a coward. Mom realized that it wasn't her dream, but his. Two weeks later, old Terry was sailing off to the Bahamas with his chow chow's groomer.

Thanksgiving dinner is subdued. Mom often invites people to spend it with us, single friends, those who couldn't make it home to families of their own. When I was younger, I would protest because I didn't want to share her with other grownups. Not when I only saw my working mother at dinner.

As I got older, I grew to appreciate the sound of laughter and interesting conversation during those meals. Unfortunately, this year, my mom hasn't invited anyone. I know it's because they'll ask about Terrance, and the breakup is too fresh for Mom to deal. I empathize. Entirely. Only I'd rather have the distraction. Now it's just Mom and me. And a quiet house.

We cook together, and I try to find something to talk about. Conversation usually isn't a problem, but since the only thing I want to do is curl up in bed and cry, I'm finding it a struggle.

My mother fills the void and talks. About her practice. About her friend Silvia, who she thinks might be depressed. About the new moisturizer she's found and loves to pieces. And it's fine. If only this aching, gnawing hole within me would fill up with each bite of food I take, instead of growing larger. If only I'd feel warm instead of cold. My walls are no longer shored up. I could topple at any moment. Right onto my mom's plush Turkish carpet.

Dessert, as always, is taken in the living room, while tucked up in front of the fire on the old chesterfield sofa that Mom had reupholstered last year in cream linen. In the frenzy of redecorating, Mom also converted the wood-burning fireplace into gas, and though the flames dance and look cheery, I miss the scent of burning wood.

Drew's house has a wood-burning fireplace. I picture him kneeling before it, stacking wood and getting the tinder ready. Is he there now? Is he with Gray? God, I hope so. The idea of Drew being alone makes my heart physically hurt. I take an extra-large bite of pumpkin cheesecake and try not to choke on it.

"What is going on with you, Anna?"

I nearly jump in my seat. I hadn't noticed Mom studying me. Though I shouldn't be surprised. Even if she doesn't always act like she's paying attention, she usually is.

I run the tines of my fork through the burnished cheesecake. I could evade, divert attention, but telling the truth is the quickest way with Mom. Like ripping off an especially sticky bandage. "I broke up with someone."

"I'm sorry to hear it, sweetheart."

My fork stabs deep.

"It didn't get too far. We weren't really right for each other."

God, the lie chokes me. I'm going to throw up my Thanksgiving dinner right here on the living room floor.

I take a deep breath. "But I think I hurt him, and I'm sorry about it." I might have also done some irreparable internal damage to myself, but we don't need to talk about that.

Mom wisely says nothing but simply rises to go make me a cup of espresso. It gives me enough time to control my erratic breathing and quivering lip. When she returns, I'm composed.

"With a little extra *crema* on top," she says, setting a tiny white cup down on the table before me. "Just as you like it."

"Thanks." The rich, deep scent of espresso is a needed comfort.

"Mom," I say after a welcome sip. "Did you think my father was...well, the one? You know, when you first met him?"

As usual, mention of my dad makes her expression go cool. She takes a sip of her own coffee. "Hard truth?"

Since I was a child, she has always asked if I want the watered-down version or the harsh one. It depresses me to realize how often I'd asked for the easy tale. Not today.

"The plainest," I say.

"Not really," Mom says with a sigh.

I sit up. "Then why did you marry him?"

She runs a hand through her artful hair, a true sign of distress; she'd never risk ruining it like that.

"Because I wanted him to be the one. And maybe..." She shrugs slightly, her dark hair sliding over her shoulder. "Maybe if he had stayed, he might have been."

The taste of coffee turns bitter in my mouth. I set aside my cup and curl my feet under me. "But if he was the one, he would have stayed. And you would have known he was from the beginning. Right? I mean, it would have felt perfect."

The very idea that my dad could have grown into her true love baffles me.

Mom's light laugh fills the room. "You think love doesn't take work? That it doesn't need to grow?" Her hair swings as she shakes her head. "Of course it does."

I sit back against the pillows with a huff. "Honestly, Mom? I'm shocked that you even believe in love at all."

"Why?" Her eyes narrow to dark slits.

"Because you..." I take a frustrated breath. I don't want to hurt her, but my unthinking mouth already started the ball rolling. Now I can't take it back. "All these guys..." I trail off, looking away. The heat of the flickering fire tightens my cheeks.

Mom's eyes are on me, burning my skin further. "Because I fail at love?"

Dully, I nod. And she drinks her coffee as she looks off into the fire. The clink of her cup against the saucer breaks the silence.

"Why do you think I keep trying, Anna?" Sadness weighs down her soft voice.

And when I dare to look at her, I see the lines deepen around her eyes.

"No, I haven't found love," she says. "Not the kind that lasts. Not yet. But it's out there. And it hurts me to think that, because of my mistakes and fumbling, you have become so cynical."

My entire face prickles with heat and the urge to cry. Fucking hell, I've never cried so much in my whole life than I have in these past few weeks. I hate that. Hate the tight ball of regret and ugliness that's taken residence in my gut. Drawing my knees up to my chest, I wrap my arms around myself. Yet I still feel cold and unbalanced, as if something essential is missing from me.

Mom's voice grows sharp. "I rather hate to tell you, but you remind me of your father right now."

It's like a punch to the gut. I exhale in a burst of breath. "That's low. And unfair. I am nothing like him. *Nothing.*" I've worked hard to be like neither of them.

Her lips purse as her brows rise. She knows she's cut me off at the knees. I'm paying for what I've said to her. Even if she won't admit to it.

"Well," she says. "He too gave up when it became difficult. He never wanted to try. Only to take the easy way out."

"If you think I find any of this easy," I grind out. "You're wrong."

Mom sets her cup on the coffee table. "Maybe so. But you're still safer in your misery than going out onto that unknown limb."

I'm on my feet before I can think about the action. "I'm going to bed."

My feet eat up the plush carpet, propelling me away from my mother's claws. But her reach is far, and I cannot block out her final remark. "That's fine, Anna. Run away. But you'll only feel worse for it."

Sometimes I really hate my mother. But not as much as I hate myself.

THIRTY

ANNA

I RETURN TO campus Saturday night and come to the realization that I need to quit my job. I decide this the moment I open an email from Dave and read the catering schedule. I'm signed up for the football game tomorrow night. What the hell?

"I've got a family thing," I blurt out when I call Dave. Besides being the poorest excuse in the world, it's a total lie. My plans for the weekend include making a large batch of brownies, watching a movie that has absolutely no romance in it, then climbing under the covers and hiding there until class starts again.

He's supremely unhelpful. "Then you should have said so two weeks ago when I was doing up the schedule."

"Can't I change shifts with someone else?"

"Who? I've got all-hands-on-deck working. This is the last game before the playoffs."

Other team losses have put Drew's team in contention. Something everyone but me takes very seriously. For Drew, this is one of the final steps to the National Championship. For a fleeting moment, I wonder how he feels, if he's nervous. Then I remember that I've put a ban on thinking about Drew.

As for the rest of the world, he's all they can talk about. Excitement over the game and discussions about the team's chances have been buzzing around campus for weeks.

Dave's tone is far from compassionate. "Sorry but you're shit out of luck."

And so I'm stuck working the luxury box during Drew's game. Fuck. A. Duck.

Usually this is a good gig. The luxury box is heated, while everyone working outside freezes their asses off. I simply have to set up the buffet and wine bar and then keep it clean. Only I can't avoid seeing the game. Or hearing it. Our college sports radio pipes in through speakers, giving me a play-by-play update on Drew's progress as I try to concentrate on my work.

University bigwigs and their friends are relaxing, stuffing their faces, and giving their opinion of Drew and his teammates.

"Grayson is looking good," one of them says. "But Baylor's off. Don't know what the hell he's thinking—throw the damn ball, boy!"

I want to tell the man to shut the hell up or get down on the field and play the game himself. But I hold my tongue.

"He's open. Johnson is open. Throw— Damn it!"

The room groans as the radio announcer calls an incompletion. I can't help but look. Drew, both the real man and his doppelganger on the TVs, has his hands on his hips and is looking down at the grass. He clearly utters a ripe curse and then turns back to his team.

"He's been off for the past few games," insists Mr. Know-It-All.

And though the guy next to him is quiet about it, I still hear him mumble, "Pussy problems."

Fucking pig.

But, *God*, is that what people think? My stomach roils.

It must be, because the pig isn't the only one who complains that Drew is off his game. The radio announcer goes on about how Drew hasn't been himself for the past month or so. And how he needs to get his head back into it, because this game is brutal.

And it is. Every hit Drew takes has my entire body clenching in sympathy. The box is close enough that I can hear the impact of flesh upon flesh, the grunts. The opposing team, big fucking brutes from Alabama, are pummeling Drew and his boys.

Grayson is limping after a particularly vicious takedown, clearly trying to shake it off, and Drew is slower to get up every time the defense hurtles into him. But he's holding it together. He's winning, even if it's obviously taking everything he's got.

When halftime rolls around, I'm a nervous wreck. My neck is aching, and I can only imagine how Drew feels. The vivid memory of his hip and torso, blue and black with bruises, cruelly shoves itself into my mind. I'd kissed and licked my way across his battered flesh. And he'd threaded his fingers through my hair and held me to him as though I was the only thing that mattered.

The truth crashes over me like a breaking wave, and I'm sucked down in the aftermath. *He* is the only thing that matters. I've known this. But until now, I never completely let myself feel the void of his loss in my life. The feeling is so hard and strong that I nearly stagger.

Tears smart my eyes as I walk back to the tiny kitchen to get another platter of chicken fingers. Staring blindly at a gloppy vat of barbecue sauce, my body goes numb, as a lump fills my throat, threatening to choke me.

I've become everything I've ever been accused of, a nobody, a shadow who sought dark corners for fear of judgment. And I'd done it to myself, believing in other people's perceptions of me, playing into it and hiding away as though I'm not good enough. The worst part is that I thought I was doing the opposite, that I was being strong, not giving a fuck.

What bullshit. If anything, I care too much. But I care about the opinions of the *wrong* people, faceless fucking people that will never mean anything to me. I've been ducking my head for fear of what they think.

"God." My fist hits the countertop with bruising force. Bracing my hands on the counter, I rock back and forth, blinking back the tears. I can't believe this. I've been so stubbornly clueless.

"God."

In the outer room, the crowd cheers at a play. I suck in a sharp breath and wipe my eyes with the back of my hand. A strange sense of lightness steals over me. My shoulders lift. But deep inside my chest, I still ache. The hole is still there.

Drew. Only he can fill that void.

After the game is over, I'm going to him. I'll tell him everything. Beg for another chance.

"We could have been so good," he'd said.

We *were* so good together. I'd been too afraid to believe in it.

As I return to the box, I feel battered but calmer, like I've cried all night but have finally caught my breath. The game is back on, and the spectators settle in.

I am about to set the platter on the table when it happens. It's as if I can feel the danger creeping up. My head turns to the wide plate windows just as the men and women in the box start to shout. Everything slows down. My gaze narrows on the massive linebacker smashing into Drew, taking him out low and to the side, while another brute comes at him from the opposite side.

Drew goes down. His leg is wrong, sticking out at an odd angle. And he is screaming. It's the sound of raw agony. It rips through the box and over the stadium. It takes the breath out of the roaring crowd, creating dead silence.

The platter crashes to the floor in a spill of fried chicken pieces. Someone turns and glares. I am already running from the room.

THIRTY-ONE

ANNA

IN THE BOWELS of the stadium, it's chaos. Reports and players are everywhere. People are shouting, and then campus security is there. My catering badge gets me far but not far enough. I'm stopped short of the locker room by a vigilant guard.

"I'm his friend," I shout, frantic. *Drew. Drew.*

"You and everybody else, honey. Give us a break and let the doctors look at him in peace." The guard moves to close the door, when I see Gray just behind.

"Gray Grayson! Gray!"

He stops and frowns through the slit in the closing door.

"Please, Gray!"

Gray's still scowling as he ambles forward and shoulders past the guard. I grab onto his arm as soon as he's close enough. His skin is cold and covered with sweat. Next to me, he's a house, a wall of white and red in his pads and uniform. His expression is grim, scared, and it scares me more.

"Is he okay?" I'm panting. My grip on his arm tightens.

Gray's throat works, and when he talks it's a rasp. "His leg is broken. Bad."

"Oh, Drew," I whisper. His season is over. Maybe his career. I ache for him. Wrapping my arms about my middle, I search Gray's face. "Can you get me in to see him?"

Gray's blue eyes fill with suspicion. It's as if he's just remembered that I am the enemy. I don't know how much Drew has told him, but it can't be good.

"He doesn't need that aggravation. If you're here to gawk."

"Fuck you." I slap a massive shoulder pad. "Fuck if that's why I'm here."

His face twists, and he takes a step into my space.

"Why are you here? You treated him like shit." He sneers. "Yeah, I know. You didn't want him before, so why are you here now?"

"Because I—"

My mouth goes dry. I'm not saying this to Gray. Only to Drew. But Gray is glaring a hole through my head, and he's the only one who can bring me to Drew.

"I care about him." It's true but not the whole truth. "I don't know if he needs me or even wants to see me. But he needs someone. He's alone and hurting, and I—" My breath hitches. "I want him to know that I'm here. For him. I... I don't want him to feel alone right now."

Gray looks at me for what feels like an eternity, and then his shoulders sag. "Look, they aren't letting anyone see him now, only the coaches. They're taking him to the hospital. Go home."

His gaze scans my front and I realize that I'm covered in honey mustard and barbecue sauce. "Take a shower, and I'll pick you up. We can go together."

THIRTY-TWO

ANNA

LEAVING DREW BEHIND is one of the hardest things I've had to do. I'm shaking by the time I get home.

An hour later, I'm in Gray's truck, and we're headed to the hospital.

Our silence is awkward and heavy. I know Gray doesn't like me, and I'm not keen on why he doesn't. Guilt is a brick on my chest.

"You were wrong about him," Gray finally says.

I stir from my vigil out the window. And he continues when I give him a questioning look. "Drew doesn't sleep around. As in, he doesn't have casual sex. Not for a while now."

I must look skeptical—and I admit, I *am* a little shocked—because Gray shrugs. "Yeah, he went a bit wild for a couple of years. We all did. And yeah, he's got girls hanging on him left and right. But that's all they do. Hang there."

"Out of the goodness of his heart." The vision of endless

toothpaste commercial candidates dancing through my head makes it all a little hard to believe.

"No," Gray says with exaggerated patience. "More like he's too lazy and too easygoing to give them the brush-off. He might fool around now and then, but he doesn't fuck them."

Gray snorts when I raise my brow. "Don't believe me. But it's the truth. Coach batters safe sex messages into our heads on a constant basis. Drew's a star, and people will do anything to catch a ride. He's got to watch out for false pregnancy accusations, potential cries of rape from women he never met, bullshit that most college guys never deal with. And well…"

"Well, what?"

Gray scratches behind his ear. "He got burned. The beginning of junior year. Jenny." This comes out like a bad word. "Drew and Jenny had been together since the end of sophomore year. She wanted to get married."

"When they were twenty?" I practically yell. "That's ridiculous."

He nods like I'm preaching to the choir. "That's what Drew told her. But Jenny wanted insurance. That he wouldn't sleep around, find another girl, as if that was even remotely Drew's style. When Drew said no, that they were too young, she gave him an ultimatum and he walked."

"Well, it's certainly an unfortunate story—"

"A week later," Gray cut in. "Jenny's telling anyone who'd listen how Drew dumped her because he was stressed over football. That he was scared of losing. That his arm was 'in agony' after every practice. She showed people their text messages. Select ones that skewed the truth to her purposes."

"That bitch."

Gray's expression turns ugly. "You said it. And they listened. The press. Other teams. You expose a hint of weakness, and they pounce. Drew was pummeled during every game we had. Now, every girl he's with, he has to wonder if she'll sell him out."

I sink back into the leather seat, deflated. "Why are you telling me all this? I mean, shouldn't you be watching his back, not spilling his secrets?"

"I *am* watching his back. You need to know that he isn't a player. And if that's all you're after—"

"There are things about me that Drew had wrong too. I'm not telling them to you. But he's more to me than just…"

"A fuck?"

My face flames. "Really? You really just said that to me?"

He laughs. "Kind of worth it to see you blush that red."

While Drew has his bone reset, Gray and I sit in the lobby. A ways down, the ubiquitous group of girls hang around like specters, clearly waiting for word of Drew. They titter when they catch sight of us, and I roll my eyes.

"Excuse me," says one of them, her voice anything but polite. "Are you Big Red Hen?"

My face prickles. Beside me, Gray mutters something ripe under his breath and rubs his big hand over his eyes.

Is that what people have been calling me? Iris and George have been sheltering me, keeping me off social media, but I know there's been endless talk. Most of it ugly.

Slowly I turn. There's four of them. Tanned, thin, smug.

"No," I say. "I'm Anna Jones."

Heavy Eyeliner smirks. "Yeah, exactly. I can't believe you're here. Isn't that kind of pathetic? Drew dumped you."

Gray shifts in his seat, wincing. I remain stone still. There's so much I could say about just who and what is pathetic in this scenario. And, yes, a part of me feels the familiar hot weight of humiliation and wants to hide from it.

But I take a deep breath and address what's really important here.

"Seriously, what is wrong with you? Have I given you any reason to be a bitch to me? You know what? I don't care. I'm done with you all. Fuck along now. Go on, fly monkeys! Fly!" I make shooing motions with my hands until they all turn beet red and stalk off, muttering various insults under their breath.

Beside me, Gray laughs into his fist. "Women are evil."

"Women are awesome," I answer, not looking at him because I'm still irked. "You've just been overexposed to the worst of our gender."

He grunts in acknowledgment, and we wait in silence. By the time Drew is resting in his room and visitors are allowed, his coach has already arrived and stands like a gryphon, blocking entry to Drew's door. When Gray escorts me up to Drew's room, his coach steps forward. I half expect him to pull a Gandalf and state, "You shall not pass!"

Which he basically does, though his delivery has southern politeness to soften the blow. "I'm sorry, young lady, but no visitors. It's best you go on home now."

Unfortunately for him, I'm not much in the mood for social graces. "I'm not leaving until I see Drew. He can tell me to go if he wants me to."

The coach is a big man, and when he crosses his arms over his chest and braces his feet apart, he blocks the entire doorway. "Drew isn't in the position to make that decision. I'm making it for him. You cannot go in."

I smile at the coach, pleasantly as if I have all the time in the world. "I am not one of your players or your daughter. You have no authority to tell me what I can and cannot do."

"Look, young lady—"

"Do not," I interrupt, "use that misogynistic, patronizing title on me again. You may call me Anna, or Miss Jones if you want to be formal. But 'young lady' is off the table." I raise a brow at him. "Unless you like to be called 'old man,' which would be the equivalent insult."

At my side, Gray clears his throat several, quick times, but I don't spare him a look. Drew's coach is staring at me like I've grown two heads.

"Well," he says in a somewhat strangled voice. "I guess you put me in my place."

"I'm not trying to do anything other than get to Drew."

"Coach," Gray interjects. "She's Drew's girl."

Drew's girl. Not really. That hurts too.

"The reason why he's been playing like the walking wounded, you mean." Coach Smith's eyes are hard, making me want to squirm.

"Which means he'll probably feel a hell of a lot better seeing her than us right now," Gray says.

I want to hug him, even if I'm not so sure he's right.

Coach Smith seems to think the same.

"I'm going in there," I say. "Try to stop me, and it will get ugly."

This time, Gray's suppressed laugh isn't as successful. Coach Smith's brows rise, but he steps aside. "If you're that insistent. By all means."

I move to the door when he comes in close. "But if I hear any hysterics, I'm hauling you over my shoulder and taking you out of here, Miss Jones."

Got to love a man who protects his players like they're his own. I nod, and then open the door to Drew's room.

Cool air and the smell of antiseptic hit my face as I walk in. At the sound of the door opening, he turns his head, but it's an abortive movement, and he quickly looks away. His bed is elevated at the end so that his broken leg can rest higher than his head.

Fading sunlight turns the picture window into a canvas of orange, and against it, Drew's profile is sharp and clean. The fan of his lashes is touched in gold as he blinks. But the rest of him is still. So still. And though he's a large guy, the hospital bed diminishes him.

He doesn't move as I walk closer, but he swallows rapidly, making a series of clicking noises in his throat. His nostrils flare, and a tremor works over him. He's trying so hard not to let go. And it kills me.

I don't make him turn, but round the bed to his good side. To face him. The clicking in his throat gets louder. He sucks air through his nose. God, he's pale and battered.

"Drew." My voice is a breath, and his lower lip wobbles. His gaze darts around as if he doesn't know where to look and is about to break.

I sink down beside him, and a shuddering breath rips out of him. He's shaking his head as if to say *no, no, no,* and his face gets redder and redder. Gently, I cup his cheek. Drew's eyes squeeze shut as he leans into my palm, and a tear leaks out.

"Baby," I whisper, full of heartache for him.

A sob escapes. He falls into me, his head burrowing against my breast as his hands clutch at the back of my shirt. I gather him close as he lets loose. The broken sounds, his full-bodied sobs, tear into me. I curl myself around his torso, protecting him with what little I have as he cries.

I don't say a word, don't try to tell him it's all right, because it isn't right now. I can only run my fingers through his hair, stroke his broad back, and rock him slowly. His grip on my shirt pulls it tight like I'm his lifeline. And I cuddle in closer so he can feel all of me. I'm a wall. No one can get through me now. I'll protect him with all that I have.

I lose track of time, and my leg grows numb. But I'm not complaining. Soon he goes heavy against me. But I know he's awake. His lashes tickle my neck as he blinks.

"I'm so sorry, Drew," I finally whisper, and it's not just about his leg.

And maybe he hears that because a shuddering sigh leaves him. I kiss his temple, the wet rise of his cheekbone, his forehead, all the while stroking him. A soft touch along his neck, over his shoulder, his jaw.

"I'm so sorry," I say again.

His big hand opens and presses against the small of my back. I feel the heat of his lips on my neck, and he's breathing me in.

"I'm so sorry, Drew."

"Anna." Just my name. But I hear the peace in it. And the need. We hold each other now. And I'm not letting go.

THIRTY-THREE

ANNA

I STAY WITH Drew until the hospital staff kicks me out. And I return in the morning to stay with him all over again. We don't say much. I sit in the big armchair that I've pulled up next to his bed. Sometimes I hold his hand. Sometimes he just sits and plays with my fingers as he stares out the window with a pensive expression. I read Emerson to him, slow and low and just for his ears. When he grows still and silent, I stop.

"More." His voice is rusty and soft, and his hand grasps mine in a warm and engulfing hold.

I read until he falls asleep. But I don't leave him. I can't. Being close like this highlights how empty I've felt without him. I know this man on so many tiny levels. In ways I hadn't realized, in the cadence of his breath, the scent of his skin, how he always makes a small sound in his throat when he shifts position in bed. Little pieces of information that make Drew wholly and uniquely him.

His hospital room quickly takes to resembling a florist shop. Seemingly endless streams of "Get Well" bouquets are brought in by beaming nurses. None of which make Drew even crack a smile. When a nurse maneuvers in a massive football-shaped balloon-flower combo, he snaps.

"Take it away." His hand waves in annoyance. "Take them all." He looks at the shocked nurse, and his expression becomes pained. "Please, just give them to people who need some joy. There's got to be plenty of candidates in this place."

The nurse, who is an obvious fan, smiles at Drew as if he's a god. "Well, of course there are. Aren't you sweet to suggest that?"

Only I can hear his muttered, "More like sick of the freaking smell," and I fight down a smile of my own.

"If any more come, can you do the same?" is all he asks.

The nurse agrees, but when she picks up the vase nearest Drew, he stops her with a quick, "Wait." The bed squeaks under him as he leans over and plucks a small, yellow rosebud from the vase. He breaks the stem off, leaving only about three inches, and then, without ceremony, tucks the rose into the meat of my high ponytail. I blush, and the nurse beams again, but Drew merely flops back onto his pillows, crossing his arms over his broad chest, and glares at the TV—which isn't even on.

"He's a natural charmer, your man," says the nurse as if she's a proud mama.

"Oh, yes," I murmur, grinning at Drew, who is blushing now. "Especially when he's grouchy."

"Humph…" Drew's brows knit tighter together. "Rather look at you, anyway."

Sighing happily, the nurse bustles out, not seeing Drew's mouth twitching at the corners. But I do, and once she's gone, I lean in and kiss his stubble-covered cheek.

"Thanks," I whisper. "I was trying not to sneeze with all of those flowers." I know exactly why he hates the sight of them, but I'm happy to pretend I was the one who didn't want them.

Drew's head tilts back as he closes his eyes. "I just want to get out of here."

"I know." Gently, I run my fingers up and down his forearm. I love the tight, satin texture of his skin and could touch him indefinitely. But a shadow from the window in the door catches my attention. "Looks like the guys are here to see you."

Drew lurches up, his eyes wild. "Oh, shit no."

"What do you mean, 'no'?"

"Get rid of them, Anna." He looks positively panicked.

"Drew, I'm not going to tell them to go. They're worried about you."

He grabs my hand. "I don't want them to see me like this." His lids lower, his gaze skating away. "I don't want to hear about the game. Or face them. Fuck!"

Because Gray is already heading in with what looks like the entire team. Evading Drew's hand, I get up and lean over him.

"These guys love you. And you love them. Don't forget that." I kiss him on the cheek and pretend I don't see him glaring at me like I'm a traitor as I walk out the door.

THIRTY-FOUR

DREW

I KEEP MY eyes on Anna's pert ass as it sways out of my room. Traitorous woman. With her gone, I face the guys, who are shuffling in like they're going to a fucking funeral. And aren't they, really? Ladies and Gentlemen, the death of Drew Baylor's college career. Unfortunately, he did not go out in a blaze of glory, light, and screaming fans. No, he was carried out, screaming in pain and wanting to cry for his mommy. Shit.

No one says anything as they stream in, a parade of legs filling my view, and the scent of deodorant, shower gel, and the faint smell of what I can only describe as "football" that lingers on them filling my nose.

Shit. Shit. Shit.

I have to look up. It hurts my neck to do it. My eyes burn as I fight to keep them open. Starters surround me, bench warmers and second strings spilling out into the hall.

"Hey," I say to no one in particular.

A unified grumble of "Hey, Battle" is returned.

It's so awkward, I'm choking on it. Beneath the sheet, I clench my fists. I don't meet my guys' eyes, and they don't meet mine. Gray steps forward and plops down on the seat Anna vacated. "Jesus, someone tell a joke or something."

A couple of guys laugh nervously. The following silence is deafening.

"Hey," says Gray into the void. "How did Darth Vader know what Luke got him for Christmas? He felt his presents!"

Everyone groans at that.

"Fucking terrible, Gray-Gray."

But they're laughing more. Rolondo comes forward and slaps my shoulder. Hard. "You all right, man?" He winces. "Aside from your busted-up leg."

We eyeball each other for a beat then both laugh. It isn't a full one but enough for now.

"Yeah. Other than my busted-up leg. And stinking of hospital."

"That nursemaid of yours can't hurt," Dex says with a smile.

Someone coughs, *"Scarlett."*

I roll my eyes, but I'm not touching that one.

Dex's smile fades. "We kicked their ass, Drew."

"For you, man," adds Simms. Cool rage simmers in his eyes, and in the eyes of my guys as I look around. For a brief moment, I almost feel sorry for the players they must have pummeled. But then I remember why, and a tight pain twists my gut. I don't want to be the team's Gipper.

"Motherfuckers had it coming," says Marshall. A louder grumble runs through the room.

"We in the playoffs, then?" I manage to ask.

No one looks at me then. "Yeah."

Without me. They didn't need me after all. Is it petty that it feels like a kick to the gut? Yeah. But I say what they need to hear.

Taking a deep breath, I force the words to come out with

conviction, to face each and every one of their eyes. "And you're gonna kick ass."

A sound of agreement goes through the room, but it's half-hearted at best.

Thank God, or whoever is listening to my pleas, that the nurse weaves through the crowd and starts to shoo them out. And they go. Having been on the other side of these sorts of visits, I know how badly they want to escape. I want to follow them.

One after another, they come forward, give me a pat on the arm or the shoulder with a murmured, "Get better," or some equivalent. And each time, it feels like another nail in my coffin. By the time it's just Gray, I want to be alone so badly, I'm sweating. Scratch that, I want Anna. I want to get lost in her warm scent, her syrup-sweet voice, or just her smooth skin.

But Gray lingers. He frowns, opens his mouth, closes it, and then tries again. "We won because our defense shut them down. We didn't score another fucking point. Our offensive productivity went to hell when you were taken out."

My throat closes, and I study the waffle weave of my thin hospital blanket.

"You're one of the greats, Drew. Don't you forget it."

"Was," I mutter.

He takes a step closer, getting into my field of vision. *"Are."* His expression is fierce. "You aren't done yet."

Anna walks in but halts, her gaze going to me and then Gray, and she hovers, clearly worried she's interrupted something. Gray glances at her but then looks back at me. Moving faster than I expect, he reaches out and musses my hair, giving my head a little shove at the end.

"Love you, you thickheaded bastard." Gray's voice is uneven, and I realize then how freaked out he's been. I would have been too, had I seen his leg broken like a twig.

"Same here," I say, something stuck in my throat.

He backs out quickly, giving Anna a small smile. "Take care of our boy. See you tomorrow, Drew."

Tomorrow. When I'll finally break free of this place. Even though I'm counting the seconds, a wave of black panic washes around the edges of my vision.

Anna sits back down in her seat. I take her hand and don't let go.

ANNA

At night, when I'm kicked out of Drew's room once again, I grab his keys and head to his house. Yes, I'm basically breaking in, but things need to be done. Drew's car is in the drive, one of his teammates presumably having dropped it off with the spare key earlier. The porch light is on, as is the kitchen light, just visible in the back. It heartens me that someone cared enough to protect his house that way.

Hauling up my load of groceries with one hand, I brace a hip against the door and let myself in. I'm halfway across the living room when a massive shape looms up from the kitchen. Naturally, I scream my head off and launch my keys at my attacker. With a loud jangle they bounce off the center of Gray Grayson's forehead before clattering to the floor.

"What the ever-loving fuck?" He clutches his head and glares.

Sheepish, and my heart still racing, I glare back. "Most people duck."

"Yeah?" Still frowning at me, he scoops the keys up with one hand. "Most people don't break into houses and launch keys at innocent victims' heads."

Since the groceries are cutting off the circulation to my hand, I push past him and set my bags on the counter. "If I have keys, it isn't breaking in, now is it?"

Gray comes into the kitchen where a pot of something is cooking on the stove. It smells fantastic. "I don't know." He gives me the gimlet eye. "Did you ask Drew if you could use his keys to get into his house?"

Busted.

I shrug. "Drew was otherwise occupied." I begin to unload the groceries. "I'd meant to come here, clean up, and make him some food to get him through the week. But I didn't know he already had a resident chef."

Surprisingly, Gray smiles wide. "It's a simple barter system. I cook and Drew lets me hang out."

The idea that Gray feels the need to barter for Drew's company has my heart squeezing for the guy. I know he doesn't much trust me, but I like him.

I take another look at the pot. "Whatcha cooking?"

"Soup." Gray stirs it like it's a fragile brew.

"Kind?" I prompt, my lips twitching.

"White bean with sausage and corn."

My stomach growls. I haven't eaten all day. "God, I love soup."

By Gray's pleased expression, I've said something right.

Leaning forward to catch another whiff, I almost dance with impatience. "When's it gonna be ready?"

Gray's blond brows rise in mock offense. "This here is for Drew, woman. Get your own supper."

"Oh, come on. One bowl isn't going to hurt. Besides—" I pull out a bag of apples "—I plan to make pies. I'm pretty sure I can share one in exchange for dinner."

Eyes gleaming, Gray licks his lips. "Can you truly bake?"

"Can I bake? Did you seriously just ask me that?"

"Ah…" He holds his hands up in surrender. "Ask you what? I don't recall saying anything other than we have a deal."

Smart guy. I smile then. "Good. And when we're done, you can help me clean."

"He had to fall for a bully," Gray mutters under his breath. But he's smiling too. And we get along just fine after that.

THIRTY-FIVE

ANNA

DREW IS CLEARED to leave, and he acts like he's been sprung from jail. "Finally! Where are my clothes?"

The doctor laughs at his enthusiasm. More so when Drew leaves his bed and hobbles toward the bathroom, the back of his hospital gown flapping in his haste and flashing his bare ass to the world. I roll my eyes while Gray snickers. He and Drew's coach are here.

Drew returns, dressed in baggy basketball shorts and a long-sleeved cotton shirt that hugs his lean frame. "I can't wait to get out of here."

"I'd worry about you if you enjoyed the hospital," says Coach Smith with a small smile. He's a stern man, but I can see his affection for Drew.

All is well until a nurse arrives with a wheelchair. "Ready to go home, Mr. Baylor?"

Drew eyes the chair as if it were a snake. "Yeah. But I'm not getting in that."

She gives him a patient smile. "Hospital regulations, I'm afraid. Even for you." There's steel in the look she pins on him, and Drew's scowl grows because we all know he isn't going to argue with her.

"Fine." He hops down from his bed and spins into position on one leg. He doesn't look at anyone as the nurse props his feet on the footrests and gives him a friendly pat on his arm. "All set?"

"Yes." He hates being in the wheelchair. Every line in his body, his sullen glare, radiates that fact. Spitting nails mad is what my grandpa would have called Drew's expression.

"Good. Now I just need to know that you have someone taking care of you at home for the next few days."

Drew's chin jerks up. "I do not need someone taking care of me. I'm fine."

Again, the nurse uses her patient-don't-fuss-with-me smile. "And I do not want to see you back in here, Mr. Baylor. Allow yourself time to become accustomed to your crutches before you go it alone."

Drew's hands curl into tight fists. I've seen that look in his eyes before. Just before he blew up at me.

I step in. "I'll be taking care of Drew."

His glare cuts to me like a swinging scythe. "No."

It echoes through the air, hard and ugly. And my back grows so tense it feels as though my spine is a steel rod. "Yes, I am."

Drew's nostrils flare. "I do not want your pity." If words were nails, I'd have been punctured.

I affect a long sigh. "All right. Gray, cross 'pity Drew' off my to-do list, would you?"

Gray chokes off on a smothered laugh, and Coach Smith has a sudden interest in his shoes. Drew's eyes narrow into slits and, for a long moment, I'm sure he's going to yell, but his mouth starts twitching.

"I told you she was a smart-ass," he says to Gray.

"Huh." Gray scratches the back of his head. "I could have sworn you said, 'pain in the ass.'"

The nurse picks the moment to cut in. "Are we all set then?"

"I'll bring the car around," I say. Bad enough that Drew has to be wheeled out. My watching will not sit well with him.

"Anna..."

I cut Drew off before he can resume his anti-pity objections. "If it were me, would you do the same?"

Everyone goes quiet.

"Yes." He says it so softly yet with such force that my breath hitches. His darks eyes stare into mine. "Yes."

And suddenly everything else fades. It's just us in the room.

"And if I needed help but didn't want to ask for it?" I ask.

His chest lifts on a breath as he looks at me. "I would never leave you."

It hurts to swallow, and my voice comes out rougher than it should. "Then don't ask it of me."

When he nods, he doesn't meet my eyes, but I know it's because there are too many people in the room. "Get the car."

DREW

Coming home has never felt so good. Not since before my parents died, have I experienced such relief when entering my house. It's warm, quiet, and the scent of leather and general cleanliness surround me as I hobble into the living room, my crutches thudding against the polished wood floor. I halt and look around before turning to Anna, who has taken an extreme interest in a remote spot on the wall.

"You cleaned." The whole house gleams.

She shrugs. "Who likes returning to a messy house?"

"Anna, you didn't have to—"

"If you tell me I don't have to help you one more time, I'll..." Her cute nose wrinkles as she trails off at a loss.

"You'll what?" I tease. "Punch me? Knee me in the balls?"

An auburn brow rises, as she looks me over, her gaze stopping at my chest. "Give you a purple nurple."

I grin, but my chest grows hot. Christ, the idea of Anna pinching my nipple is getting me off. "As long as I get to return the favor, Jones."

Just as I'd hoped, she blushes. "Perv."

"I prefer egalitarian lecher." I thump further into the room and set aside my crutches before plopping on the couch. The padded leather gives around me, a familiar comfort that I sink into.

I expected Anna to follow; she's been hovering over me like she was afraid I'd topple. But she's still standing by the door and looking at me with a strange expression, her mouth tilted on a nervous half smile.

"What?" I shift a bit in my seat, hauling up my injured leg to rest it on the chaise.

Now that we're alone and not distracted by things like hospital monitors, nurses coming and going, and my intense pain, there's a certain amount of awkwardness between us. She's broken my heart, and I vowed to stay clear of her. A statement that crumbled like dry sand the second she walked into my hospital room and looked at me as if I was the most important thing in her life. I've been waiting months for that look. But it doesn't erase everything.

"Nothing," she says, still watching me. "I just missed your humor."

I've missed a lot more from her. "Most people don't really get my humor."

And then she smiles full out. "I'd believe that."

Finally, she comes into the house, closing the door behind her. It's then I notice the small bag in her hand. She flushes when I spot it.

"I thought maybe I'd..." The flush washes down her neck. "Well, maybe you'd like some company for a while."

So, she's unsure as well. I should ask her right now what she expects from me. If she wants what we had before, it will kill

me. I can't go back to that. But she has to know that. And she's
stayed by my side in the hospital when, before, she would have
run in the other direction.

The moment stretches, and she shifts from one foot to the
other, her expression going pinched and pale, as if she's afraid I'll
tell her no, tell her to leave now. Not happening.

"I want you, Anna," I say in a low voice. "I always have. If you
want to stay, you must know I'd want that too."

Her lashes sweep down, hiding her eyes from me as she gives
a brisk nod. "That's what I want."

The answer is barely above a whisper, but I hear it and my
body responds with a burst of warmth and satisfaction.

"Well then…" I don't know what to say exactly. Get your
sweet butt over here and sit in my lap would probably sound too
needy, even if that is what I crave. Hell, it's been over a month
since I've properly touched her.

Anna, however, has other things on her mind. "You want
something to eat?"

Behind the familiar scent of home, something savory and
something sweet linger in the air. "Was Gray here?"

She moves into the kitchen. "Figures you'd know it was Gray
who cooked. Yeah, he was here too."

I imagine Anna and Gray in my house together and frown.
While doctors were putting me back together, they were going
on with life. Neither of their lives has been smashed to pieces.
And the difference between them and me is painfully clear.

Unaware of my growing anxiety, she eyes me slantwise. "You
should have told me you had a personal chef. I wouldn't have
bothered."

I twist in my seat to look at her fully. "You cooked for me?"

"Don't look so shocked. I have before." She's scowling now.

"I'm grateful every time, Anna."

My honesty is rewarded by her smile. "I didn't actually cook.
Gray did. He made you bean soup." Her lips twitch. "Said the

pain meds might leave you 'backed up' and in a state that you'd need some roughage."

"That asshole."

She laughs. "What? No need?"

"Hardly. But I'm starving, so I'm not turning down his damn soup."

"Shocker." Her expression is cheeky as she gets a bowl. "I baked."

"She bakes." I grin up at the ceiling, earning an eye roll from Anna. "What'd you bake me, Jones?"

"Apple pie."

"Awesome. Bring that too." Now that I'm out of the hospital with its disgusting, flavorless food, I'm so hungry I could eat the whole pie. That Anna made it for me makes it even better. Whatever the case may be, she cared enough to clean my house, bake me a pie, and stay by my side.

The sounds of her puttering around my kitchen, reheating the soup, and getting a tray ready make me sleepy. I relax against the couch, my lids growing heavy. It feels right having her here, like the house is suddenly a complete home. She's only here for a while. But I know in my bones that I want her here forever.

I'm twenty-three years old, my carefully built life has just been smashed to pieces, yet I know with complete clarity that I never want to be parted from Anna Jones.

I watch her walk toward me, and my chest clenches. Pale from lack of sleep, her red hair flying wildly in all directions, she's not at her finest, and she's still the most beautiful woman I've ever seen.

"You're supposed to be elevating that leg." She sets the laden tray on the coffee table before grabbing some couch pillows to stuff under my leg. Not that she gets far. A grunt of annoyance escapes her as she tries to carefully lift my leg and struggles.

"Jesus, it's like a tree limb," she grumps.

I snort and help her haul the dead weight that is my leg up so she can place the pillows beneath it. "Does that mean you won't be carrying me to bed?"

She shakes her head, suppressing a smile, but then catches my eye. "Are you tired?"

"Yeah." Exhaustion has me by the balls. If I allowed myself, I'd sink down and be out for weeks. "But all I've been doing is sleeping."

She nods in understanding and slips another pillow behind my back. "Then we'll hang out for a while."

Before we go to bed. Together. And though I'm feeling like shit warmed over, the idea of sleeping in a bed with Anna tightens my gut with longing. I need to touch her. Just feel her next to me.

"Sit," I say. "You've done enough for now."

Anna hands me a bowl of soup then takes her own before complying. Without hesitation, she snuggles down, her shoulder leaning into mine as though she too needs comfort. Before I can say a word, she hands me the remote, and I grin. "You know how to take care of a guy."

"No," she assures. "I don't. I've never done this before."

Anna takes a spoonful of soup before talking again. "I just know guys like their TV."

But I don't turn on the TV. Not yet. Frankly, I'm afraid it will be on the sports channel, and I don't think I can stand seeing any sports right now. I sure as shit don't want to see a replay of my leg being broken on national TV, or hear the sports casters' opinions about my chances of recovery and what this means when it comes to the draft.

The soup turns to lead in my stomach, and I bend forward to put it down. Only I can't reach the table with the bulk of my leg sticking straight out. I grit my teeth and itch to toss the bowl across the room.

Anna takes it out of my hand and neatly sets it on the table.

"Lie back," she says softly.

I do it because the alternative is raging and hitting the side of the couch.

She turns the TV on, hits mute, and then changes the channel before I can register what was said. She knows me too well. And I like it.

When the volume comes on again, it's some cooking show, and she takes up her position at my side. I wrap an arm around her shoulders and draw her close. She rests her head on my chest and places her warm palm on my abdomen.

We eat and watch cooking shows, and Anna grows heavier and softer at my side as she relaxes. It's quiet, warm, and the most peaceful I've felt in ages. With the tips of my fingers, I draw patterns along her arm and the curve of her hip. She's so quiet that I wonder if she's nodded off, but then her fingers mimic mine and she's tracing little circles along my stomach. Lust unfurls like a tinder within me, but I don't do anything about it. Just hold her.

And when she makes a soft, half-stilted yawn, I kiss the top of her head. "Why don't you lie down? Rest your head in my lap."

Her green eyes look up at me, hesitant.

"I promise to behave." It's sort of the truth.

She scoots down. "You say that like it's a good thing." Then she's resting her head in my lap with a satisfied sigh. "Forget I said that. I want to rest here for about forty weeks, if that's okay."

"Anything you want, baby." I mean it to sound like a tease, but it comes out husky. I clear my throat and grab the remote to change the channel.

Absently, I stroke her hair. The wild curls are thick silk, springing around my fingers with a life of their own. The mass of dark red is so dense that I can only concentrate on a section. I let myself indulge; I've wanted to touch her hair like this for ages.

"You're going to make me look like a clown," she says quietly, but she's not moving.

"Do you want me to stop?" The strands rub along my skin with pleasurable friction.

"No." Her lids flutter. "Never."

Which is fine by me. My favorite girl and my favorite movie.

Sometimes life is good. It gets better when Anna smiles as the movie starts. "*Top Gun*. Excellent."

"You like *Top Gun*?" I continue to run my fingers through her hair.

Her mouth curls, which pushes her plump upper lip out in that upside-down pout that makes me lustful. "Yeah." She turns her head slightly to glance up at me. "Is that so surprising?"

Softly, I laugh. I'm warm all over now. "Everything about you is a surprise. But in a good way."

She snuggles down deeper into my lap; I love the sensation, love feeling like I'm protecting her by providing a place to rest.

"So let me guess," I tease. "The infamous volleyball scene turned you on to it?"

The leather squeaks as she rolls on her back, her head now fully cradled in my crotch, which has the expected effect on my dick. It stirs, and I will the horny bastard down. If she notices, she isn't saying anything. Instead, she looks up at me with wide green eyes the color of holly leaves.

"Actually, it was Tom racing on his motorcycle." Her smile is smug. "Where do you think I got the desire to buy my little Vespa?"

Inwardly, I groan in appreciation for the woman who appreciates all things automotive.

Then she shrugs, not meeting my eyes, as if she's shy. "I used to fantasize about doing something like that."

"What? Getting on a motorcycle and just riding off?"

Maybe I'll do the same thing. Take Anna with me. As soon as this fucking leg heals. Panic touches the edges of my mind with black fingers. Her light laugh brings me back.

"Not quite." Her hair pools against her shoulder as she turns toward me. "You ever watch Ewan McGregor's series on motorcycling around the world?"

"*Long Way Down*, and so on? Yeah, sure."

"I used to think about how fun it would be to document something like that, you know?"

She laughs again, an uncomfortable sound. "Or maybe it was the idea of following Ewan McGregor around. Iris has such a crush on him. Calls him her 'cutie daddy.'"

I play with one of her red curls. "Bet you'd kick ass at film production."

Anna's cheeks pink. "I don't know anything about film."

"So, you learn. We all start off ignorant."

She shrugs again. "Maybe."

I place my palm against her cheek. "Babe, whatever you set your mind to doing, you'll nail it. You're so perfect and you don't even know it."

"Pish." She rolls her eyes. "You're forgetting that I can't stand watching sports."

I haven't forgotten a thing. Unease settles over my shoulders, but I shrug it off. I don't want to think about why we broke up, but it's there, and it will need to be addressed, but not now when I'm finally relaxed.

"What I don't get is Iris," I say instead. "Ewan McGregor, really? I pegged her as more a lover of boy band types."

The corners of those gorgeous eyes crinkle as she smiles. "Iris loves boy bands. But she has a major thing for blond guys."

"But that guy she was with… Henry, right?"

Anna's head moves against my cock as she nods, and I repress the urge to squirm.

"She's back with him. The idiot."

"Henry or Iris?" I quip, but it bothers me how we've missed out on each other's lives.

"Both?" she offers.

I can't help but smile at her disgruntled look. "Henry has dark hair," I point out.

"Yeah, well, I keep waiting for her to realize she's going against type."

Her cheek is silken against my fingertips. I stroke along her temple and then trace the curved arch of her brow. And she simply watches me as if she takes pleasure in the act. Her breathing is soft and steady, her body warm where it meets mine.

The bruised area around my heart begins to ache. The sack, the leg break, all of it has left me unsettled and just touching her, just lounging here with her like this affects me. I want to cry. I want to laugh. I want to bury myself so deep inside of Anna that I'll forget my name.

Fucking fluctuating emotions. The doc warned me about them. But, hell, at this rate, I'm going to be a wreck by the end of the week.

"And what's your type?" I find myself asking.

Part of me curses myself for looking weak and needy. But, fuck it, the other part of me *is* needy. I know why I left. I don't truly know why she came back.

Her eyes darken as she searches my face, as if she knows I'm no longer teasing. It's too quiet between us, the sound of the TV blaring in the background. Slowly, she reaches up and runs her fingers along my jaw. Her expression changes, opening. Fear, I can see it flickering in her green irises, but something more, something that makes my insides clench.

"You are." Her voice is low and smoky. But her touch grows stronger as she wraps her fingers around the base of my throat where my pulse is beating hard. Her chin lifts, stubborn, sure. "You are the only one I want, Drew. In all things."

Nothing can stop me from slipping my arm under her shoulders and pulling her up to me. Her lips are soft and yielding, but I haven't truly kissed her in so long that it hits me like a punch to the gut.

I suck in a sharp breath, steal one of hers, and angle my mouth to go deeper. Her tongue slides against mine, and I'm dizzy. I feel like I'm falling into her. My abs tense on a shudder, but I can't stop the kiss. I need more. Always more.

And she's giving it to me, kissing me back with the same need. I'm happy to give her anything she wants, but when I move to bring her further into my lap, a sharp pain shoots through my leg. It's enough for me to draw back and take a breath. But I don't let her go.

Her fingers run through my hair, as I cup her cheek and hold her close. For a long moment we just breathe, and then I find the strength to talk. "I've missed you."

Her lips tickle the corner of mine. "I've missed you too. So much it hurt."

I shouldn't feel satisfaction, but I do. Not that I want her to hurt. In fact, nothing would please me more than to bring her pleasure. Right now would be nice. Lying here on the couch is no longer enough. If I had the strength, I'd pick her up and carry her into my room. But I can't, which sucks. I need help getting there. While I'd ordinarily hate asking for help, this is Anna, which makes all the difference. If any guy tells you that he doesn't like the woman he adores taking care of him when he's hurting, he's probably lying.

"Take me to bed," I whisper against her cheek.

"Or lose you forever?" There's a smile in her voice.

I grin, slow and wide. "Did you just quote *Top Gun* to me?"

"Maybe."

This girl. Jesus, she does it for me.

All those luscious curves move at once, and she's up, reaching for my crutches. I hate the sight of them, hate the way that my leg throbs, that I am helpless.

But I push it all aside because she's here. I'm not alone, and I don't care if I have to down five painkillers, I'm having her tonight.

THIRTY-SIX

ANNA

DESPITE THE FACT that he's on crutches, Drew makes short work of getting into his room. A familiar gleam is in his eyes, one that makes me go all hot and fluttery inside. I have my concerns about having sex with him right now. He's got to be hurting. Inadvertently jostling his leg and injuring him further is the last thing I want to do. Then again, kissing him on the couch has me so worked up, I know that if he touches me all my good intentions will topple like a house of cards in a stiff breeze.

Drew reaches the center of the room before he stops. I cleaned here too, and though I don't think he minds, part of me still worries. I took over his house with impunity, making myself at home before we've even settled things. At the time, I pushed this all aside in favor of assuring his comfort, but he's here now, seeing what I've done.

His golden eyes find mine and they're smiling, soft and tender.

"My mom used to give me fresh sheets when I was sick. It always felt good to slide into a clean bed." His mouth quirks. "I'm not saying I think of you like my mom, just that…well, I appreciate it."

"My mom did that too. Maybe it's a mom thing."

He holds my gaze. "If you're ever sick, I promise to change the sheets for you."

Warmth floods my veins. One small statement, promising a future.

He heads to the bathroom. "I'm dying for a shower. I swear to God, I stink like hospital."

"Just a little," I tease, following. I've got the room set up for this eventuality.

Drew's bathroom is gorgeous. Heated floors of a dark, distressed wood, white glass tiles, and a massive walk-in shower encased in frosted-glass panels, the space resembles a luxury spa. A white bowl sink rests on a teak cabinet base. He lays his crutches there as he reaches in to turn on his shower, and water falls from the big rain showerhead. Almost instantly, the air begins to grow sultry and humid.

His eyes glint again as he turns. "Gonna join me, Jones?" He wags his brows like a stage villain before tugging his shirt over his head.

Good God, but I'm never going to get over the splendor that is his chest, or the way those taut muscles move and flow beneath his honeyed skin.

"Not today." I picture his chest all wet and glistening, running my tongue along the groove in his abdomen, right down the happy trail of dark hair that leads to his thick—

"Spoilsport." He sighs. "Though I'm guessing we'd end up on our asses when I'm in this condition."

Blinking rapidly to clear my dirty mind, I reach over and grab the garbage bag and surgical tape I've set on a shelf.

"Speaking of…" I hold them up and give his leg a pointed look. While the doctor said Drew could get his cast wet, it will take hours to dry off and won't be comfortable for him.

"Kinky." Keeping his eyes on mine, he hooks his thumbs on the waist of his shorts and eases them off, revealing those long, strong legs of his and the weighty cock that has brought me so many hours of pleasure. I swallow hard. I've missed this part of him too. He's already growing thicker, his cock curving as it begins to rise under my stare.

With effort I raise my gaze up to his face, which is currently wearing a smug yet hot expression. I give him a level look. "Behave."

"What?" He's all innocence. "I'm taking a shower here, Jones. Gotta get naked to do that."

"Whatever." And because I can be a tease too, I kneel before him, my face inches from the heat of his cock. It twitches, the musky scent of him filling my nostrils. I look up at him, my smile sweet. "Lift your leg."

A pulse visibly beats at the base of his throat as he gazes down at me. Slowly he lifts his cast-covered leg an inch. The garbage bag rustles as I ease it under his foot and begin to pull it over him. Drew's flat abdomen lifts and falls in a steady, quick cadence.

His leg is so long, the bag barely makes it to the top of the cast. With quick movements, I wrap the ends up with surgical tape, not missing the way his cock is now standing proud and waiting. Longing fills me. I know how he will taste, salty and sweet, how he will feel against my tongue, heavy and firm. Instead, I look into his eyes. "There now, all set."

Drew swallows audibly, his hips canting just a bit as if he can't help it.

"You love torturing me, don't you?" It's a husky whisper, barely heard over the steady rush of the shower.

I lick my dry lips, noting the way his breath catches as I do. "It's only fair, you know."

"Why is that, Jones?" But he knows. I can see it in his eyes, those fuck me eyes that both challenge and make promises.

I cup his ass, that fantastically firm ass that features prominently in so many of my dirty dreams. My finger strokes his little battle axe tattoo, and his nostrils flare in a sharply drawn breath.

"Because," I say, "you only have to be standing there to torture me."

"You've just made countless painful hours of exercise worth it."

A teasing note lightens his tone but shadows creep into his eyes. Drew doesn't work out to impress people. His body is a tool, finely honed to perform at the optimum level. And now it's broken. I know he's fighting off the fear and has been since the sack.

My knees protest as I rise. On my way up, I pause and kiss the smooth, hot tip of his cock, and he hisses. Before I'm fully standing, he cups my neck and pulls me in. His biceps bulge as his arms bend, and then his mouth is on mine, his kiss tempting me with little licks, soft sucks, and sharp needy breaths. His cock pokes my belly as I lean into him, and I'm so hot, so wet that I nearly forget why this is a bad idea.

He sways on his feet, the long length of his body threatening to topple.

I pull back. "Drew…"

He doesn't let me go, but sighs. "All right, all right. I'll be good for now." His eyes meet mine, and I see the heat in them. "But you're going to pay for that one, Jones."

"I'll be waiting for it, Baylor." Tenderly, I kiss his mouth, lingering just enough to have him follow when I pull away. I smile at him. "Now, take your shower."

He gives my upper lip a soft nip before backing away. "Heartless wench." And then, before I can change my mind and grab him, he hobbles into the shower and stands under the spray.

No, I will not watch. I will not. My mouth goes dry. Those fine muscles are defined by taut skin, all slick and shining. Water runs in rivulets off his still half-hard cock. I suck in a breath and close the door on his knowing laugh.

Fleeing to the relative safety of Drew's room, I pull back the covers on the bed and arrange the pillows so he can lie comfortably. It feels good doing this for him, yet anticipation bumps around in my belly. I am going to sleep here with him. I've done so before. Though never like this, never planned and without the promise of sex. I prefer this way, knowing that I'm here because I simply want to be with him. Letting go frees me more than I thought possible.

I'm smiling as I catch a glance in the mirror, then halt in horror. My hair has a fuzz factor of ten.

"Holy hell." Mad snarls stand out around my head. I'm like a girl version of freaking Carrot Top. And I've been flirting with Drew like this. I almost moan in distress, but stifle it when I hear the shower stop.

I grab my toiletries bag as he comes into the room.

Drew, of course, does not bother with a towel. No, he's perfectly fine limping in butt-naked and giving me a cheeky grin.

"I'm taking a shower," I say as I edge past him, dying to hold down my angry hair.

He raises a brow. "Then why didn't you shower with me?"

"You know why."

I'm almost to safety.

"Wasting water is a crime in some states, Jones," he calls, as I scuttle into the bathroom.

"Good thing we don't live in one of those states." I close the door on him.

Despite my hair nightmare, Drew's shower is heaven. I bend my neck and let the hot water pour down on my aching muscles. But I don't linger long. I want to be with Drew now.

Putting on enough product to make my hair behave, I look around for my nightshirt and curse. I've forgotten it. And while I'm not shy about Drew seeing me naked, it seems like a tease to do it now. Not that going out wrapped in a towel won't be either. I could put on my clothes, but they stink of hospital too. Then I spy one of his shirts hanging on the back of the bathroom door. It smells clean, so I take it, only to realize that it's one of his jerseys.

I slip the jersey over my head, and it falls to my knees, the sleeves flopping around my elbows. I dither, wondering whether to keep it on when I hear him from the other room.

"Did you get lost in there, Jones?"

Rolling my eyes, I put some lotion on my legs. "Impatient much?"

"Hey," he says from the room. "What's with this little jar here?"

I crack the door open. "It's olive oil." I'd left a small jar of it on his bedside table. "The team physical therapist said you might be sore, and I didn't have any massage oil so..."

"You talked to my PT?" He sounds surprised, but not angry.

"Of course." I walk into the room. "I wouldn't be much help to you if I didn't. I can massage your leg now if you... What?"

I stop at the foot of the bed. "Why are you looking at me like that?"

Because he's hauling himself up from his slouch in the bed, his muscles bunched and tense, and he's gaping at me. For a moment we simply stare at each other. God, but he's a sight. The lamplight glows warmly on his golden skin, a sharp contrast to the white bedding that lies low over his narrow hips, the cover more a tease then a barrier.

Drew breaks the silence.

"You..." He clears his throat. "You're seriously trying to kill me, aren't you?"

"Are you high?" I laugh softly, but my heart rate has increased to an excited flutter.

"Maybe." His lips curl into a tilted smile. "You look utterly, spectacularly hot in my jersey, Anna Jones."

"You *are* high."

"Come here." He holds his hand out to me. "Like now."

Shaking my head, I go to him, and promptly yelp when he grabs hold of my wrist and yanks me onto the bed.

"Easy," I admonish as I straddle his lap, facing him. "I'm not going to be happy if you make me kick your leg."

"Screw the leg." His hands settle on my hips.

Since I have him all to myself, I explore the silken skin of his chest with my hands, loving the dense muscles and the heat he gives off. Drew is always warm.

"Feeling all right?" My voice is soft with a protectiveness I hadn't known myself capable of.

"Feeling pretty damn fine now, Jones." He lifts a hand and gently traces one of the ironed-on numbers that rests over my right breast. My nipple stiffens under his touch, and he lingers there, drifting back and forth. "This looks a lot better on you than it does on me."

And though heat is in his gaze, I hear the hitch in his voice and the darkness. My heart clenches. I try to shift away, but he holds me tight, a frown working between his brows as he looks at me in question.

"I shouldn't have worn this. It was insensitive." Why didn't I realize he'd remember his loss when he saw the jersey?

He gives my hip a squeeze. "Yes, you should. Every damn night, if I have my say." He fights valiantly for a smile.

Wanting to soothe him, I caress his shoulders. "All right. If you wear this every night."

"But I'm not wearing anything, Jones."

"I know." I give him a soft kiss.

Our lips cling, and he threads a hand through my hair.

"You're so beautiful to me," he says against my mouth.

I pull back to look him in the eyes. "To you?"

He often says that, and part of me wonders if others have said something contrary to him.

"To me." His fingers trace the curve of my shoulder, brushing a lock of hair over it. "When we're together, it's just you and me. No one else exists."

He makes me want to cry, to tell him things I've never allowed myself to think, much less say aloud.

"Drew." I press my fist against his chest. "You can't keep saying these perfect things to me." I give him a wobbly smile. "I mean, how am I supposed to match that?"

He chuckles. "Are you giving me grief for being too romantic?"

"No." I kiss his cheek, high up by the corner of his eye. "Maybe. I find that, when it comes to you, I'm competitive too."

Another laugh rumbles in his chest. "Game on, then?"

"Yeah." I kiss his other cheek.

He sighs, touches my neck, a light stroke. "Hit me with it, Jones."

"Drew?" I nuzzle his ear.

"Yeah?"

"I think you're real cute," I drawl.

He bursts out laughing. "Oh, wow," he deadpans. "I've just been schooled."

"You know it."

I've missed him. Happiness is a blade that cuts into my heart.

His warm palm skims up my thigh until his thumb brushes the curls between my legs. Immediately, my insides clench. More so when his voice lowers roughly. "Ah, I missed this. I missed the perfection of your pussy."

"Oh, that's smooth."

"Classy too."

We snicker, but another light touch of his thumb makes me utterly wet. He feels it and sighs, resting his forehead against mine. "Anna Jones's pussy. Total perfection."

"I'm thinking of having a T-shirt made up that says just that." I'm trying not to squirm against his roaming finger.

"At the very least, have it imprinted on your underwear." He flickers a thumb over my clit.

"I've decided to forgo underwear altogether." I'm breathless. "Seems a shame to cover perfection, you know?"

"Good plan. Don't want to smother our girl here."

"You're so thoughtful, Drew."

Though we're joking, and he's doing his best to turn me on, that somber air still hangs over him. His breathing is too slow and heavy, as if he has a massive weight on his chest. And my heart hurts for him. Especially when he absently traces the numbers on my chest once more.

"Hey." I cup his cheek. "You *will* wear one again. Don't you dare think otherwise."

"Yes, ma'am."

"I mean it, Drew. You will."

The corners of his eyes crease with worry. "What makes you so sure, beautiful?"

"Because it isn't in you to quit."

Drew's smile is slow, but wide. "Kiss me, Anna."

We meet halfway. Instantly, I open to him, and his tongue dips in to taste me. I shiver, loving the way he touches me, and he breathes into me on a sigh.

Under the sheet, his cock rises hard and strong, nestling between my legs. I rock against it, and we both groan. Drew cups my cheeks, holds me where he wants me.

"I love your lips." He suckles my bottom lip, plays with my mouth in that delicious way of his.

"I love the way you kiss," I say.

He hums, the vibration making my mouth tinge. He kiss goes deep then light. "I love *you*."

The words slap into me, and my entire body seizes. I'm shaking as I pull back to look at him. His expression is tender but wary. He knows he's turned my world on its ear.

"What did you say?" I choke out.

"You heard me." His tone is cautious, as if he's waiting for me to run away but hoping I won't.

Tears blur my vision. My body feels like lead. I sag in his arms and slump against his chest. Gently, he lifts me up a bit until he can see me.

"Hey." He thumbs away a tear. "I didn't tell you to upset you. I told you because holding it back is too hard." He leans in until our breaths mingle. "I want to tell you every day."

Drew pauses and vulnerability tightens the corners of his eyes.

"And you need to know what this is for me, because I wasn't clear before." Deep gold eyes hold mine. He's leaving himself wide open, revealing his soul. "You have my heart, Anna. And every time I had to walk away from you, every time you walked away from me, it felt like it was being ripped out of my chest. It fucking hurt, Anna."

His confession mirrors my feelings so closely that a fresh wave of hot tears well in my eyes. "It hurt me too. So much. I felt so empty I couldn't stand up straight."

Drew's dark brows furrow. "Why didn't you—"

"I was afraid. *Shit.*" I take an unsteady breath, feeling sick. "You shine so brightly, Drew. And it's beautiful to me, but I didn't know how to live under your light."

He frowns, his expression growing fierce. But his words are low, strong. "What people see? That is only gloss. But, Anna, you light *me* up. Drew. Not the player. You didn't know how to live under my light? I don't have a light anymore unless you're there."

"Drew." With a trembling hand, I stroke his neck then rest my palm in the center of his chest. "I'm not..."

I squeeze my eyes shut. I don't want to admit my weaknesses out loud. But this is Drew, and I trust him. More importantly, he deserves to know. I open my eyes and face him.

And he's watching me, uncertain now, likely hurting again, because of me and my fucking issues.

"I never went to prom," I blurt out. "I was never asked on a date, guys never even looked at me in high school."

His expression shifts from shock to confusion to an understanding that makes my insides pitch. My fingers curl against the dense rise of his pecs as I forge on.

"No one really liked me. I was the weird girl. The sullen one they wanted to pretend didn't exist." I snort, an ugly, pained sound. "Or maybe they really didn't know I existed."

I shrug, not wanting to meet his eyes, but I do. "Mom called me a late bloomer. Which means dick-all when you're sixteen and dying inside."

Viciously, I wipe at my eyes. "And you..." My voice cracks before I can bring it under control. "When I say you shine, I mean just that. You're the sun around which people orbit. If you had been in my school, you'd have been the one everyone looked toward to lead. You never would have seen me hiding in the shadows."

"Anna…" His voice is so gentle it sets my teeth on edge.

"No. Just…let me finish."

He gives an awkward nod.

"I know it wasn't fair to treat you the way I did," I say. "Or to put you in some category that I created due to bad experience and old teen angst. But it's hard, Drew."

My mouth trembles, I bite down on my lip. "It's hard nullifying all of that, because it came back every time you paid attention to me in public and people stared. When they'd ask why you're with me."

"I don't give a shit what people think," he cuts in on a rasp. "Only what you think."

My chin drops. I can't look at him anymore. "Don't you understand? I felt like an impostor. I kept waiting for you to realize that you'd got it wrong. That I was the girl you were never supposed to see."

"Not possible," he says with quiet fierceness.

"But—"

"Anna, baby, you would never be the girl I didn't see, whether we had met now or in high school." He pulls me in close, rubbing his nose along the tip of mine. "Don't *you* understand? I know you wouldn't be because, since the moment I laid eyes on you, you're all I *can* see."

Drew kisses me, lingering before he pulls back to study me. His eyes are clear and filled with so much emotion that my throat closes up.

As if he too is overcome, he swallows hard. "I love you, Anna Jones. That's not going to change. I loved you when I thought we'd never be together, and I love you still."

I let go of a sharp breath and then lean into him. I don't kiss his lips but the tender spot on his neck where his pulse beats. "I should have told you earlier."

His throat moves under my lips as he swallows. "Yeah." His lips brush my temple, his warm, rough palms smoothing down my thighs. "But I understand now."

"I'm so sorry, Drew." I place a tender kiss on the center of his chest.

His voice is thick. "Don't need that."

No, he needs the words, at the very least to know that I care for him too. I owe him so much more. Sitting back on his lap, I meet his eyes. Emotion clogs my throat, makes my heart speed up to a desperate thud, thud, thud.

He appears almost stern, his mouth relaxed but not smiling. God, he's everything. *Everything.*

I touch his cheek, grazing the beard-roughened skin there with my fingertips. My mouth opens yet nothing comes out. With a garbled sound, I throw myself on him, hugging him hard and burrow my face into the smooth crook of his neck. He's warm, his scent familiar and comforting in a bone-deep way that has me crying harder.

And though I've clearly shocked him, he wraps his arms around me and holds on tightly.

"Hey," he says softly. "Anna..."

"I'm sorry." I gulp down air, trying to calm. "I'm sorry."

But I can't stop shaking. His arms are steel supports against my back, his chest a solid slab that bolsters me. I snuggle in deeper. "I was so scared," I whisper against his damp skin. "I saw you... the hit. I needed to get to you, and..."

I can't say the rest.

Beneath me, his body relaxes a little and his big hand cups the back of my head before stroking it. "Shhh. It's okay."

But it isn't. How can I explain to him? If he hadn't gotten up from that hit, something vital inside me would have died. The truth chokes me, burns my throat.

"It's okay, Anna. I've got you." His smooth, deep voice rolls over my skin like a caress. "I won't let you go."

He won't. He never truly has.

I press my forehead to his. "This wasn't supposed to happen."

"What wasn't, baby?"

I run my shaking fingers along his jaw. "Finding you now. Before I got all of my shit together."

"But it did," he whispers. "And I'm not sorry."

Neither am I.

I look at him. Really look, my eyes wide open, letting him see all of me. Every hidden vulnerability. In return, I see the world in his. A tremor runs through me, and I cup his cheek.

"I love you, Drew Baylor. No one has *ever* meant as much to me as you have. I adore you, need you, crave you—"

His lips meet mine, his kiss deep and demanding.

I sink into it, clutching his neck and shoulders like a lifeline. And there is no more talking, just long searching kisses, and short, frantic ones. Places to touch and rediscover. Emotion and need surge in like the tide. The sheet covering his lap is tugged away, and his hot cock presses against my sex, slipping against the wetness there.

"Put me inside you," he breathes into my mouth, his lips nipping at mine. "I need to be inside you."

I rock against him, making him groan. I lift up and the thick, rounded crown of him presses against my opening. Our gazes lock. We both shudder as I sink down onto him. It feels so damn good, like everything I've missed and like nothing before. It's better. Truer.

The muscles along his chest strain as he pushes in further and a flush works over his cheeks. "God," he rasps, "I've missed being surrounded by you. So perfect. This is what I needed. You. Here."

"I know. I needed this too." I cup his cheeks with my hands. "I've missed you. I've missed you so much."

His eyes squeeze shut at the words, his throat working. His hands ease up to hold me as I hold him. And he thrusts up, meeting me halfway. Our foreheads touch, our breath mingling hot and uneven.

I ride him slowly, working my hips in an undulating rhythm that has us both trembling. My sex feels swollen, full of him. The pace is torture. I'm acutely aware of every inch of his thick girth moving in and out of me.

My skin steams, and I wrench the jersey off, the cool air tightening my nipples. Drew captures one in his mouth, sucking it with sharp tugs that I feel down to my core. My breath catches, and my insides clench. A move I know he feels when he groans and answers with a sharper thrust. His big hand clamps down on my butt, clenching and kneading it as if he's making up for lost opportunities.

God, he's so delicious looking, all sweaty and flushed, his muscles moving as his body rocks into mine. I lean down, lick along the strong column of his throat. His scent surrounds me, a comfort and an aphrodisiac. I love the way he smells, feels.

Both hands cup my butt now. His finger brushes against the entrance to my ass, and I hiss. Sensation, dark and forbidden, skitters through me at the touch.

Our eyes meet. Because Drew is paying attention to my every move, and because I am watching him, I see the understanding and the heated knowledge dawn in his eyes.

Slowly, deliberately, he strokes the spot again, an exploration that circles the area. And again, my insides tighten. It feels illicit, this touch, and despite my pounding heart, or maybe because of it, I push back against his finger. Just enough. His throat works on a swallow, his skin prickling. Within me, his cock swells.

Holding my gaze, and moving slow enough for me to stop him, Drew reaches over to the bedside table. I don't look at what he's doing. Part of me knows, and I go both hot and cold. Anticipation has my heart leaping within my chest and my throat going dry. We've both gone so still and tense, I feel his cock pulsing inside of me. Our mingled pants sound overloud in the silence. And then I see the gleam of his fingers now coated in olive oil.

The first touch is a slow, insistent push. I swallow hard, my clit throbbing and my entire lower half clenching. *God.*

The thick tip of his finger breeches the tight ring of my ass. I moan, my head falling forward. Oh God. What we're doing is something new for me. Something I never trusted anyone to do. It's personal, naughty, decadent. I want more.

Watching me with dark eyes, he sinks in further. My lids flutter, pleasure and a feeling of fullness overwhelming me. I'm so hot, so turned on, I can barely breathe. My chest is heaving now, my thighs shaking.

He shakes too, his heavily-lidded gaze never leaving mine, and I know he's never done anything like this either. He pants like he's run miles, sweat making his golden skin glisten.

With every thrust of his cock, his finger slides away, then pushes back in as his cock retreats. In and out, a slow, inexorable rhythm of dual attack that gets me hotter. I'm so weak, I can only lie prone against his chest and take it as I shiver and sweat.

Our lips brush, our breath shared. I kiss him, trusting my tongue in his mouth, fucking it just as he fucks me. Drew groans. His hips slam into mine, harder, aggressive.

Another finger plunges into me, and I whimper. The invasion aches, a sore heaviness that I both want to escape and push into further. I feel it everywhere, running up against my skin, licking down the valley of my spine. I'm going to melt right here, dissolve and sink into his flesh.

His next thrust wracks my body. My breasts slide over his slick chest. He wiggles his fingers. And I lose all sense of myself as I begin to come on a long, keening wail. I arch back, my hands braced on his shoulders.

But he doesn't stop tormenting me. He pushes deeper. The orgasm ratchets higher with each hitch of my breath. Frantically, I rock my hips, needing the friction. "Oh, shi— Oh, shi—"

I bow over Drew, my face burrowing into his neck, my entire body going so tight it shakes. Weakly, I grasp his shoulders as my hips grind against his. I need release. I'm still coming, pleasure tearing through me.

"Drew." It's a helpless plea. "Drew…"

On a deep groan, he turns his head, grabs the back of my neck. His kiss is frenzied, messy as he thrusts into me, hard and wild. The orgasm breaks over me like cold fire. I whimper into his mouth. He swallows it down, his breath coming out in fierce exhalations through his nostrils. His entire body shakes, his grip in my hair going tight as he bucks against me. He comes with a bellow that vibrates his frame.

For a long moment, we lie boneless and sweat-slicked. My body rises and falls with his chest as his breathing slows down. Then he holds me against him, one arm wrapped around my shoulders, the other about my hips, and peppers my face with tender kisses.

"Baby. You okay? That was…" A luscious shiver goes through him.

"Yeah," I rasp. "It *so* was."

Smiling, I play with the ends of his hair and weakly kiss him back. Finally. *Finally*, everything feels right.

Drew presses my hand against his sweaty chest where his heart still beats a fierce rhythm.

His voice is whisper-quiet but crystal clear. "My world lives in your palm, Anna."

And I'll fill it with all the love I have. We fall asleep that way, him still deep inside me, our bodies so entwined that we've become one.

THIRTY-SEVEN

DREW

I HAVE ANNA all to myself for seven days. Seven days of living by what I start to call the holy trinity of S—sex, sleep, and sustenance. It's all we really need. My bed is base camp, though we've made forays onto the couch, the kitchen counter, and that one time on my weight bench, though I can't recall how we even got there. I can, however, recall with perfect clarity the way Anna came, how her inner walls clutched me as she cried out. Which makes me horny all over again as I hobble out to the kitchen for more sustenance.

As a guy who has always operated under a schedule, I thought I'd grow antsy, need to get out and about, but I'm loving the break. As long as I don't think about football, I'm happy. Relaxed. When was the last time I was relaxed? I don't even remember. I do know one thing: it's because I'm with Anna. Anna who loves me. God, having her love does me in. It makes me feel as weak as a fucking kitten and as big as a fucking mountain.

As if my thoughts pulled her in, Anna enters the living room. Only she's carrying her overnight bag. Like that, my stomach bottoms out.

"You're going?" I think I sound casual, but I can't be sure. I'm too off balance to gage it.

She plops the bag down on the couch to put her hair in a ponytail. "I need to do some laundry."

"You can do it here." Smooth. That didn't sound at all needy.

She gives me a quick smile. "I know. But I'm kind of sick of these clothes too." Right. Well, there goes that argument.

Walking with her usual casual grace, she heads for the kitchen. "After breakfast, I think I'll head home and get a few things done."

I flick the back of my nail against my orange juice glass. "Okay."

I don't know what is wrong with me. I like my solitude. Anna ought to be able to take off whenever she wants. And I ought to be fine with that. I just know that the moment she walks out of this house, she'll take the sunshine of my day with her.

A loud, long buzz sounds, and the scent of coffee fills the air. The espresso maker. Gray brought it back earlier, pretending he'd been borrowing it while I was laid up in the hospital, a lie for which I'm still extremely grateful. Especially when Anna squealed over the thing like a kid on Christmas morning and tackled me when I'd told her I had bought it for her.

Anna takes her newly filled cup over to the counter and sits on one of the bar stools. She's wearing a white muscle shirt and boy short panties. It's fucking hot. I'm tempted to push the top over her breasts and suck the sweet tips, but there's a pit in my stomach that won't go away.

Oblivious of my souring mood, Anna rakes a tumble of curls from her face and takes a sip of coffee. "Tonight, I'm going to go out with Iris and George." She eyes me, and I don't miss the hesitation in her expression. "You ought to go out too. Maybe hang with your friends. Dex keeps calling."

She's afraid I'll become a hermit. Too late.

"Subtle, Jones."

Unrepentant, she grins. "It's one of my many qualities."

"Fine. I'll go out." I don't want to, but I'll be damned if I'll give her a reason to start pitying me.

"Good." She grabs a banana, frowns at it, then puts it down before hoping off the stool. Her pert ass lifts in the air as she rummages around in the depths of the fridge. "I guess I'll see you tomorrow."

My hand tightens on my glass.

"You can come back here tonight, Anna. It's fine. You have a key."

She doesn't look at me as she helps herself to the yogurt. "Naw. It will be late." Not something I care about. "And, anyway, I should get out of your hair for a while. Give you some space."

Shit, her hands are moving too quickly, putting away the yogurt, messing with a dishrag, toying with the handle of her spoon. I watch her flutter about, and my heart sinks down into the cavity of my chest.

"Do you need space?" I say this as carefully as I can. But she still freezes like a caught thief and eyes me warily. I feel like we've stumbled onto a minefield.

"Do you?" she volleys back.

Despite my unease, a smile pulls at my lips. "Are we going to talk in circles now?"

Some of the starch leaves her shoulders. Her tilted smile mirrors mine. "Maybe. Why don't you define your idea of space, and I'll tell you mine."

This is one of those girl traps, designed to leave you wide open to fall in a hole of your own making. I know it, and she knows it. But her direct gaze tells me I'd better answer or I'll just fall into yet another hole. Damn female logic. I run a hand through my hair.

"'Space' would be we do stuff together because we want to be together. We do stuff apart because we want to do stuff apart."

Slowly she nods, her eyes never leaving mine. "I'd say the same."

Some of the tension eases from my chest. "To be clear," I tell her, "being with you is the highlight of my day."

Anna bites the bottom of her lip, but she can't hide the pleased expression blooming over her features. "You're the highlight of my day too."

It's my turn to nod, not quite looking at her because I don't want her to see my relief.

She's staring at me again. "That isn't all you want to say though, is it?" She waves an idle hand as if to draw the rest out of me. "Come on, I know there's more."

I grip the back of my neck. "Move in with me."

The words are out of my mouth before I even fully process them. And they hang there between us, a detonated smoke bomb that makes her squint at me.

Her mouth opens and closes before a weak "What?" rips from her throat.

I don't back down, don't look away. "I know you probably have tons of very good, very logical reasons that we shouldn't live together so soon. Hell, I can think of a dozen right now. But here's the thing—" my fingers spread wide on the counter, the granite cold beneath my palm "—in the beginning, I moved with caution, not wanting to spook you or push you—"

"And you don't mind pushing me now?" she cuts in, her voice wry but accompanied by a wobbly smile.

It's that smile that gives me some hope that she won't turn on her heel and run any second.

"That's not it. I wasn't honest with you then. With what I wanted." I take a step closer, my hand trailing over the counter towards hers. "And everything went to hell."

Dark shadows creep into her eyes. Guilt. I know this, but I'm not going to take back what I've said.

I lower my voice, make it gentle, persuasive. "So I figure, I lay everything on the table now. Because, Anna—" My fingers touch her cold ones, and I thread them with mine, holding on tight. "When I said I wanted everything, that's what I meant. I want to go to sleep with you, to wake up with you. Every day. The thought of you going home tonight, and me sleeping without you? I hate it."

"You do?"

"You sound surprised."

Lips slightly parted, she shakes her head. "No. I... I hate that idea too. I didn't know if you'd want me to stay or go or..." She trails off looking flustered.

More than a fucking glimmer of hope.

I give her fingers a light squeeze. "I should probably finish stating my intentions."

"There's more?" She's fighting a smile.

"Yeah." I draw her around the counter to stand in front of me. Her head tilts back as she looks up, and I touch the curve of her cheek with my thumb. My heart pounds against my ribs. I'm going all in. But it's what I do best. And I've learned my lesson; Anna is too important to go at with half measures.

"One day," I tell her, "I want to marry you."

Her whole body gives a reflexive jerk, her mouth dropping open. "Marry me?"

I can't help but smile at her shock. "Not now. We're not ready for that yet." I trace her bottom lip with the tip of my thumb. "But one day. One day, I will ask you and hope that you say yes." I palm her cheek. "You're it for me, Anna Marie."

She steps into my space, her hand landing on my waist while her other hand smoothes over my forearm to clasp tight. My heart squeezes before something deep within eases. She's searching my face, a small smile breaking over her. "Because sometimes you just know?"

A grin pulls tight at my cheeks. "You *have* been paying attention."

And then she's easing into my embrace, her hands sliding over my chest and around my neck. Everything inside me goes warm as I bend down to meet her lips, but I stop just shy of them. "Is that a yes?"

She halts too, her cheeks plumping on a smile. "You know, you didn't have to persuade me. I was going to say yes."

My gut tightens. She snuggles closer, nibbling along my jaw, up to the sensitive corner of my mouth. I feel it at the base of my balls.

"You were?" I follow her mouth with mine, trying to capture it, but she's evading, a smile gracing her lips as she brushes them across mine.

I grasp the curve of her hips and pull her hard against me. "*Jones.*"

"*Baylor.*" She laughs, and then gives in, her fingers playing with the leather cord around my neck. "Of course I was."

Her thumb caresses the sliver of wood I carved out of my parent's house. When her eyes find me, they're wide and deep green. "You're my home, Drew."

I let out an unsteady breath. "We'll be each other's home."

ANNA

Telling my friends that I'm moving in with Drew goes about as well as I expect it to, which is not very. Right in, Iris starts on me.

"Are you fucking crazy?" She follows me into my room, watching as I open my closet and haul out the steamer trunk my mother sent me off to college with. "You just got back together. Why would you move in with him?"

"Because he asked?" I heave the trunk onto my bed. "And because I want to?"

George saunters into the room. "What about Iris? You can't leave her in a lurch."

I glance at him before going to my dresser. "You think I'd do that?" It hurts that he does, but I get it; he's watching out for his sister. "I'll still pay the rent here until Iris moves out for grad school."

"So Drew's gonna be like your sugar daddy?" Iris sneers at the very idea.

"Yeah, because that's so me." I roll my eyes. "He owns the house outright and only pays utilities. I'm paying for groceries."

I'd wanted to pay for more, but Drew insisted. His name is on all the bills, and he has the money, so we'd compromised.

Iris plops down on the bed and idly flicks the trunk's lock. "I get that you're happy to be back with Drew, Banana, but, come on, you've been avoiding commitment like the plague, and now you're going to move in with him?"

I can't blame Iris for her skepticism. If I had heard myself even a few weeks ago, I'd have thought the same thing. But things change. People grow up.

"For months I've been resisting letting Drew in, convinced that I'd lose who I am if I did. That he'd crush my heart. But I was the one destroying my soul. I was fucking miserable."

Even the shadow of that memory hurts. I brush it aside with a deep breath. "I'm happy with him."

"That doesn't mean you have to live with him," she says.

"No, it doesn't. But if being with him makes me happy, then why stay apart for fear that it might not work? *That* would be a mistake."

"But you're so young. Don't you want to see what the world has to offer?"

As if life is somewhere just around the corner, and I'll find it if only I keep searching. It's what we've all been promised, an elusive brass ring that's always just out of reach, and one day, one day it will pop up in front of us. Well, I don't want a treadmill life. I've tried it and it sucks.

I shake my head. "I used to think that if I figured out what I wanted to do with my life, everything would fall into place. Now?" I shrug. "Now I'm thinking that happiness is never going to be having the perfect job, house, life. It isn't a destination, you know? It's a series of moments. I mean, isn't that what life is? Moments? The here and now?"

I stuff my underwear into a bag. "Yeah, I still have to discover what I want to do with my life. I could end up with the greatest career in the world, but at the end of the day, who I come home to, who I share my accomplishments with is what makes the struggle worth it. And for me, that's Drew. So, yes, it's reckless and it may blow up in my face, but I am not afraid. I'm more excited than I've ever been. So just…support me, will you?"

"Shit," George drawls on a smile. "We've got her monologuing." He ducks a sock I chuck at his head. His expression turns serious. "If you're that sure about it, then you have my blessing, young Anna."

I kiss the top of his head. "Thanks, Georgie." Then I give his head a light whack. "Smart-ass."

He laughs. But Iris doesn't. Her dark eyes are still troubled. Which troubles me. "'Ris?"

Slowly she shakes her head. "I still say you're making a mistake. But I'm with George. If you're that sure, I'll support you."

"I've never been more sure of anything." I thought I had lost myself in Drew. But the truth was that I'd found myself in him.

It never occurs to me that Drew might be the one to lose faith.

THIRTY-EIGHT

ANNA

I DON'T SEE the trouble at first. All I see is Drew. The only thing that occupies my time is the way we instantly click together when I move in. We get along so well, it's like having an endless sleepover with my favorite person in the world. So of course I miss the signs.

It isn't until another week passes and his friends start showing up that I notice something's wrong. For one thing, Drew doesn't want to see them. These are his teammates. These guys practically live in each other's pockets. And now? Now Drew is hunched on the far recliner, staring off at nothing, while his boys hang out on his couch, watching an NFL game. They're a boisterous lot, shouting and laughing and trading good-natured insults. I like them.

They also eat. A lot. I'm bustling back to the kitchen for more chips when Drew snags my arm.

"You don't have to feed them, babe."

I run a hand over his hair. "I'm half Irish, half Italian, and all southern, Drew. It's physically impossible for me not to offer food and drink to company." Honestly, I think I'd die of shame if I didn't.

His brows snap together as he glances over at them. "Then I'll tell them to leave. Problem solved."

Laughing, I kiss his forehead, and his arm instantly wraps about my waist. I lean into him, because he seems to need it.

"But I like that they're here. They're your friends. Which means they're mine too."

He grumbles something under his breath, but I ignore it, hoping that his mood will elevate now that he knows I'm not put out by company.

It doesn't. It gets worse. He sinks into a silence that somehow shouts loud and clear that he's displeased.

"Yo, Drew," his friend Rolondo calls over to him. "Man, you need to settle down over there. I swear, you talk any more and you gonna bust a gut." He grins as he says this and chucks a cheese puff at Drew's head.

Drew swats it away. "Pretty sure you do enough talking for all of us, 'Londo."

There's no humor in his tone. I haven't had much interaction with the star wide receiver, but I know Drew and Rolondo are close. Rolondo's glaze flicks to mine, and I see the worry there, and it feeds my own.

It gets worse when halftime comes on, and one of the guys changes over to ESPN. As luck would have it, they're talking about Drew and his chances of still being a top draft pick. Apparently, most experts had slated him to be the number one pick. Now, with his injury, it's all up in the air. Everyone stiffens, Drew most of all, but no one seems capable of changing the channel.

The light of the screen flickers off Drew's stony expression as he watches some oversized guy in a slick suit speculate about his leg. And my heart aches for him. Until they mention their visit to campus. Instantly, my gut plummets. Shit. I've been the one who's gone out for food—or sustenance as Drew's taken to calling it—and I hadn't exactly been left alone.

I edge closer to the remote. "Maybe we should watch—"

"Here's what Anna Jones, Drew Baylor's girlfriend, had to say," announces the reporter.

My face shows up on the screen, microphones being shoved under my nose as I try to escape from the parking lot at the Piggly Wiggly. I feel my cheeks heat. God, does my face really look that round?

Instantly, everyone perks up, shooting glances as me, then back at the TV. I can't even meet Drew's eyes. I want to cry. I stare at the TV instead. The footage splices to my face, the very moment I'd broken, tired of hearing the doubt in the reporters' voices, of seeing them turn against their hero. I'd wanted to punch each and every one of them.

"You named him Battle for a reason," my voice snaps through the speakers. I look angry. I remember that anger. It had fueled me, made my words come out hard. "Because he never quits. You're going to have to trust that he won't give up on this either."

I pushed past them then and escaped in Drew's car.

My face is positively on fire now. Every eye is on me, but I only care about one set, and he isn't looking my way. And then I notice that the rest of the guys are grinning.

"You tell 'em, Scarlett," says Marshall, which for some reason earns him a bap on the head by Dex.

"Ain't nobody messing with our boy," Rolondo insists. "Not with our girl kicking ass."

Gray catches my eyes, and a small, bemused smile plays about his mouth. I blush harder.

And then they're all laughing and talking as if nothing happened.

I stare at Drew until he finally lifts his head. I can't tell what he's thinking, and that scares me. I move close to him, afraid to touch him. I shouldn't have talked. Never talk to the press. Even I know that.

Still not quite meeting my gaze, Drew collects my hand. His is cold and dry as he links his fingers with mine and brings them up for a kiss. "You defended me." It's a quiet murmur.

"Of course I did. I'll always defend you, Drew."

He presses his lips against my fingers. "I'm sorry you had to deal with that."

"I'm not. I'm only sorry that they had to ask. Of course you're coming back."

He looks away. Not long after, he hobbles into our room, claiming that he's tired. He doesn't come back out. And from then on, he doesn't ask the guys over. Avoids them all with a skill that would be impressive if it didn't worry me so much.

"I only want you," he whispers against my neck in the dark cocoon of our bed. "Only you."

It should please me. But it doesn't.

DREW

As long as I don't think about football, I'm all right. But the world doesn't want me to stop thinking about football. I'm beginning to resent the claim the game and its fans have on me. I've given it my all. I'm tired now.

Coach expects me to come to practice, there's only one game left, and it's the National Championship. I need to be there, show my support. The coward in me wants to hide. I don't want the pitying looks. But my team deserves better from me. So I'll go. But Coach also wants me to go to physical therapy. I need to stay in form as my leg heals.

I promise to go to PT, but I don't. I don't do anything. And it becomes a weight on my chest. But I can't seem to snap out of it. I know Anna notices. She hasn't said anything, but it's coming. She wouldn't be Anna if she kept her opinions to herself.

Worse? The nightmares. They hit me like a sack. I wake shaking and sweating. It takes me too long to realize that I'm not on the field, my mask buried in mud, turf in my mouth, and my leg bone snapped in half.

But I'm okay. As long as I don't think about football, I'll be okay.

Hard not thinking about something you love.

Anna has gone out with Iris. She was antsy as she left, fidgeting with the car keys and kissing me almost absently as she bustled out of the door.

I sit on a stool at my kitchen counter and spin a bottle cap. Is she disappointed in me? Does she want me to go out more? I rub my fingers against the stubble on my jaw. Hell, I haven't gone anywhere in weeks, not wanting to see people. The last time I ventured out for a checkup, the sheer number of pity pats, get well soons, and you were the best we'd ever had—one incident accompanied by a grown man literally crying on my shoulder, God help me—was an absolute nightmare. I'd broken out into a sweat and almost threw up before Anna had reached the house.

She hadn't said much then, just that people were fucking weird. When we were safe at home, she'd taken me to bed and kept me occupied for the night. It isn't right, the way I'm leaning on her. It's yet another thing I can't seem to stop.

A knock on the door jerks me out of my funk. I literally flinch, my back tightening and my heart beating too hard. With a snarl of irritation at myself, I push back from the counter and get the door.

Coach stands on the threshold, his weathered face shadowed by a baseball cap. He's going casual, which, for him, means slacks and a polo shirt. It also makes me suspicious. Coach is probably not aware, but he has tells. A suit means he's going to kick your ass in a hurry. Casual means he'll come at you as a friend, hoping to sneak past your resistance before you realize you've been played.

"Hey, Coach." I step back to let him in.

"Drew." He heads for the kitchen. He's been here enough to know where it is. Coach helped me pick the place. Helped me pick my ass off the floor when my parents died. And I don't want him here. The smell of his expensive cologne makes my throat close up.

He turns and looks me over. "How you doing?"

"Good." I limp to the counter. A half-empty beer bottle rests on it. I want to drink it down, and at the same time, shove it away, hide it from Coach.

I settle for resting my hands on the cold marble. "You want a beer or something?" God, I just want him out of my house. His presence is choking me.

He gives me a level look. "You drink often?"

I can't help but snort. "I'd like to think I'm not so prosaic as to become a drunk. Or a druggie," I add because I know his next question will be about my painkillers.

Annoyingly, he smiles in that way of his, like I've made him proud. Which makes me want to smash things. But the smile falls. "You've missed another PT session."

What can I say? Nothing. The weight on my chest grows. I feel him watching me.

"Want to tell me why you missed? And practice too? You might not be able to play, but you are still a member of this team. It reflects poorly on you and the team when you don't show."

Never have I heard such subdued disappointment from my coach. I clear my throat.

I can't tell him the truth. How can I tell this man that I don't want to return?

The giant clock my mom salvaged from a downtown building in Chicago ticks away in the dining room. And then Coach takes a step toward me.

"If you could see yourself the way I do." He shakes his head. "I just don't want all that potential to go to waste, Drew."

"Yeah, well neither do I." Unfortunately, some things aren't under my control. I shift my weight further onto my good leg, and say what I need to say to get him out of here. "Look, I won't miss another PT."

The choking sensation grows, clogging my throat, filling my lungs.

"The break is clean," he says. "You're young and strong. You'll heal and be back to top form in no time."

I make the mistake of meeting his eyes. I know he sees everything. That he gets what's going on in my head, that I'm spooked. That the instant I heard my leg snap, something within me did as well, and I'd realized everything I'd ever relied on was as solid as smoke.

Maybe he too is thinking of my dad, whose pro career was snatched away by a college injury. My dad wasn't a bitter man, but the loss haunted him. I'd seen it in his eyes, in the way he'd grow distant sometimes when we talked about me going to the NFL. My dad was the best man I've ever known. But I don't want to become him, not that way.

Coach had to understand this. He'd been friendly with my dad. The silence between us stretches tight, and I want so badly to look away that I grind my teeth.

"Drew." Coach pauses, and I know it's going to get worse. "Maybe it'd be good if you saw a counselor—"

"No," I shout despite my desire to keep calm. "I'm not fuckin—" I take a sharp breath and hold up a hand. "I'm not going to a counselor, all right? So just get that off the table now."

"There's no shame in talking to someone."

"You think I don't know that?" I hobble over to the kitchen island with enough force to make my leg ache. "I was there enough when my parents died. I'm fine." I glare at him. "Fine."

Coach sighs. "Just think about it, son."

"I'm not your son." Great, I sound petulant now. I grip my hair to keep from shouting again.

"I know that," he says quietly. "But that doesn't mean I can't care about you and what you're going through." His gaze pins me. "And I promised your parents that I'd look out for you. I don't go back on my promises. Neither do you."

A low blow. Because, when I'd agreed to play under Coach's

program after he'd vowed to do right by me, I'd promised my parents that I'd respect the man's rules. Now there's nothing I can say that won't come across as defensive. I pinch the bridge of my nose, pushing against my aching eyes. I just want to sleep.

Coach's heavy hand lands on my shoulder and gives it a squeeze. "Just think about it, okay?"

Duly, I nod, but it's an empty promise and we both know it.

It might have helped if Anna came home. She can distract me better than anyone. In truth, she's the only one I want around me these days. Something I know should worry me.

The only distraction I can find is doing some upper body-work on the weight bench. When I hear the phone ring, I set the weights down with a clang. Unfortunately, it isn't Anna but Gray.

"Hey, man. I'm coming over and making lasagna tonight. And before you say no, Anna says you're free. Shocking, isn't it?"

I frown down at my cast. "You talked to Anna first?"

"Uh, yeah. How else am I going to get an invite anymore?" The annoyance in his voice is thick, and it irks me.

"Then why bother telling me? Why not just show up?"

"Because I'm not a dick?"

"You sure about that?"

The silence on the other end of the line is total.

Okay, that was shitty. But I can't help it. The little fucker is plotting behind my back. With Anna. My chest clenches tight. Fuck it, did they know Coach was coming over too? Heat crawls up my neck. I'm pretty fuck-all sure they did.

When Gray finally speaks, his voice is sharp with anger. "What's your problem, Drew?"

I have a long list right now. "Forget it."

"Right," Gray snaps. "I'll do that."

Which means he'll glare at me when he gets here and make me feel like shit. I rake my hand through my hair, pushing down on my scalp. My head is a steady throb of pain now. "You need a ride?"

Because it occurs to me, with a sinking feeling, that not only has the punk offered to cook for me again, he's also lent me his truck, which has an automatic drive, so I'm not stuck in the house. Guilt sucks.

"Naw," Gray says, lighter now. "Anna said she'd bring me."

My teeth meet with a loud clack. Right. Because they're communicating. My grip on the phone goes knuckle white. "Gotta go. See you later."

There's another awkward pause, then Gray speaks. "See you." He hangs up.

The phone is a brick in my hand. I want to call Anna and ask her why she thinks it's okay to sic my friend on me. Is this some sort of sympathy party? Or does she no longer like hanging out only with me? Is Gray here as a buffer?

"Shit."

I hate being paranoid. Hate this feeling of dissatisfaction crawling through me at all hours. I need to get out of the house.

Taking Gray's truck—which brings on a fresh wash of guilt— I head out. Anna likes wine, so I'm going to get her some for dinner.

Unfortunately, once at the store, it's clear I have no idea what I'm doing. I know she'd like red with lasagna, or at least that's what my parents always drank with it. But there's like five hundred bottles of red. What type would she prefer? Merlot? Cabernet? Pinot Noir? What's the difference?

"Hell."

"Can I help you... Drew?"

I turn to find Jenny staring up at me. Double hell.

I've managed to avoid seeing her for over a year. Which was fine by me. It's strange seeing her now. Every inch of her is both familiar yet strange.

Jenny has that flawless type of beauty. Perfect bone structure, brilliant blue eyes, glossy dark hair, and a model's body. These were the things that drew me to her in the first place.

I saw myself as a demigod back then, and thus needed to have the proper window dressing to go with my elevated status. Goes to show you what being an arrogant dick will get you.

"Do you work here?" It's all I can think to say.

She blushes, ducking her head, and her hair falls over her shoulder in a wave of shining brown. "No. I…well, I saw you standing here frowning at the wine…"

She gives me a helpless shrug, pressing her arms close to her sides as she does it, which makes her breasts thrust out and her ass lift.

The ducking of her head, the shrug. I've seen these moves a thousand times. I used to wonder if she did them to highlight her looks. Now I'm almost sure.

"I thought I'd talk to you," she says softly, coming a bit closer.

The scent of artificial strawberry fills my nose. I know it well. Strawberry body butter. After a shower, she'd stand naked in front of me and rub it all over herself in slow, meditative moments designed to entice. Only she was always coy about it, pretending that she was merely getting ready while not so subtly shaking her ass. One night Jenny jacked me off using a handful of the stuff. Ten minutes after I came, my dick turned bright red and fucking burned like fire. No matter how much I rinsed the poor bastard off, my skin remained irritated for a week.

My balls clench in remembered terror.

"I'm so sorry," she murmurs. Somehow, she's now inches away from me. My back is to the wine rack. "About your injury. I know how much playing meant to you."

She's sorry about my injury? The second I'd heard the words *I'm sorry* coming out of her mouth, I'd assumed she was apologizing for showing the world our personal correspondence, or maybe for making people believe I was a whiny wimp after every game. That still pisses me off.

Then again, I shouldn't be shocked at her focus on football. Jenny always wanted me to succeed. She wanted to hear my name chanted as much as I did, until it became clear that she would no longer be part of the show.

She wanted to be my wife. *Wife.* The second I'd heard that word come out of her mouth, I'd wanted to run as fast as I could in the other direction. I had cared for her, liked the way she took care of me, but I hadn't been in love with her. And in that moment, I knew I never would be. I still don't know if my rejection broke her heart or simply pissed her off. Jenny always kept her feelings close.

"It is what it is," I mumble. The back of my neck feels hot again, the perfumed scent of strawberry making my nose twitch.

"You'll be back." Her blue eyes gaze up at me sweetly. "I know you will."

Anna had said the same thing. Only she'd glared at me when she did, as if I'd better not defy her by arguing.

Tentatively, Jenny reaches out. Her fingers are cool, the tips of her manicured nails pressing into my skin. "I've missed you, Drew."

One nail traces up my forearm. Her breasts are almost touching my chest, her lips parted in invitation. I could have her. I could follow her home and fuck her blind. Sex with Jenny was all about what she could do for me. Which sounds good in theory, but no matter how many times I asked, she'd never give me an opinion of her own. Knowing Jenny, she'd still let me do anything I want to her.

And I feel exactly nothing. Nothing except the ever-present creepy-crawly mix of anxiety and anger that has writhed under my skin since the hit.

She's looking at me with a glimmer of victory in her eyes. As if she thinks she's irresistible.

Maybe she is to some. She might appear flawless on the surface, but it's what is underneath that I find lacking. And looking my fill of her has never given me the visceral punch of want that I get from just one glance of Anna.

Anna who, with her wild curls and generous curves, is more beautiful to me than Jenny ever will be. Anna who smells of exotic spices, warm skin, and home. Anna who brings me peace yet can wind me up hotter and tighter than a suspension coil.

Anna who is staring at me from across the wine rack.

My whole body seizes, going prickling hot then ice-cold.

Her syrup-rich voice comes out rough. "I just thought I'd get some wine for dinner." With a shaking hand, she holds up a bag of wine bottles as I gape at her in mindless horror. "Looks like you were doing the same."

Her green eyes flicker to Jenny before going back to me. "I'll leave you to your...chat."

And then she's walking away, and the floor feels like it's falling out from under me.

THIRTY-NINE

ANNA

FUCK, FUCK, fuck a duck. I stride through the parking lot, paid wine in hand, my head pounding in time with my frantic heart-beat. I hate what I just saw. Hate it. My stomach turns and my mouth fills with saliva. I want to go back there and grab that little skank by her hair and smash her face into the cabernet section.

My fingers fumble with the car key, which shakes as I turn the lock and wrench open the door.

I know who she is. Jenny. The nasty little bitch who tried to ruin Drew's life when he wouldn't roll over for her. I know be-cause the twat had on a pink football jersey—a size too small—with the name "Jenny" printed along the back. Gag. I cannot believe Drew went out with someone who wears clothes with her name on them.

Obviously, she wants to try again now that he's vulnerable.

God, the way she looked at him, like some cat all set to lick up the cream. Bitch.

"Anna!" Drew can move pretty fast on crutches if motivated. He practically flies across the parking lot, his eyes wild and his face pale. "Wait."

I get in the car and turn it on, loving the way it roars to life beneath me. This is Drew's car, and I don't really care, because I'm about to drive away from his ass in it. Before I can slam the door closed, however, he grabs it, hopping a little as he leans a hip against the car.

"I can explain." He is panting now, sweat dripping down his temple.

"Just the words a girl longs to hear," I mutter. Heat prickles behind my eyes. Not now. I need a breather.

The bitch walks out of the store, hovering there and watching us with interest.

She'll be here to pick up the pieces should I lay into Drew now.

He doesn't even look her way. His eyes, wide and pained, drill into me. "You have to know that—"

"At the house," I say. "Now get out of the way."

"No." He leans in, grabbing at my hand with his clammy one. "Talk to me."

"Not. Here." I give a pointed look in the bitch's direction. "I am not doing this with an audience."

Shockingly, he steps back and gives a short nod. "Okay." He holds up a hand. "Okay, but I'm following you."

Good to his word, he follows right behind me as I drive home. Even though I long to do it, I don't speed but keep a steady pace and take deep breaths the whole way home. My hands are cold and sweaty on the steering wheel.

I want to throw up. I want to cry. Drew is slipping away from me. And I don't know if I can handle the situation.

Once home, I slam out of the car, only to hear Drew drive up and do the same. I say nothing as I let myself in and set the wine on the kitchen counter. By the time he's inside and shutting the door, I'm rinsing off my hot face with cool water.

"Anna." His voice is soft, coaxing as he comes closer. "Baby, I know that looked bad, but—"

"It's okay." I turn to face him, taking in his pasty complexion and confused frown. "It's okay, Drew."

His heel thumps against the floor as he limps up to me.

"Not that I want to fight," he begins slowly, "but I've been close to losing my mind with fear for the past twenty minutes, so can you explain this to me?"

His brows rise, but he looks pained as he stares down at me. "Because I'm at a loss here."

I rest my hand over his cold one, and instantly he captures it, threading his fingers through mine and holding tight as if I might run. The gesture makes me smile even though I'm suddenly so exhausted that I want to lie down. He's in a panic. Not that I blame him. The scene that I stumbled into looked very cozy to someone on the outside.

"I saw the way you looked at her," I tell him.

"How did I look at her?" His voice is a rasp, his gaze darting over my face in rampant curiosity.

"Like she was an insect."

A short, humorless laugh leaves him. "Yeah, that about sums it up."

With a quick tug, he hauls me into his arms and holds me tight as he burrows his nose into my hair.

"Christ. I saw you standing there, and I thought…" He snuggles in deeper, his lips pressing on the top of my head. "I love the way you smell."

It's a rather odd change of subject, but I don't question it. I wrap my arms around his waist. Simply doing that settles the rampant jittering within my chest.

"You thought what?" I ask. "That I'd leave you?"

I can feel the tension gathering in his back.

"Maybe," he mumbles into my hair. "I don't know. I wasn't

thinking past the initial panic. Definitely thought there'd be yelling, maybe a wine bottle smashed over my head."

I laugh against his shoulder where my face is currently being smushed. But I'm fine where I am, warm and secure.

"I trust you, Drew." If he had been looking at his ex the way he looks at me, there would have been a fight. It would have destroyed me. But I didn't doubt him for a minute, because I saw his distress and the way he angled away from the little witch.

Surprise ripples over him, and he pulls back a bit to meet my eyes. "Why'd you drive away like that then?"

I shrug. "I needed a moment. Otherwise, I might have smashed that little shit's face in."

He's clearly struggling not to smile. Smart guy. "So no catfight jokes?"

"Not if you want to live."

His eyes are clear and warm. "Do you know what I was thinking just before I saw you?"

"Do I want to know?" I say with a half frown.

He grins. "I was thinking that you were my home and my peace."

"God, I sound positively provincial. Was I wearing an apron in this image?" I pretend to roll my eyes, but happiness fills me up.

"If I did picture that, it would be all you were wearing." Pulling me back in, he wraps his arms around me until we're pressed hip to hip. Close enough to feel the bulge growing behind his jeans. "I was also thinking that you make me hotter than anyone ever has."

"Sweet talker." But I kiss him. Because it's impossible to be this close to him and not kiss him. Happiness swells within me. "Love you, Baylor."

"Love you more, Jones." He takes over the kiss, angling his head and delving in deeper, appreciating me with his mouth.

"Drew," I say between hot, searching kisses.

"Mmm?" He suckles my upper lip before licking my bottom one.

"How did your talk go with your coach?" I have to ask. If I let him distract me, I'll forget and it's important.

Drew, however, stiffens and lets me go with a frown. "You knew he was coming over."

I'm not going to apologize about it. He needs someone to talk to besides me.

Someone who might understand how it feels. Sympathetic I am, but I haven't been there. I'm not a competitive athlete.

"Did you discuss therapy?"

"Jesus," Drew snaps, running a hand through his hair. The golden-brown ends stick up at the top. He falls back against the counter and glares. "I don't want to talk about this."

Of course not. He never does. I open my mouth to tell him as much when the door opens.

"Hey, hey, hey!" Gray saunters in with a big bag of groceries under his arm. Oblivious, he sets it on the counter. "You." He points a finger at me. "Forgot to pick me up."

I wince. "Oh, hell, Gray. I'm sorry. I got distracted."

"Yeah, yeah, just leave the poor, defenseless tight end sitting on the curb while you get busy with the QB."

He grins though before giving me a kiss hello on the cheek.

Over his shoulder, Drew's scowl deepens as he glares pointedly at my cheek. A prickle of annoyance hits me. So I can overlook his slutty ex rubbing herself against him, but he's pissy about a kiss on the cheek? I glare back, as Gray turns and gives Drew a pat on the shoulder.

"Hey, man. How's it going?"

"Great." Drew sounds like he's grinding down a tooth.

If Gray notices, he doesn't mention it. "Cool. But hold up, I've got to piss like you wouldn't believe."

Drew rolls his eyes as Gray runs off to the bathroom. "Why did you invite him here?"

"Hush." I give his waist a quick pinch, and he yelps, skirting away from my reach. "He's here because he's your friend, you ass."

"He's just feeling sorry for me."

"Well, who wouldn't when you've decided to revert to being five?"

Drew gives me a warning look, which I ignore.

"He's here because he cares. And since when have you not liked Gray's company?"

"Since he started kissing my girl?" he offers with false pleasantness.

I gape at him. This isn't Drew. He isn't overly possessive or irrational. He doesn't turn on friends.

"You're going to regret that statement," I tell him quietly. "You're going to realize what a shit you're being."

His lips flatten into a line, but Gray's already walking down the back hall. He eyes us but doesn't miss a step. "Now, then," he says as if nothing's wrong. "Let's get cooking."

Drew is sullen as Gray cooks. He's sullen when we sit down to dinner. And he's sullen when we eat it.

My hand clenches around my napkin, the urge to chuck it at his head running high.

All I can do is struggle to keep the strained conversation going with Gray.

"All right," I tell Gray. "You make an admirable lasagna. It's not as good as my mom's, but it will do."

"Don't kill me with praise now." Gray laughs then shakes his head. "I'm not trying to beat your Italian mama in a lasagna cook-off, Jones."

Drew scoffs. The sound sudden and harsh. "'Jones'?"

Jones is his nickname for me. But I hadn't thought he'd be territorial about it.

He levels a look at Gray, and my chest grows tight. "And here I thought you didn't like my girl."

I frown at Drew. So, being a dickweed is on the menu for tonight. Good to know.

Gray doesn't flinch. "Naw, man—" He grins at me as he answers. "It's all good. Anna and I worked out our issues over pie."

He's trying to reassure Drew, but even I know he's said the wrong thing.

The high crests of Drew's cheeks turn rusty. "Apparently so," he says with a sneer.

Gray's shoulders bunch as he goes still and stares at Drew. When he speaks, his voice is cold and flat. "What are you implying, man?"

"Gray, he doesn't…" I begin.

But Gray holds up a hand, not taking his eyes off Drew. "Let him say what he wants to say, Anna."

Gray's nostrils flare a bit. "So, tell me, are you accusing me of trying to make a play for your girl?"

He's pissed, more than I've ever seen him, but behind it is intense hurt. I hurt for both of them.

The corded muscles along Drew's forearms stand out as he clenches a fist. They stare each other down, a combined four hundred plus muscled pounds of growing male aggression. Neither of them appears to be willing to break eye contact first. Then Drew moves, so fast, I flinch.

His fist slams down on the table, rattling the plates.

"No," he snaps, then takes a harsh breath before shoving back from the table. "No, all right?"

His movements are not with his usual grace when he rises, bumping his leg on the chair. "I'm just fucking tired of you two sneaking around trying to fix me."

"Sneaking around?" I almost shout the words, I'm so irate, but I'm not going to fight with him in front of Gray.

Gray snorts. "We're trying to help you."

"Well, don't."

"Tough shit, Baylor. That's what friends do."

Drew's jaw clenches. "There's nothing wrong with me. Or am I expected to waltz around shooting daisies out my ass all the time?"

"I don't care what you shoot out of your ass," Gray says. "Just as long as you aren't accusing me of betraying my best friend."

Drew flinches, his mouth pinching. But he doesn't apologize. He walks away, his stride determined, awkward, and angry. "I'm going to bed."

Gray stands. "I'll go."

"Don't bother. Do whatever you want." Drew pauses at the door to our room. He doesn't turn but his fist curls on the door frame. "Thanks for dinner." The words are curt and clearly torn from him out of force of habit, and then he's shutting the door behind him with a dull thud.

My shoulders sag. "I'm sorry, Gray."

He shakes his head, his blue eyes still full of hurt and anger. "I expected it. Damn if he hasn't been alluding to it for a while."

"He doesn't mean it, you know." I'm not sure if he does or not. I do know that, were Drew his old self, he'd never have picked a fight with Gray.

Gray shakes his head. "He's not jealous of us." His voice is low, as if he doesn't want Drew to hear. "He's jealous of me, which just plain sucks."

I frown, and he sighs.

"He's injured, Anna. And I'm not. Simple as that."

Gray rolls his shoulders and heads for the door. "Get him to talk to that therapist. I don't blame him for avoiding it." His eyes crease with tired humor. "But he's got one too many daisies stuck in his ass."

DREW

Anna doesn't come to bed when Gray leaves. I'm not surprised. I fucked up. I knew I was doing it every step of the way. It was as if the rational Drew was locked up tight within my mind while asshole Drew took over.

Lying in bed, I stare up at the ceiling and curse myself for being an asshole. Again.

It's almost pitch-black in here because Anna insists on closing both the blinds and the curtains. Apparently, she likes to sleep in darkness so complete it's like we've crawled up into a womb.

Which is fine by me at the moment. A sensory oblivion would be nice.

A slab of gray moonlight cuts across the bed as Anna opens the door. She must have killer night vision or be part vampire because she doesn't turn on a light as she pads through the room and into the bathroom.

My heart pounds loud in my ears as I listen to the running water of the sink and wait for her to return. Coach's suggestion swirls around in my head. Therapy? I'm only injured, not depressed. Yeah, I tend to overanalyze things, but I didn't exactly love going to counseling before.

"Tell me about your parents, Drew."

"They're dead, Doc. What else is there to know?"

"How does that make you feel?"

Like I'm free-falling from the darkness of space.

How do I feel now?

Like I'm free-falling from the darkness of space.

Without my permission, my fingers end up clutching the sheets. I force myself to let go and calm the hell down. It's just a fricking broken leg. It will heal. I'll get back in form.

On the next breath I'm on the field, the scent of grass, chalk, and my own sweat filling my nose. I hear the defensive end's footsteps, feel them reverberating through the ground as he comes upon me. My stomach clenches, acid rising in my mouth along with the soul-deep terror of knowing that this sack is going to be catastrophic. Then the lightning-hot pain and the sound of my bone snapping like hard wood. Stomach-turning pain.

That snap, that sick sound echoes in my ears even as I take another sharp breath.

Then Anna is there, climbing into bed, the mattress barely dipping under her slight weight.

For the first time, I regret buying a king-size bed. She might as well be in Siberia, hugging the edge of her side, while I'm laid out on my back like a slab of beef on mine.

Because I've been in the dark longer than she has, I can see the shadowy shape of her shoulders, hunched over and drawn away from me. Her curls spill across the pillow in a dark, rambling mass.

Regret swells in my throat. "I'm sorry."

My words hang loud and uncomfortable over us.

Bed sheets rustle as she turns, and then she's next to me, her warm hand smoothing over my lower belly.

I love the way she touches me, the way she finds the exact spots that are most sensitive. I slide my arm under her neck and draw her closer, comforted when she lays her head on my shoulder. The curve of her luscious ass fills my palm. I give it a light squeeze.

"I'll apologize to Gray tomorrow." Which won't be easy, because we almost never fight, and I was a colossal dick.

Anna's breasts press against my side as she sighs. She's wearing one of those thin nightshirts she favors, which does nothing to block the warmth of her body, and I struggle to ignore that as her fingertips trace a circle under my navel.

"We are, all of us, fucked-up in some way," she says. "The only difference is a matter of how deep our crazy goes and how we handle our shit. Frankly, I think the crazy comes and goes in cycles."

I make a sound. It's supposed to be a laugh, but it sounds like despair. "It must be my time of the month, then."

"Mmm…" Anna strokes me again. "I shouldn't have invited Gray here without asking you. I'm sorry."

I can't hold back. In one move, I roll over onto her, and her thighs part instantly, cradling my hips as I brace my forearms on either side of her so I won't crush her chest. Her eyes gleam in the dark, her hair a wild halo around her pale face.

"Your leg," she protests against my seeking mouth.

"Is fine." I nuzzle her lips then dip my tongue into her sweet mouth. She tastes faintly of mint toothpaste, but underneath is pure, delicious Anna. Kissing her plump, pouty mouth makes my head light. It spins when my erection rubs over a tickle of curls and slick desire. That she gets wet for me as easily as I grow hard for her is a high I'll never get over.

Gently I rock against her, sliding over the place where I long to be inside. My hands hitch up her shirt and stroke her silky skin. Her curves are soft and warm and giving beneath the hardness of my body.

"Anna." I kiss one corner of her mouth, then the other one. "I don't deserve you."

She clasps my cheeks, her thumbs brushing my jaw. "Probably not," she says into another kiss. "I can be a pain in the ass."

"Always with the jokes," I whisper before I kiss her deeper and lift my hips enough for the head of my cock to find her wet core. On a groan, I sink into her. So tight. So perfect.

A shivering heat licks down my spine. I go easy, making love to her with an adoration that has me trembling, sweating. Her hands caress my back, my ass, a gentle exploration as she makes little noises that send lust burning through my veins. It is perfect.

I feast on her soft mouth and slowly pump in and out of her welcoming body. Here and now, I am whole. Healed.

If only it could last forever. But nothing does. And it soon becomes apparent that although Anna's responding to my touch, she isn't into it the way she normally is. I start to feel the tension in her, the way she holds back. It reminds me of those early days when I'd try to move in for a kiss, and she'd evade me. My insides go cold and heavy, and I lift my head.

"What's wrong?"

It's too dark to fully see her expression, and I hate that. Hate the way she stiffens further. The way she pauses for a moment too long. When she speaks, it comes out stilted, off.

"Nothing... Drew..." Her breasts press against me as she takes a breath. "I'm just tired."

A lump fills my throat. "You should have said so. You should have stopped me."

Her eyes glimmer in the gray dark. The sadness in them has my chest clenching.

"It isn't as bad as all that," she says, reaching up to touch my cheek.

But I've seen enough. I try to ease off her. It's awkward, my chest crushing into hers, my bad leg tweaking and sending pain up to my hip and down to my toes.

I bite back a curse, even as Anna tries to pull me back.

"I don't want a pity fuck," I whisper, as I roll away and sit on the side of the bed.

Anna's hand barely touches my back, as if she'd been reaching out to me, but then it's gone, and her voice snaps like a whip through the dark. "And I don't want to be accused of giving them."

I'm not going to apologize. I'm done apologizing tonight. I run a hand through my hand and lift off the bed. "Forget it."

"Where are you going?"

"I can't sleep." I grab a discarded pair of shorts. I'll put them on in the living room. The hell will I bobble around in here, helplessly trying to dress. "Go back to sleep."

"Drew—"

"Please, Anna." My voice is broken, desperate. "I can't do this anymore tonight."

I don't wait for her response, but flee to the safety of the other room where it's quiet and free from any expectations. For the first time since I met Anna, I wonder if it would be better if I handled this alone.

FORTY

ANNA

SOMETHING HAS TO GIVE. Drew is hurting inside, and I can't help him. Nor can I just sit back and ignore it any longer. The tension it creates is an ever-inflating balloon, growing tight and swollen. I'm so afraid of the inevitable burst that I don't dare to touch it. But the only thing avoidance has ever brought me is grief.

Lying in bed, I watch the morning light sneak in through a crack in the curtain to stretch its pale fingers across the ceiling. My heart is a stone weight in my chest. I need to tell him how I feel. It isn't going to be pretty. Drew's pride is a powerful thing. And much more sensitive than I ever gave it credit.

A crash from out in the living room has me sitting up quickly. I toss on a robe and run out.

Drew is crouched over a broken glass. Bending at an awkward angle, he attempts to sweep up the pieces.

"Here," I say, coming forward. "Let me."

"I can do it." His tone is short, as he shoos me away.

I stand back, watching as he clears up the mess. Storm clouds brew over his expression. And when I pick up a stray sliver of glass with a napkin, the storm breaks.

"Jesus," he snaps, "I said I could do it. Would you quit hovering over me like a bee?"

Stung, I fight to keep my expression neutral as I throw out the glass. "You missed one, and I saw it. That isn't hovering."

"Oh no?" His dark brows rise with incredulity. "So you haven't been walking around on eggshells with me this whole time?"

Pausing, I take a breath. Calm. I need calm. "If I've had to walk around on eggshells it's because you've been spoiling for a fight."

A mulish set lifts his chin, and he doesn't meet my eyes. "Maybe you've been waiting for me to snap."

"Maybe I have."

He flinches at that, his gaze darting to mine.

I don't look away. "Maybe I'm looking for the Drew I fell in love with. Because, if you ask me, he's gone into hiding."

The color drains from his face, but I can see the wheels turning in that keen mind of his. I know he's going to avoid this, pretend like everything is okay, and it's all in my head.

Like clockwork, his expression eases. "Anna…"

"Don't—" I take a step forward, pointing a finger in his direction. "Don't you dare, fucking, 'Anna' me. You do not get to placate me any longer."

"What do you want from me? I'm trying not to fight."

"I don't care if we fight, if it means you acknowledge the fact that you've got a problem going on inside your head at the moment."

My heart is racing now. I hate confrontation. I loathe it with Drew.

The muscles along his neck tense as his color darkens. "Jesus, what is with everyone?" He rakes a hand through his disorderly hair before slapping his good thigh. "Would you give it a rest? I'm not some problem for everyone to solve."

"Oh, bullshit."

His brows wing up. "Excuse me?"

"You heard me. That is utter bullshit. You know damn well that if it were me, Gray, or any one of your friends, you'd do the same thing. So don't start that whole 'why won't you leave me alone' line again."

Drew backs up, his ass hitting the counter. "I don't even know why you care."

"Of course I care! Why wouldn't I care?"

"Isn't it better if I never play again, Anna? Huh?" He takes a hard step in my direction. "I mean, it's not like you wanted me to be a quarterback. You didn't want anything to do with me in the beginning. You took one look and decided I was just some meathead jock that wasn't worth your time."

"That's not fair. You know that I didn't want to want you—"

"Well, now there's the difference. I wanted all of you the moment I laid eyes on you. But you were so damned closed off, I didn't know how to approach you."

"Why are you dragging this up?" I hate that I hurt him so deeply with my fear that he can't let it go.

"Why?" He laughs without humor. "Does it bother you to remember that you only wanted me for one fuck?"

I've always said he was too quick. My jaw hurts from keeping my mouth shut. Arguing about this now won't help. Not that Drew has any intention of stopping. A vein bulges along his throat as he continues to yell.

"That first night. It was the best damn feeling I'd had in my life. And I've won the fucking Heisman!"

"Just stop," I say. "Stop changing the subject. This isn't about me."

But he ignores me. "Every time is like that with you. Like my heart's going to explode. Like I might pass out, but I've got to hold on because I need to feel this for as long as I can."

"It's the same for me. You know that."

"Maybe that's the only place I'll be good enough for you. Maybe all you want is Drew the Fucking Hook Up."

Frustration is an ugly bubble beneath my breastbone. "You call me clueless? For months I've thought about nothing but you. You walk into a room, and I feel you."

"What does that have to do with wanting me for me?" He jabs a thumb against his chest.

"It has everything to do with it!" I yell. "You think I can cut pieces of you up and put them into categories? Drew the man. Drew the player. Drew the super fuck? I tried and, believe me, it doesn't work that way.

"When I say I want you, I want all of you. And when I say I love you, I love all of you. You're the one who wants to put a label on everything now."

"Just following protocol, sweetheart." His tone is so snide that my eyes water.

"Stop being an ass." I take a step into his space. "You say you don't want my pity. Well, it sure as shit seems like you do."

He scoffs, and I press closer. "Do you want my pity, Drew? Is that it?"

"Why are you really here," he shoots back. "To play nursemaid?"

Rage I can handle. But I'm not equipped to handle his resentment. Not when I know I'm the cause of it. The hurt is a kick in my stomach, making my body want to sag in on itself.

"You're never going to forgive me, are you?"

"Maybe I'm not."

For a long, hard moment, we glare at each other. Drew's nostrils flare, his tight chest lifting and falling with agitated breaths.

And then I step back. "You know what? I can't do this with you right now. It's exhausting."

He blinks, his head jerking as if I've slapped him.

"You're right. I think you should leave." There's so much disdain in his voice, it's like dry ice. His eyes are cold, dead. And I feel the chill down in my guts.

I think you should leave. I have to say the words over again in my head before I can process them. I can't even respond; I've gone so numb.

I know he doesn't want to deal. He wants to hide away where nothing can hurt him, lash out when he's challenged on it. I know because that's how I've been for so long. And I know what it will do to him if he gets his way. Drew wasn't meant to sink into the dark.

And if I leave, he'll think he deserves it. For once in my life, I'm not going to take the safe way. I'm not going to protect myself in a shell, even though I know this is going to be awful. Already his rejection is searing away my skin. But I'm willing to let it go to the bone for him.

As if it's all been decided, Drew moves to go, his expression closed off and dark.

"No."

He stops in his tracks and turns. "Excuse me?"

"You heard me fine. I live here."

"No, I live here. You've just been hanging around."

Like dead weight, his tone implied.

Nice, Drew. Nice. I know what he's doing and why. So it shouldn't hurt. But, of course, it does.

"You asked me to move in with you. Which means I live here."

His dark brows lift nearly to his hairline. "Have you been listening to a word I've said? I don't want you here."

"Well, that's just tough shit, isn't it?" I cross my hands over my chest to hide their shaking.

Drew takes a step in my direction, his color returning with a vengeance. "What the fuck is wrong with you? I. Don't. Want. You. Here."

It takes all I've got not to cry, to lift my chin up to meet his eyes. "I. Don't. Care."

For a moment, he just looks at me, his color blooming over his cheeks. Then he grabs the hairs on the back of his head like he's going to rip them out. His biceps bulge, and his teeth flash in a grimace.

"Why are you just standing there? Go." He waves a hand as if I'm a fly, and he needs to swat me away.

"Why won't you fucking leave!" He's shouting so loud now my ears ring. Veins pop out along his neck. His face is so red with rage that it's contorted.

I should be frightened of him. He's looming over me, six feet four inches and two hundred and thirty pounds of raging man. One blow could break my face. But I'm not frightened because everything about his quivering body speaks of restraint. He's coming apart at the seams, but he will never, ever physically lash out at me.

It doesn't stop my own rage, though. It's a lit fire in a dry forest. "You want to get away from me so bad, you fucking leave."

"It's my fucking place!" he bellows. And his arm punches the air for emphasis. "You stubborn ass—"

Even now he can't call me a name. A strangled shout breaks free. "Just leave me the fuck alone."

"No!" I get in his face. Maybe I want him to hit me. I sure as hell want to hit him, hit something. "And there isn't a thing you can do about it."

"Oh, yes I can." In full beast mode, he stomps into our bedroom. Before I can follow, he's out again, carrying an armful of my clothes.

Shock has me rooted to the floor. I want to cry. I want to laugh. I want to punch him when he wrenches open the door and tosses my things out.

"You motherfucker," I shout.

Not to be outdone, I go to the room and get a handful of his things. His own shock, when he sees me, is nearly comical, were it not for the fact that he's breaking my heart.

"You're being the asshole," I retort, tossing his things onto the lawn. "So you get out."

Maturity has officially left the building. Along with our clothes.

Nostrils flaring, he moves to go into our room again. I know he's after more clothes. I dodge in front of him, blocking the way. Drew skids to a stop, teetering before he snarls.

"No," I snap. "You don't get to manhandle any more of my stuff."

He's so angry now, he vibrates. "Get. Out!"

"No!" We are nose to nose now. "I'm not fucking leaving. Do you hear?" My throat hurts from the force of my words. "I'm never leaving you, Drew. No matter what you say. I'm. Never. Fucking. Leaving!"

It's the truth. I won't leave him. But I don't have to look at him. Not when hateful tears are pricking behind my lids. Not when my lip is quivering. Angry crying is a curse. I turn from him, but it's too late. He's seen it.

I march away. I was wrong. I can't do this. I'm not strong enough; I don't know what the hell I'm doing.

"Anna!"

I ignore him. The door to our room, when I slam it, rattles the windows. I lock it for good measure, just in time, because he's on the other side.

"Anna, damn it!" He smashes his fists into the wood with enough force that something cracks. But the door holds.

"Get bent," I shout in a voice way too high-pitched.

With a snarl, he pounds once more, and adds a "Fuck!" for emphasis. Then he's gone.

I'm pretty sure if his leg weren't broken the fucking bastard would have kicked down the door and physically tossed me out by now. Like he did my clothes. God, that hurt. It still does.

Our dresser drawers are tilting haphazardly, half torn from their housing. T-shirts, and one of my bras, hang from them like streamers. I focus on that lone bra. A ridiculously expensive La Perla sky blue bra that Iris gave me on my twenty-first birthday. The bra Drew slipped his fingers under the night he'd asked me to move in with him.

He emptied my lingerie drawer? That dick. My fucking bras are on the street, probably being ogled by some fucking frat boy.

The thought, for some inane reason, makes the damn burst. I sob, great big hulking sobs that I try to contain by shoving a pillow into my face. Smothered by down and hunched over on the floor, I almost don't hear him.

"Anna." His voice is ravaged, but so close and clear, he has to be leaning on the door. "Anna, baby. Let me in."

I hate myself that my whole body vibrates with the need to do as he asks. I just want this fight to end. I want him to hold me. I want to hold him. And then I remember that my panties are likely hanging on the bushes and curl tighter into myself.

"Anna." It's a long plea. "Please, honey. I just... Please."

God, he sounds so broken. He is broken. And I don't know how to fix him. He doesn't want me. But he's on the other side of the door. Calling my name.

Snot-nosed and red-faced, I crawl across the floor, flick the lock and then scurry back to the safety of my pillow. A second later, he opens the door, but I can't look at him. I'm too raw. Too humiliated.

Only his legs, one bare and the other in a cast, are in my line of sight as he limps over to me. With each step he takes closer, the more I tremble. I will not cry in front of him. I will not. But it costs me to keep it in. My bottom lip throbs against the clench of my teeth.

He hunkers down next to me, his cast making the descent ungainly and slow. I don't look. But I feel his body heat. And I smell him, clean and warm and delicious. Drew.

It takes him no effort at all to pick me up and put me in his lap. Tears start streaming again as he wraps his arms about me. Arms so thick and corded with muscle they feel like iron. His hands are in my hair, on my back, as he nuzzles against my neck.

"I'm sorry," he whispers. "I'm so fucking sorry. I've never lost it like that. I don't know what..."

He's kissing me. My eyes, my cheeks, my swollen lips, all the time saying, "I'm sorry."

I don't kiss him back, just let him do what he will. My hand falls against the hard swell of his chest where his heart beats fast and strong.

"I'm so messed up." The words are pulled from him, a raw agony. "I'm so fucking messed up about this, Anna. I'm afraid. Every time I think of holding the ball, or playing, I feel sick. And it pisses me off. It's just an injury. I shouldn't be freaking out like this. I—"

I move then, wrapping my arms around his neck and pressing my cheek to his. "There's never going to be a right way to feel. And you don't have to go it alone. I'm here."

He holds me tighter. Tight enough that he trembles, that I can barely breathe.

I squeeze him harder, wanting to be his anchor. "I'm *here*."

We hold each other, our breath steaming in the small space between us.

Drew sighs. "I don't want you to leave me. Ever." His voice is muffled against my hair. "I'm just terrified that you will. How can you not when I'm this pathetic mess? And I'd rather…"

He takes a ragged breath. "I'd rather it happen now if it's going to happen."

Now. So he can hit rock bottom. I kiss him then, clasping his face in my hands. I kiss him like he kissed me, over his cheeks, his closed eyes, his chin. He's doing the same, and it's a fumbling mess of lips trying to make contact. But then our mouths meet, and I melt into him. The kiss is tender yet fierce. There is no end to it, just a slow liquid glide and a gentle exploration. I put everything I am into the kiss. And I am rewarded. I feel his love down to the soles of my feet.

When the kiss ends, our lips still touch, and we share the same breath, soft and slow. His big, rough hands are cradling my jaw, and I'm holding on to his neck so I can feel his life's blood move through his veins.

"I love you so much it hurts," he says. "But everything I love gets taken away."

My breath hitches in a choppy hiccup. "You can do a preemptive strike, Drew. You can try to throw me away—"

"No." His forehead presses against mine, his grip growing tighter. "No, I don't want that. I don't—"

"Just listen."

He squeezes his eyes shut and nods. And the sight is an arrow through my chest.

"I love you, Drew. All of you, the good and the bad." My thumb glides along the crest of his heated cheek. "I won't leave you. But if you treat me like shit, it will be you leaving me."

"Fuck," Drew says brokenly. "Fuck, Anna." He gathers me up again, secure in his arms. "I was an asshole. A huge, fucking asshole."

"Yeah," I say, but I'm smiling now. "But I was one to you long before."

Drew stills, and I know he's remembering the words he tossed at me. I'm remembering them too. He's wanted me from the first. My whole body grows tender at the thought, then hurts at the way I had rejected him.

"You should know," I say against his shoulder, "I wanted you from the first too. The second I saw you, I thought, yeah, that guy, he's the one. I just didn't let myself believe that I could have you. Because of my own shit. Not because of you."

His hand encompasses the back of my head. "Anna."

I go on. It's important he knows. "I was coming to tell you that before you got hit. Because I had realized that you were the best thing that had ever happened to me or ever would. Because what I felt for you was stronger than my fear. You won, Drew. You will always win with me."

He swallows hard, and then pulls back. His smile is golden. It's a true Drew smile.

And I'm so glad to see it return that I almost miss his next words.

"Good. Because I'm keeping you, Anna Jones."

DREW

Asking Gray to meet me outside the stadium was a mistake. I can feel the damn place looming over me, pressing upon my back in a silent taunt. *Turn around. Look at me.* And when I don't, *Coward.*

A cold sweat breaks over me, and I press my ass back against the cab of Gray's pickup, as if it can anchor me. An early frost has sugared the world with ice. I draw in a deep breath and welcome the burn in my lungs.

My attention drifts to a bubblegum-pink Fiat headed my way. The lot is fairly empty, which makes me wonder if the person driving has spotted me in particular. If it's a fan, I swear to God or to whoever's listening that I'm leaving. I can't deal with that now. Not even a little.

When the car parks next to mine, my fists curl within the pockets of my jacket.

Shit.

A second later, Gray awkwardly unfolds his long bulk from the tiny car, and I. Lose. It.

I laugh so hard, I double over, my hand braced on the side of my cast.

"Yeah, yeah, laugh it up," Gray grouses as he slams the pink door.

Wiping my eyes, I try to stop, but can't.

"Man…" Gray sighs, but I can see his lips twitching. "Asshole."

I clear my throat, sputtering, but managing to choke down my glee. "What the absolute fuck?"

Gray's scowl grows. "I needed a car, didn't I?"

That sobers me. God, I've been a jerk. I love this guy. He is my brother in all ways but blood. And I've treated him like shit.

"We can switch," I offer with thick awkwardness. I don't deserve to be driving Gray's truck anyway.

He snorts. "Like you'd be able to squeeze into that fucking box with your cast. Besides, it's a stick shift."

"Uh…why are you driving that particular car?"

Gray leans against his truck. "Got it from an agent."

"An agent?" I bobble as I whip around to fully face him. "What? Why?" Neither of us has interacted with them on the level of asking for things. We'll make our choice free of any obligations.

He doesn't look at me as he answers, but squints into the pale winter sunlight. "It's like this. I needed a car, so I asked my top three agent picks for a loaner." He shrugs. "Have to whittle down my choices anyway, so why not see how they'd react, you know?"

Stiffly I nod.

"So I get an offer for a Merc. A sweet-ass AMG SLS coupe."

I whistle. Now that is a car I'd love to drive.

Gray's knowing look says the same. "Next guy says he'll send over 'his own, personal' Ferrari California, and a girl to keep me company."

"Two ladies for the price of one. That's…ah…generous." I still can't believe some chicks go along with that shit.

"Yeah." Gray crosses his legs at the ankles and then gives a dark laugh. "So the next guy, Mackenzie," he adds for clarification, "tells me, 'look, kid, I'll go to the mattresses for you come draft day, keep the press off your ass, and bail your sorry butt out of jail if you're ever foolish enough to get thrown into one, but I don't like the taste of dick, so don't expect me to suck yours.'"

I blink for a second and then grin wide. Gray does too.

"So," Gray finishes, "Mackenzie says I can drive his daughter's Fiat for a few weeks because she's studying abroad. And there you go." He extends a hand toward the pink nightmare. "One hideous bubblegum clown car at your service. Oh, and if I wreck it, I bought it."

Gray rolls his eyes. "It'd be so worth it to drive the thing off a cliff, but there aren't any around."

"The guys must be giving you hell." I try not to smile as I say this.

Gray's brows draw tight. "They're calling me Glamour Gray."

"Ahh…" I glance at the car, which is far from glamorous. "Is that supposed to be ironic?" Whatever their inspiration is, I know it will be evil.

His cheeks go ruddy. "No. Marshall, that fuckstain, said that his kid sister plays with these tiny dolls called Glamour Gals, and that they drive a car like mine. Hence…" He rolls his hand in the air in an irritated fashion.

I won't laugh… I crack up.

"You're a fuckstain too," Gray mutters.

"Whatever, Glamour."

Reluctantly, Gray grins, but it doesn't reach his eyes.

"Seriously, though," I say, "good on you for not selling out."

"You should consider Mackenzie too. I know he's interested."

My laugh dies on a breath. Mackenzie had been my top choice, mainly because he seemed a straightforward guy, and Gray's story certainly nails that down. But I can't stop the uncertainty within me from rearing its ugly head. I force myself to nod.

"Yeah." I clear my throat. "Yeah, he sounds like a good guy."

We go quiet, the faint sounds of activity from within the stadium filling the space between us.

"About last night. I'm sorry." I can't look at him. Not yet. A hot pressure builds behind my nose and lids. "I was a dick."

From the corner of my eye, I see Gray turn his head my way.

"Yeah, well, you're a pretty good dick as far as dicks go… Fuck." He grimaces. "That did *not* sound right."

We both laugh, strained. And then I face him. "I mean it, Gray."

He colors, his mouth going into a straight line. "I know."

"I never thought you'd make a play for Anna. Never."

Absently, he nods. "I know, man. And I know you're freaking. I'd be doing the same."

"I…" Words get stuck in my throat, and the prickling pressure grows. "You're… Hell."

I grab onto him, likely shocking the shit out of him, and haul him close. My hug is hard. "I love you, all right?"

He hugs me back, just as hard, a fist pounding into my shoulder. And then we both shove each other away with a laugh.

"Shit," he says, surreptitiously wiping at the corner of his eye, "you're going to have me bawling like some oversized man-baby."

"Cuz you are an oversized man-baby," I answer, rubbing my forearm over my own eyes.

The wind blows again. It's too cold to be standing around.

"Well come on, then." Gray goes to his Barbie car and grabs something from within. My insides dip but my heart speeds up when I see the football.

Gray gives me a challenging look and throws me the ball. I either have to catch it or let it fall.

I catch it.

"We're tossing around the ball." Gray's tone brooks no argument.

The ball feels so good in my hand that I want to clutch it to my chest like it's a baby.

"You going long?" I ask.

"You gonna throw down?"

My arm tightens with the need to let the ball fly. "Like a hammer." Some of my cockiness leaves as I glance back at the stadium. "But not here."

"We'll go to the park." Gray moves to the passenger side of the pickup.

"Not in the glamour mobile?" I say as we both get in the truck.

He looks disgruntled as hell, but he's smiling. "You owe me big for that car, you know."

I do. I owe him for more than he'll ever know.

"Anna's making bourbon pecan pies. I told her to bake four." She'd called me a greedy Gus, as if that would be some kind of deterrent. "I'll give you two of them."

Gray grins wide. "That's a start."

FORTY-ONE

ANNA

THE CAR ENGINE ticks as we sit in front of the brick town-house. Neither of us moves to open a car door. Drew takes a slow breath. His profile is to me as he stares out of the window.

"Last night," he says, "I had a nightmare. I was in the house, trying to find you. But you were gone. Your stuff was gone. Like you'd never been there."

His mouth quirks bitterly. "Suddenly, I'm tearing through campus trying to find you, when I realize that I'm running. My leg is perfect, there's no pain. Coach appears and he tells me it was all a dream. The bad sack, my leg getting trashed. It never happened."

I turn toward him in my seat, and he swallows hard.

"Then I see you. You're with Mr. Yuck, and you look at me like I'm scum."

I reach for his hand, and his warm fingers link with mine.

He gives me a little squeeze of reassurance, like I'm the one who needs comfort. He's gone silent, just looking down at our hands, his so much bigger than mine that all you can see of me are my pale fingers threaded through his darker ones.

"You should know," I say, "I left Mr. Yuck at the bar. He never stood a chance. I was in love with you."

A sad smile plays on Drew's lips, but it grows into one of satisfaction. He pulls our linked hands onto his thigh and his thumb glides over mine. "Well, in the spirit of sharing and honesty, I hung around all those girls to make you jealous."

My eyes flick up. He has the grace to look sheepish. "It was shitty, I know." His expression grows somber. "But I never touched them."

But then his lashes sweep down, hiding his eyes. "One of them kissed me, and—" he shakes his head "—I couldn't stand it. You don't know how much that pissed me off at the time," he says with a wry laugh.

"I bet," I say sourly, but I'm not really mad, and he knows me enough to get that.

Because he's smiling at me now. The smile turns tender, and his thumb continues to stroke mine.

"The thing is, when I saw you in the dream, walking away from me like we never were and never would be..." He goes pale. "It tore me in half, Anna."

"Drew, no..." I cup his cheek with my free hand.

He leans into it a little as he keeps talking. "I felt so empty. Even when I woke up. Like I'd never experience happiness again."

"I'm here," I say softly. "I'm here." I hate that he's felt that sinking empty pain again.

"That's the point, baby," he answers. "Ending my college football career the way I did? Facing the idea that eventually an injury might end everything one day? Yeah, it's doing a number on me. It scares the shit out of me. Football made me what I am. But I'll have to deal with it regardless. No one plays ball forever. And at the end of the day, when the game is over?" His golden eyes hold mine. "I'd rather have no football and feel whole with you than play and feel empty and at sea like before."

"Drew." I wrap my arms around his neck and hug him hard. And he hugs me back, his breath warm against my cheek as he nuzzles it, breathing me in like he always does.

I press my lips against his temple. "You're wrong about one thing. Football doesn't make you. You make football."

He grunts in wry disagreement, and I shake my head, brushing my lips over his ear. "Anyone can pick up a ball and throw it. But you? You turn the act into something magical. Something wonderful."

A sigh escapes him. The sound is equal parts sadness and relief. I hold him tighter, kiss his jaw.

"It's you, baby. Your light. Your joy. Your soul. You bring that to everything you touch. To the game, your friends, me. It won't end with football, I promise."

"Anna." He drags me across the armrest and into his lap to bury his face in the crook of my neck. "I love you so much. It's like my life truly started when you walked into it. I want what my parents had, Anna. I want it with you and only you."

He strokes my hair, his breath a burst of heat against my skin. "I'm going in there today to get my shit together for me, and for us."

"Drew." I kiss his cheek, his mouth, his nose, slowly softly, and he lets me, closing his eyes as if each touch is a balm.

Cupping his jaw with my hands, I press my forehead to his. "You are the best man I've ever known. You helped me become the person I've always wanted to be. You're everything, Drew." My breath leaves in a huff of frustration. "I don't even know how to tell you how much you mean to me."

He smiles as he kisses me, a gentle easy kiss, as if he's finally breathing free. "Just be with me and I'll know. Just be with me."

How could I not? He is part of me now. "Always."

EPILOGUE

ANNA

Two Years Later…

IT'S SUNDAY NIGHT and I'm bathed in brilliant white light. The air is crisp and fills my lungs with a sweet burn as I take in the scents of fried food, beer, and human sweat. Electricity buzzes around me, created by the joy and cheers of eighty thousand people. This is high theater. It's human drama, and we're all riveted to the twenty-two men on the emerald green field.

But my attention is drawn only to one. His helmet obscures his face but he's still gorgeous to me. Tall and strong, he is poetry and grace in motion. He owns the ball. He throws and it listens.

And I'm so excited I barely can keep still.

"Keep bouncing around like that," says a voice in my ear, "and you'll fall out of your seat."

Gray laughs as he says it, and I can't help but grin. He's flown in from San Francisco, where he was drafted to play, to be here.

"He's blowing it up, Gray."

"Yeah, he is," Gray says with his own grin.

Two years of working toward this moment. Rehab, the fear of not getting signed, then trying to fit in as a rookie, and tonight Drew finally gets his chance to start, filling in for the team's injured starting quarterback.

As if he's been waiting for it, he explodes out of the gate. He's born for this, and his team knows it. They respond to his confidence, playing with precision and verve. Already they're up three touchdowns against the better team.

And though he'd once insisted it was okay if he never played again, I know what this means to him. Tears blur my vision as I scream his name, my voice lost among the many.

"Everything is going to change," Gray warns me, though he doesn't really look worried.

"I know." It will be *more*. More press. More pressure.

But we'll weather it. We still can't keep our hands off each other. Do we fight sometimes? Of course. Drew has his dark days, and I have mine. I barely saw him when I began to intern at a cable production company on a whim. I'm now an associate producer for a cooking show. It's something I'd never envisioned for myself but love with a passion.

Our stress levels rose to a pitch during the days before the draft. Would he go quickly like some thought? Or languish in the third, fourth, or fifth rounds as Drew secretly feared? When he was the fourth pick in the first round—to New York, thank God—we celebrated for an entire week.

But it full-out sucked living in New York City those first few months before his draft. Because I refused to let Drew dip too far into his savings, we could only afford a walkup in the Lower East Side. I can't even think about the number of roaches Drew smashed without shuddering. We both cried a little in relief when we finally bought our apartment in Chelsea. But the dark days are few. We have more fun than anything else.

He's my best friend, and I'm his.

I clap my hands, and the ring on my finger catches the light with a glint. It's a brilliant round diamond surrounded by a ring of black emerald-cut diamonds on a platinum band. Drew gave it to me last month, asking me to be his forever. And it's perfect.

But I don't really need a ring. I just need Drew. The moment he asked me the question, the only answer I wanted to give was yes and how soon?

At first my mom was worried. We were too young. Did I know the divorce rate for pro athletes? The constant travel and temptation Drew will deal with?

Yeah, I know. And yet I will never treat Drew as a stereotype again. Taking Drew means taking the good, the bad, and the in-between. Just as he takes me.

After the game, when I finally get to him, I fling myself into his arms, and he holds me tight before spinning me around, the high of kicking ass infectious. Our kiss is messy, broken up by giddy laughter—mostly mine.

"I'm so proud of you," I tell him when he puts me down. "You were awesome." Already there is talk. And I know his team is going to make him starting quarterback now.

Drew's grin lights up his face. His touch is tender on my cheek, and then he tells me what I know is his absolute truth, because it's mine too. "It means nothing without you."

★ ★ ★ ★ ★

EXCLUSIVE NEW BONUS SCENE

This takes place *after* the events in the main story of *The Hook Up* but *before* the events in the epilogue. Drew and Anna have graduated, and Drew has begun training camp for his new NFL team.

Now and then, I've thought how Drew and Anna would get along outside of college, and I realized that this is when they'd truly grow wings and live life to the fullest.

I loved getting the opportunity to visit with them again by stepping back into their world. I hope you do too!

—*Kristen Callihan*

I'M WALKING DOWN Fifth Avenue, an iced Americano in one hand, when "Ride of the Valkyries" blares out from the depths of my purse. An older woman in a white silk turban and oversized Dior glasses gives me a look and snorts as she walks her wolfhound toward the park.

I smile thinly, struggling with my purse. "Valkyries" is in full pageantry by the time I find my phone.

"Seriously, Baylor?" I say, laughing as I answer.

His deep, rolling chuckle comes through the phone. "What? No good?"

"It's terrible." But I'm laughing, and he knows he got me good.

I step past a couple of tourists and sip my coffee. "I liked 'Immigrant Song' better."

"Who doesn't?" There's still a tinge of devious glee in his voice. "But it doesn't have the same…impact as this one."

"Understatement of the year."

Ever since coming to New York, Drew has been messing with my ringtones. I could block him out with a new password, but where's the fun in that? I'm never tempted to peek, but instead wait with anticipation for the next song.

"One day," I warn darkly, "you're going to tell me how you manage to change my ringtone remotely."

"Never! I'll take the secret to the grave."

"Hmm." I bite back a laugh. "I guess it's just coincidence that the changes coincide with visits from our friends?"

Last night, George had been in town and dropped by to say hello. The other week, Iris visited.

Drew adopts a tone of indignation. "Don't go pulling our innocent friends into your wild conspiracy theories, Jones."

I kind of love that our friends are in on it.

"Okay, okay," I say with a dramatic sigh. "Well, this one was inspired. Love the Nordic gods theme."

"Aw, Jones, you noticed."

Snickering, I sidestep a stroller. "I shudder to think of what you'll come up with next."

"Breathless in anticipation?"

"You know it, baby."

We text frequently, but Drew prefers the phone. His new teammates give him shit about it, calling him old-fashioned. He just grins and shakes his head at them.

"They don't get it," he'd told me later. "I hear your voice, and my day is better. Anything is possible."

Every time he says something like that, I fall more in love with him. My man can call me whenever he wants. Fact is, if I can't see him, I need to hear his voice too. A lump grows in my throat. The summer heat swaddles me like a wool blanket, and I take a long pull of my icy coffee. But it doesn't cool me down or ease my feelings. I miss Drew. Badly.

I'll never tell him how much it hurts to be away from him. Not when he's stuck in training camp and needs to focus. I tell him I love him every day. But not about the longing. I think he knows, though. Drew has always read me like a favorite book.

His voice goes soft. "You out getting your coffee?"

I'm currently staying in the Central Park West condo of Drew's agent while I wait for Drew to finish training camp. Then we'll find a place of our own. Soon, he'll be back. Soon.

"Yep. Walking toward the park to finish it."

"Well, watch where you're going. You almost got run over by that lady with the stroller."

I halt. My heart thumps hard in my chest. And then I hear it. The distinctive rumble of Drew's Camaro. I whirl around and spot him coming up the block. Thank God it's a Sunday, or he'd never get to the curb. Yes, he would. He always finds a way.

I'm afraid I squeal. Loudly. Coffee splatters as I drop the cup and run to him. That gorgeous smile of his goes wide, his one dimple popping up. He barely has time to get out of the car before I tackle him. But he gathers me up and holds me tight.

God. The feel of him. His familiar clean scent surrounds me. My eyes well up.

"Drew."

He breathes in and then exhales on a contented sigh. "Anna."

We stand like that, soaking each other in, until some asshole honks and breaks the moment.

I pull back to look at Drew's face. "Why are you here? Is everything okay? They didn't cut you, because if they did, I'll personally go down there and—"

He kisses me softly. Slowly. I lose myself in him, soak up all that is good and strong and beautiful about him. Until some other asshole honks.

Drew gives the guy the finger while he nuzzles my cheek. "Everything's good. We let out a little early."

"Yay!"

Grinning, he leads me to the car. "Want to get out of here?"

"Absolutely."

It takes us a while, but we finally leave the city. Drew came prepared with lunch for the road, and I'm soon handing him a sandwich and a bottle of his weirdly glowing but beloved Green River soda.

"Where are we going?" I ask before eating a chip.

"The Hamptons. I rented a house for the week."

"But I didn't pack."

"I picked up some things at the apartment before I hunted you down. We can buy the rest."

"Did you bring all my products?"

"Please," he says with a look of horror. "I want to live, don't I?"

"Har." I curl up in my seat, half facing him. "How was training camp?"

"Exhausting. Fun. Weird." He shrugs. "Take your pick."

I place a chip in his mouth as he is driving. "They give you shit for being a rookie?"

Crunching on the chip, he nods before swallowing. "Made me play the guitar and sing a sappy song."

A laugh bursts free. "Which one?"

Drew sends me a sidelong glance full of mischief. "Which one do you think?"

I know that look. I'm practically dancing in my seat because I can imagine the whole thing. "You didn't."

"I sure did."

I bite my lip to hold in my smile. But it doesn't work. "'Crash into Me'?"

Chuckling, he nods again. I laugh and lean close to him to pat his arm. "I bet you looked very emo and deep."

"Well, I should hope so. I thought of you the whole time," he says with mock solemnity before his lips quirk. "And then someone threw a jockstrap at my feet in adulation."

We both burst into laughter as the car speeds along the highway.

By the time we get to the sprawling beachfront home, the sun is high overhead and hot on my skin. It's a pretty place, the house done in New England cottage style, with cedar shake shingles weathered silvery gray, white trim, high gabled roof and dormer windows. Cottony balls of white hydrangea bushes line the property.

"It's cute," I say. "You know, for a multimillion-dollar house." Because while it resembles cottages up here, it's also enormous, with two wings, multiple porches, and fronting about an acre of wild green meadow that reaches for the pale sandy shore and the deep blue ocean beyond.

Drew huffs out a laugh. "You should have seen the owner's house." Drew's new team owner had invited them to a welcome party. "It had a ballroom. An honest-to-God ballroom."

"Well, I suppose if you host a lot of parties..." I shrug. It's a strange sensation to go from hearing about extreme wealth to seeing it up close and personal. There's a sense of disorientation, as if you've fallen into Wonderland. Because everyone on the inside seems just a bit eccentric.

Drew pulls out the bags he packed from the trunk and slings them easily over his shoulder. He takes my hand in his free one and leads us up the flagstone walkway.

"I don't want to be like that," he says as he unlocks the front door by punching in a code on a keypad.

"Like what?"

"Immune to it all." He says this as we enter an expansive entry hall of soaring whitewashed arches and wide plank floors. And then he laughs a little, shaking his head in that self-deprecating way of his. "I realize the irony of that statement in this particular moment."

I lift to my toes and kiss his cheek. "The fact that you do makes it clear that you aren't immune to it all. And this..." I wave a hand around. "This is one of the fruits of your labor."

He's worked hard, suffered a lot, to get here. But Drew is never going to be easy about success; he's too pragmatic about those things. And I get it. Sometimes, I feel like a child in this new world—ignorant of the rules, an outsider. We both are right now.

Drew sets the bags down and, without warning, swoops me up in his arms. I yelp then laugh. I'm never going to get used to his ability to effortlessly carry me around at will.

"You, Anna Jones," he says, striding us to the bedroom, "are the reward for all that I've done."

The bedroom faces the ocean with a little deck just beyond a wall of windowed doors. It's bright and airy, with an enormous wicker-and-beechwood bed done up in white linens. Gently, he sets me down in the middle of it, crawling in after me. My heart warms a little at the fact that, although Drew could have easily tossed me on the bed, he's always careful of his strength and how he might accidentally hurt me should he misuse it.

I flop back and sigh with contentment. The linens are cool; the sunlight shining through the windowpanes is warm. Drew stretches out beside me and rests his head in his hand.

"Well, hello," he says, easing a curl away from my face.

I beam back at him. "Hello yourself."

We smile at each other, wide and happy. He's been gone from me for a little over two weeks. But it felt longer. Now I study the familiar lines of his face, the strong angles of his jaw, the straight bridge of his nose, the little dimple on his cheek. I know these lines, but they are more dear to me after the separation. I know there will be many more times we're separated. Drew's job will take him away a lot. But he comes back to me, and that's what matters.

As if he's thinking something similar, Drew's gaze travels over my face as well. His fingers tremble as he lifts a hand and gently touches my mouth.

"Anna."

Just that. Just my name. It sparks something deep inside and ignites. Desire blooms so hot and fast that I suck in a breath and feel a little dizzy. Drew never fails to see what he does to me so very well. His nostrils flare on a breath. A small grunt escapes him.

The next breath, we're crashing into each other, a desperate tangle of deep kisses, hands seeking and reassuring. I'm panting into his mouth, licking up his flavor.

He groans behind it all. "God, you taste good." A greedy

taste. Another searching kiss. "How is it that you always taste so fucking good?"

I can only whimper and give him more—take more.

His big hands coast up my thighs, under my skirt. "And this ass. This perfect, peachy ass." He palms my butt with utter appreciation.

I choke out a half laugh, breathless and fast. He gives me a squeeze. Then his fingers slip beneath my panties.

He finds me slick, and he shivers as though he's the one being touched. "Fuck, Jones." The blunt tip of his finger slides along my sensitive flesh. "You need me here, don't you?"

"Yes. Yes. Please—I can't... That's so... I want..."

I don't know what I'm saying anymore. I'm burning up. He feels so good. All of him. Solid and warm and *here*. Finally, here with me. The long, smooth line of his strong back is hot and damp. I wrench his shirt off, mussing his hair and making him grunt again. He's distracted by trying to recapture my mouth. I open to him, needy and wanton. And he makes a sound of satisfaction. Then he's pulling down my panties with sharp tugs. I want my shirt off too—everything off, but I'm too impatient.

My fingers fly to his jeans, fumbling with the button.

"Hurry," I pant. "Hurry."

He pushes my hands away to take care of it because I'm shaking too hard. A tight, short smile plays on his mouth as he does it. He knows we're a mess, the both of us clumsy and uncoordinated with our lust, but he's used to that. It's always this way between us.

I cup the back of his neck and pull him into another kiss. Drew's tongue slides along mine, and he gets himself free. The hot, round crown of him glides over my wetness and notches into place. Everything stops: the frenzied movements, the sound of our breathing.

Our gazes clash, his golden and so filled with love that my vison goes blurry. I blink back the tears and look up at him. His expression is taut, pained even. But behind it all is a tenderness that makes my insides flutter. God, I love this man.

"Anna." It sounds like a song. A tone only I get to hear.

My voice is barely a whisper, but the conviction behind it is strong and sure. "I love you, Drew."

With a sigh, he sinks in deep. And it is perfect. No longer frantic, we're slow and sinuous with intent. He fills me up, makes me whole. I wrap my legs around him and hold him closer. Closer still, kissing along his jaw, the tip of his nose, his parted lips.

He cups my head between his hands, gently as though I am infinitely precious, and whispers soft words of encouragement. Until it's too much for him, and he simply gives in to the feeling, watching me with a steady gaze.

We move together, relearning each other, coming home.

In the heavy silence of the light-filled room, we find each other again. Inch by inch, breath by breath, we fall into that space where nothing else matters. There is only him, me, us.

Drew dips his head. His words, rough with emotion, tickle the shell of my ear. "Always."

Later, after we've had our fill and lazed around in bed, contented to just be, we shower and investigate the rest of the house.

We end up in the kitchen, which is fully stocked for the week ahead. I make us sunset smoothies, while Drew fusses around in the bedroom, "looking for his shirt."

"Just wear a new one," I call as I pack up the smoothies and grab a beach blanket and some towels from the mudroom, which houses everything one could want for the beach.

Drew comes jogging out. Barefoot and flustered, he's got on a button-down shirt halfway done up and a pair of jeans hanging low on his hips. Effortlessly gorgeous. With an almost shy smile, he pushes his still-damp hair back from his forehead. "Sorry, I'm ready now."

"I don't mind."

He seems almost nervous, which is weird. But maybe I'm

making things up in my head. Because Drew is never nervous around me. Whatever it was goes away quickly, and he takes the towel tote and the smoothie bag.

Hand in hand we make our way along the hot sand. And when I yelp, doing a little dance to save my toes, he sweeps me up again.

"I could get used to this," I tell him.

"Counting on it," he says with a cheeky look.

We drop our things on the beach and spread out the big blanket. Then I head straight for the ocean. Cold, briny water flows over my toes as I stretch my hands wide and take in the breeze.

Drew flops down on the blanket, watching me with a pleased expression. "That's what I was picturing the whole week."

"The ocean?"

He gives me a knowing look. "You. Beaming like the sun."

I go to him and make myself comfortable, straddling his lap. Drew draws me closer and kisses his way along my cheek. "I missed you," he says. "So fucking much."

"I did too." I kiss his mouth, softly. Taking my time.

"You didn't want to tell me, did you?" There's no judgment in his tone. Only knowing.

Wryly, I smile. "Didn't want to make it worse."

He rests his forehead against mine and rubs my back. "The reunions are good, though."

"The reunions are the best."

He kisses me again, little tastes that feel like he's luxuriating in me. I melt against him.

"We'll have to make do with a lot of reunions for a while," he says. He's trying to keep his voice light. But I know it gets to him when we part.

"Unless I go to more away games," I say. When he draws back to look at me with a hopeful expression, I smile tentatively. "I'm just figuring out this whole documentary business. I can work anywhere right now. So, whenever you want me with you—"

He rolls me onto the sand and hovers over me, his expression fierce but tender. "I will always want you with me. Always. But if you want to stay in one place and wait for me to come back, I'll want that too."

I know that. I've known that for a while. I touch his cheek. "I want to be where you are."

His gaze wanders over my face. "We could buy this place. To get away. A condo in the city. A place out here."

He has money. Stupid money, my mom calls it. Because it tempts you to do foolish things. But Drew's been careful, investing wisely and waiting to see how he settles before making big purchases.

"You can buy this place." I run my fingers over his brow. "But home is always going to be where you are."

Lightness steals over him. "Anna Jones," he says. "I have something in my pocket for you."

My breath hitches. Suddenly my heart is tripping. "That's not a pickle?"

He grins. "Not a pickle."

I tremble, fighting a smile. "Oh?"

He trembles as well as he pulls a little black box from his pocket. "Got a question I've been wanting to ask you, Jones."

I hadn't expected this. Not quite yet... And *yet*... I know I want it. With all that I am, I want this life with this man. The good, the bad, and the in-between. I don't need anything official. That won't change how I feel about him or alter my level of commitment. But it means something to Drew. He told me early on he wanted this. And that makes me want it too.

I'm floating. Happiness bubbles through me, so swift and effervescent, I fear I'll laugh with sheer giddiness before I can get the words out. "Ask me, Baylor."

And so, he does.

AN EXCLUSIVE Q AND A WITH AUTHOR
KRISTEN CALLIHAN

What inspired you to write *The Hook Up*? At the time, I understand you were writing historical romance.
There were two things. I was talking to [someone] and said off-hand I was thinking about trying to write contemporary. She laughed and told me there's no way you can do that because you're writing historical. You can't switch. You don't have the voice for it. Which only made me think, *Oh, really?* Well then, that's a challenge...

But as for the actual story? Around that time, a lot of people were really into Channing Tatum, but I wasn't getting it. Nothing personal, I just didn't see the appeal. Then I read an article about him in *People* and he sounded so sweet and funny. So I thought, What if there's this guy who everyone idolizes, but this girl doesn't? But then she finally gets to know the guy, and she realizes that there's more to him than just a nice body and pretty face.

Why did you write about football heroes?

I wanted to set the story at college, and I began to wonder, Who would be the big man on campus? Who would everyone know about? It *had* to be a football player. I couldn't think of anyone else who would be that popular.

And for Anna, someone who was shy and did not want attention, I wondered how bad it would be if she got together with the huge star on campus, where you're in the public eye all the time...

Your heroes are super sexy and they know how to pleasure their partners and they're very comfortable in their masculinity. Is that intentional? In other words, is it important to you to create heroes that, in their own way, challenge or dismantle toxic masculinity?

I think it's about conveying a balance of respect and emotional growth. It's important to show the good parts of what a man can be, that strength of character comes from the inside. Heroes don't have to act the exact same way, and they should be fallible in some form or other. But if you show that these guys are coming from a good place and want to do right by their love interest, even if it's being vulnerable, that's what's attractive to me.

To that point, there are common elements in some of your heroines. They're often smart and independent, but also kind of messy. Is it important for you to reflect some sort of emotional growth or journey in your main characters?

The more I've hung out with successful women, the more I found we're all secretly a bit messed up and still kind of a perpetual work in progress, you know? Like you can't just shed so easily all the stuff that happened in high school or childhood. I think it's powerful to be honest about what a mess we are instead of hiding it. We have to keep reinventing ourselves throughout our lives. We're still discovering ourselves at whatever age. And that's normal. That's okay.

How does it feel to revisit these books now?
It was kind of weird. I put so much of my own college memories in there. The part where Anna's in the office, thinking, *I don't know what I'm gonna do*, that was directly taken from what I called my young-life crisis. I distinctly remember freaking out around that age because I didn't yet have a set plan of what my life would be. It's kind of what you go through.

What I like about these books is that they are kind of messy and it still resonates with me. I hope it does for readers as well.

Can you give us any tidbits about the new Game On book, *Only On Gameday* (releasing summer 2025)? Who are the main characters?
I'm just getting to know them, so it's still coming together. I've noticed there are families with a few football players, like a football dynasty. There's definitely a football culture in August's family—August [the hero] and his brother are players.

I'm thinking with August, he's kind of stilted and nervous around Pen [the heroine], but very charismatic around other people. I kind of like the idea of how you can become that way when you're enamored.

Which leads me to the next question, and I think I know the answer. Are you a pantser or a planner?
Every time I try to plan, it's like, oh yeah, I can't do it right in a straight line. It often comes in different stages, like a nebulous cloud of ideas. I'll write a chapter toward the end, one around the middle, the opening…and then I have to go back and flesh things out and pull it all together.

One last question. What role does music play in your writing? It tends to be very present in a lot of your stories.
I started writing when my daughter was a baby, and I would put music on so she could nap. Eventually, I grew used to listening to music while I write. More importantly, though, is that music conveys emotions and moods so well. If I manage to work what I'm listening to into the books, the reader can then listen to those songs as well and experience the story on another emotional level. I kind of like that idea.

Be sure to check out Kristen's playlist for
The Hook Up, *exclusive to this edition!*

PLAYLIST FOR THE HOOK UP

A SELECTION OF SONGS THAT INSPIRED KRISTEN CALLIHAN IN WRITING THIS BOOK.

"Dear Prudence," Siouxsie and the Banshees

"Norwegian Wood," The Beatles

"Crash into Me," Dave Matthews Band

"We Will Rock You," Queen

"Closer," Nine Inch Nails

"Little Ghost," The White Stripes

"Kashmir," Led Zeppelin

"Bitchin' Camaro," The Dead Milkmen